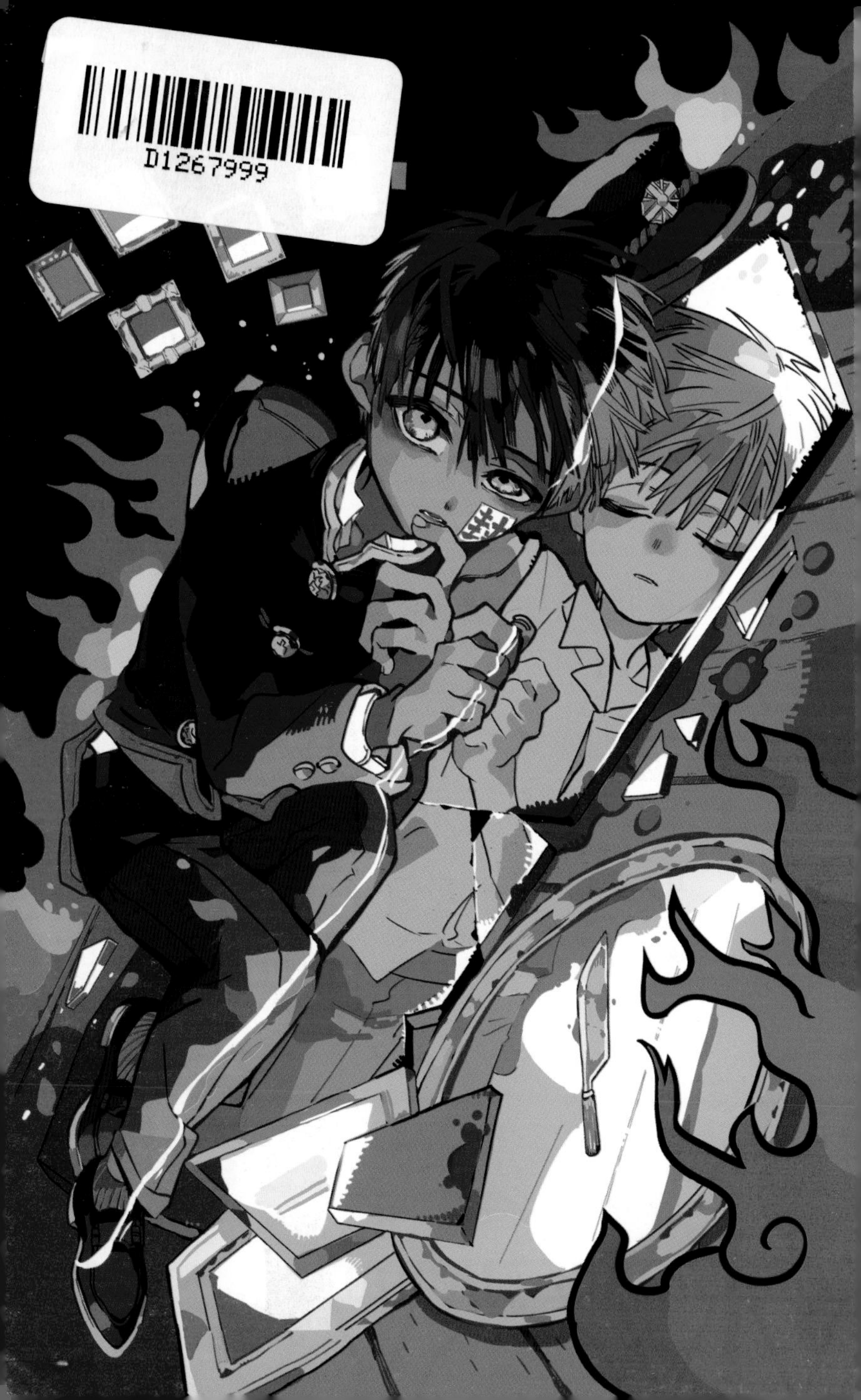

# Contents

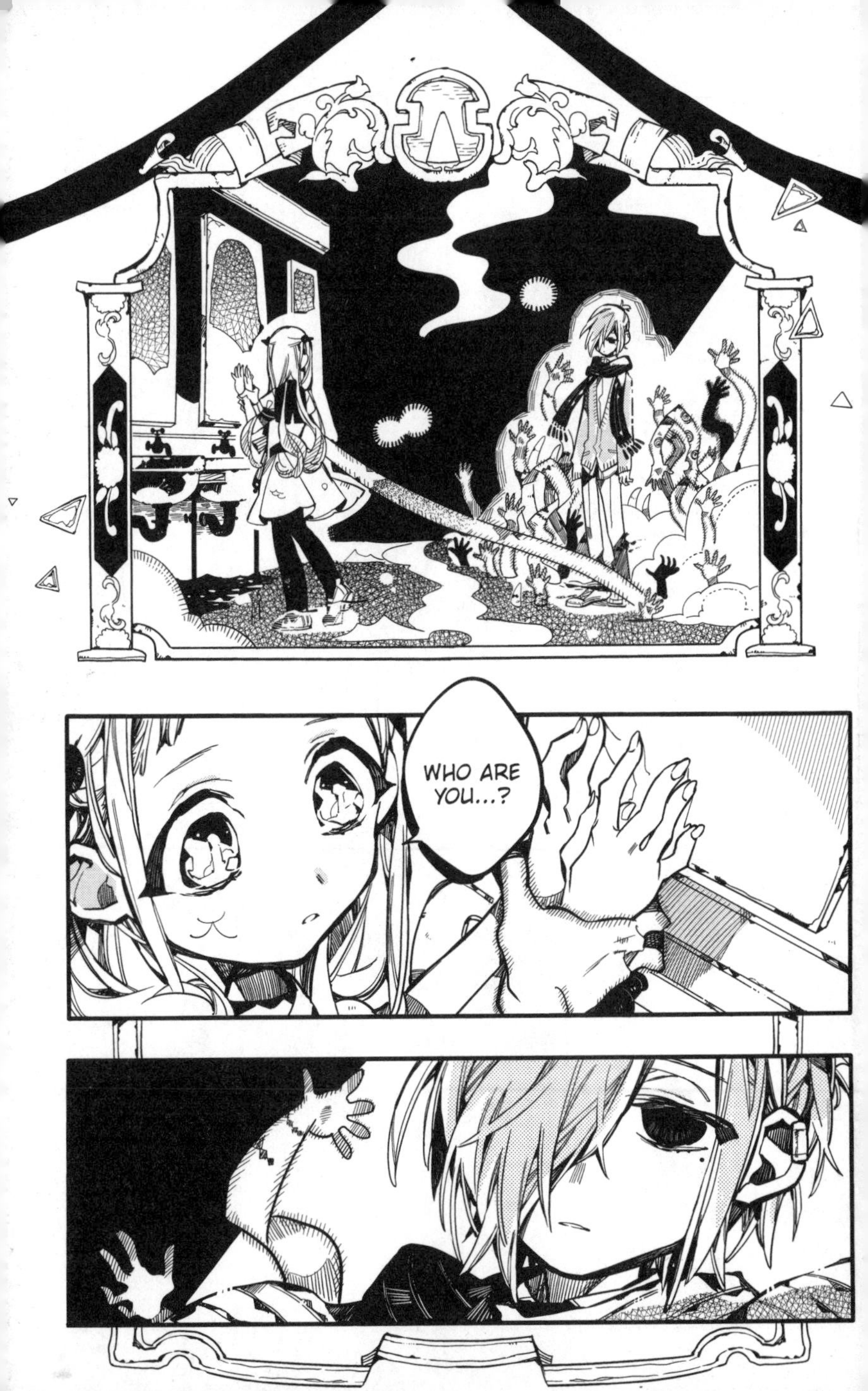
WHO ARE YOU...?

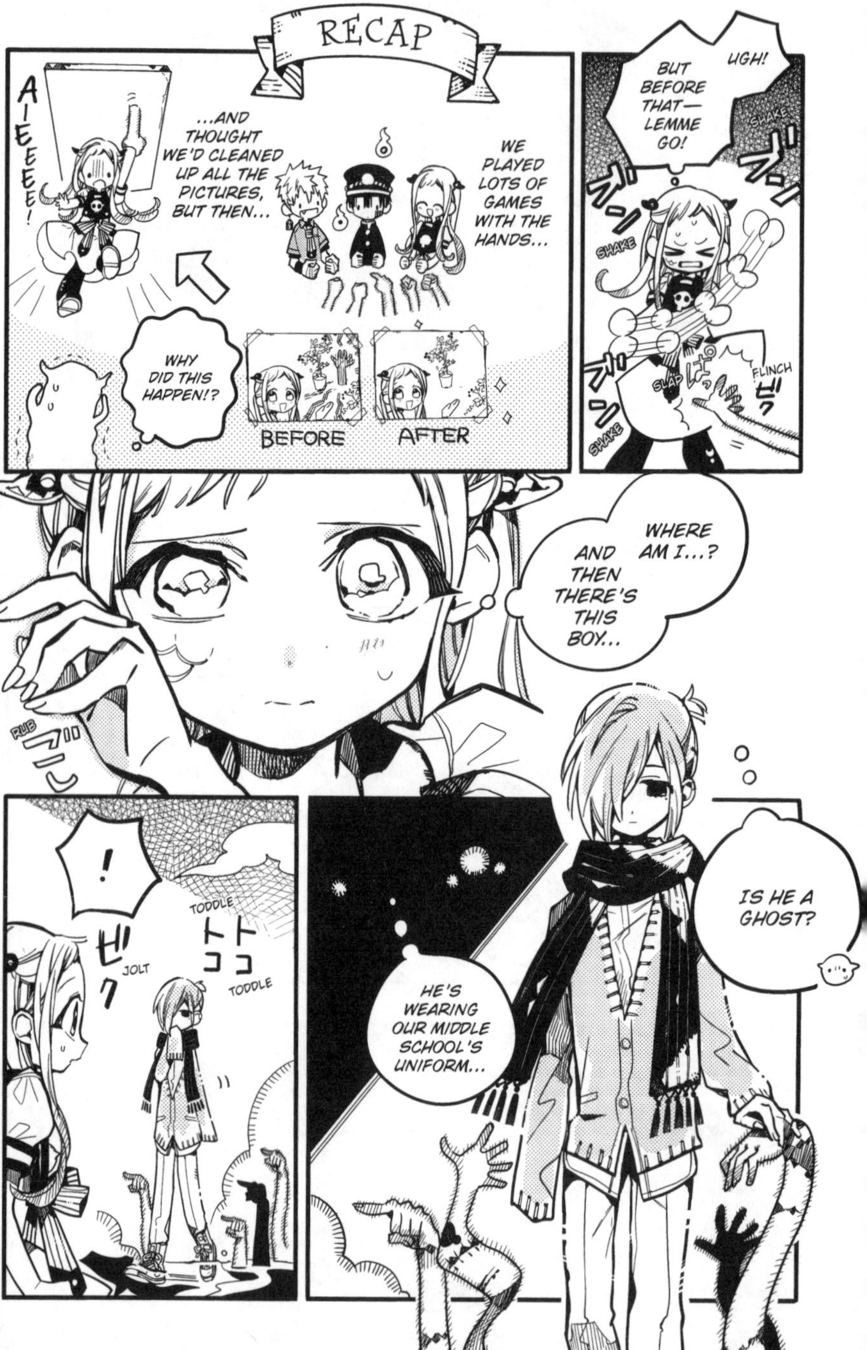
UGH!
BUT BEFORE THAT— LEMME GO!
SHAKE
SHAKE
FLINCH
SLAP
SHAKE
RECAP
WE PLAYED LOTS OF GAMES WITH THE HANDS...
...AND THOUGHT WE'D CLEANED UP ALL THE PICTURES, BUT THEN...
AIEEEEE!
WHY DID THIS HAPPEN!?
BEFORE
AFTER
WHERE AM I...?
AND THEN THERE'S THIS BOY...
RUB
IS HE A GHOST?
HE'S WEARING OUR MIDDLE SCHOOL'S UNIFORM...
!
TODDLE
TODDLE
JOLT

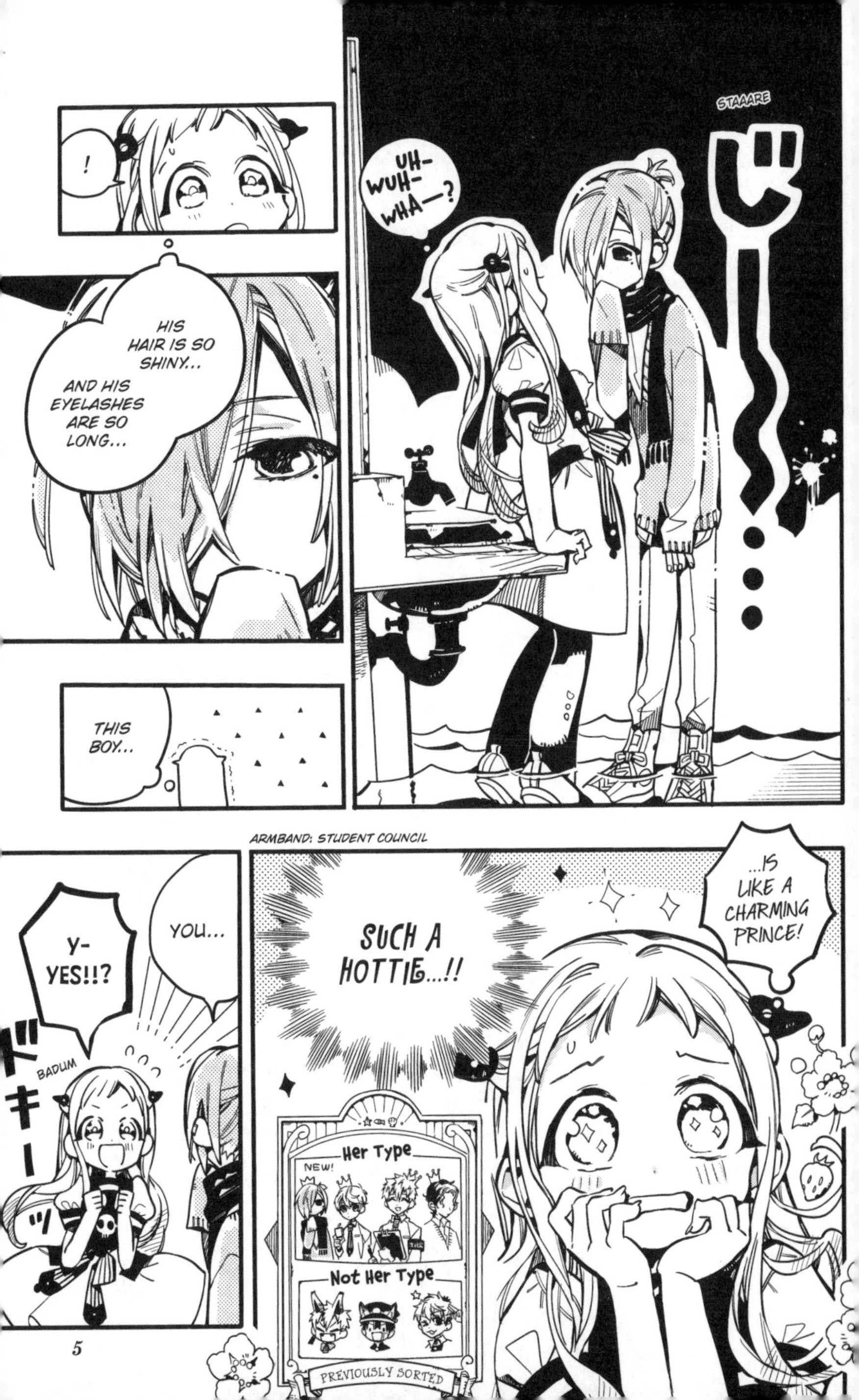
STAAARE
じー
...
UH-WUH-WHA—?
!
HIS HAIR IS SO SHINY...
AND HIS EYELASHES ARE SO LONG...
THIS BOY...
ARMBAND: STUDENT COUNCIL
...IS LIKE A CHARMING PRINCE!
SUCH A HOTTIE...!!
Her Type
NEW!
Not Her Type
PREVIOUSLY SORTED
YOU...
Y-YES!!?
ドキーッ
BADUM

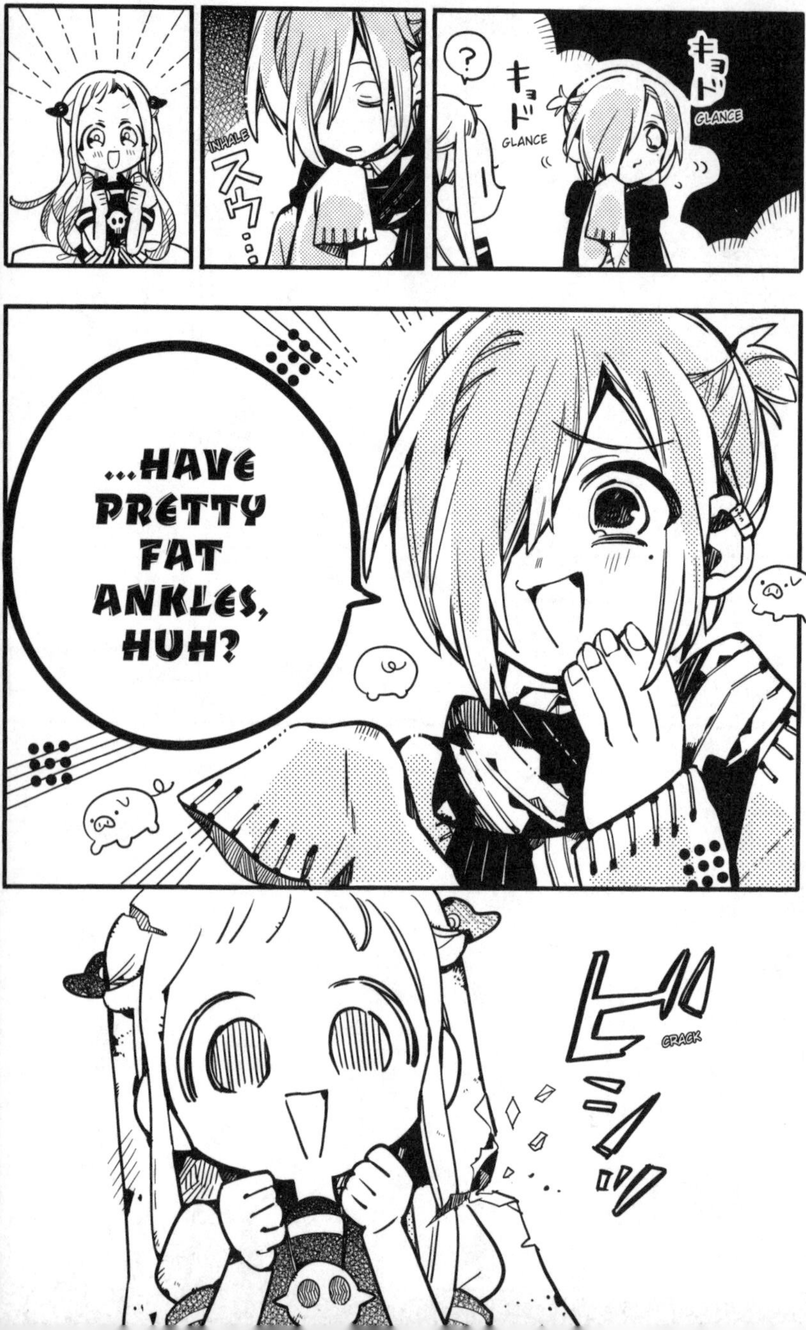
キョド
GLANCE
?
キョド
GLANCE
INHALE
スゥ…
...HAVE PRETTY FAT ANKLES, HUH?
ビシッ
CRACK

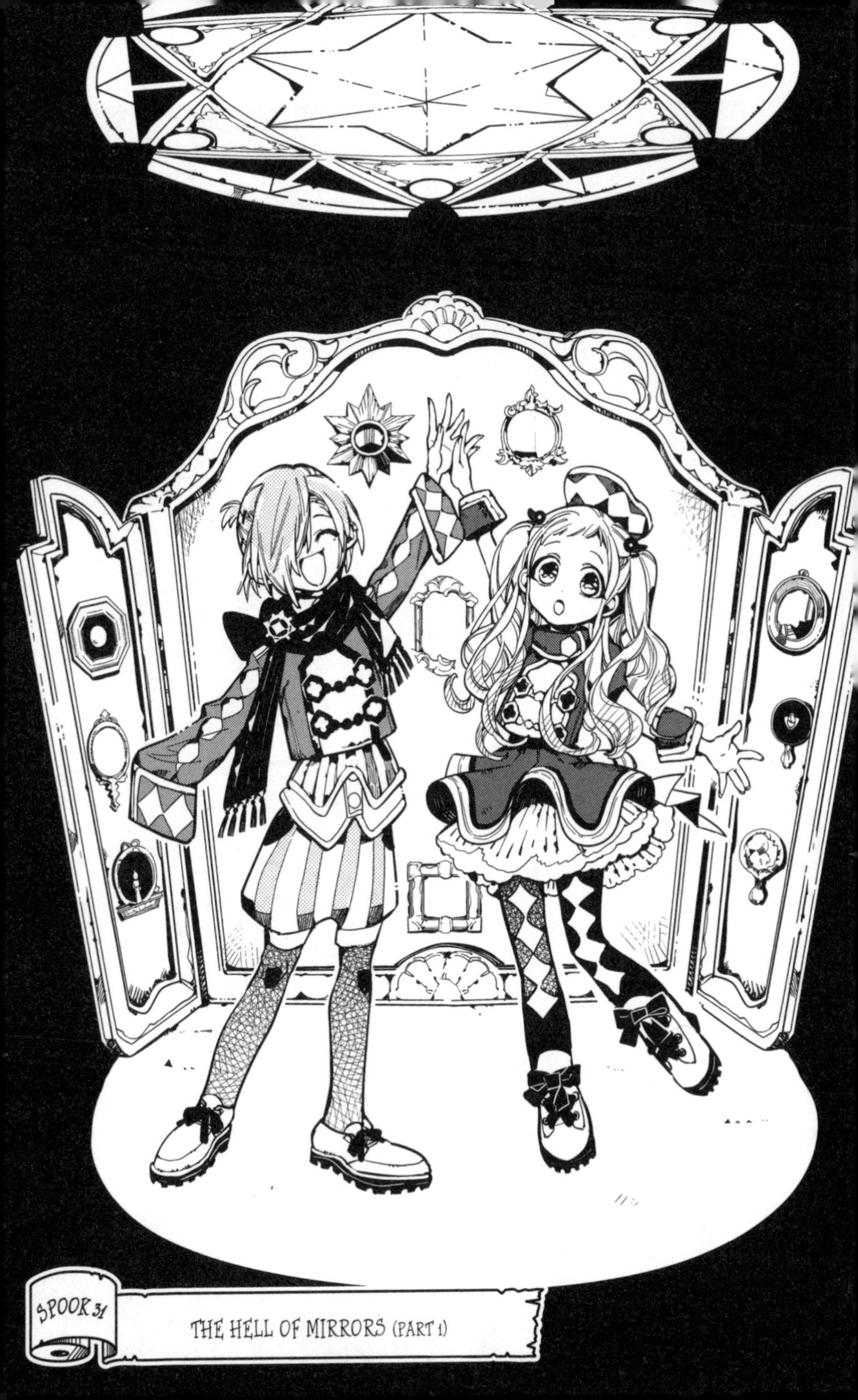
SPOOK 31
THE HELL OF MIRRORS (PART 1)

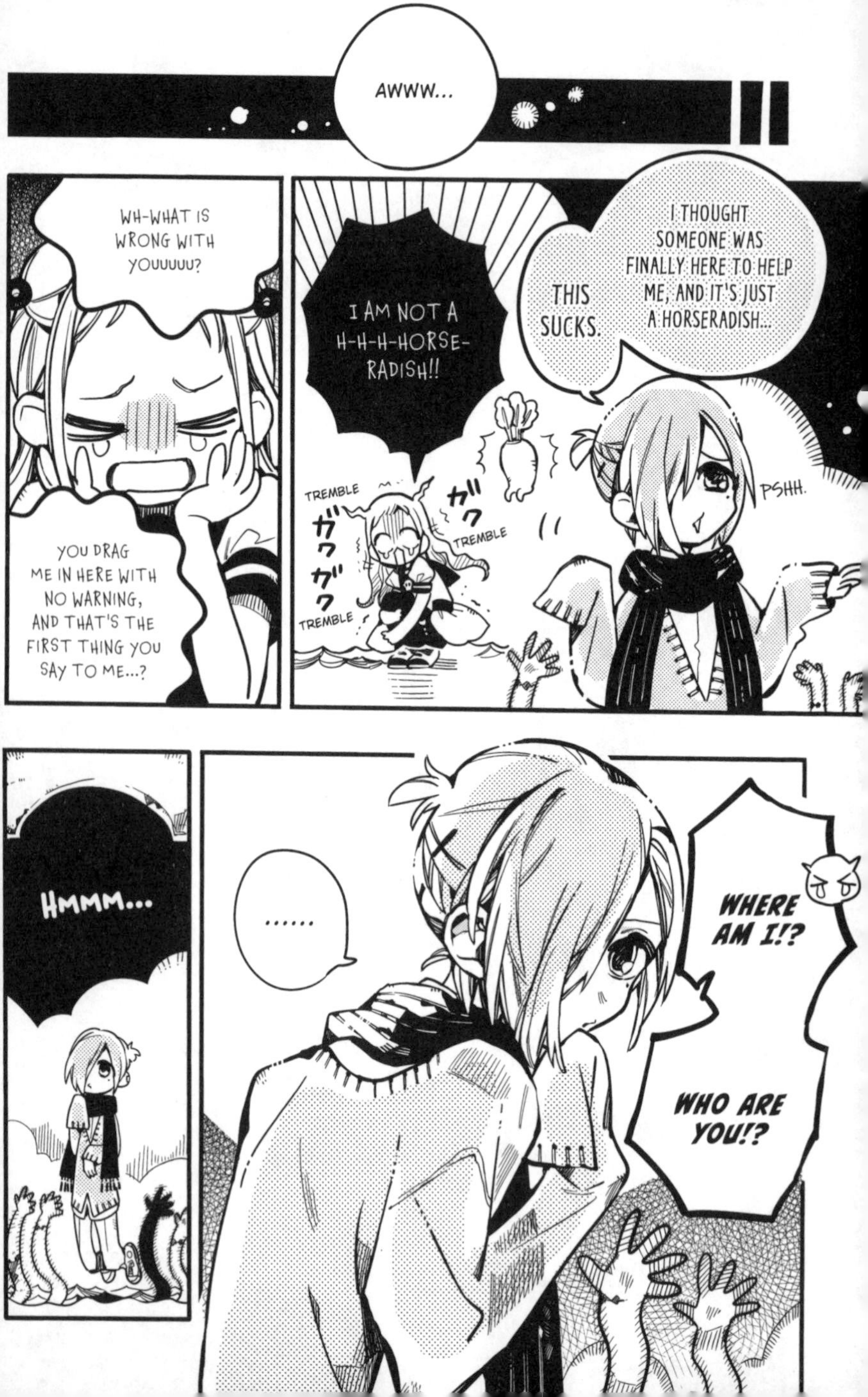
AWWW...
I THOUGHT SOMEONE WAS FINALLY HERE TO HELP ME, AND IT'S JUST A HORSERADISH...
THIS SUCKS.
PSHH.
I AM NOT A H-H-H-HORSE-RADISH!!
ガク
TREMBLE
ガク
TREMBLE
ガク
TREMBLE
WH-WHAT IS WRONG WITH YOUUUUU?
YOU DRAG ME IN HERE WITH NO WARNING, AND THAT'S THE FIRST THING YOU SAY TO ME...?
WHERE AM I!?
WHO ARE YOU!?
......
HMMM...

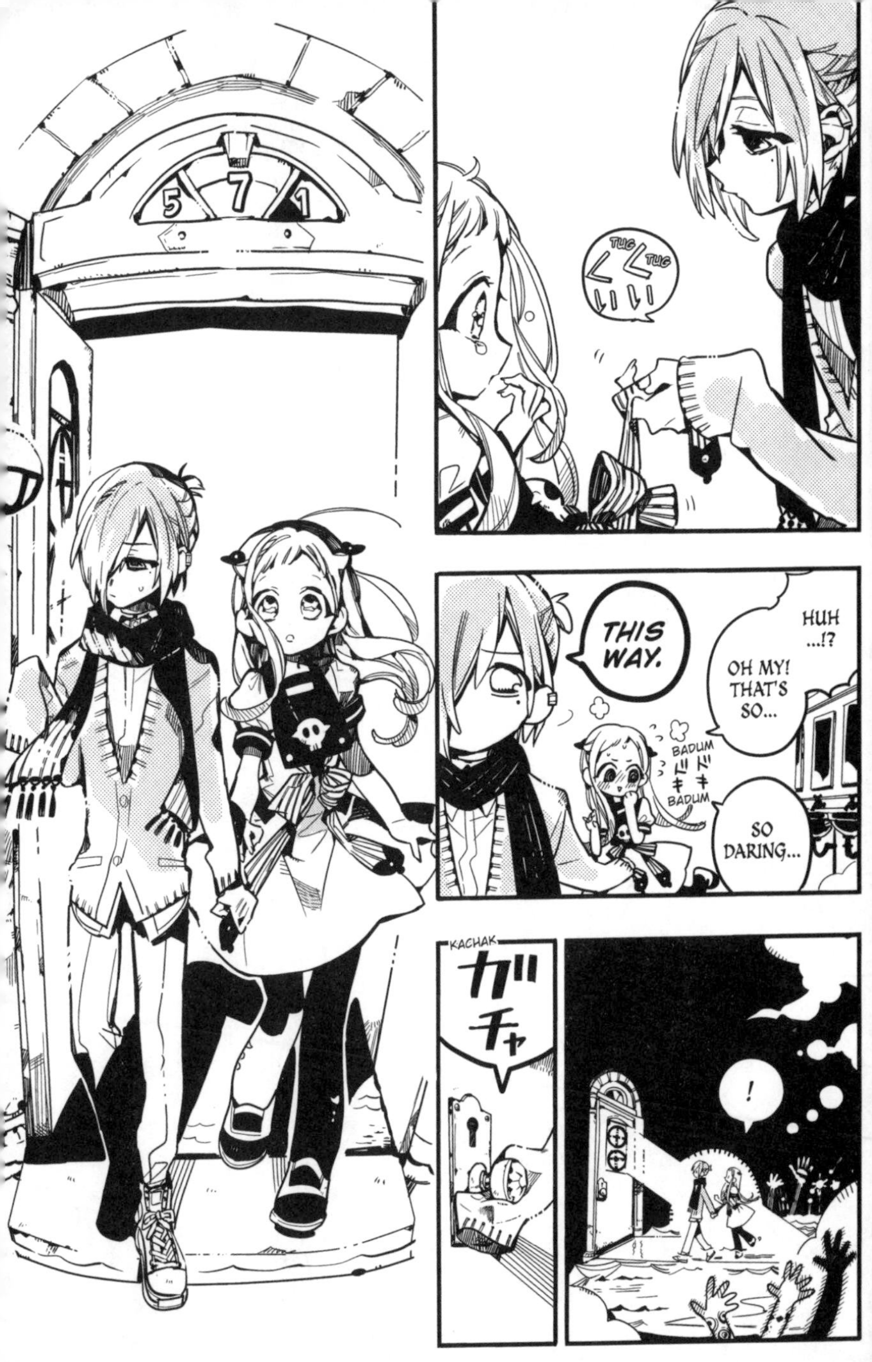
TUG TUG
くいくい
THIS WAY.
HUH ...!?
OH MY! THAT'S SO...
BADUM ドキドキ BADUM
SO DARING...
!
KACHAK
ガチャ
5 7 1

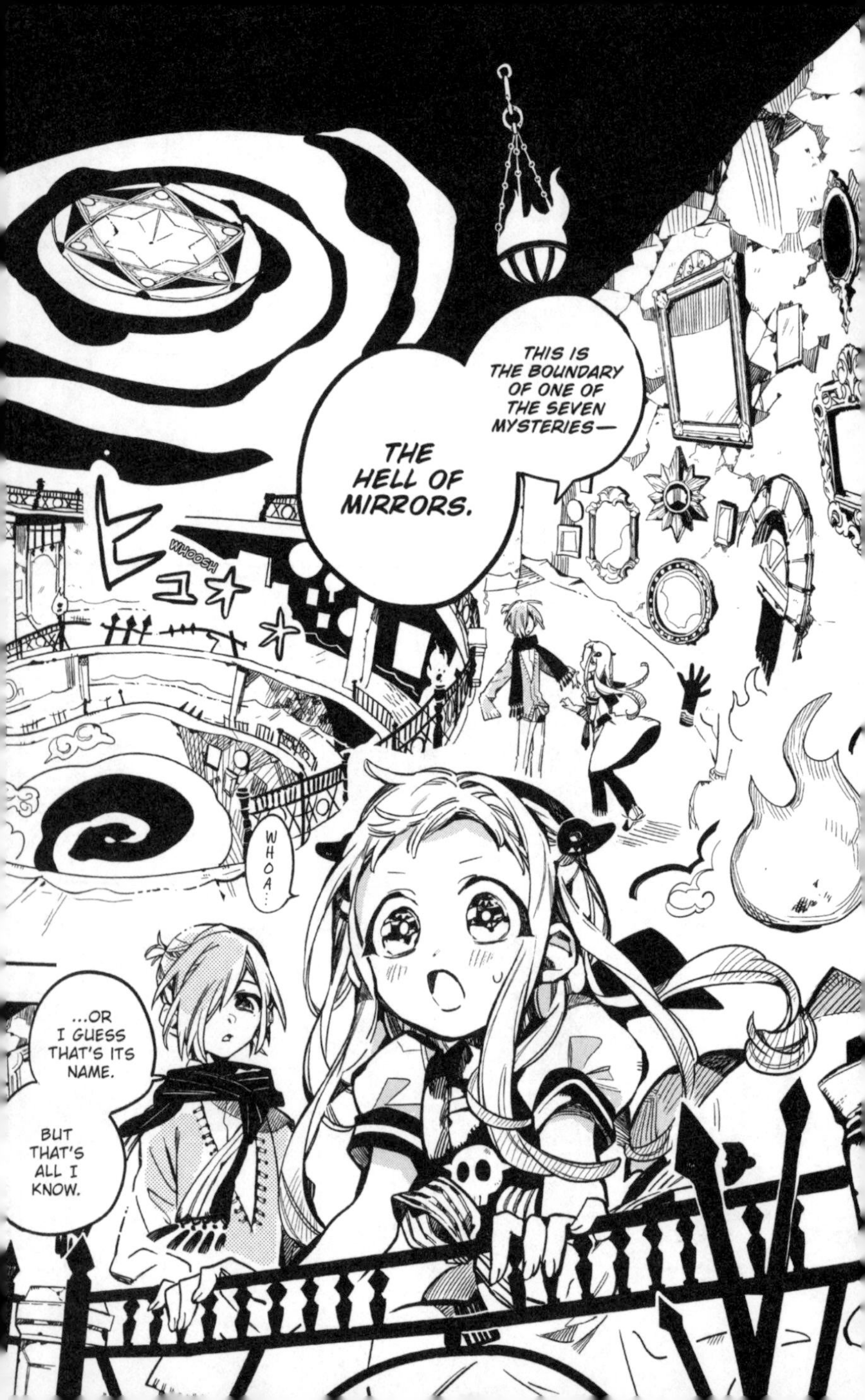
THIS IS THE BOUNDARY OF ONE OF THE SEVEN MYSTERIES—
THE HELL OF MIRRORS.
ヒュオオ
WHOOSH
WHOA...
...OR I GUESS THAT'S ITS NAME.
BUT THAT'S ALL I KNOW.

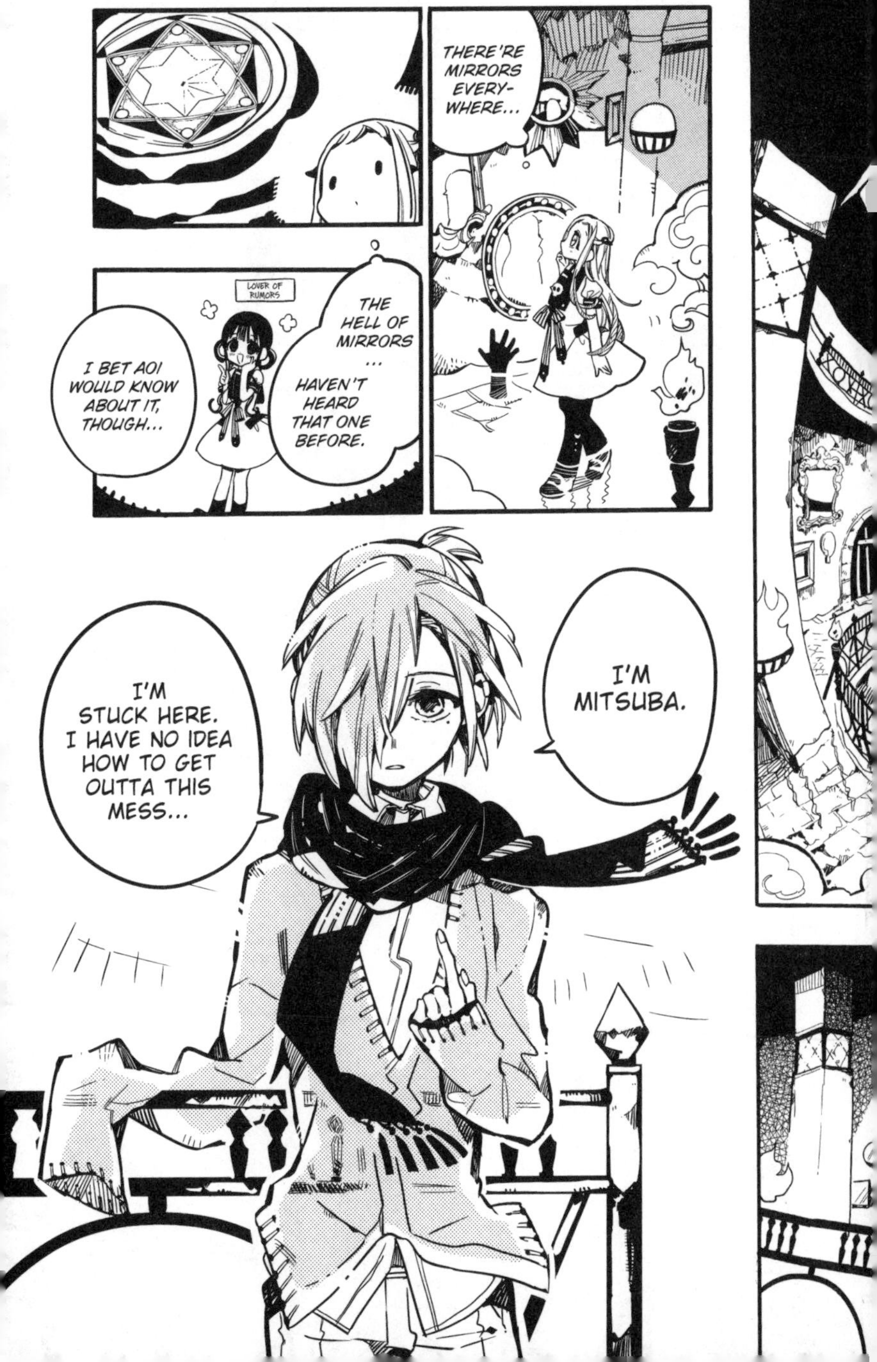
THERE'RE MIRRORS EVERY-WHERE...
THE HELL OF MIRRORS... HAVEN'T HEARD THAT ONE BEFORE.
LOVER OF RUMORS
I BET AOI WOULD KNOW ABOUT IT, THOUGH...
I'M MITSUBA.
I'M STUCK HERE. I HAVE NO IDEA HOW TO GET OUTTA THIS MESS...

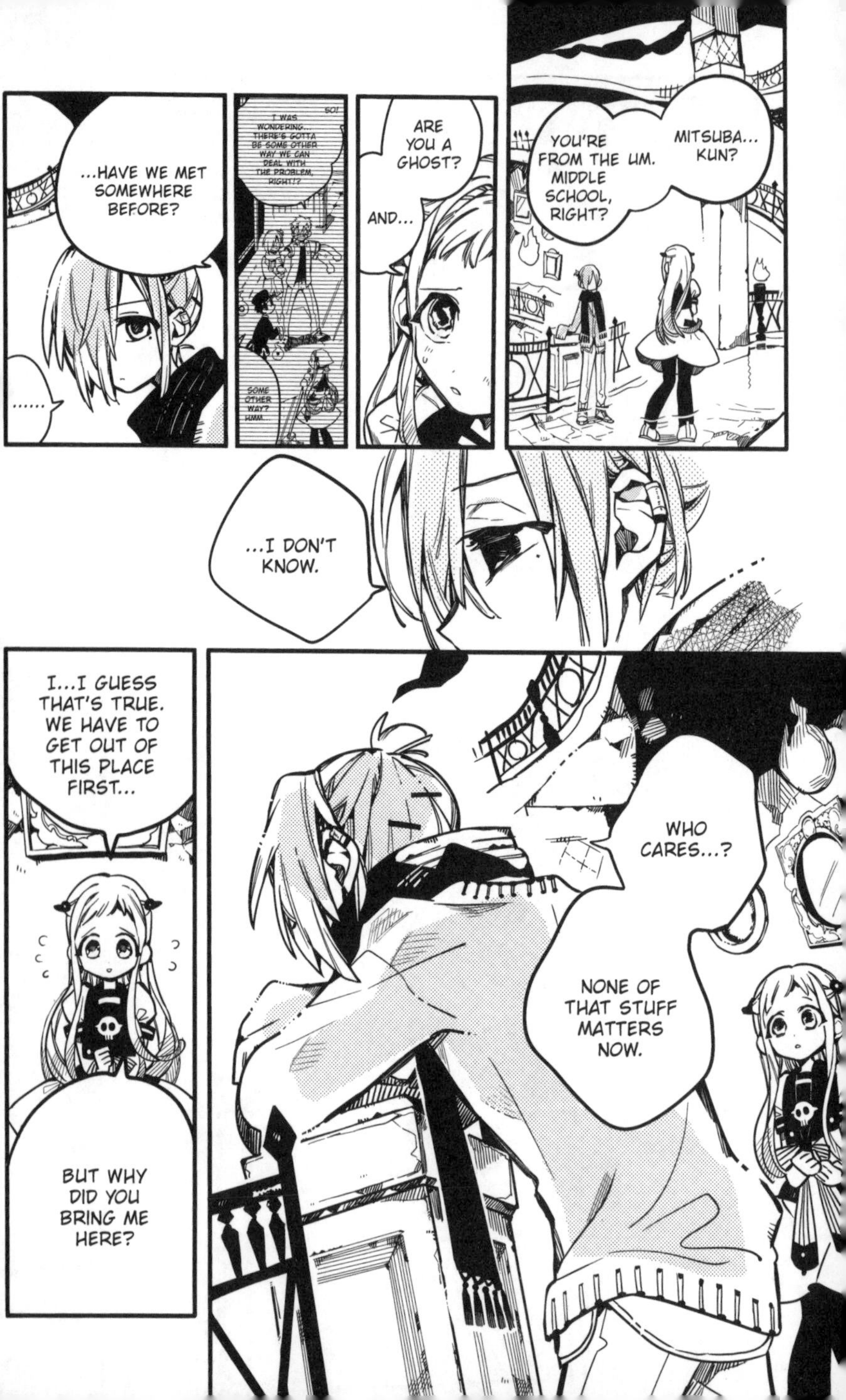
MITSUBA... KUN?
YOU'RE FROM THE UM. MIDDLE SCHOOL, RIGHT?
ARE YOU A GHOST?
AND...
SO!
I WAS WONDERING... THERE'S GOTTA BE SOME OTHER WAY WE CAN DEAL WITH THE PROBLEM, RIGHT!?
SOME OTHER WAY? HMM...
...HAVE WE MET SOMEWHERE BEFORE?
......
...I DON'T KNOW.
WHO CARES...?
NONE OF THAT STUFF MATTERS NOW.
I...I GUESS THAT'S TRUE. WE HAVE TO GET OUT OF THIS PLACE FIRST...
BUT WHY DID YOU BRING ME HERE?

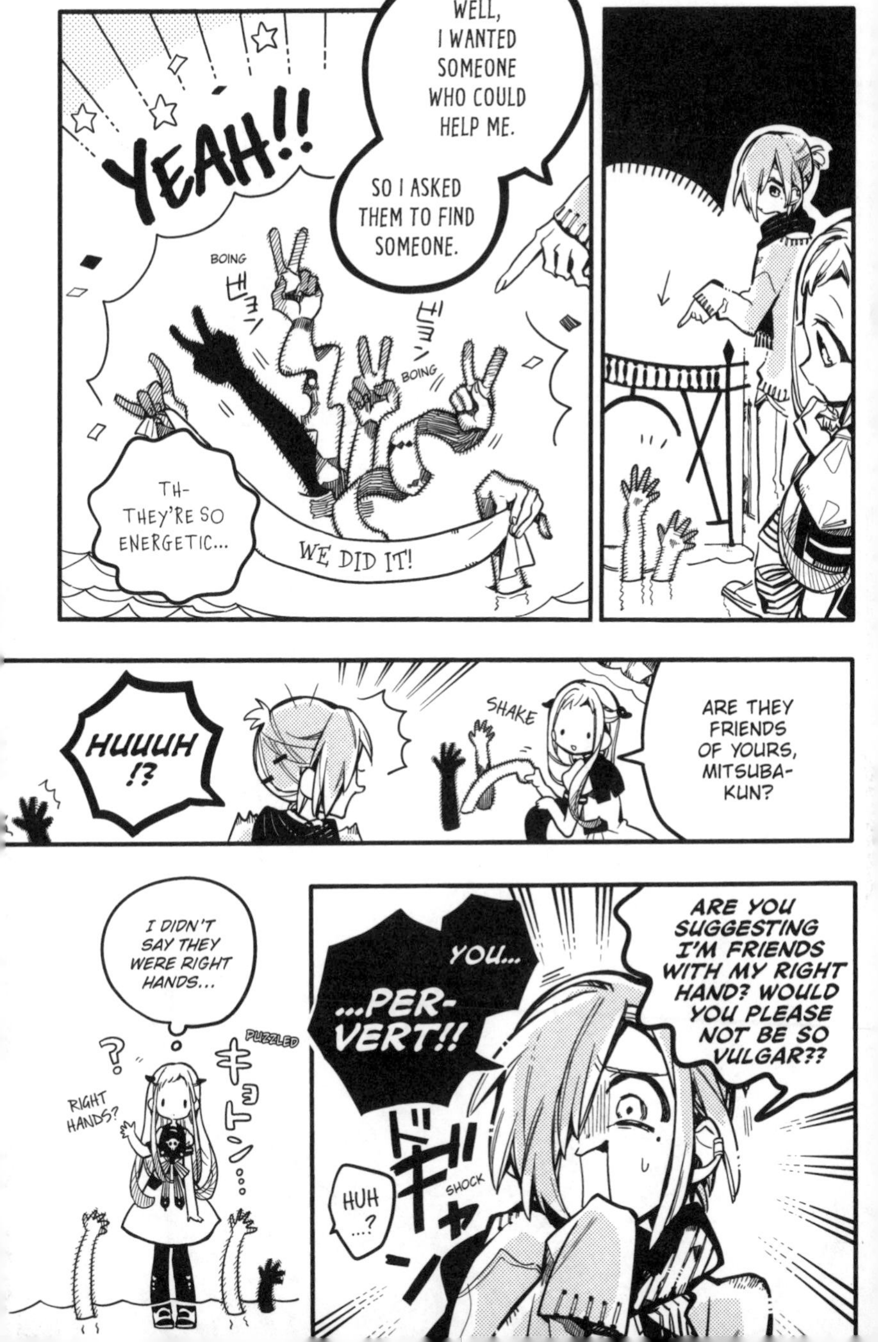
WELL, I WANTED SOMEONE WHO COULD HELP ME.
SO I ASKED THEM TO FIND SOMEONE.
YEAH!!
BOING
BOING
WE DID IT!
TH- THEY'RE SO ENERGETIC...
ARE THEY FRIENDS OF YOURS, MITSUBA-KUN?
SHAKE
HUUUH!?
ARE YOU SUGGESTING I'M FRIENDS WITH MY RIGHT HAND? WOULD YOU PLEASE NOT BE SO VULGAR??
YOU... ...PER-VERT!!
SHOCK
HUH ...?
I DIDN'T SAY THEY WERE RIGHT HANDS...
PUZZLED
RIGHT HANDS?

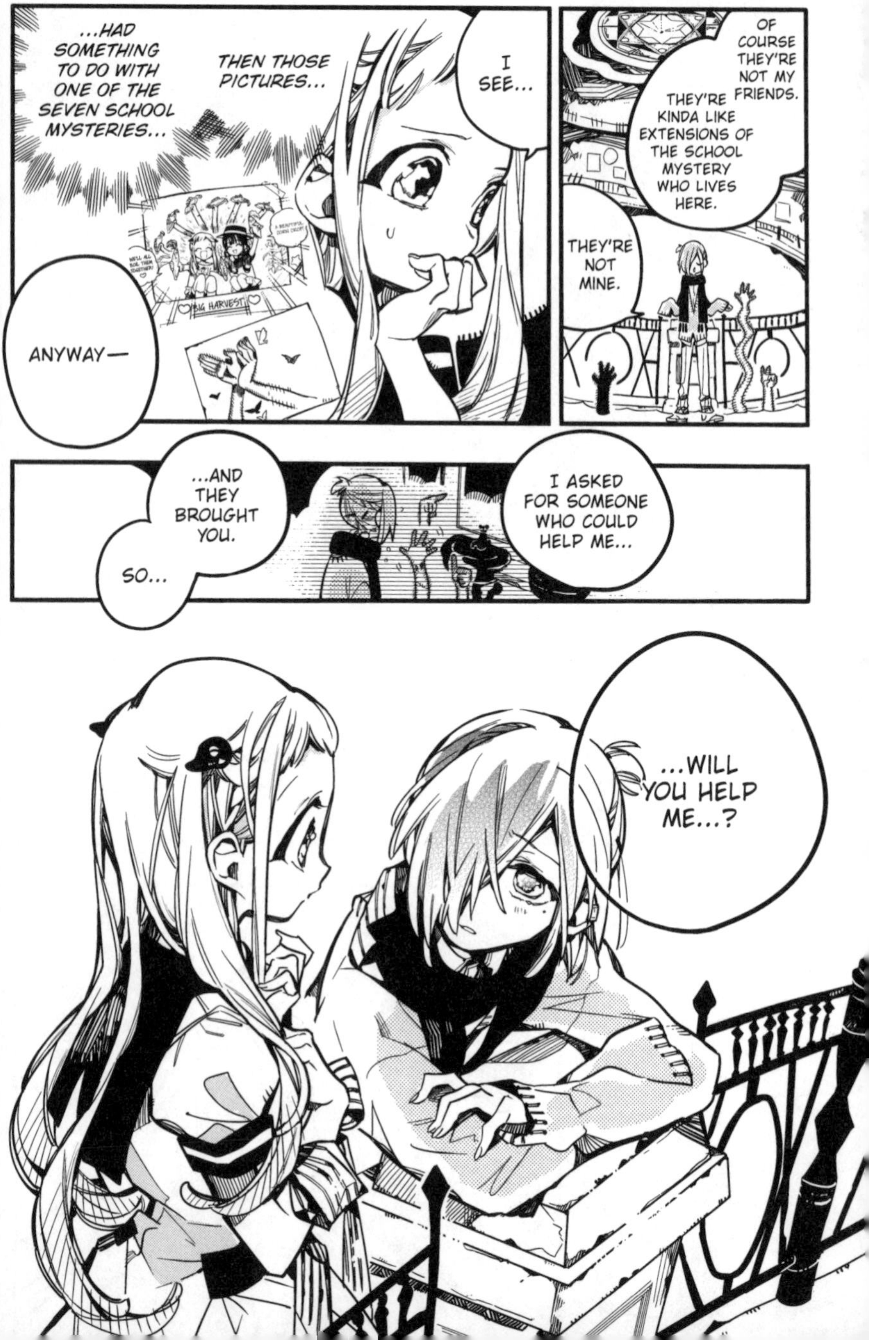
OF COURSE THEY'RE NOT MY FRIENDS.
THEY'RE KINDA LIKE EXTENSIONS OF THE SCHOOL MYSTERY WHO LIVES HERE.
THEY'RE NOT MINE.
I SEE...
THEN THOSE PICTURES...
...HAD SOMETHING TO DO WITH ONE OF THE SEVEN SCHOOL MYSTERIES...
BIG HARVEST
ANYWAY—
I ASKED FOR SOMEONE WHO COULD HELP ME...
...AND THEY BROUGHT YOU.
SO...
...WILL YOU HELP ME...?

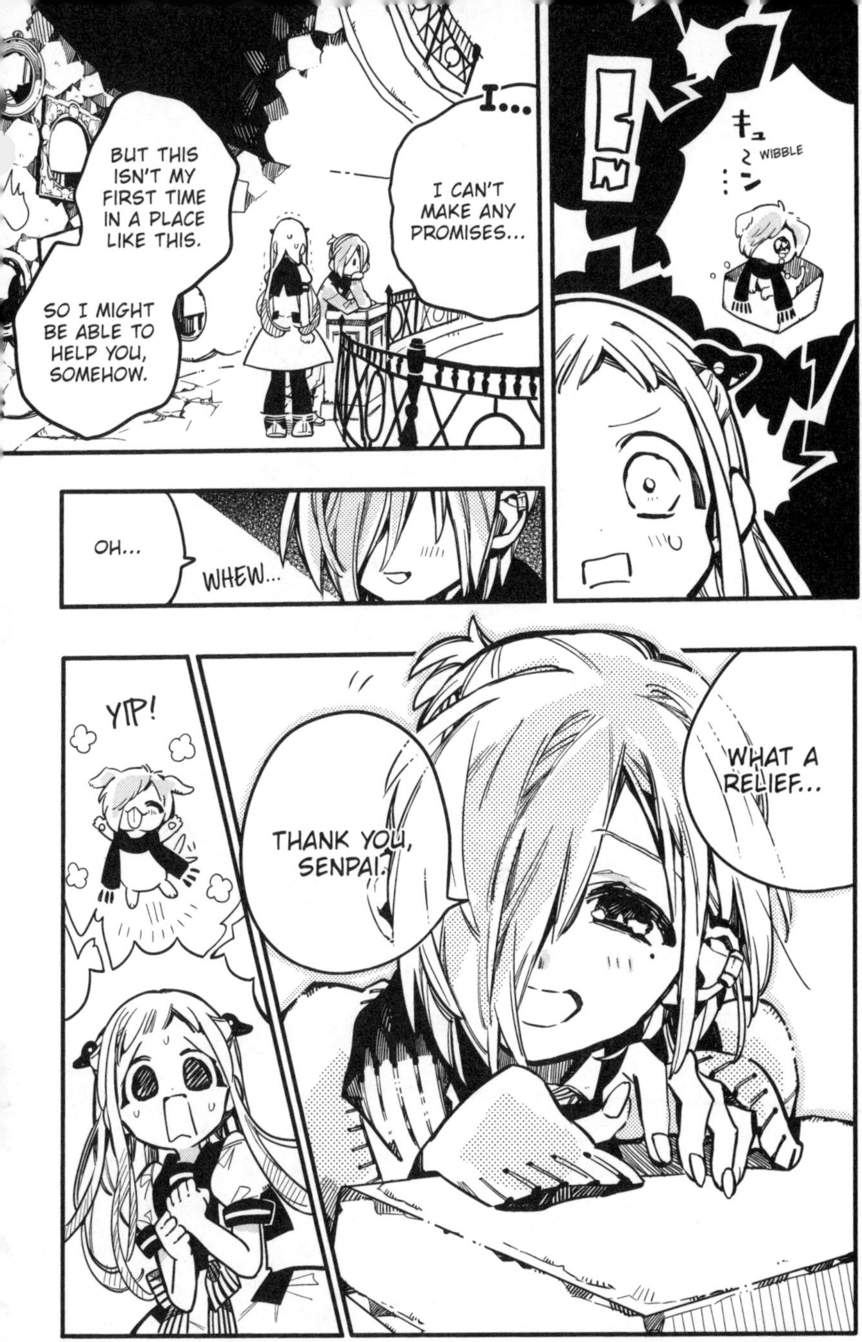
キュ～ン
WIBBLE
I...
I CAN'T MAKE ANY PROMISES...
BUT THIS ISN'T MY FIRST TIME IN A PLACE LIKE THIS.
SO I MIGHT BE ABLE TO HELP YOU, SOMEHOW.
OH...
WHEW...
WHAT A RELIEF...
THANK YOU, SENPAI.
YIP!

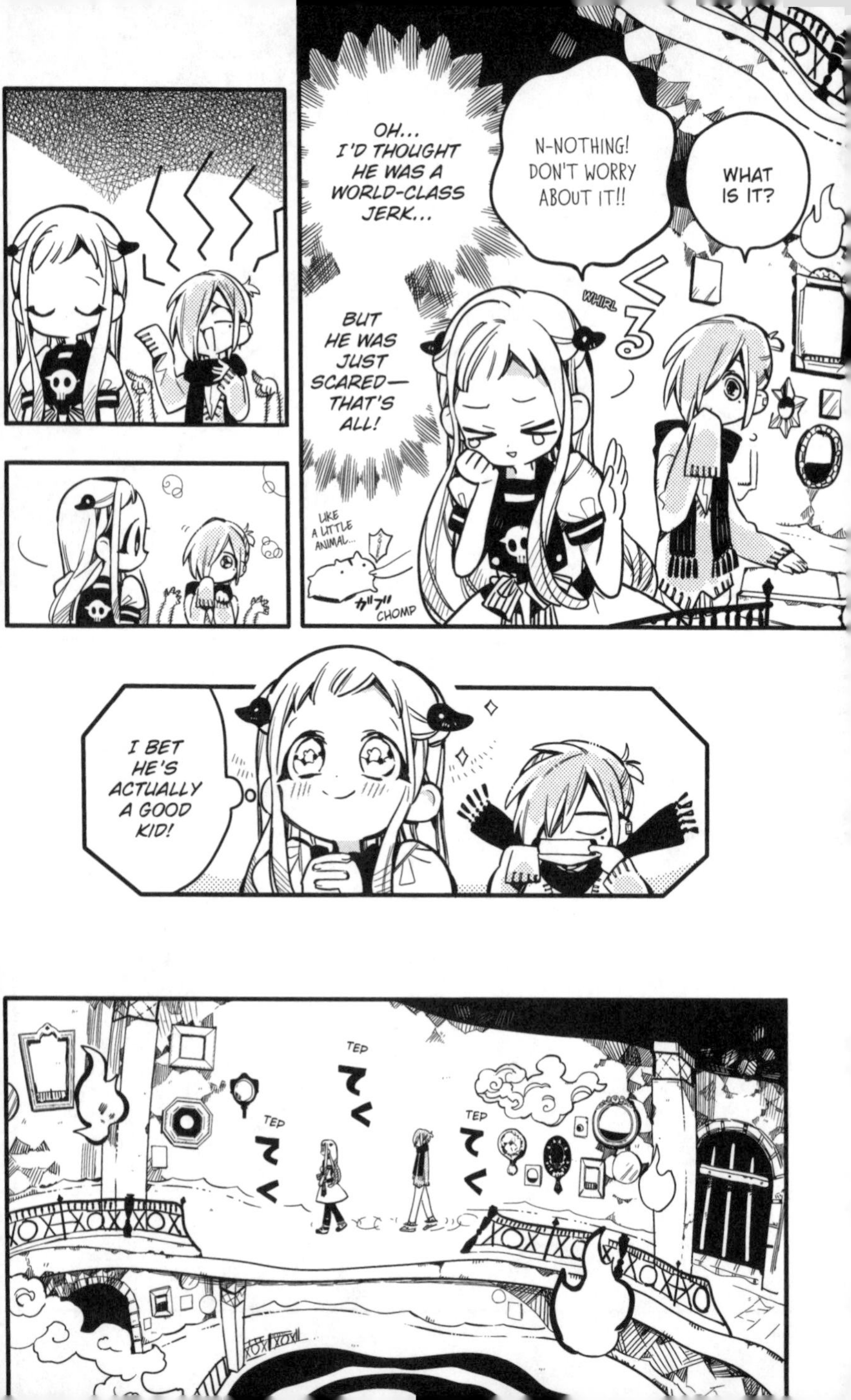
WHAT IS IT?
N-NOTHING! DON'T WORRY ABOUT IT!!
OH... I'D THOUGHT HE WAS A WORLD-CLASS JERK...
WHIRL
BUT HE WAS JUST SCARED—THAT'S ALL!
LIKE A LITTLE ANIMAL...
CHOMP
I BET HE'S ACTUALLY A GOOD KID!
TEP
TEP
TEP

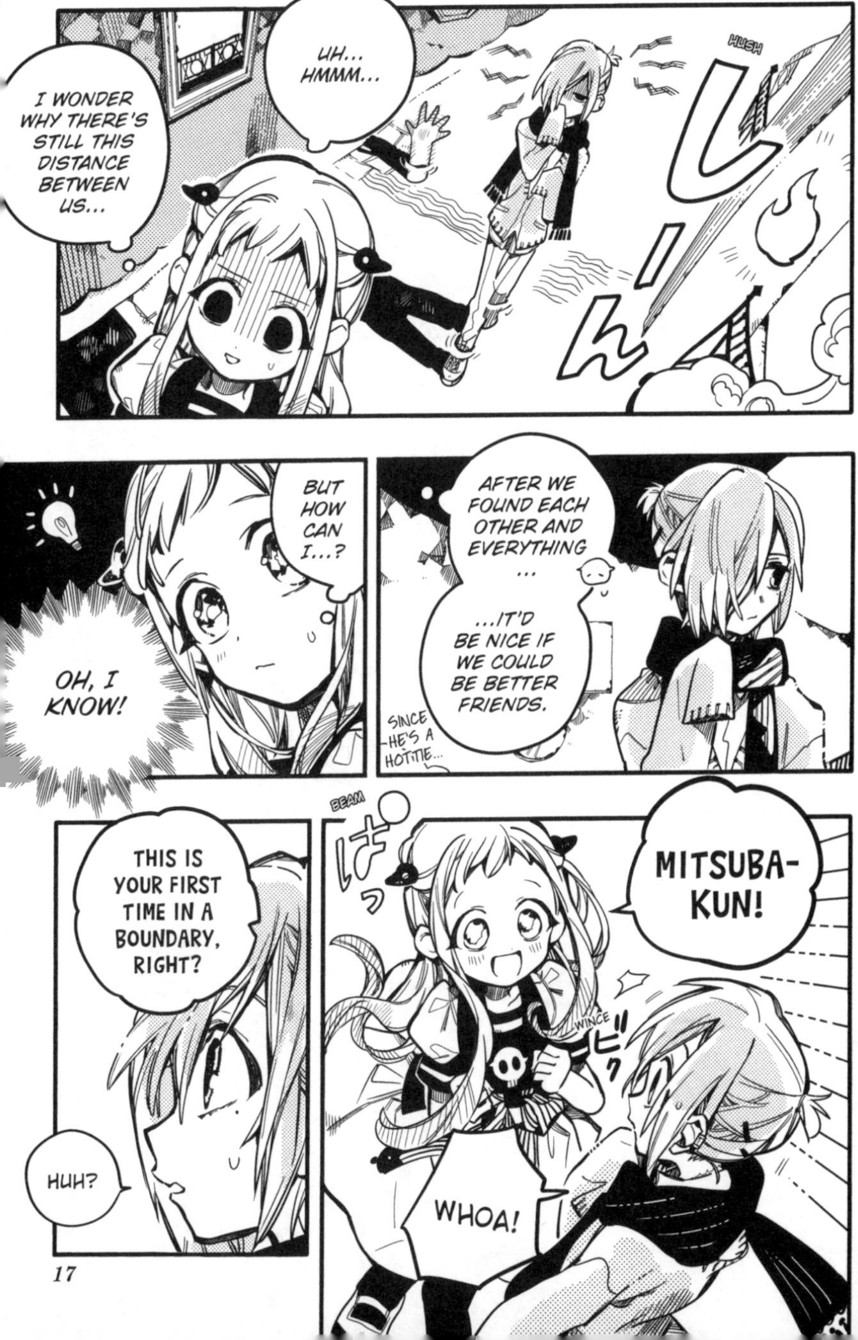
HUSH
UH... HMMM...
I WONDER WHY THERE'S STILL THIS DISTANCE BETWEEN US...
AFTER WE FOUND EACH OTHER AND EVERYTHING ...
...IT'D BE NICE IF WE COULD BE BETTER FRIENDS.
SINCE HE'S A HOTTIE...
BUT HOW CAN I...?
OH, I KNOW!
BEAM
MITSUBA-KUN!
WINCE
WHOA!
THIS IS YOUR FIRST TIME IN A BOUNDARY, RIGHT?
HUH?

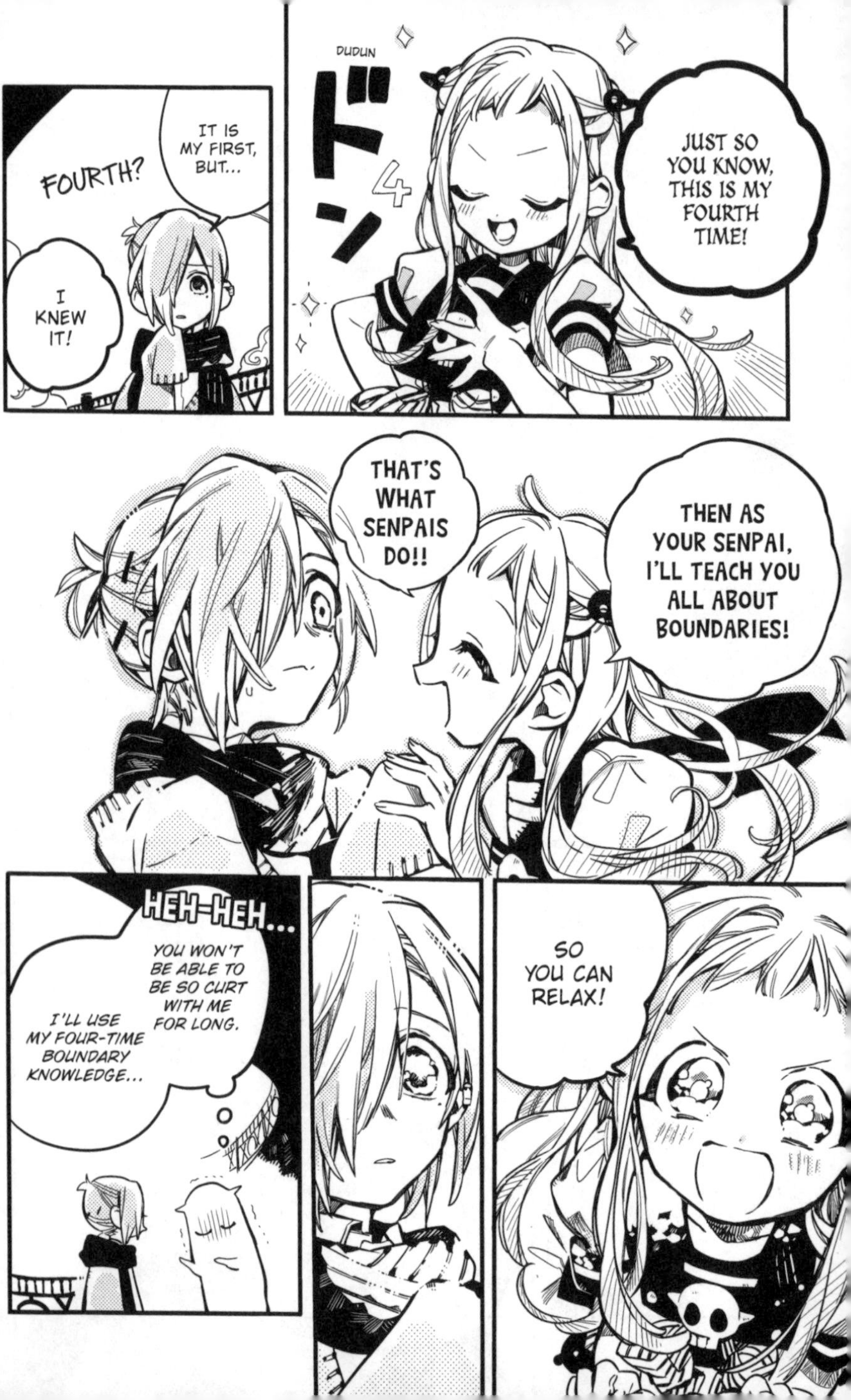
DUDUN
ドン
4
JUST SO YOU KNOW, THIS IS MY FOURTH TIME!
IT IS MY FIRST, BUT...
FOURTH?
I KNEW IT!
THEN AS YOUR SENPAI, I'LL TEACH YOU ALL ABOUT BOUNDARIES!
THAT'S WHAT SENPAIS DO!!
SO YOU CAN RELAX!
HEH-HEH...
YOU WON'T BE ABLE TO BE SO CURT WITH ME FOR LONG.
I'LL USE MY FOUR-TIME BOUNDARY KNOWLEDGE...

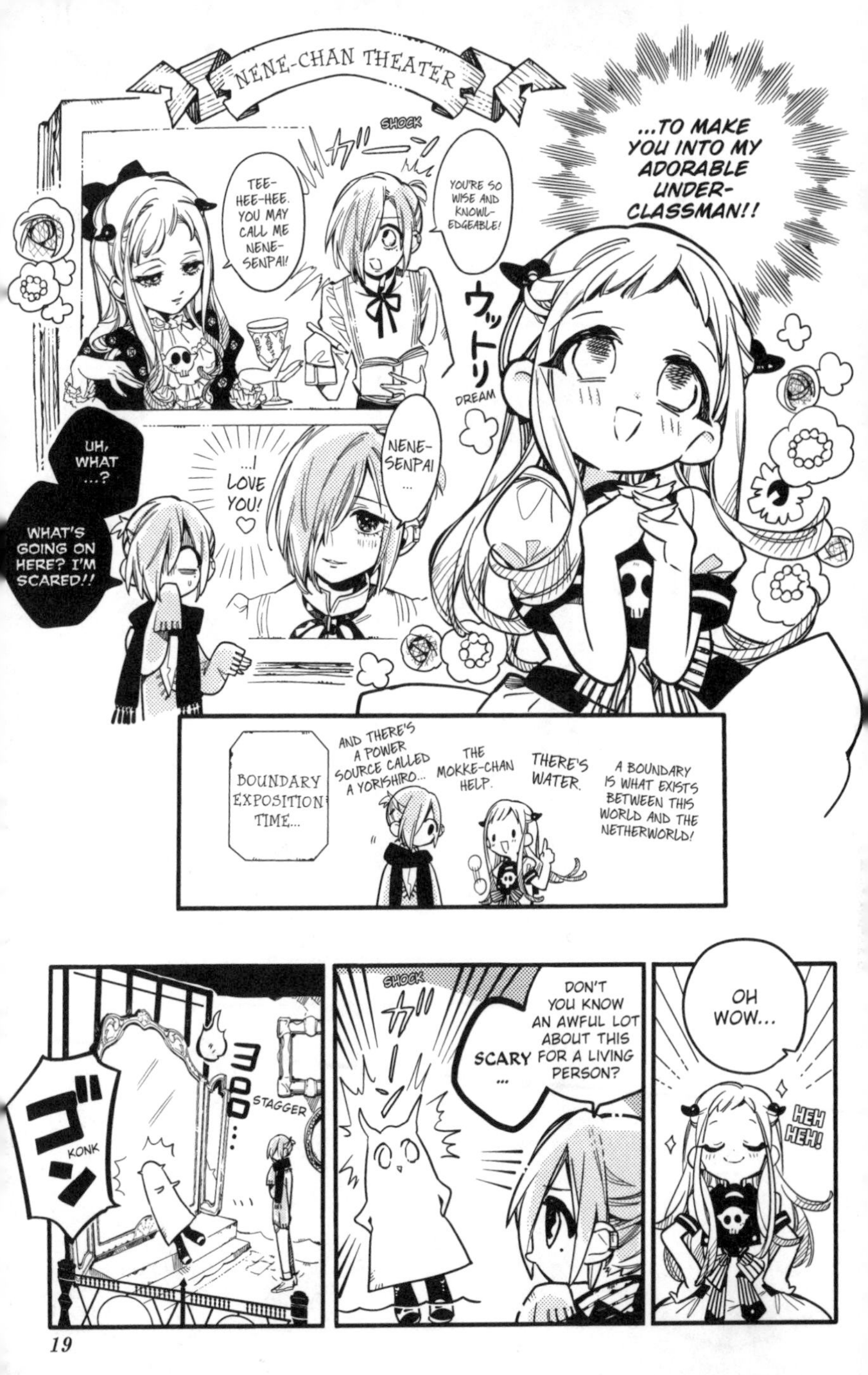
...TO MAKE YOU INTO MY ADORABLE UNDER-CLASSMAN!!
DREAM
NENE-CHAN THEATER
YOU'RE SO WISE AND KNOWL-EDGEABLE!
SHOCK
TEE-HEE-HEE. YOU MAY CALL ME NENE-SENPAI!
NENE-SENPAI...
...I LOVE YOU!
UH, WHAT...?
WHAT'S GOING ON HERE? I'M SCARED!!
A BOUNDARY IS WHAT EXISTS BETWEEN THIS WORLD AND THE NETHERWORLD!
THERE'S WATER.
THE MOKKE-CHAN HELP.
AND THERE'S A POWER SOURCE CALLED A YORISHIRO...
BOUNDARY EXPOSITION TIME...
OH WOW...
HEH HEH!
DON'T YOU KNOW AN AWFUL LOT ABOUT THIS FOR A LIVING PERSON?
SCARY...
SHOCK
STAGGER
KONK

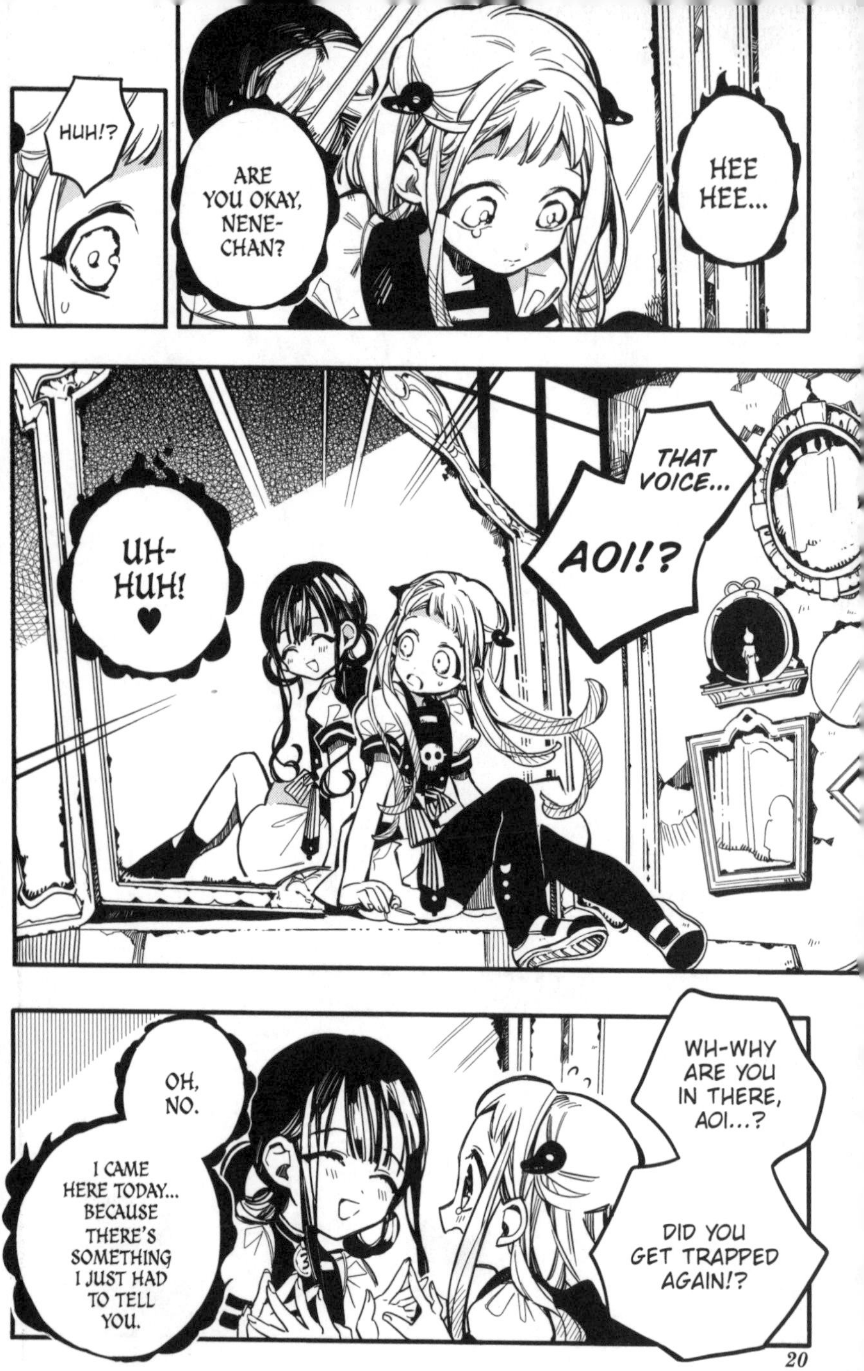
HEE HEE...
ARE YOU OKAY, NENE-CHAN?
HUH!?
THAT VOICE...
AOI!?
UH-HUH! ♥
WH-WHY ARE YOU IN THERE, AOI...?
DID YOU GET TRAPPED AGAIN!?
OH, NO.
I CAME HERE TODAY... BECAUSE THERE'S SOMETHING I JUST HAD TO TELL YOU.

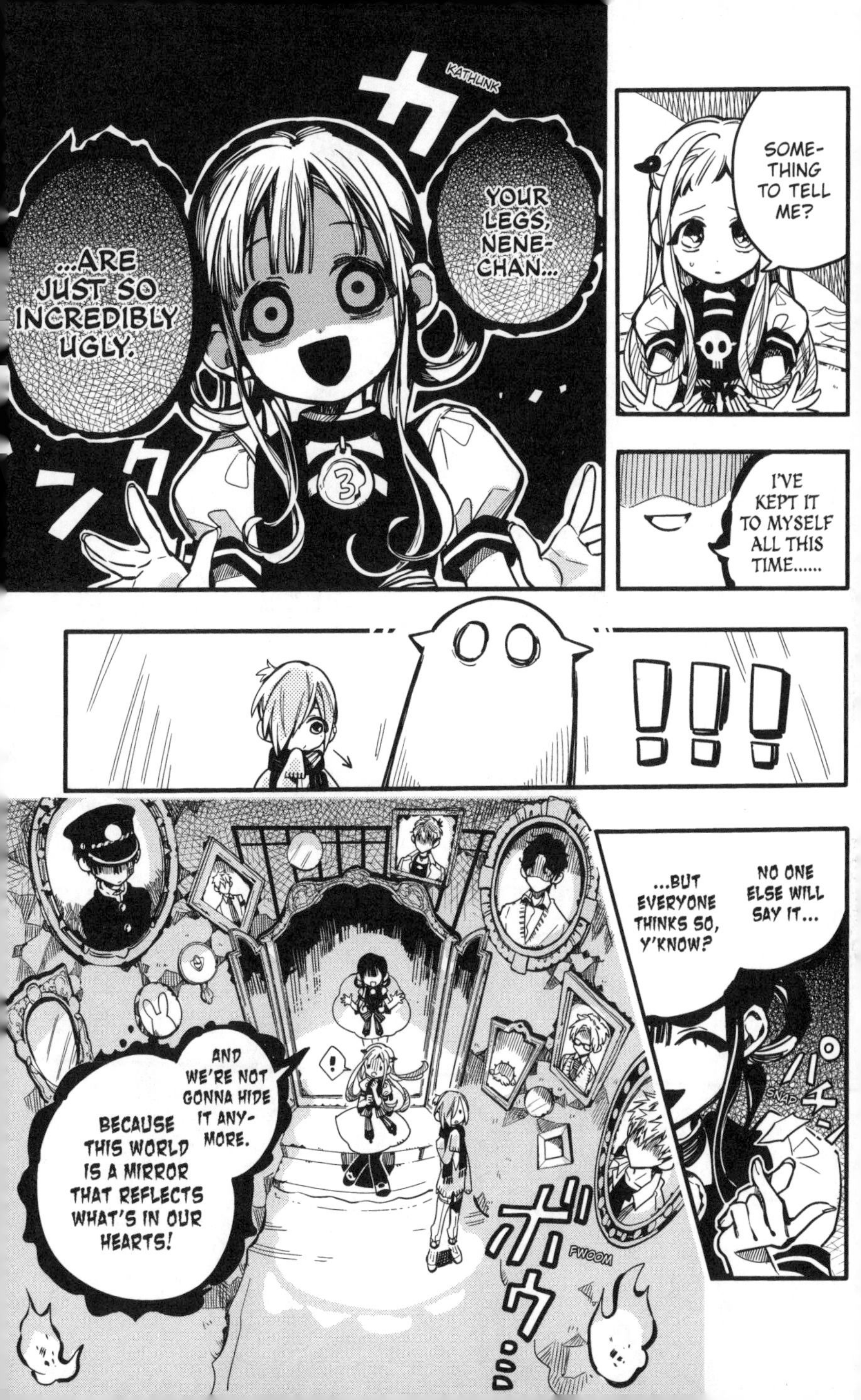
SOME-THING TO TELL ME?
I'VE KEPT IT TO MYSELF ALL THIS TIME......
KATHLINK
YOUR LEGS, NENE-CHAN...
...ARE JUST SO INCREDIBLY UGLY.
NO ONE ELSE WILL SAY IT...
...BUT EVERYONE THINKS SO, Y'KNOW?
SNAP
AND WE'RE NOT GONNA HIDE IT ANY-MORE.
BECAUSE THIS WORLD IS A MIRROR THAT REFLECTS WHAT'S IN OUR HEARTS!
FWOOM

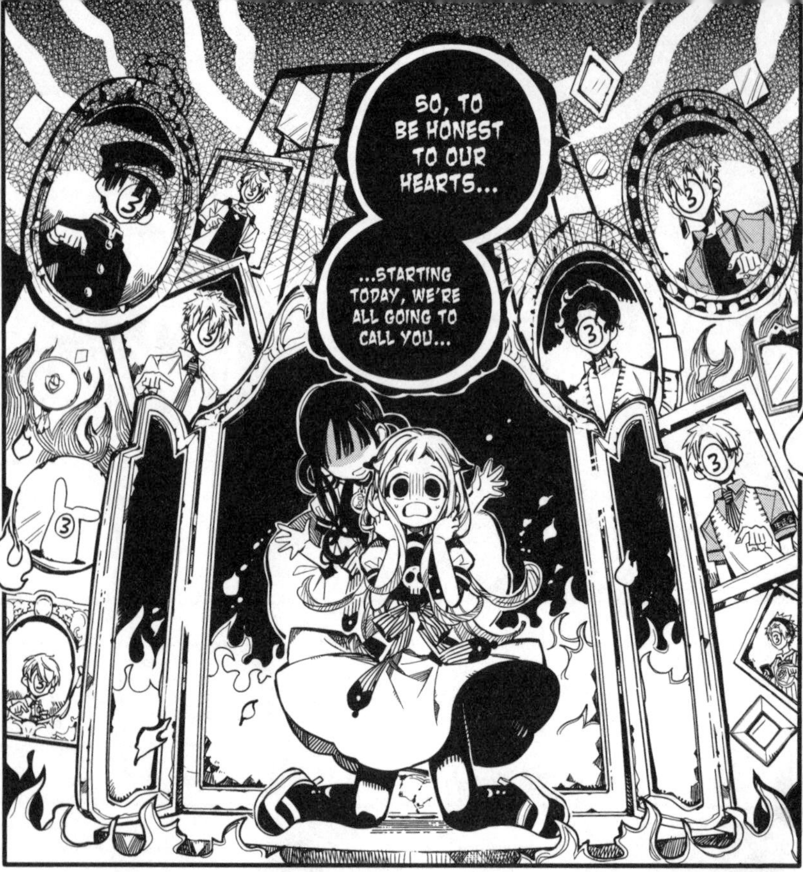
SO, TO BE HONEST TO OUR HEARTS...
...STARTING TODAY, WE'RE ALL GOING TO CALL YOU...
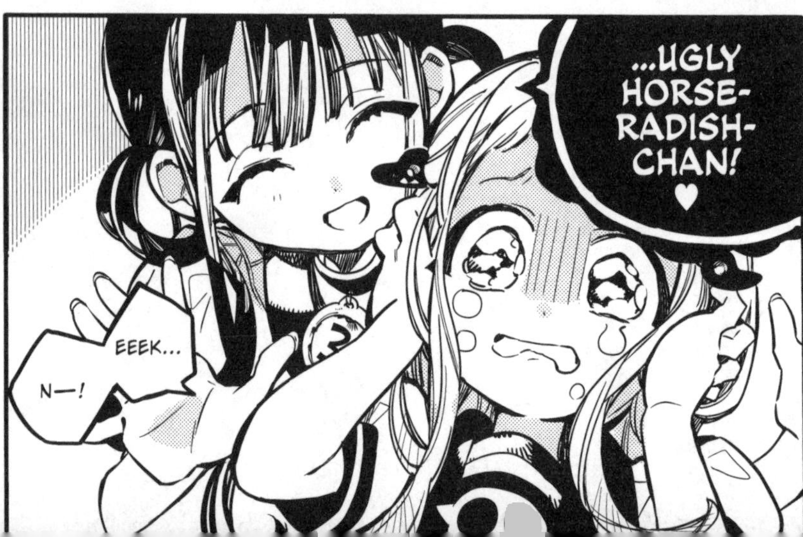
...UGLY HORSE-RADISH-CHAN! ♥
EEEK...
N—!

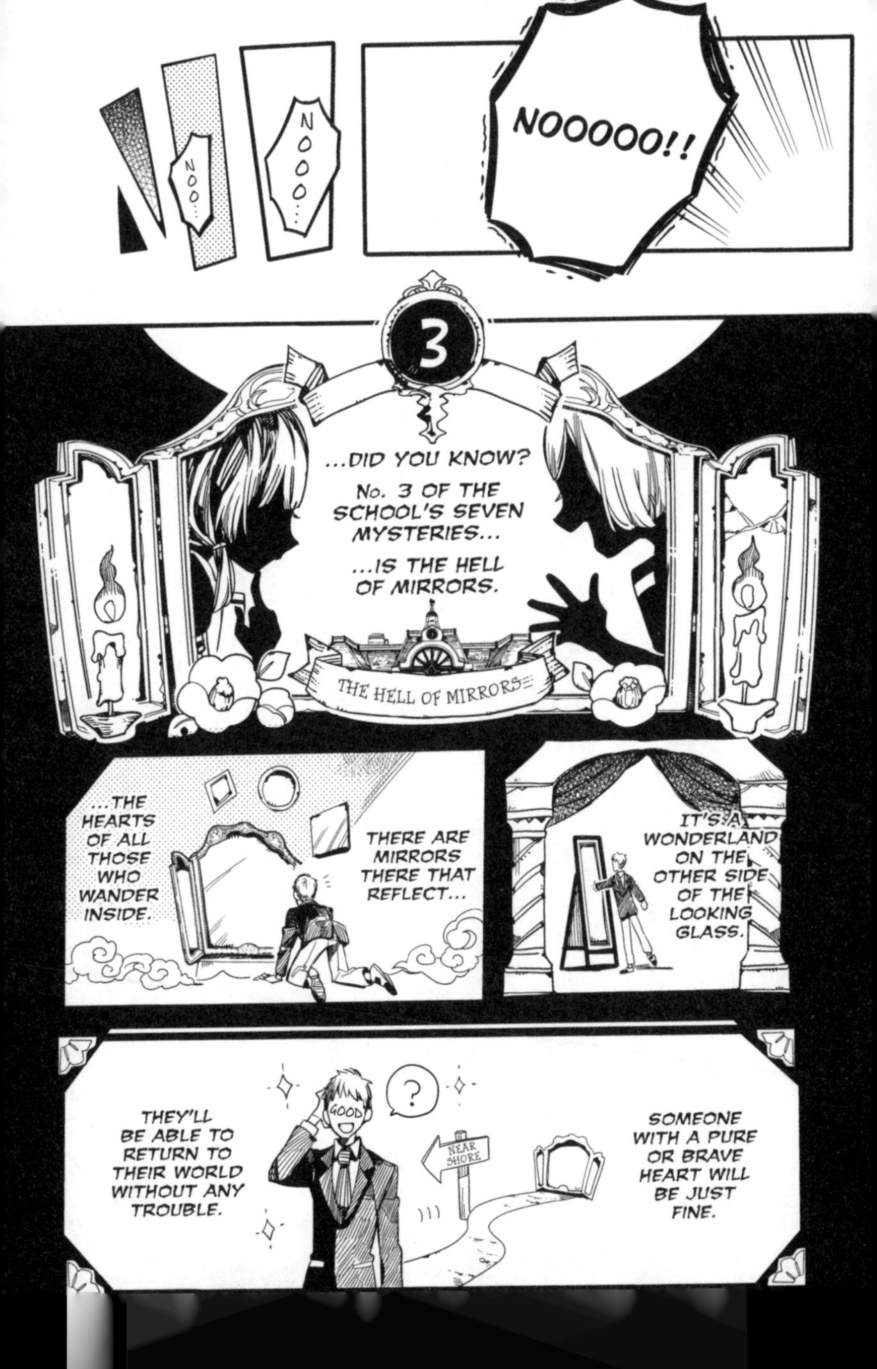

NOOOOO!!
NOOO...
NOO...
3
...DID YOU KNOW?
No. 3 OF THE SCHOOL'S SEVEN MYSTERIES...
...IS THE HELL OF MIRRORS.
THE HELL OF MIRRORS
IT'S A WONDERLAND ON THE OTHER SIDE OF THE LOOKING GLASS.
THERE ARE MIRRORS THERE THAT REFLECT...
...THE HEARTS OF ALL THOSE WHO WANDER INSIDE.
SOMEONE WITH A PURE OR BRAVE HEART WILL BE JUST FINE.
NEAR SHORE
?
GOOD
THEY'LL BE ABLE TO RETURN TO THEIR WORLD WITHOUT ANY TROUBLE.

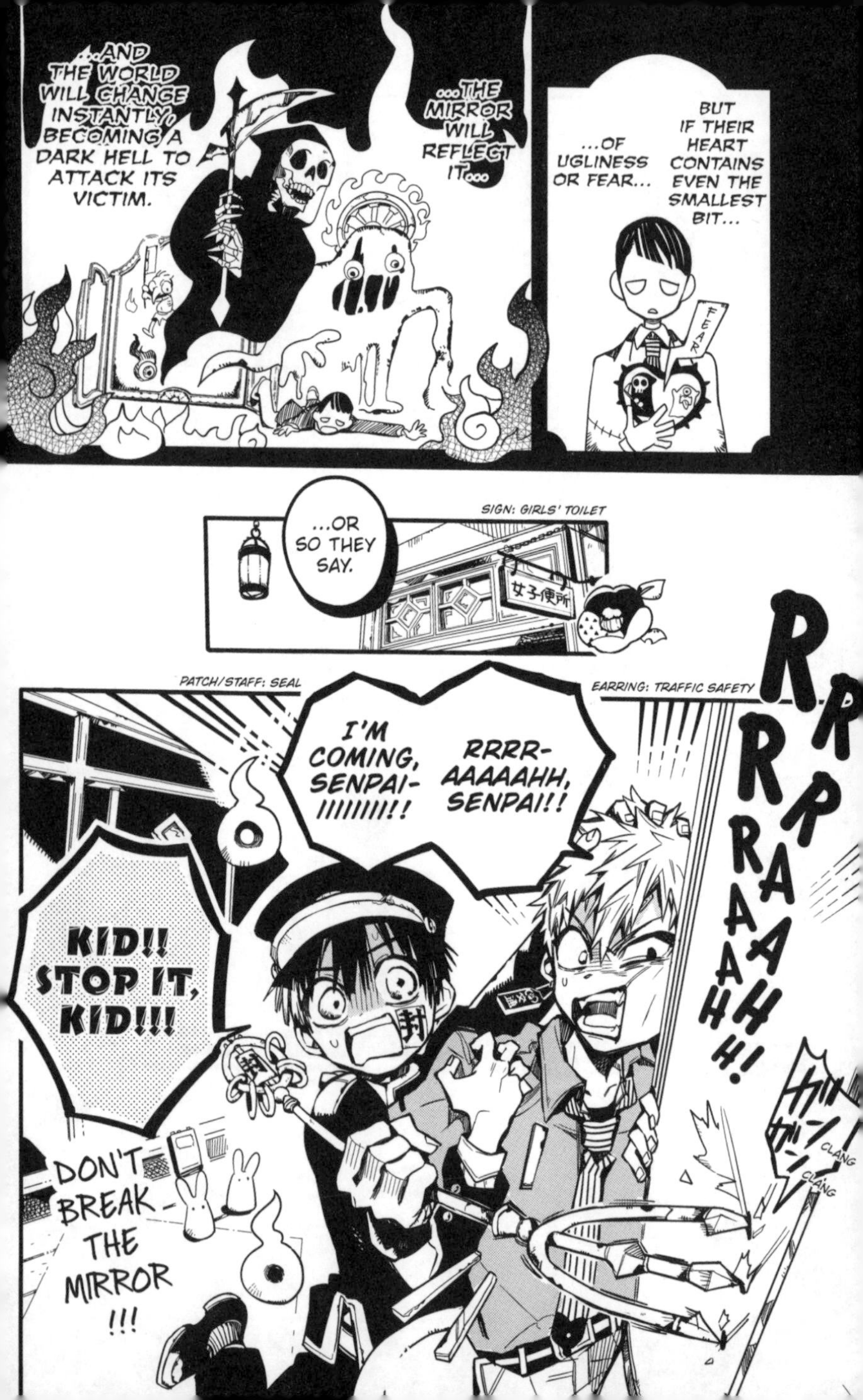
BUT IF THEIR HEART CONTAINS EVEN THE SMALLEST BIT...
...OF UGLINESS OR FEAR...
FEAR
...THE MIRROR WILL REFLECT IT...
...AND THE WORLD WILL CHANGE INSTANTLY, BECOMING A DARK HELL TO ATTACK ITS VICTIM.
SIGN: GIRLS' TOILET
女子便所
...OR SO THEY SAY.
EARRING: TRAFFIC SAFETY
PATCH/STAFF: SEAL
RRRRRAAAAHHH!
RRRR-AAAAAAH, SENPAI!!
I'M COMING, SENPAI-!!!!!!!!!!
KID!! STOP IT, KID!!!
DON'T BREAK THE MIRROR!!!
CLANG
CLANG

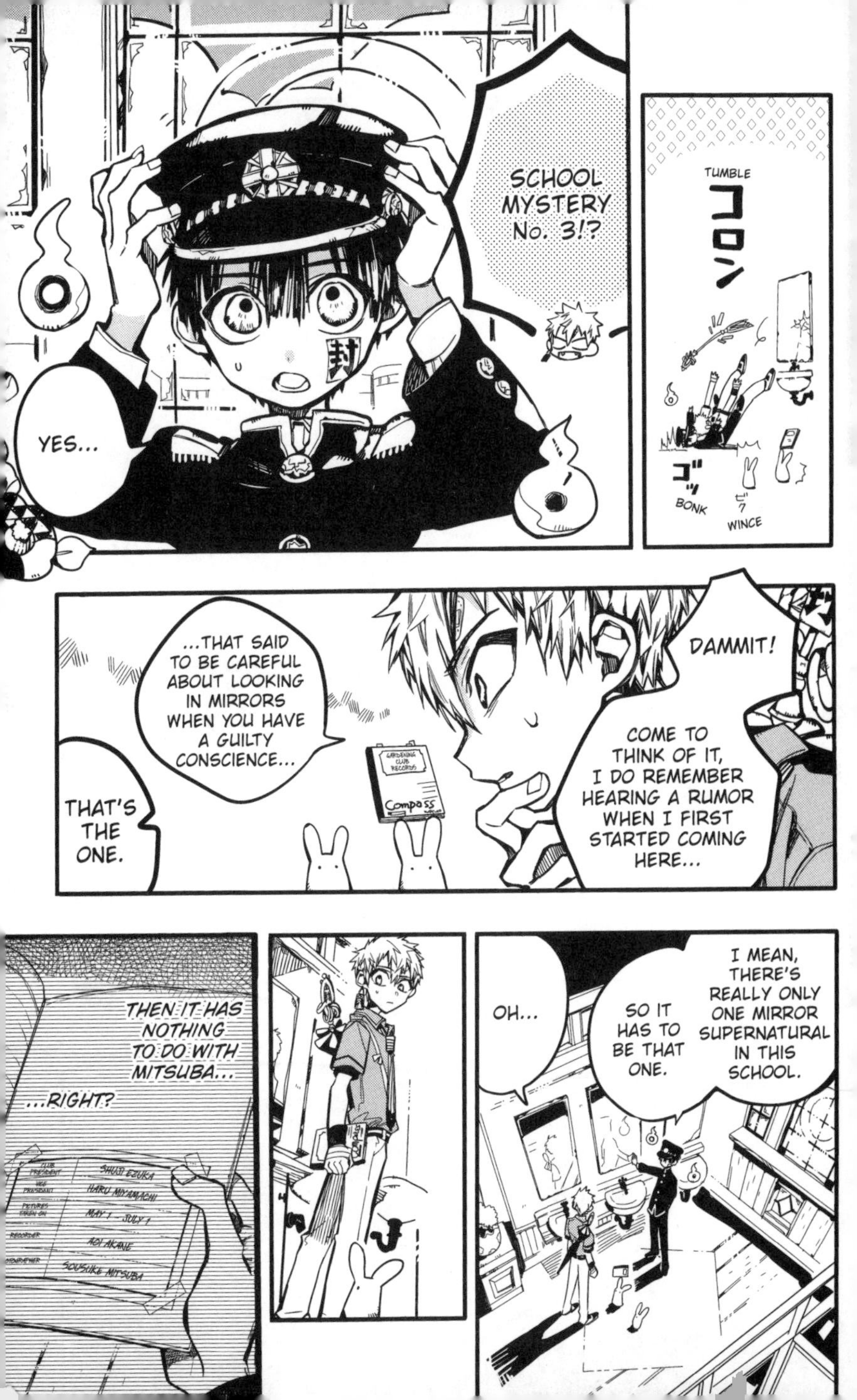
TUMBLE
コロン
ゴッ
BONK
ビク
WINCE
SCHOOL MYSTERY No. 3!?
YES...
DAMMIT!
COME TO THINK OF IT, I DO REMEMBER HEARING A RUMOR WHEN I FIRST STARTED COMING HERE...
...THAT SAID TO BE CAREFUL ABOUT LOOKING IN MIRRORS WHEN YOU HAVE A GUILTY CONSCIENCE...
GARDENING CLUB RECORDS
Compass
THAT'S THE ONE.
I MEAN, THERE'S REALLY ONLY ONE MIRROR SUPERNATURAL IN THIS SCHOOL.
SO IT HAS TO BE THAT ONE.
OH...
THEN IT HAS NOTHING TO DO WITH MITSUBA...
...RIGHT?
CLUB PRESIDENT
SHUJI EZUKA
VICE PRESIDENT
HARU MIYAMACHI
PICTURES TAKEN ON
MAY 1 – JULY 1
RECORDER
AOI AKANE
SOUSUKE MITSUBA

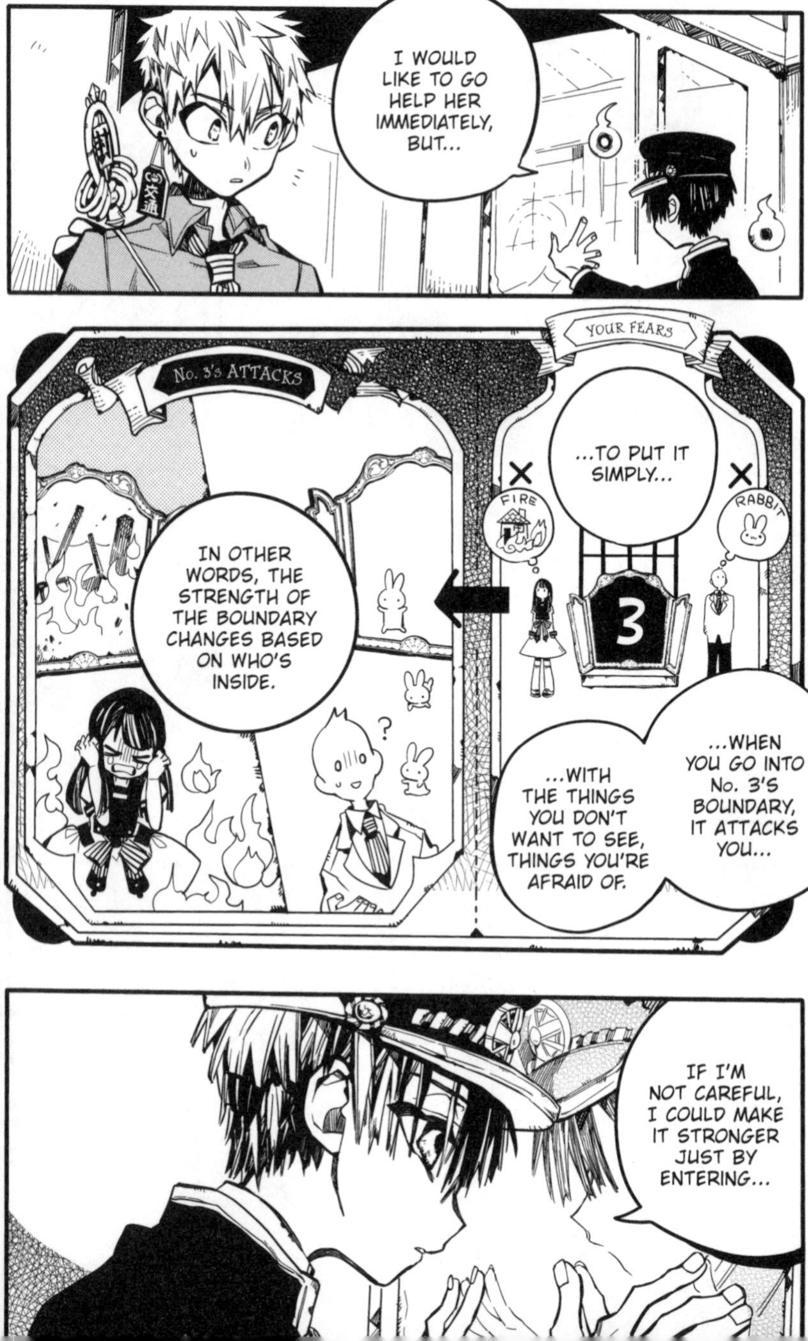
I WOULD LIKE TO GO HELP HER IMMEDIATELY, BUT...
YOUR FEARS
...TO PUT IT SIMPLY...
FIRE
RABBIT
3
...WHEN YOU GO INTO No. 3'S BOUNDARY, IT ATTACKS YOU...
...WITH THE THINGS YOU DON'T WANT TO SEE, THINGS YOU'RE AFRAID OF.
No. 3's ATTACKS
IN OTHER WORDS, THE STRENGTH OF THE BOUNDARY CHANGES BASED ON WHO'S INSIDE.
IF I'M NOT CAREFUL, I COULD MAKE IT STRONGER JUST BY ENTERING...

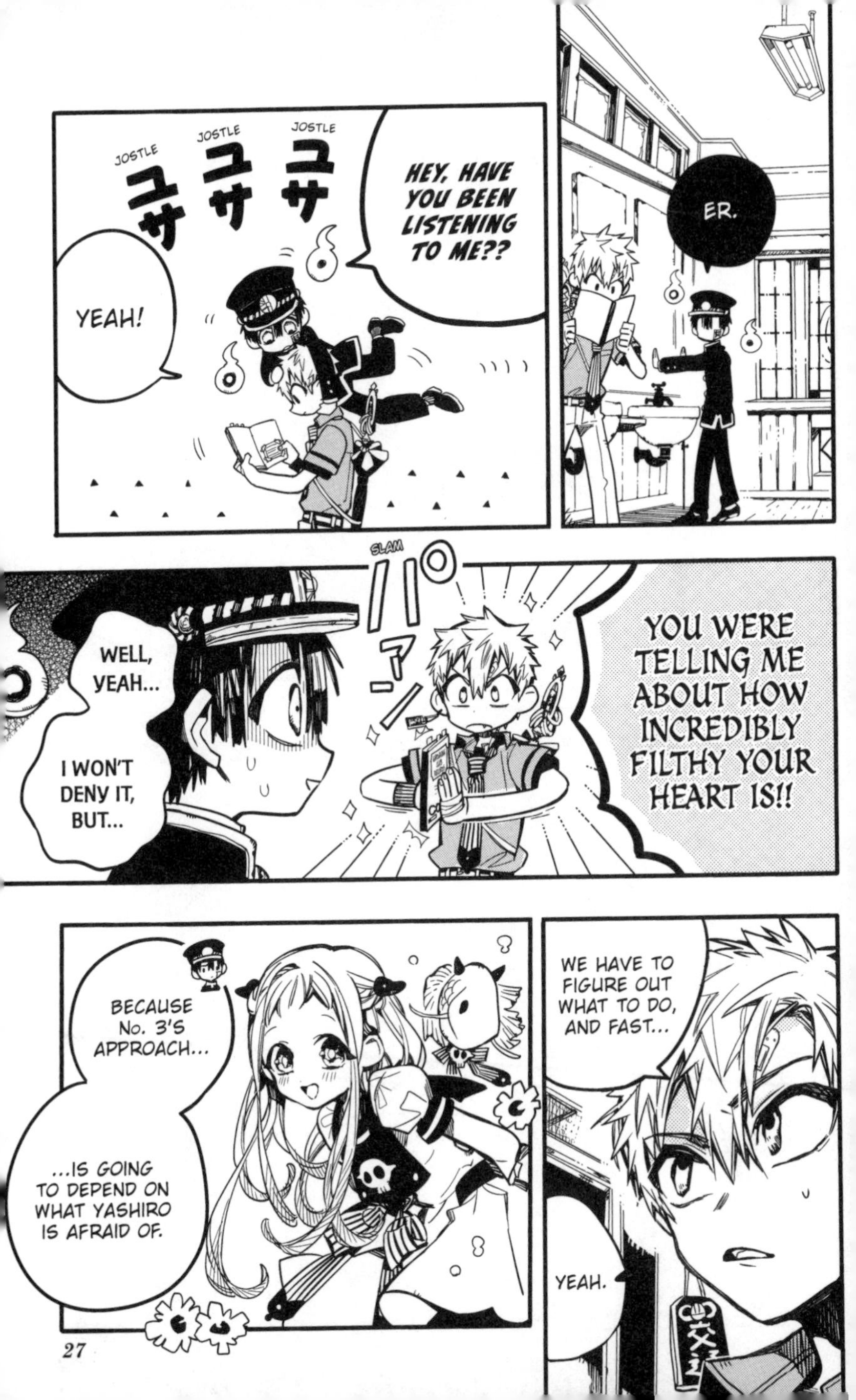
ER.
JOSTLE JOSTLE JOSTLE
HEY, HAVE YOU BEEN LISTENING TO ME??
YEAH!
SLAM
YOU WERE TELLING ME ABOUT HOW INCREDIBLY FILTHY YOUR HEART IS!!
WELL, YEAH...
I WON'T DENY IT, BUT...
WE HAVE TO FIGURE OUT WHAT TO DO, AND FAST...
YEAH.
BECAUSE No. 3'S APPROACH...
...IS GOING TO DEPEND ON WHAT YASHIRO IS AFRAID OF.

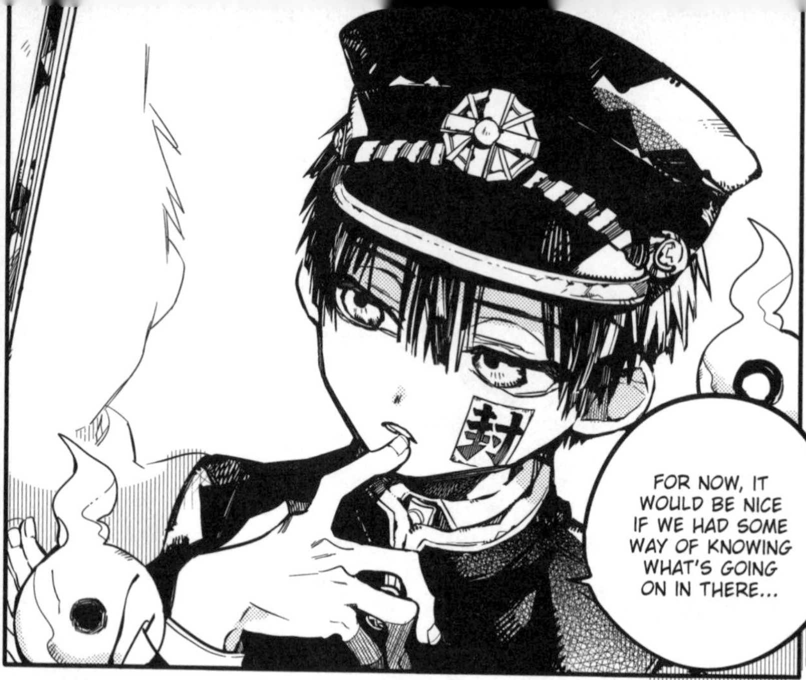
FOR NOW, IT WOULD BE NICE IF WE HAD SOME WAY OF KNOWING WHAT'S GOING ON IN THERE...

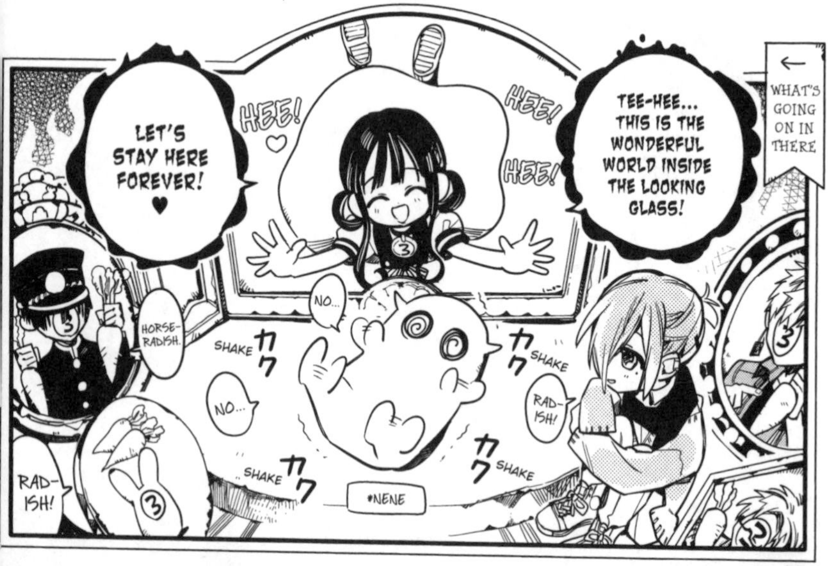
← WHAT'S GOING ON IN THERE
TEE-HEE... THIS IS THE WONDERFUL WORLD INSIDE THE LOOKING GLASS!
HEE!
HEE!
HEE! ♥
LET'S STAY HERE FOREVER! ♥
SHAKE
RAD-ISH!
SHAKE
NO...
SHAKE
HORSE-RADISH.
NO...
SHAKE
#NENE
RAD-ISH!

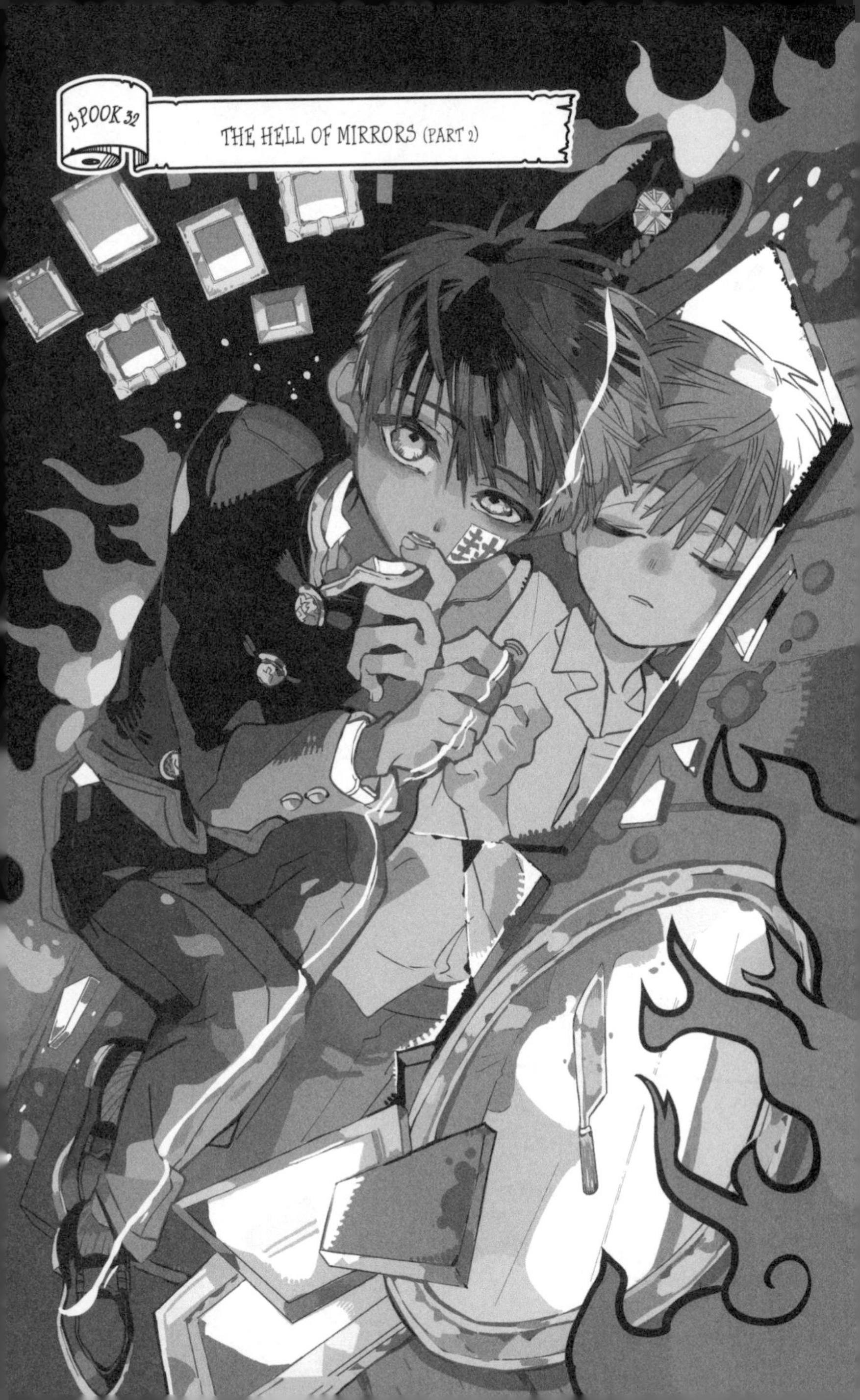
SPOOK 32
THE HELL OF MIRRORS (PART 2)

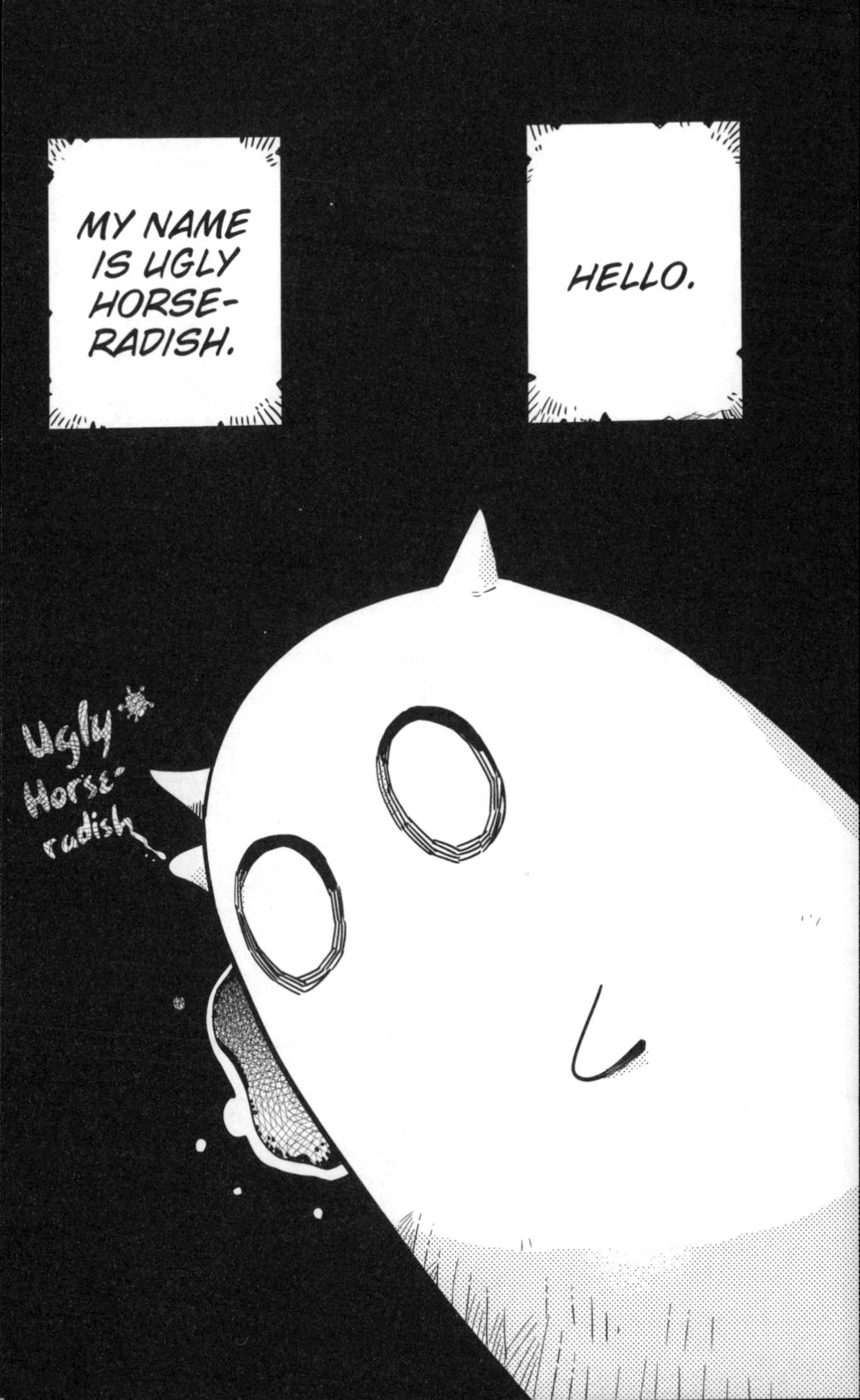
HELLO.
MY NAME IS UGLY HORSE-RADISH.
Ugly Horse-radish

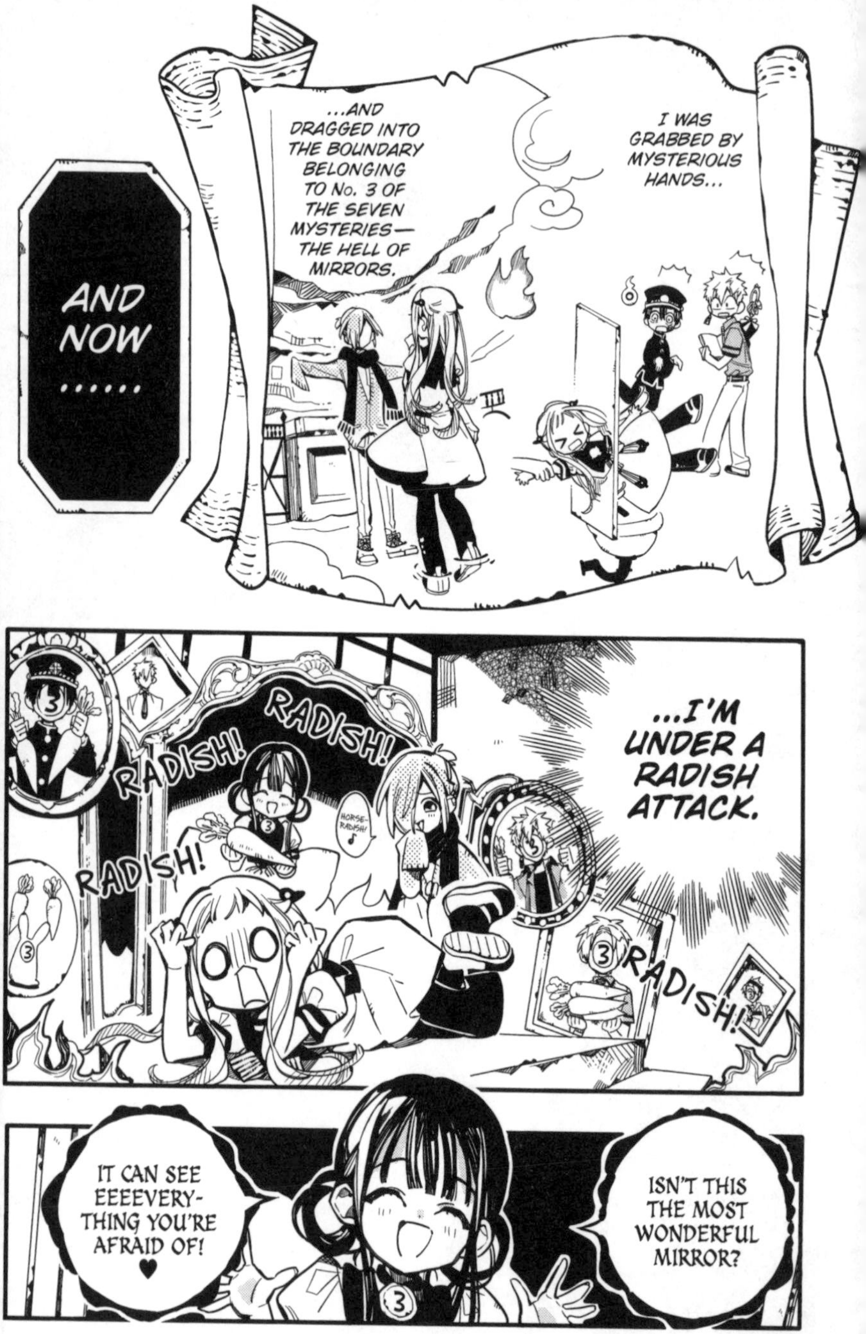

I WAS GRABBED BY MYSTERIOUS HANDS...
...AND DRAGGED INTO THE BOUNDARY BELONGING TO No. 3 OF THE SEVEN MYSTERIES—THE HELL OF MIRRORS.
AND NOW......
...I'M UNDER A RADISH ATTACK.
RADISH!
HORSE-RADISH! ♪
RADISH!
RADISH!
RADISH!
ISN'T THIS THE MOST WONDERFUL MIRROR?
IT CAN SEE EEEEVERY-THING YOU'RE AFRAID OF! ♥

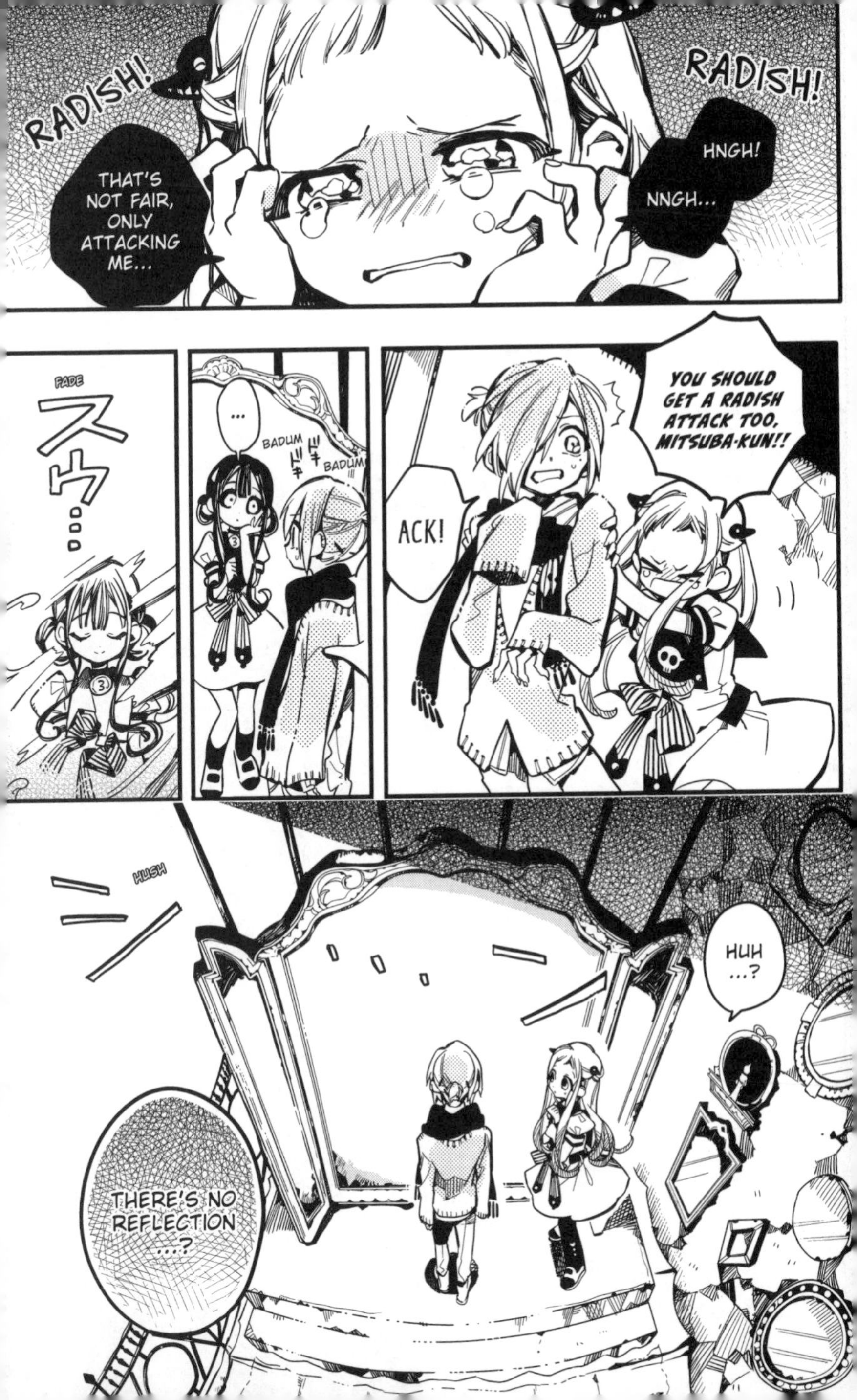
RADISH!
HNGH!
NNGH...
RADISH!
THAT'S NOT FAIR, ONLY ATTACKING ME...
YOU SHOULD GET A RADISH ATTACK TOO, MITSUBA-KUN!!
ACK!
...
BADUM
ドキドキ
BADUM
FADE
スウ...
HUSH
HUH ...?
THERE'S NO REFLECTION ...?

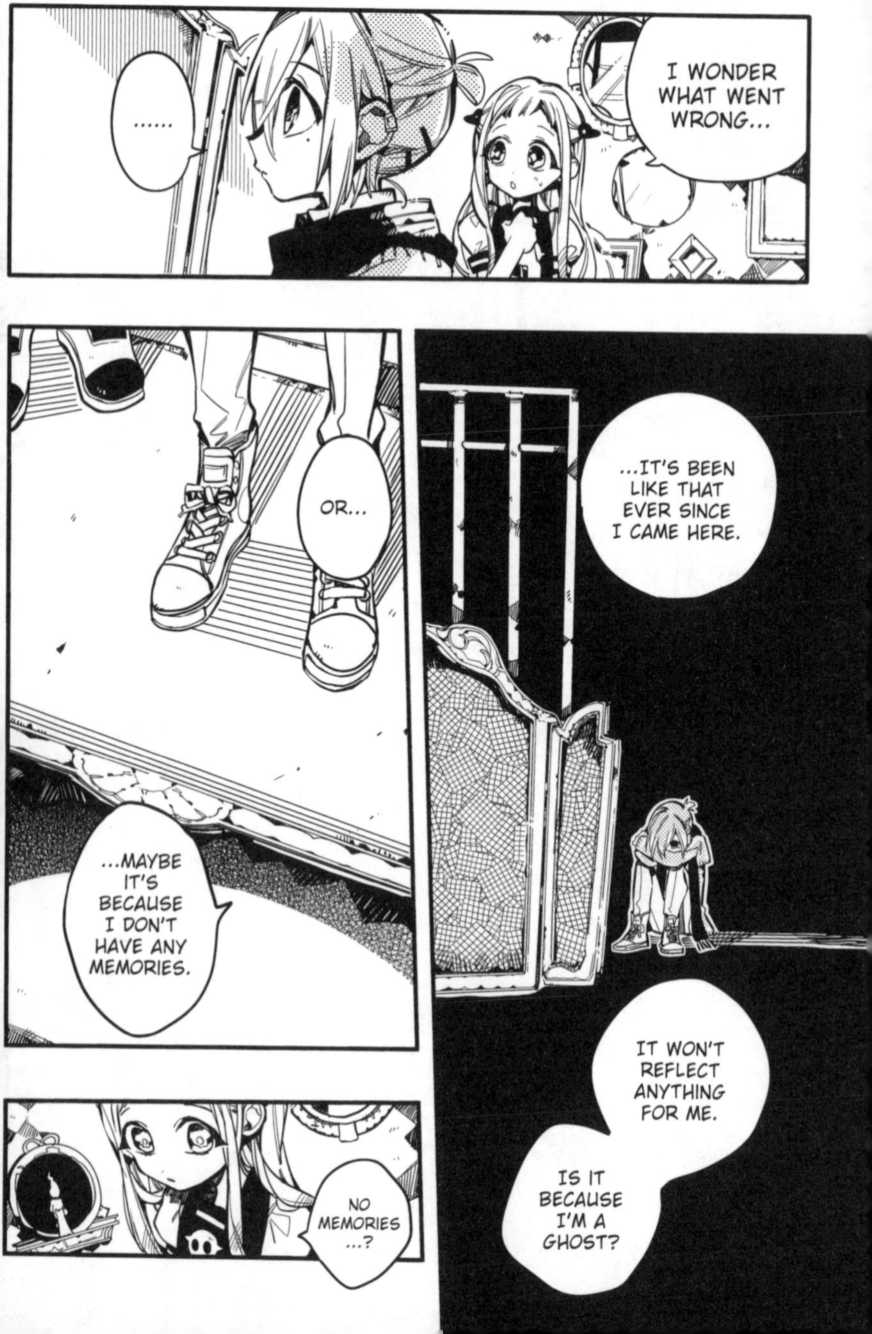
I WONDER WHAT WENT WRONG...
......
...IT'S BEEN LIKE THAT EVER SINCE I CAME HERE.
IT WON'T REFLECT ANYTHING FOR ME.
IS IT BECAUSE I'M A GHOST?
OR...
...MAYBE IT'S BECAUSE I DON'T HAVE ANY MEMORIES.
NO MEMORIES ...?

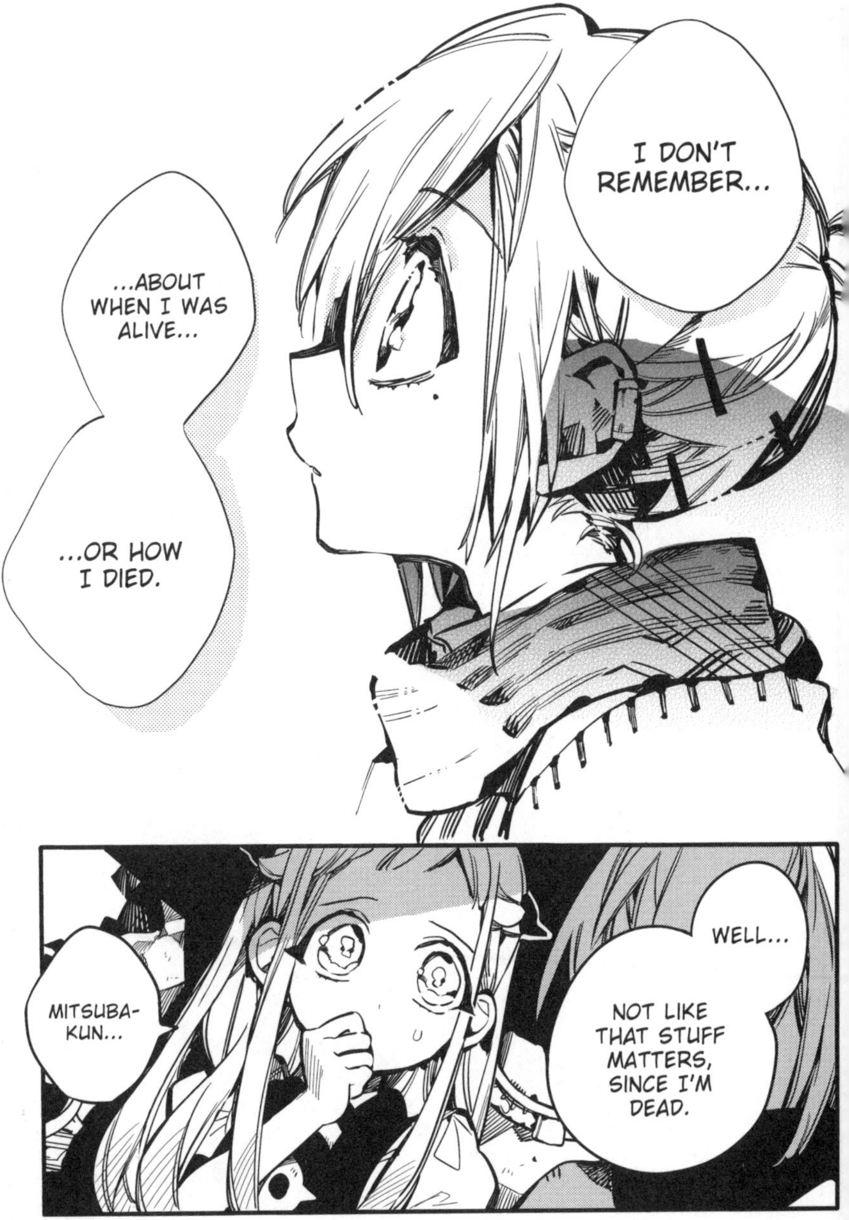
I DON'T REMEMBER...
...ABOUT WHEN I WAS ALIVE...
...OR HOW I DIED.
WELL...
NOT LIKE THAT STUFF MATTERS, SINCE I'M DEAD.
MITSUBA-KUN...

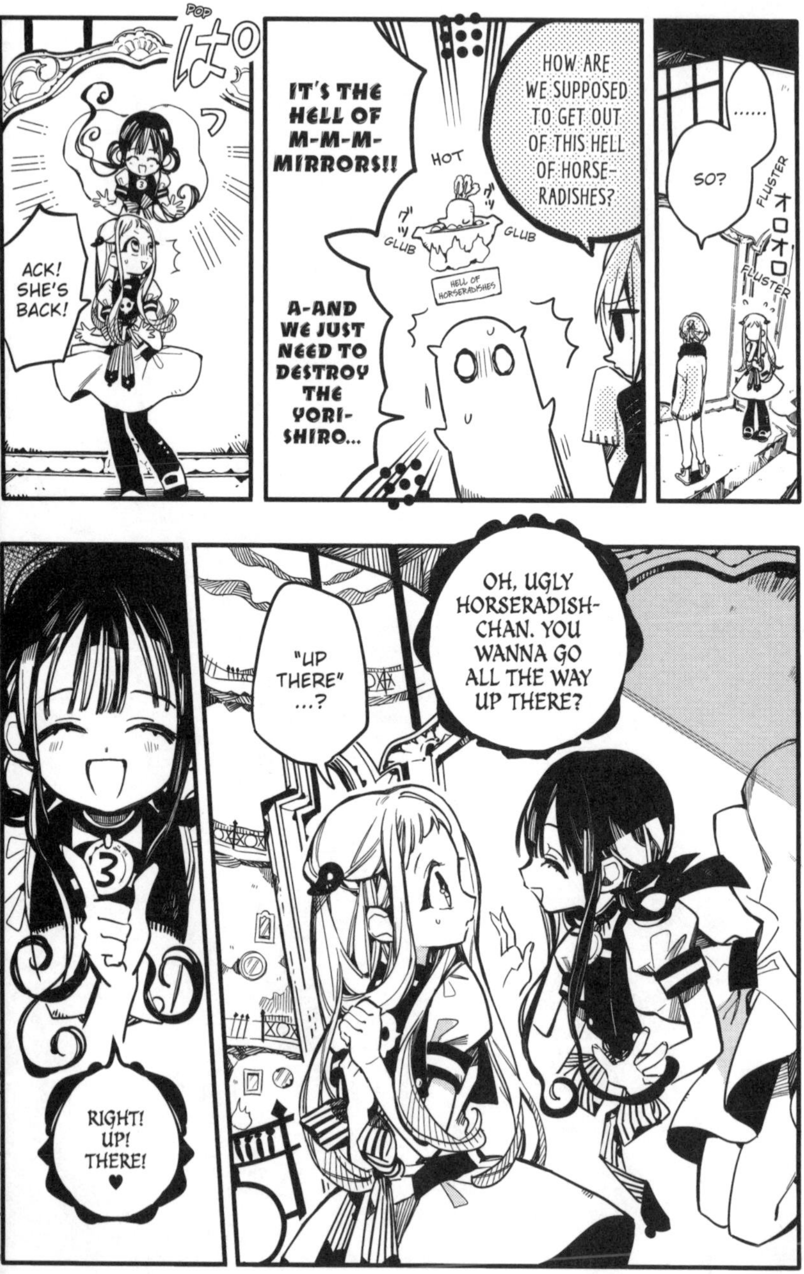
......
SO?
FLUSTER オロオロ FLUSTER
HOW ARE WE SUPPOSED TO GET OUT OF THIS HELL OF HORSE-RADISHES?
IT'S THE HELL OF M-M-M-MIRRORS!!
HOT
GLUB GLUB
HELL OF HORSERADISHES
A-AND WE JUST NEED TO DESTROY THE YORI-SHIRO...
POP
ACK! SHE'S BACK!
OH, UGLY HORSERADISH-CHAN. YOU WANNA GO ALL THE WAY UP THERE?
"UP THERE" ...?
RIGHT! UP! THERE! ♥

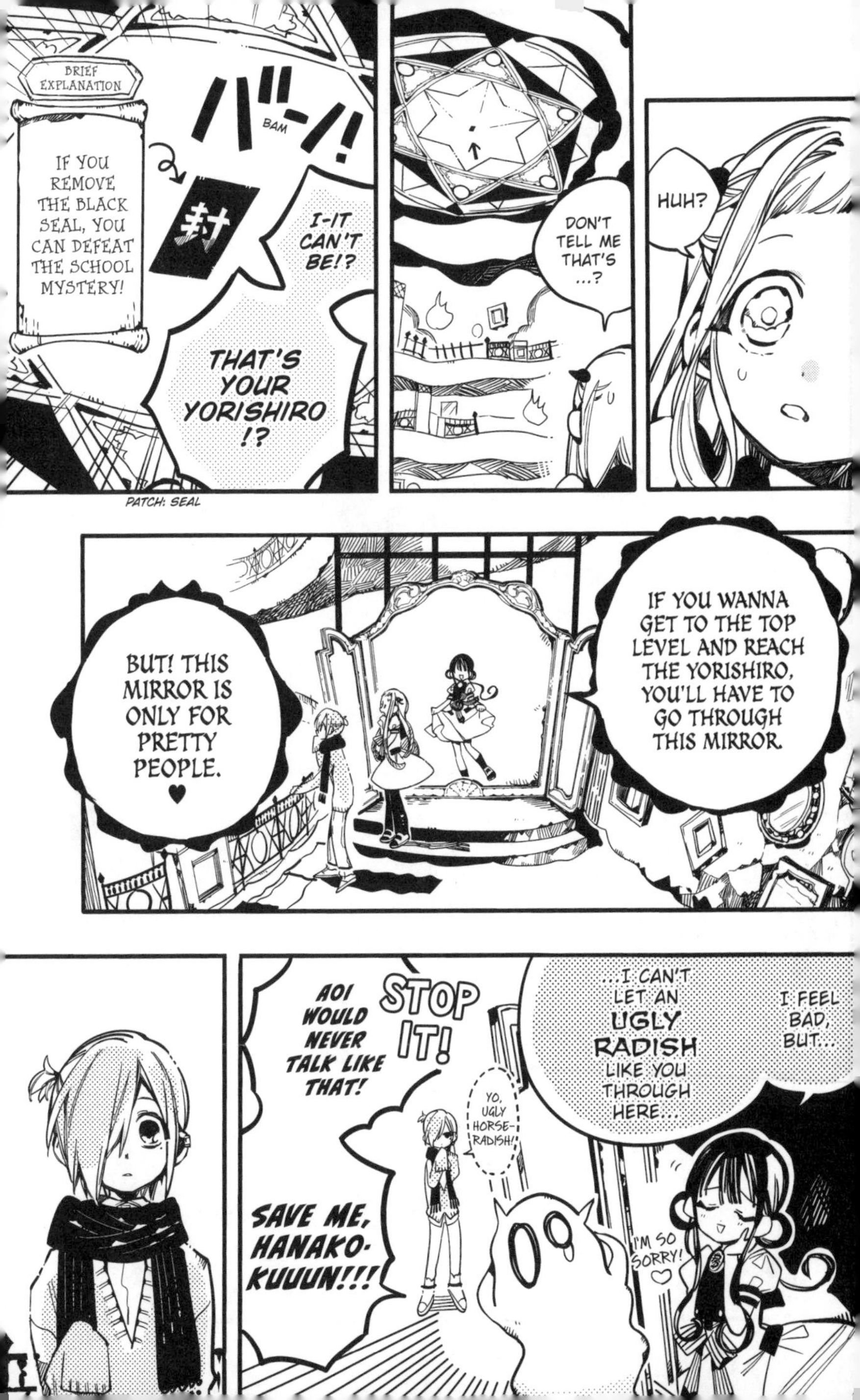
HUH?
DON'T TELL ME THAT'S ...?
BRIEF EXPLANATION
IF YOU REMOVE THE BLACK SEAL, YOU CAN DEFEAT THE SCHOOL MYSTERY!
バーン!
BAM
封
I-IT CAN'T BE!?
THAT'S YOUR YORISHIRO !?
PATCH: SEAL
IF YOU WANNA GET TO THE TOP LEVEL AND REACH THE YORISHIRO, YOU'LL HAVE TO GO THROUGH THIS MIRROR.
BUT! THIS MIRROR IS ONLY FOR PRETTY PEOPLE. ♥
I FEEL BAD, BUT...
...I CAN'T LET AN UGLY RADISH LIKE YOU THROUGH HERE...
I'M SO SORRY! ♡
YO, UGLY HORSE-RADISH!
STOP IT!
AOI WOULD NEVER TALK LIKE THAT!
SAVE ME, HANAKO-KUUUN!!!

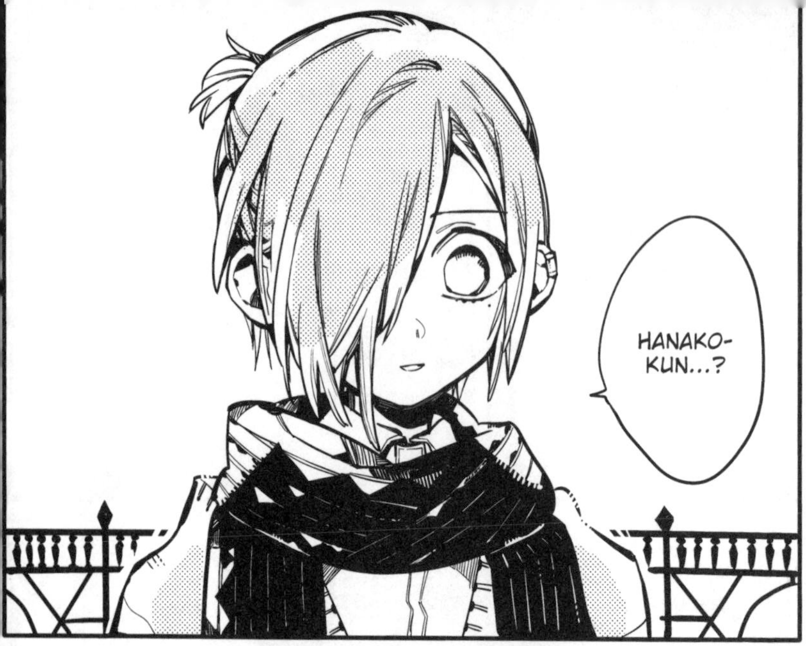
HANAKO-KUN...?

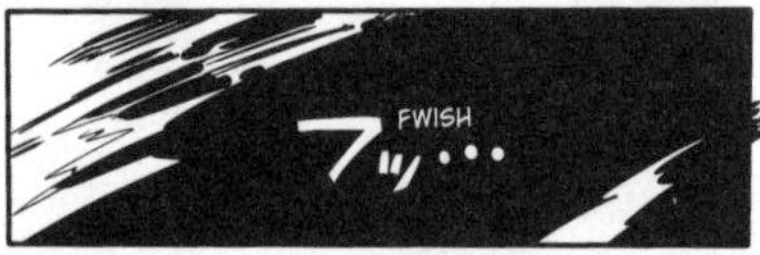
FWISH

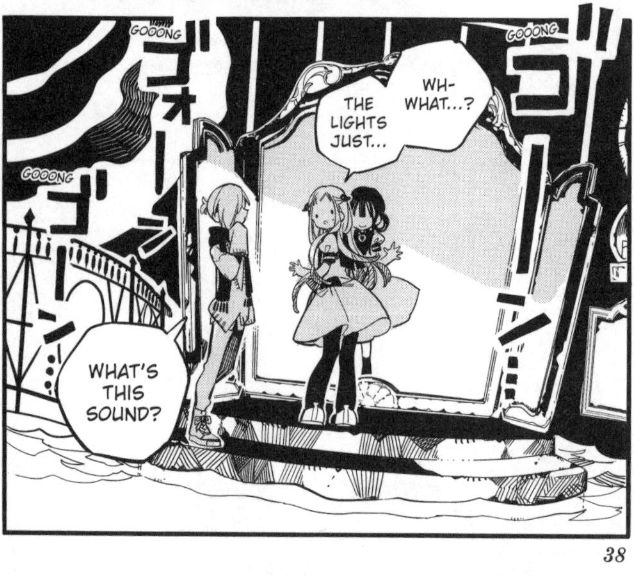
GOOONG
WH- WHAT...?
THE LIGHTS JUST...
GOOONG
GOOONG
WHAT'S THIS SOUND?

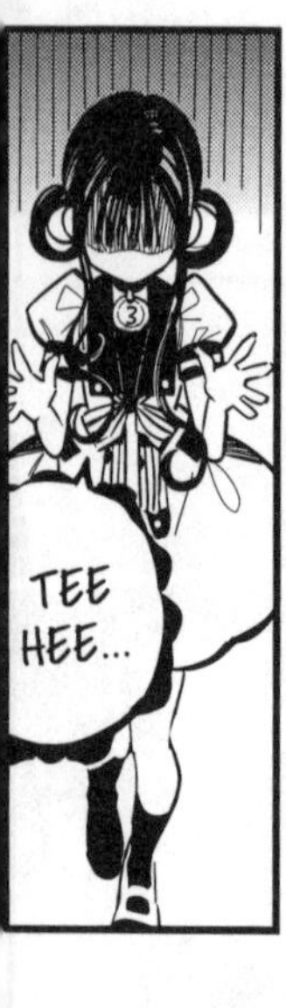
TEE HEE...

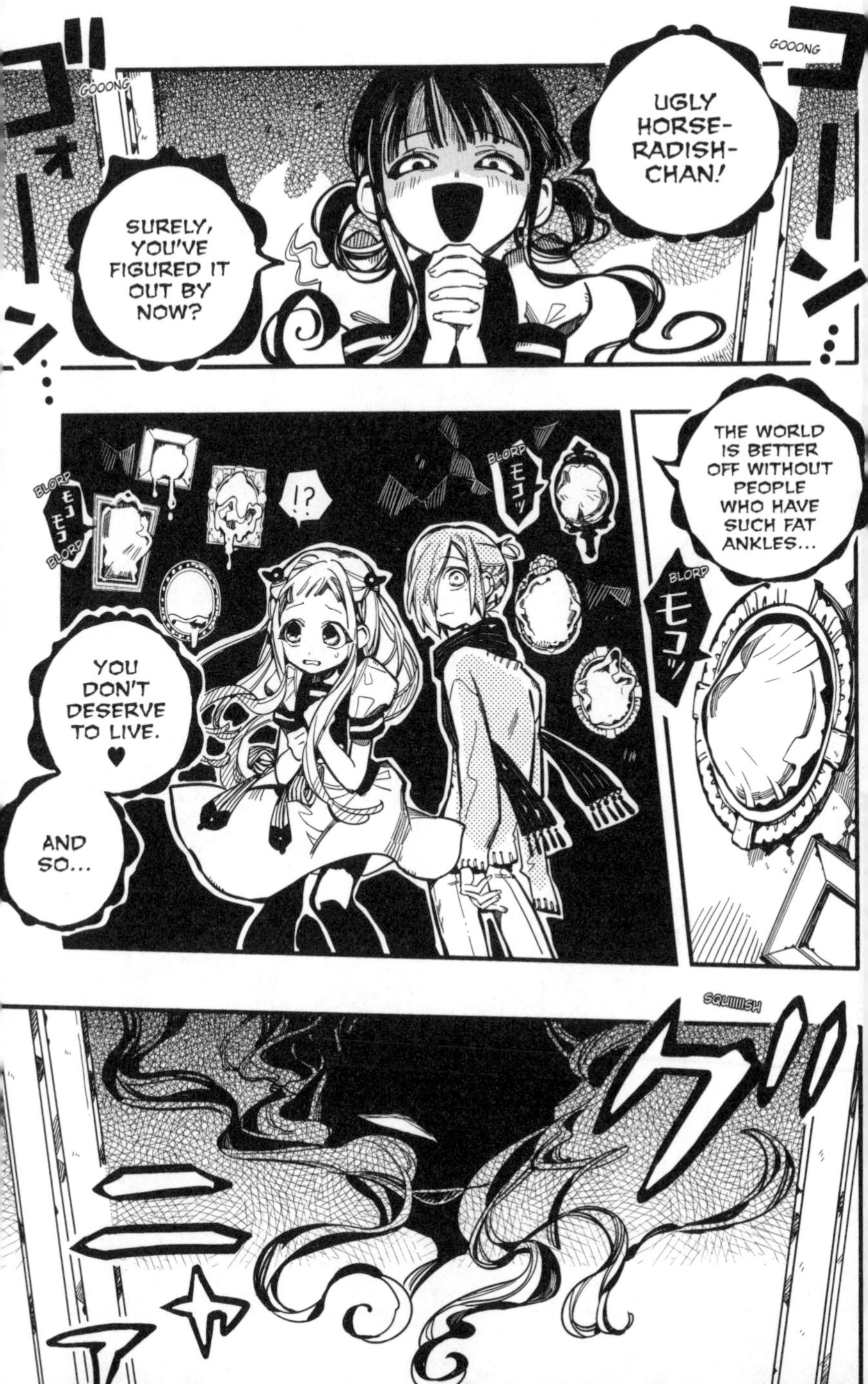
GOOONG
UGLY HORSE-RADISH-CHAN!
SURELY, YOU'VE FIGURED IT OUT BY NOW?
GOOONG
THE WORLD IS BETTER OFF WITHOUT PEOPLE WHO HAVE SUCH FAT ANKLES...
BLORP
BLORP
!?
BLORP
BLORP
YOU DON'T DESERVE TO LIVE. ♥
AND SO...
SQUIIIISH

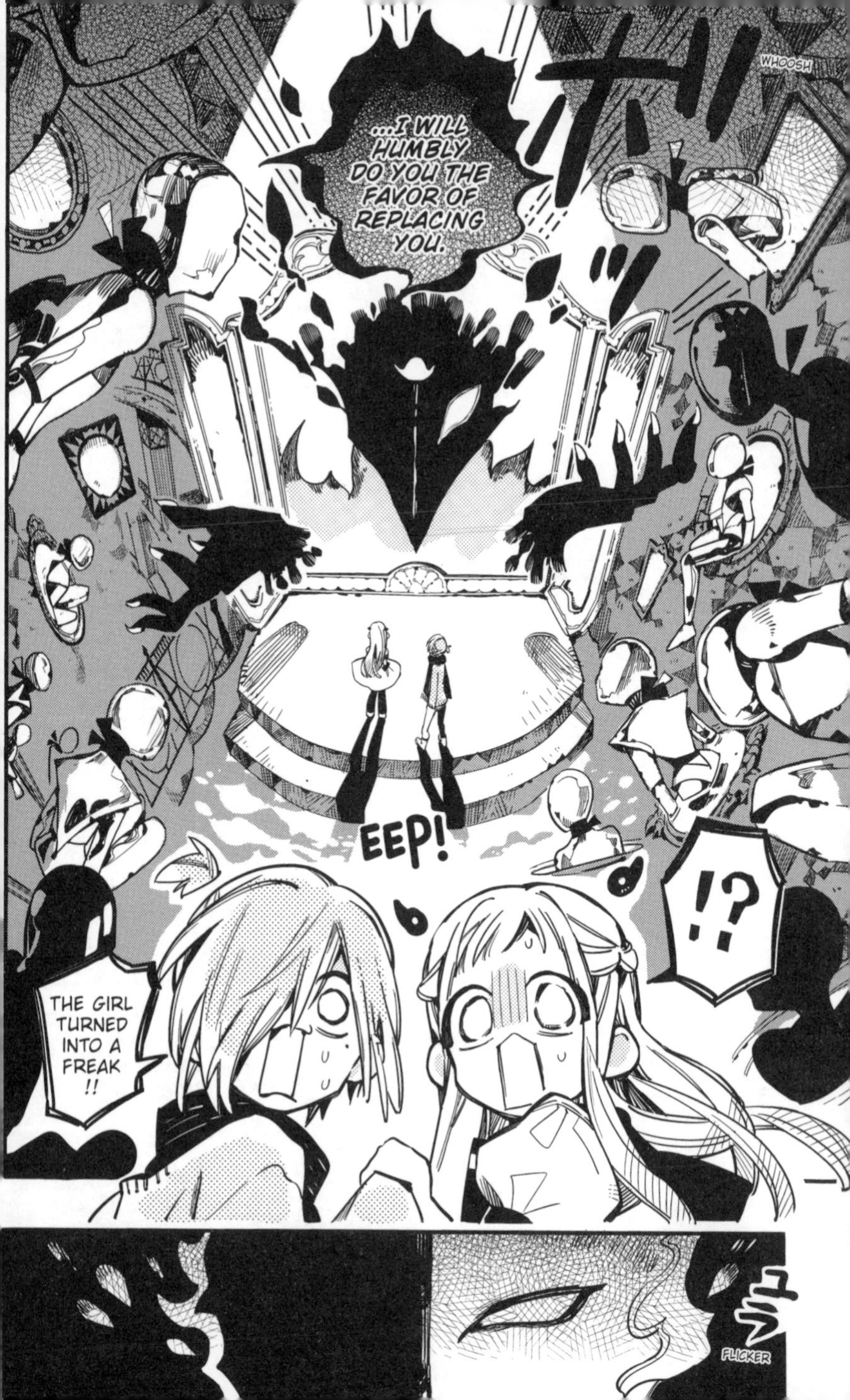
WHOOSH
...I WILL HUMBLY DO YOU THE FAVOR OF REPLACING YOU.
EEP!
!?
THE GIRL TURNED INTO A FREAK !!
FLICKER

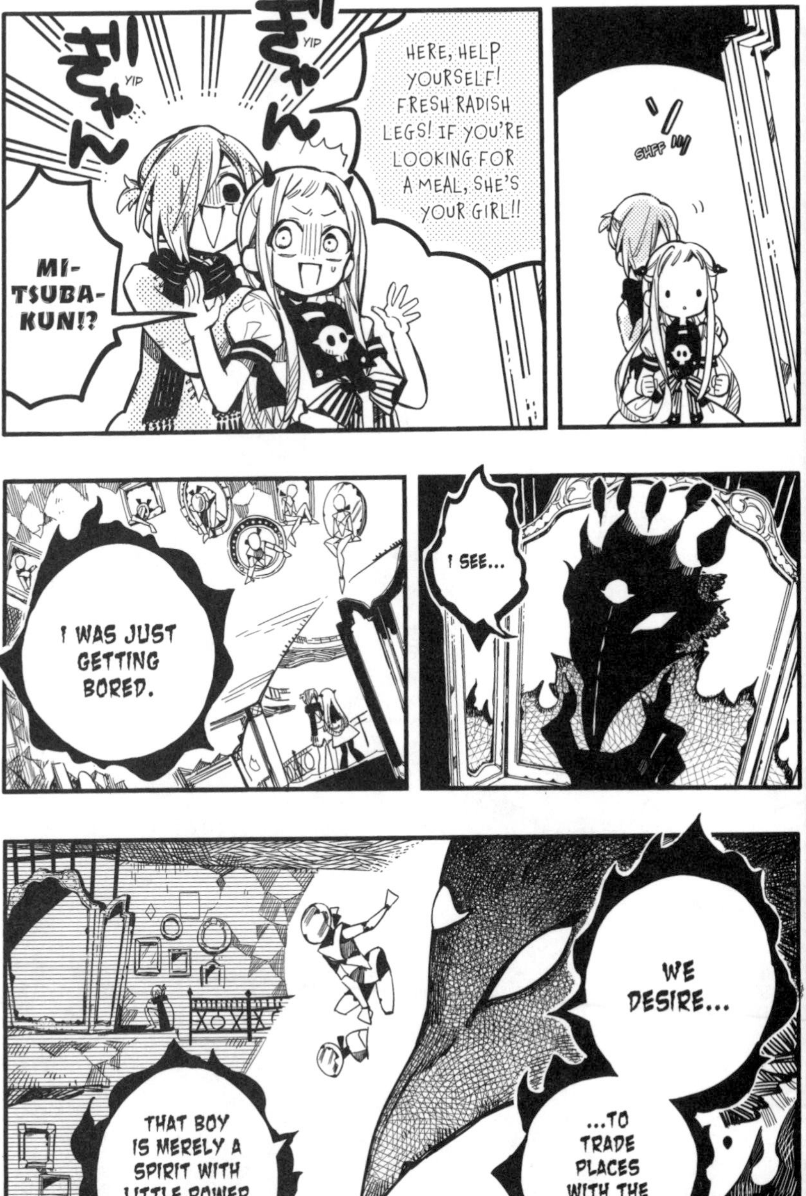
SHFF
ぎゃん
YIP
HERE, HELP YOURSELF! FRESH RADISH LEGS! IF YOU'RE LOOKING FOR A MEAL, SHE'S YOUR GIRL!!
ぎゃん
YIP
MI-TSUBA-KUN!?
I SEE...
I WAS JUST GETTING BORED.
WE DESIRE...
...TO TRADE PLACES WITH THE LIVING.
THAT BOY IS MERELY A SPIRIT WITH LITTLE POWER TO SPEAK OF...

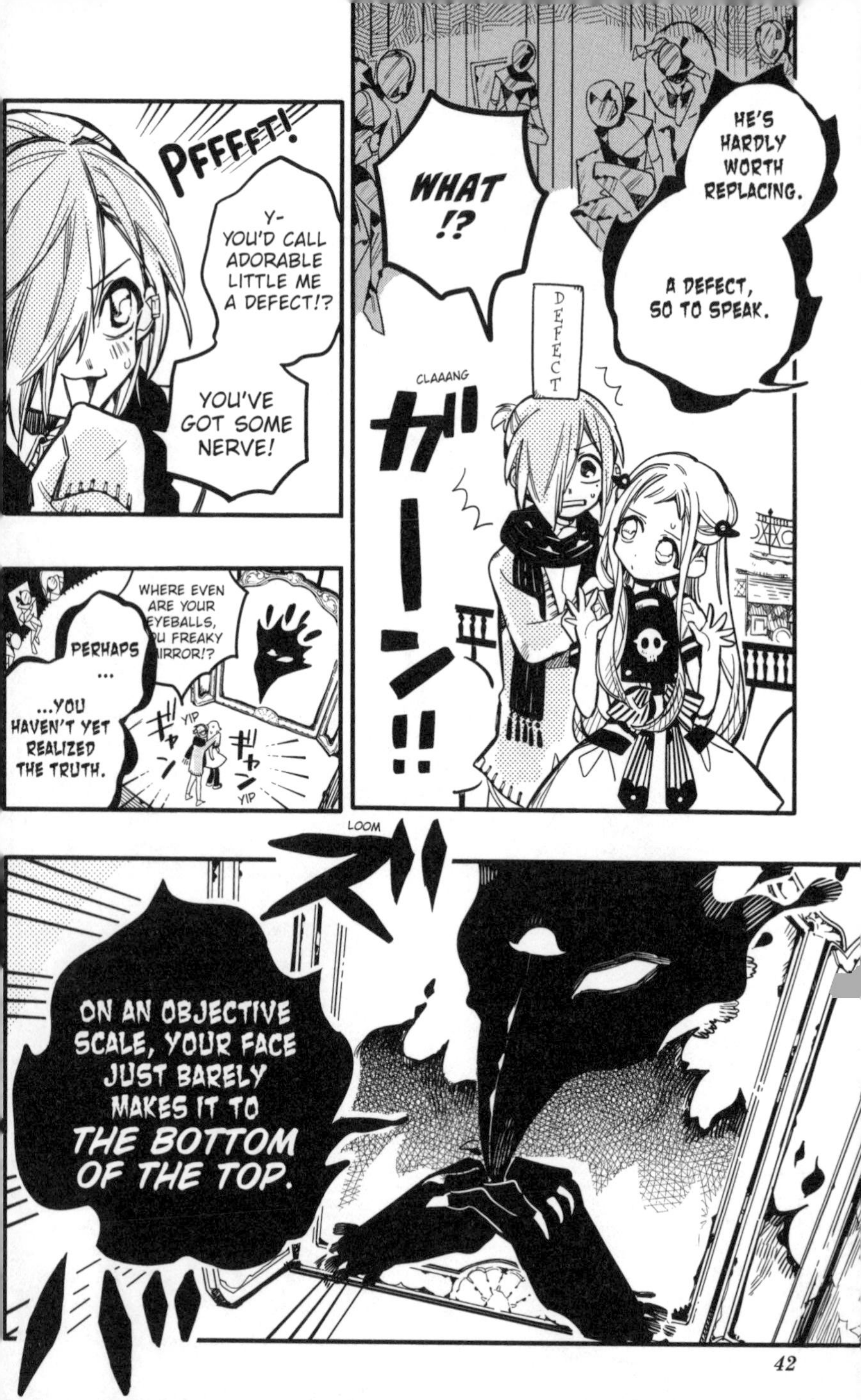
HE'S HARDLY WORTH REPLACING.
A DEFECT, SO TO SPEAK.
WHAT!?
DEFECT
CLAAANG
ガーン!!
PFFFFT!
Y-YOU'D CALL ADORABLE LITTLE ME A DEFECT!?
YOU'VE GOT SOME NERVE!
WHERE EVEN ARE YOUR EYEBALLS, OU FREAKY IRROR!?
YIP
ギャン
YIP
ギャン
PERHAPS...
...YOU HAVEN'T YET REALIZED THE TRUTH.
LOOM
ズ
ON AN OBJECTIVE SCALE, YOUR FACE JUST BARELY MAKES IT TO THE BOTTOM OF THE TOP.

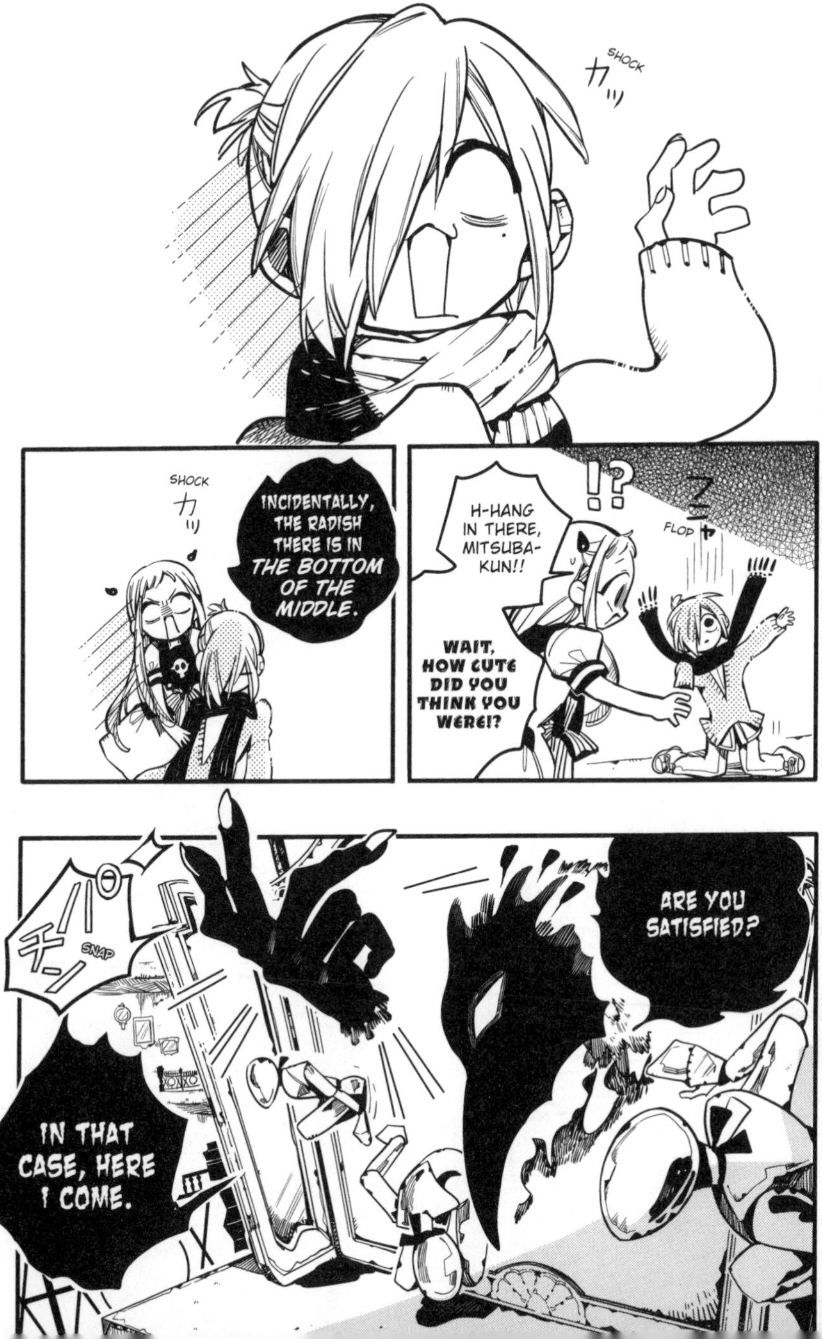
SHOCK
カッ
H-HANG IN THERE, MITSUBA-KUN!!
!?
FLOP
WAIT, HOW CUTE DID YOU THINK YOU WERE!?
SHOCK
カッ
INCIDENTALLY, THE RADISH THERE IS IN THE BOTTOM OF THE MIDDLE.
ARE YOU SATISFIED?
パチーン
SNAP
IN THAT CASE, HERE I COME.

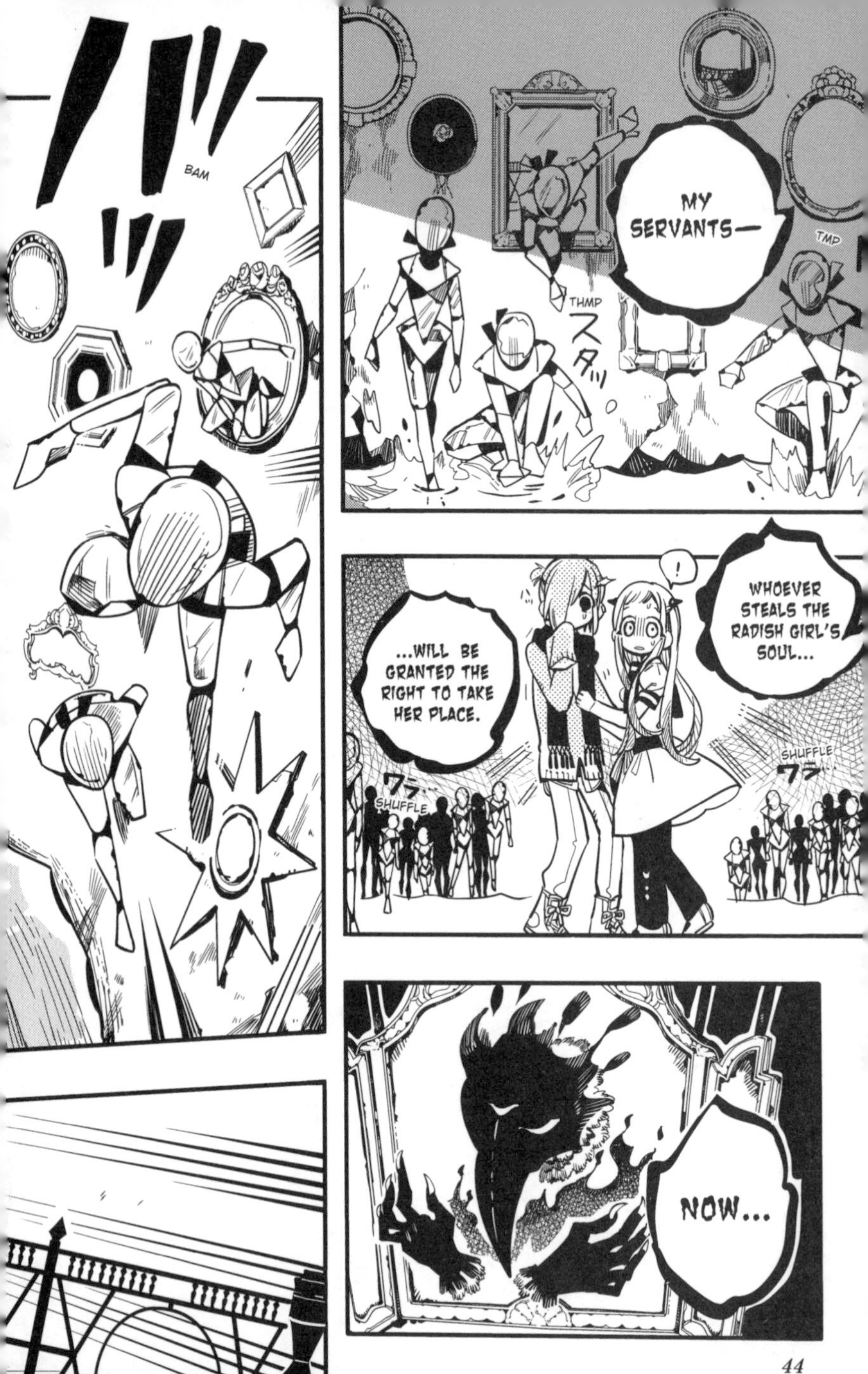
MY SERVANTS—
TMP
THMP
スタッ
WHOEVER STEALS THE RADISH GIRL'S SOUL...
!
SHUFFLE
ワラ…
...WILL BE GRANTED THE RIGHT TO TAKE HER PLACE.
ワラ…
SHUFFLE
NOW...
BAM

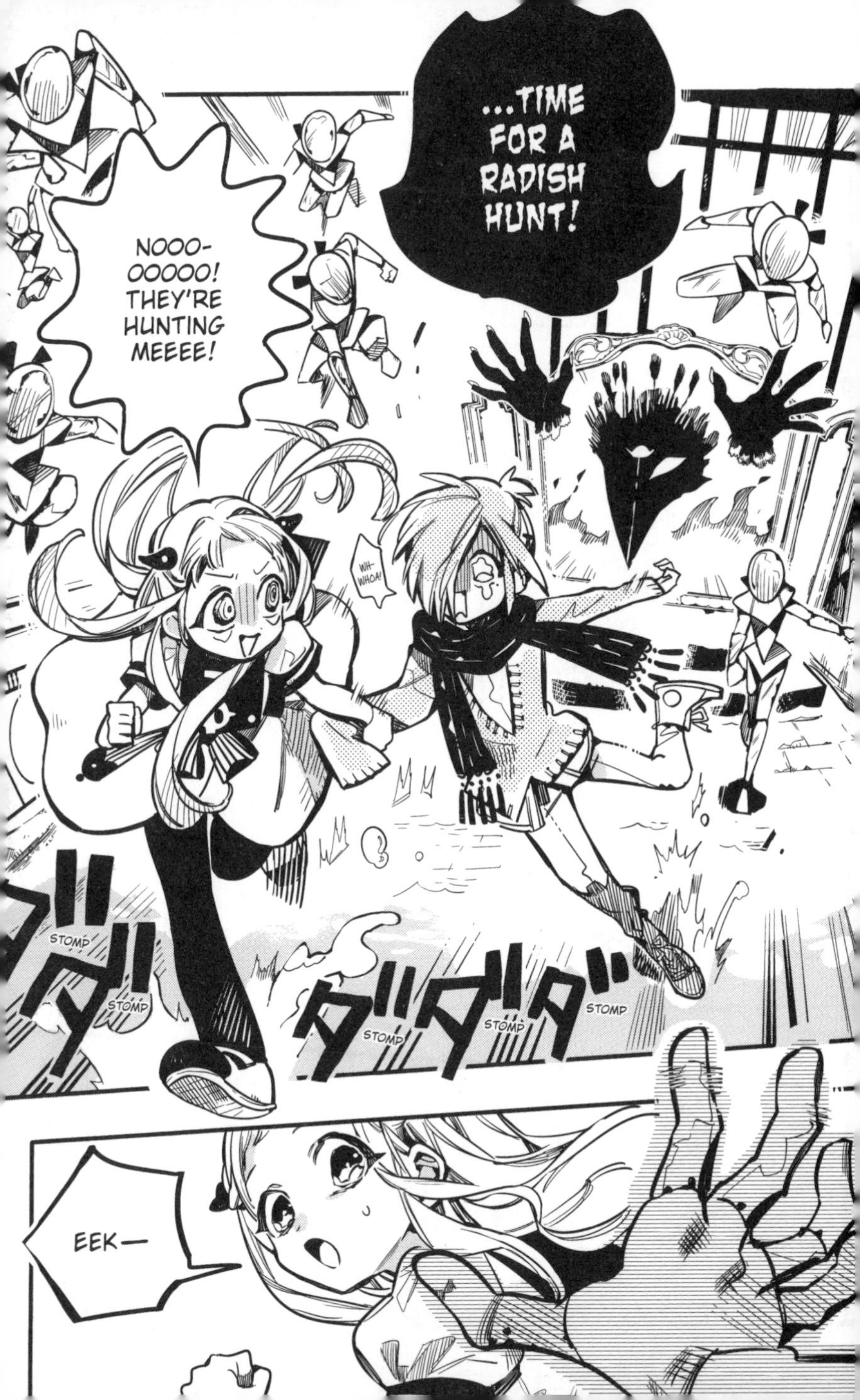
...TIME FOR A RADISH HUNT!
NOOO-OOOOO! THEY'RE HUNTING MEEEE!
WH-WHOA!
STOMP
STOMP
STOMP
STOMP
STOMP
EEK—

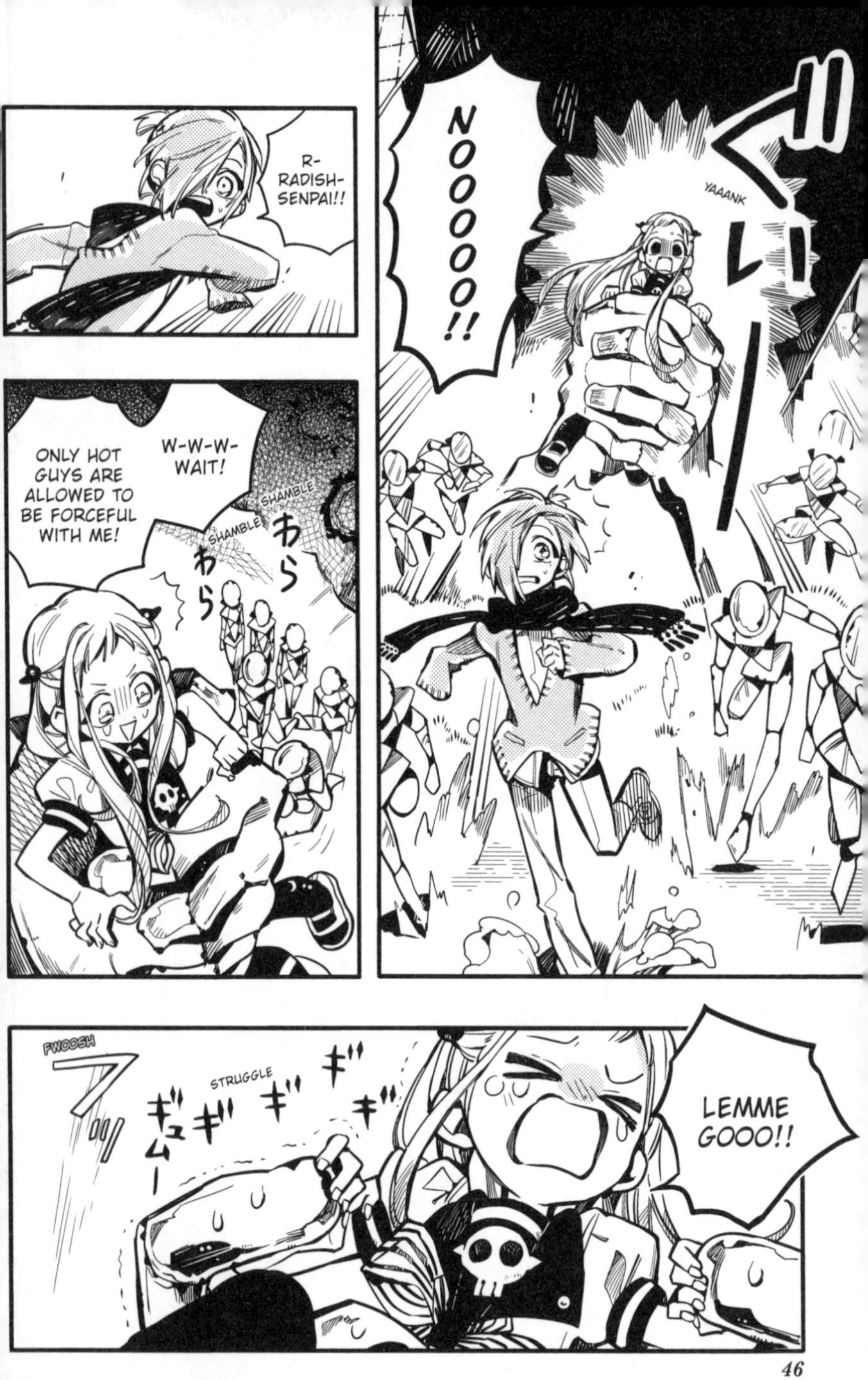
NOOOOOOO!!
YAAANK
R-RADISH-SENPAI!!
W-W-W-WAIT!
ONLY HOT GUYS ARE ALLOWED TO BE FORCEFUL WITH ME!
SHAMBLE
SHAMBLE
あら
あら
LEMME GOOO!!
STRUGGLE
FWOOSH

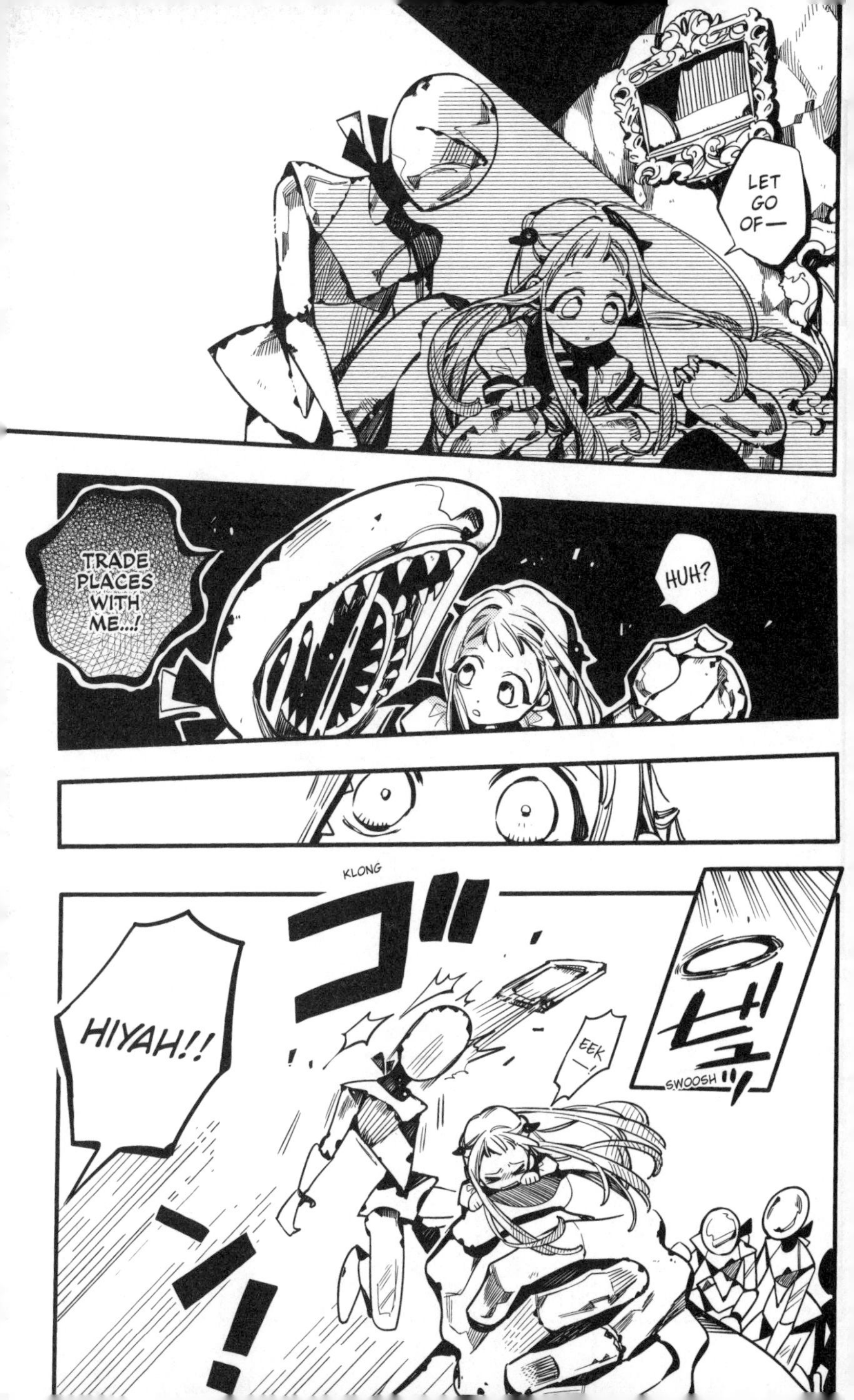
LET GO OF—
TRADE PLACES WITH ME...!
HUH?
KLONG
HIYAH!!
EEK—!
SWOOSH

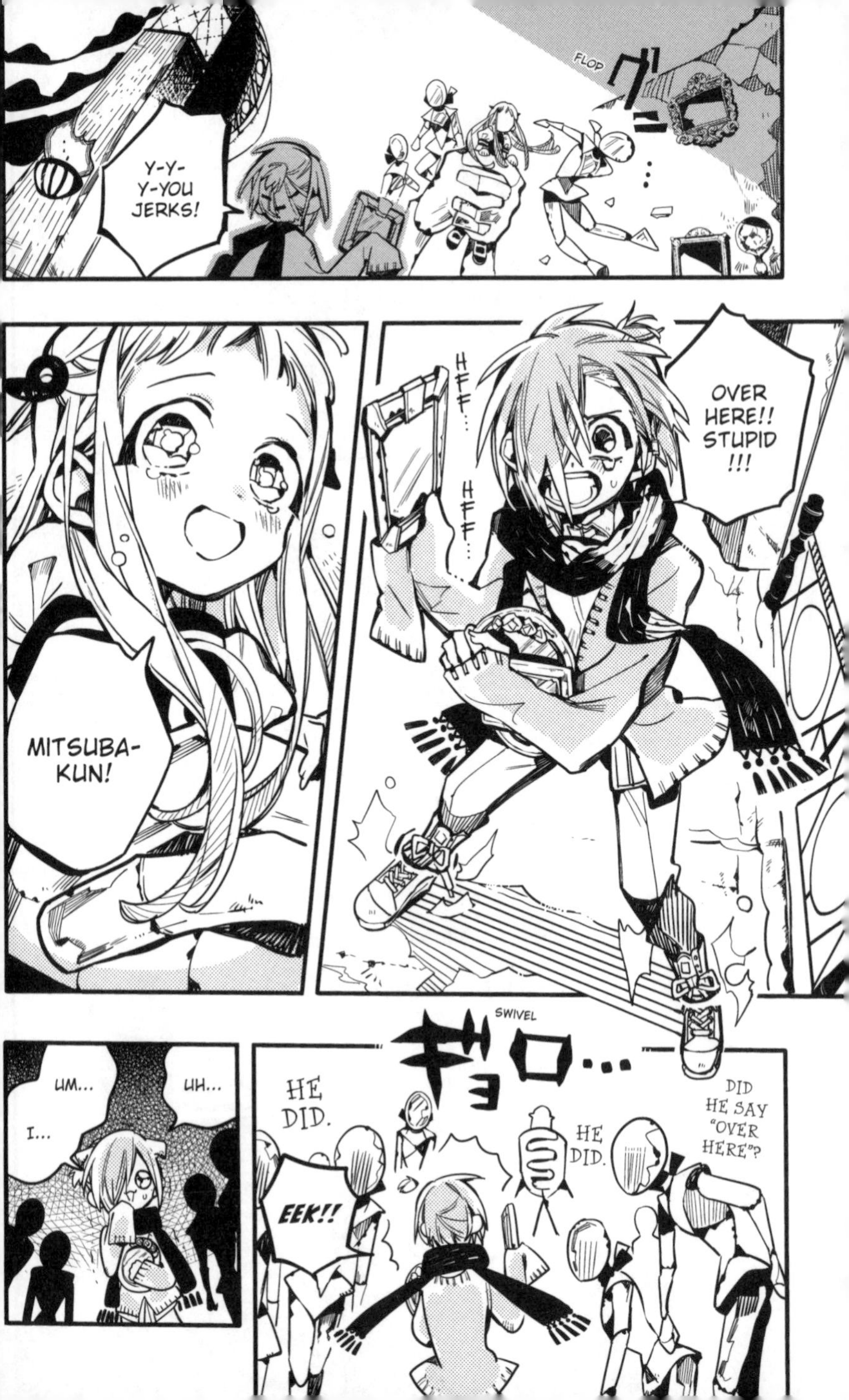
FLOP
Y-Y-
Y-YOU
JERKS!
OVER
HERE!!
STUPID
!!!
HFF...
HFF...
MITSUBA-
KUN!
SWIVEL
DID
HE SAY
"OVER
HERE"?
HE
DID.
HE
DID.
EEK!!
UH...
UM...
I...

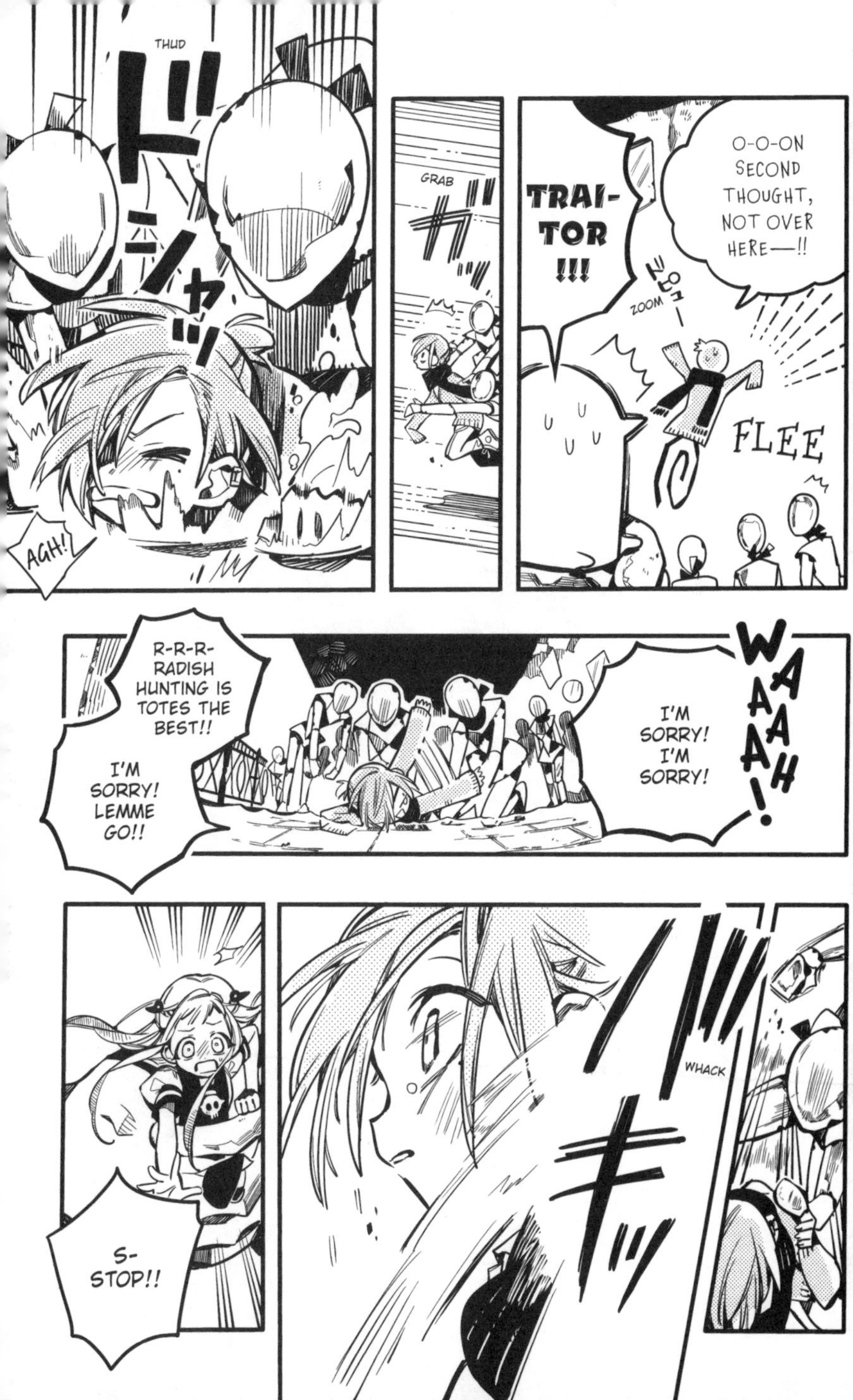
O-O-ON SECOND THOUGHT, NOT OVER HERE—!!
TRAI-TOR!!!
ZOOM
FLEE
GRAB
THUD
AGH!
WAAAAH!
I'M SORRY! I'M SORRY!
R-R-R-RADISH HUNTING IS TOTES THE BEST!!
I'M SORRY! LEMME GO!!
WHACK
S-STOP!!

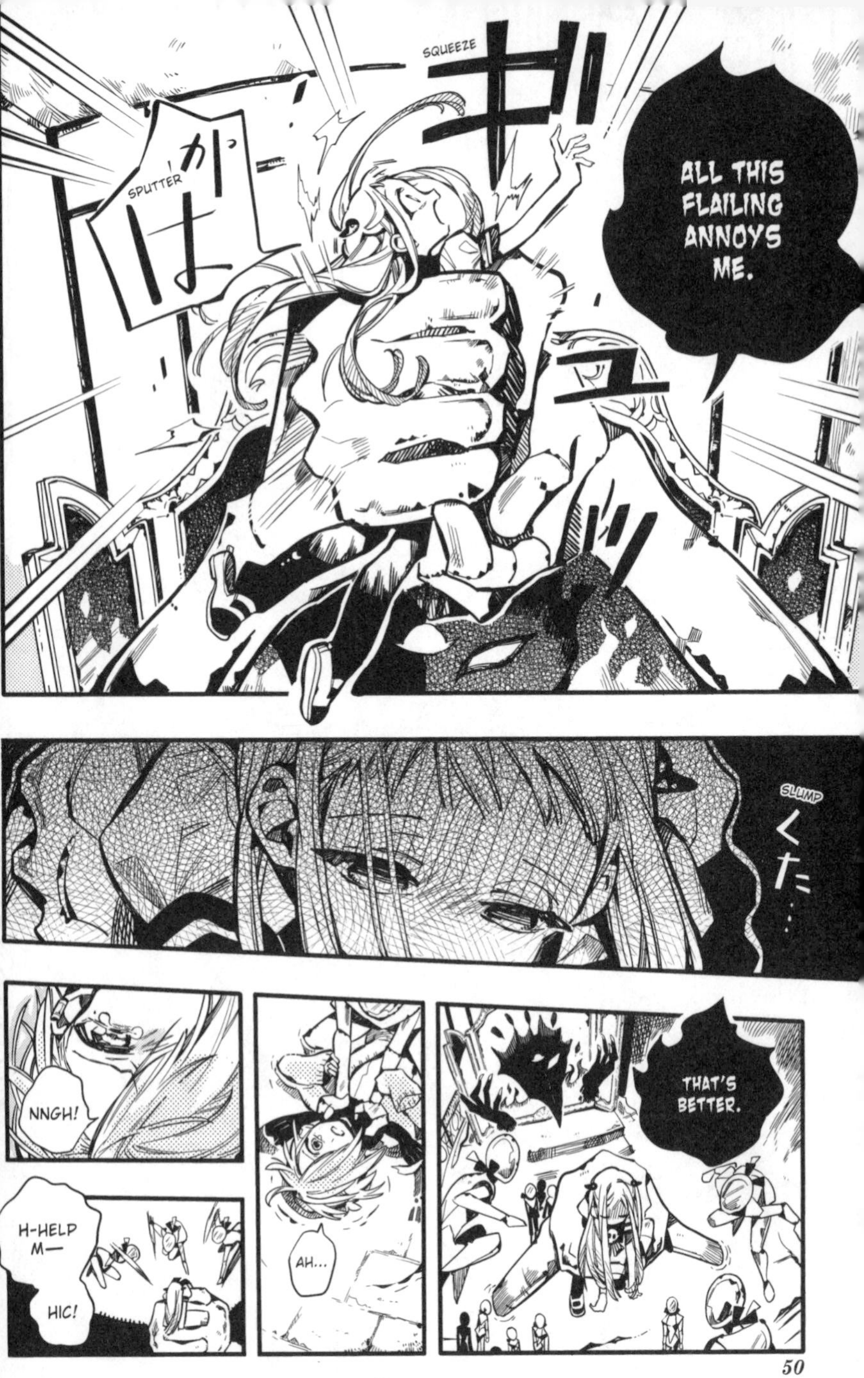
SQUEEZE
ALL THIS FLAILING ANNOYS ME.
SPUTTER
SLUMP
THAT'S BETTER.
AH...
NNGH!
H-HELP M—
HIC!

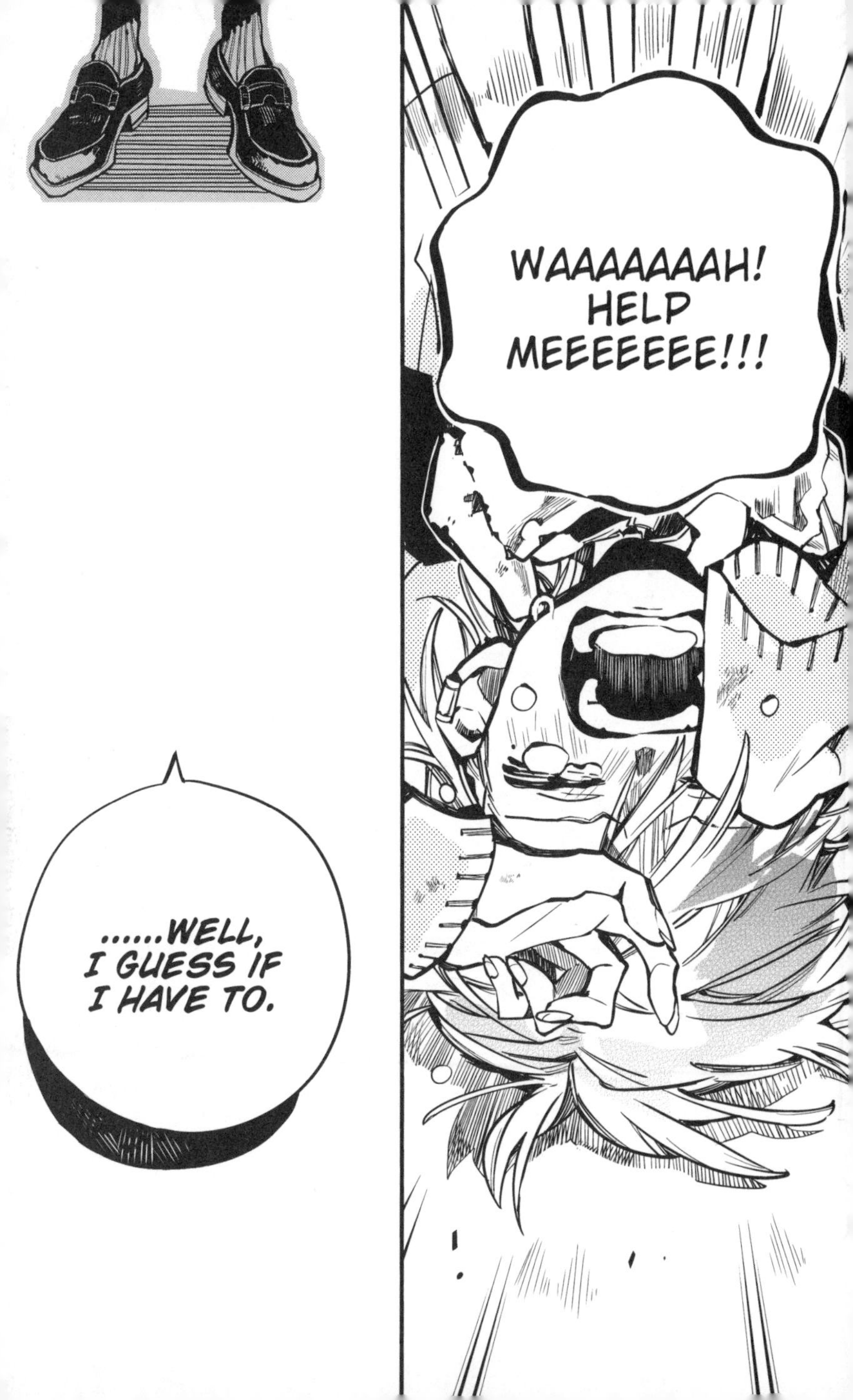
WAAAAAAAH! HELP MEEEEEEE!!!
......WELL, I GUESS IF I HAVE TO.

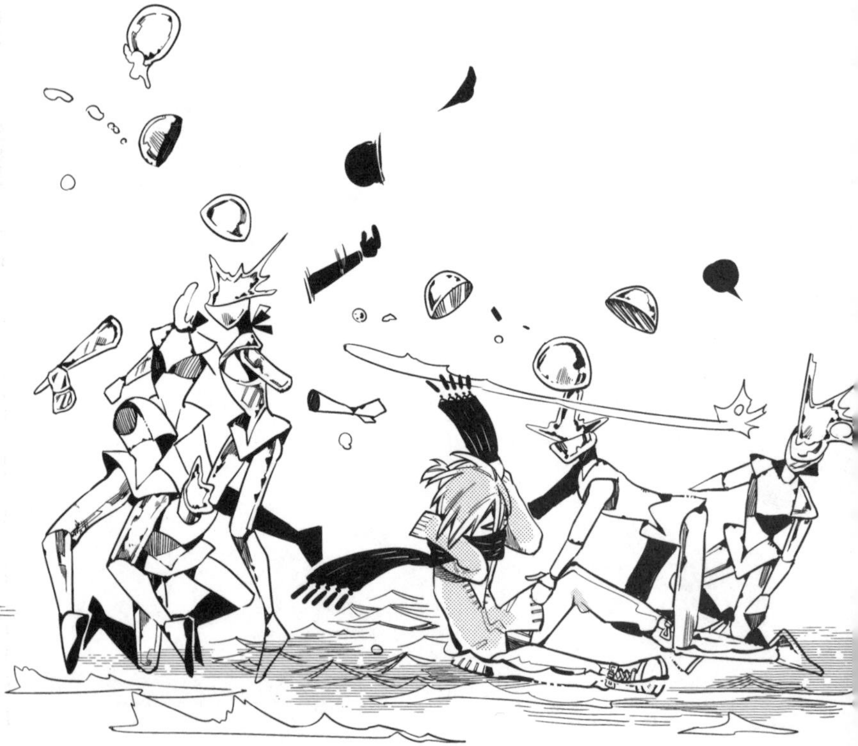

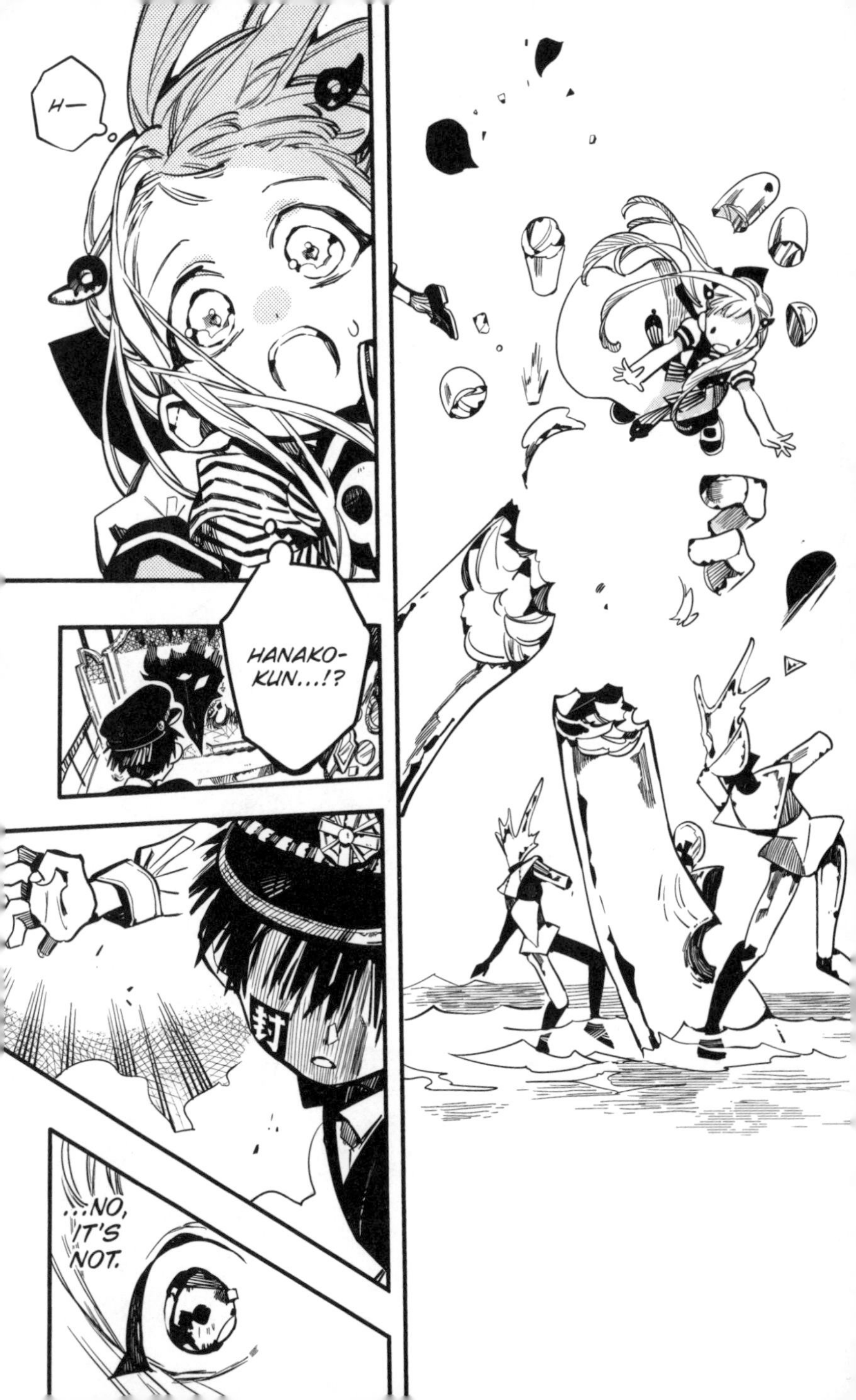
H—
HANAKO-KUN...!?
...NO, IT'S NOT.

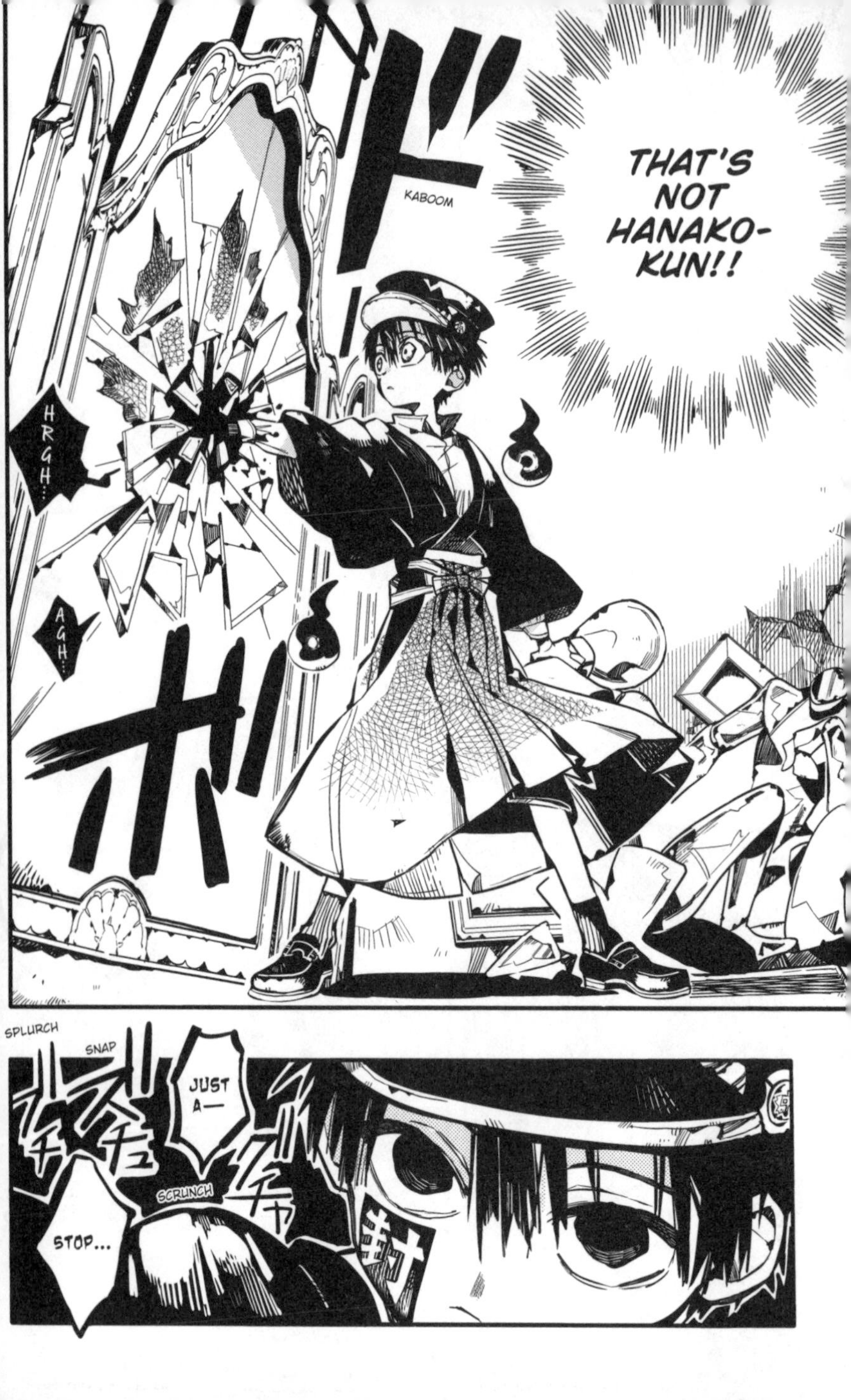
THAT'S NOT HANAKO-KUN!!
KABOOM
HRGH...
AGH...
SPLURCH
SNAP
JUST A—
SCRUNCH
STOP...

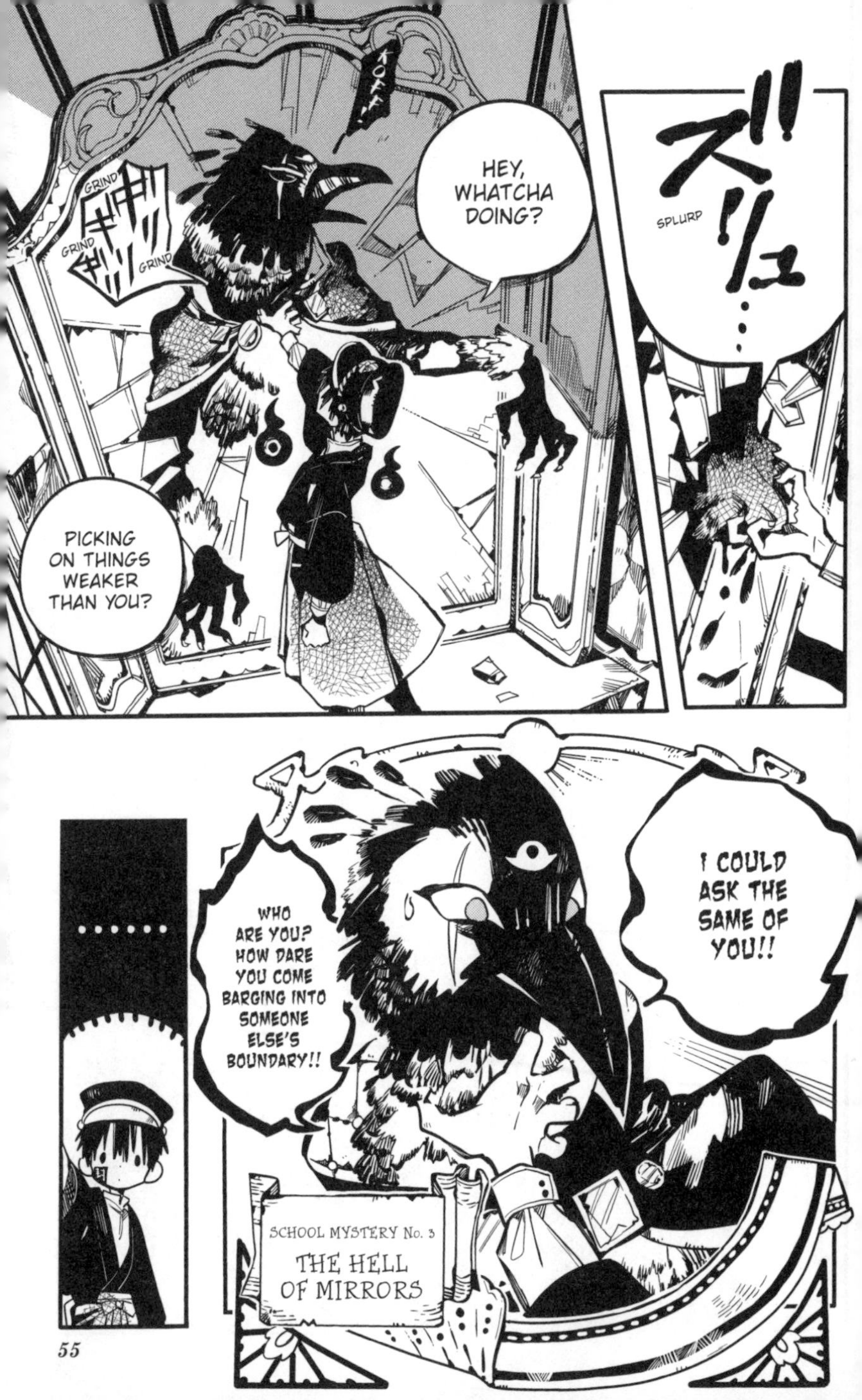
ズリュ
SPLURP
...
KOFF!
HEY, WHATCHA DOING?
ギャリ
GRIND
GRIND
GRIND
PICKING ON THINGS WEAKER THAN YOU?
I COULD ASK THE SAME OF YOU!!
WHO ARE YOU? HOW DARE YOU COME BARGING INTO SOMEONE ELSE'S BOUNDARY!!
SCHOOL MYSTERY No. 3
THE HELL OF MIRRORS
......

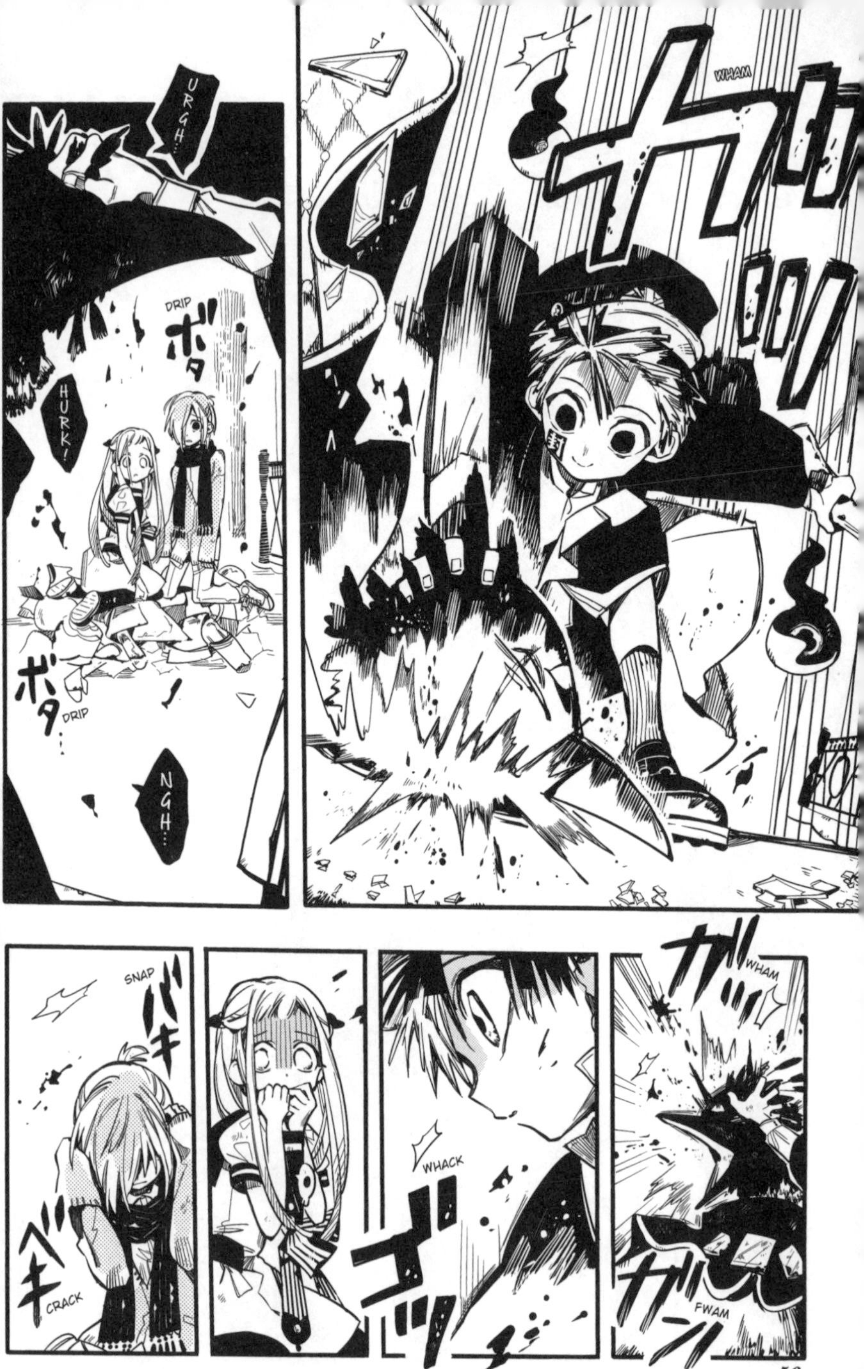
WHAM
URGH...
DRIP
HURK!
DRIP
NGH...
WHAM
FWAM
WHACK
SNAP
CRACK

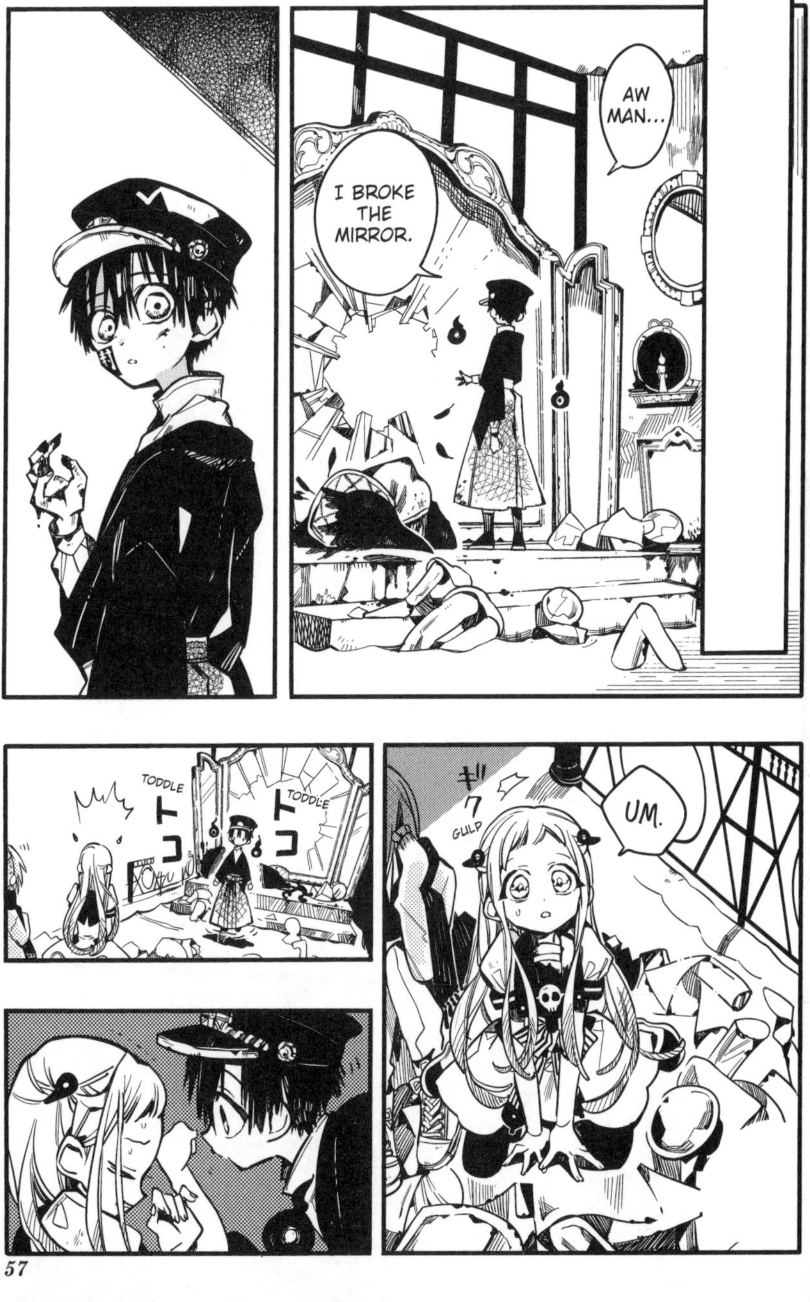
AW MAN...
I BROKE THE MIRROR.
UM.
ギク
GULP
TODDLE
トコ
TODDLE
トコ

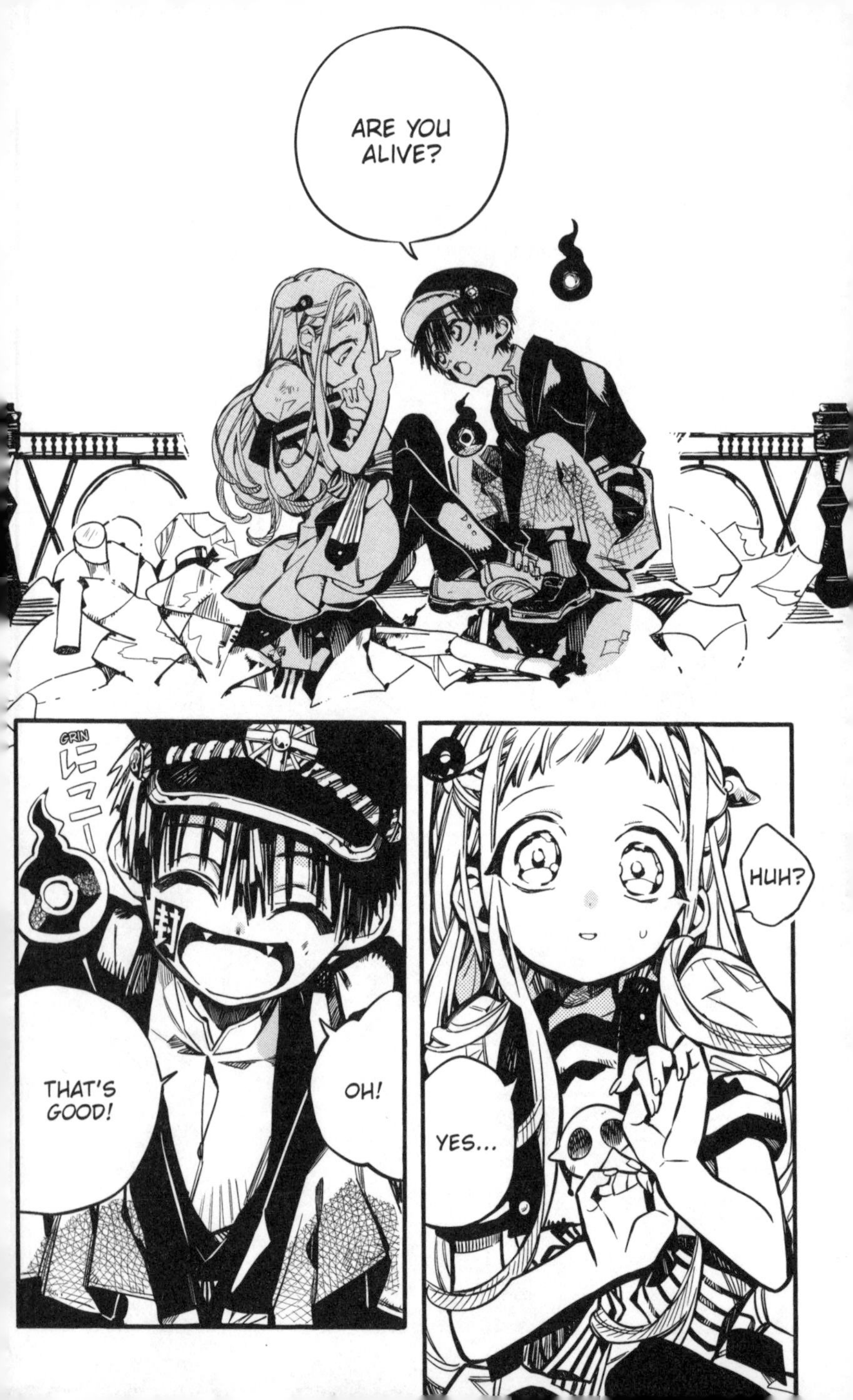
ARE YOU ALIVE?
HUH?
YES...
GRIN
OH!
THAT'S GOOD!

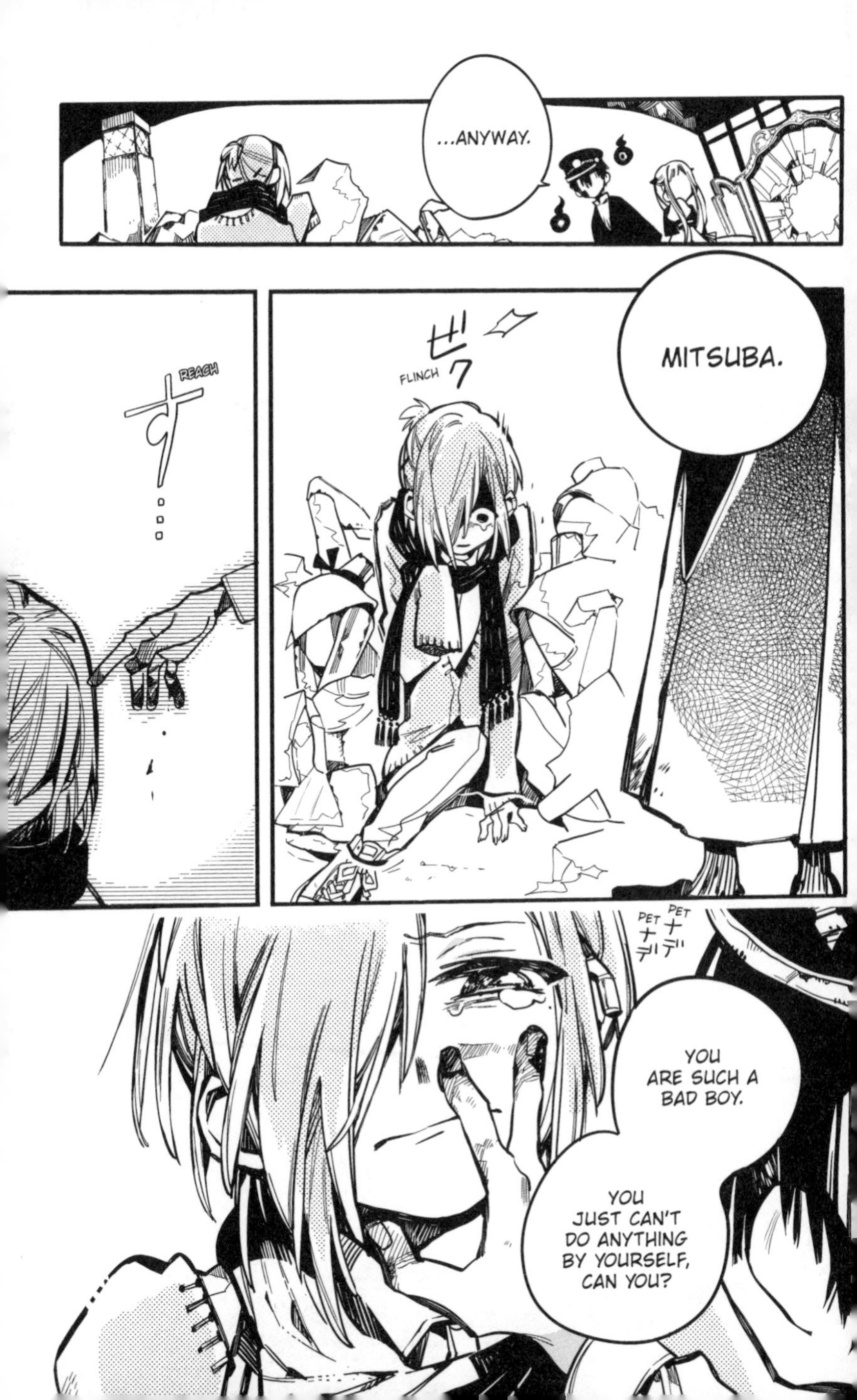
...ANYWAY.
MITSUBA.
ビクッ
FLINCH
す…
REACH
ナデナデ
PET PET
YOU ARE SUCH A BAD BOY.
YOU JUST CAN'T DO ANYTHING BY YOURSELF, CAN YOU?

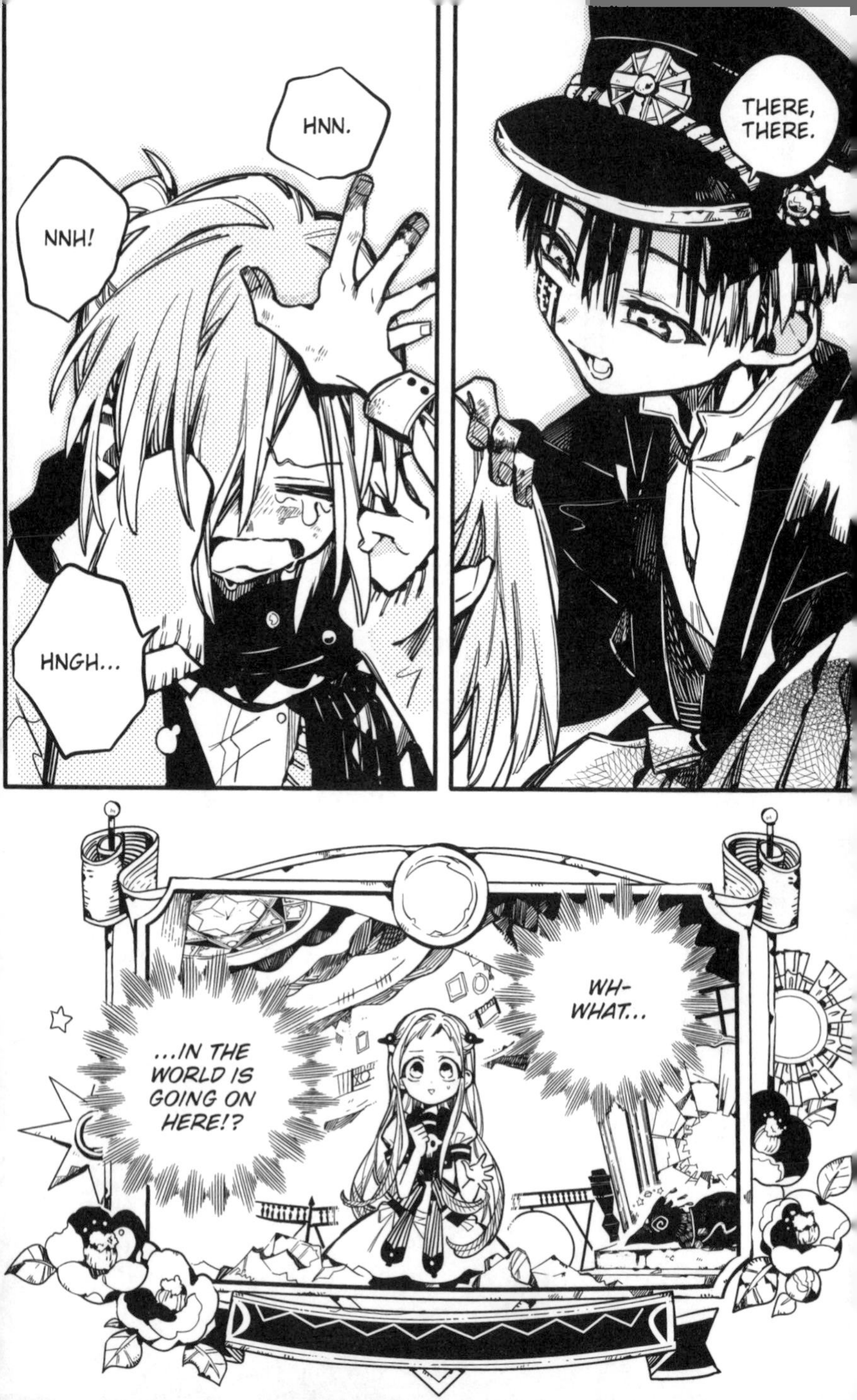
THERE, THERE.
HNN.
NNH!
HNGH...
WH- WHAT...
...IN THE WORLD IS GOING ON HERE!?

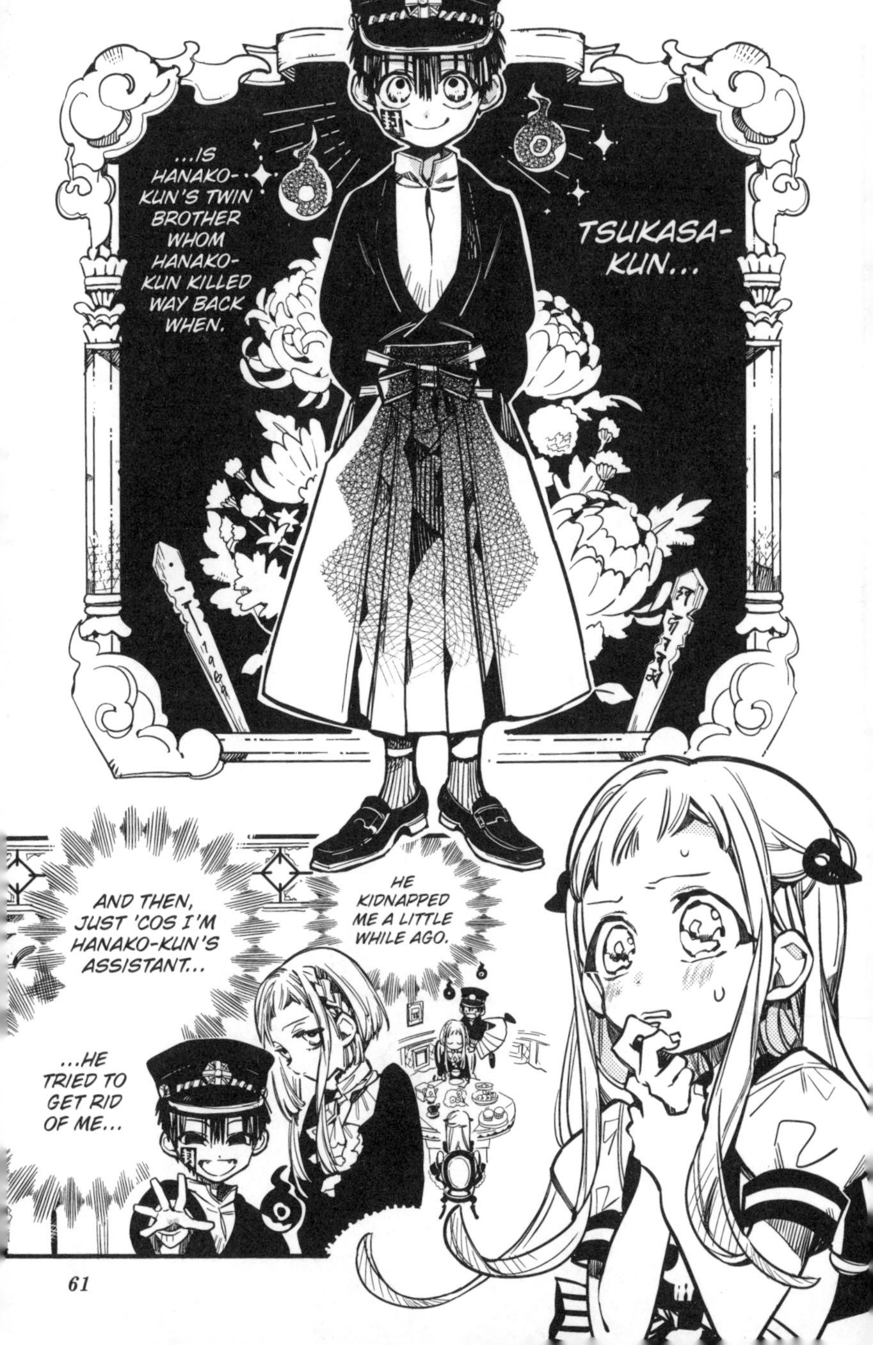
TSUKASA-KUN...
...IS HANAKO-KUN'S TWIN BROTHER WHOM HANAKO-KUN KILLED WAY BACK WHEN.
HE KIDNAPPED ME A LITTLE WHILE AGO.
AND THEN, JUST 'COS I'M HANAKO-KUN'S ASSISTANT...
...HE TRIED TO GET RID OF ME...

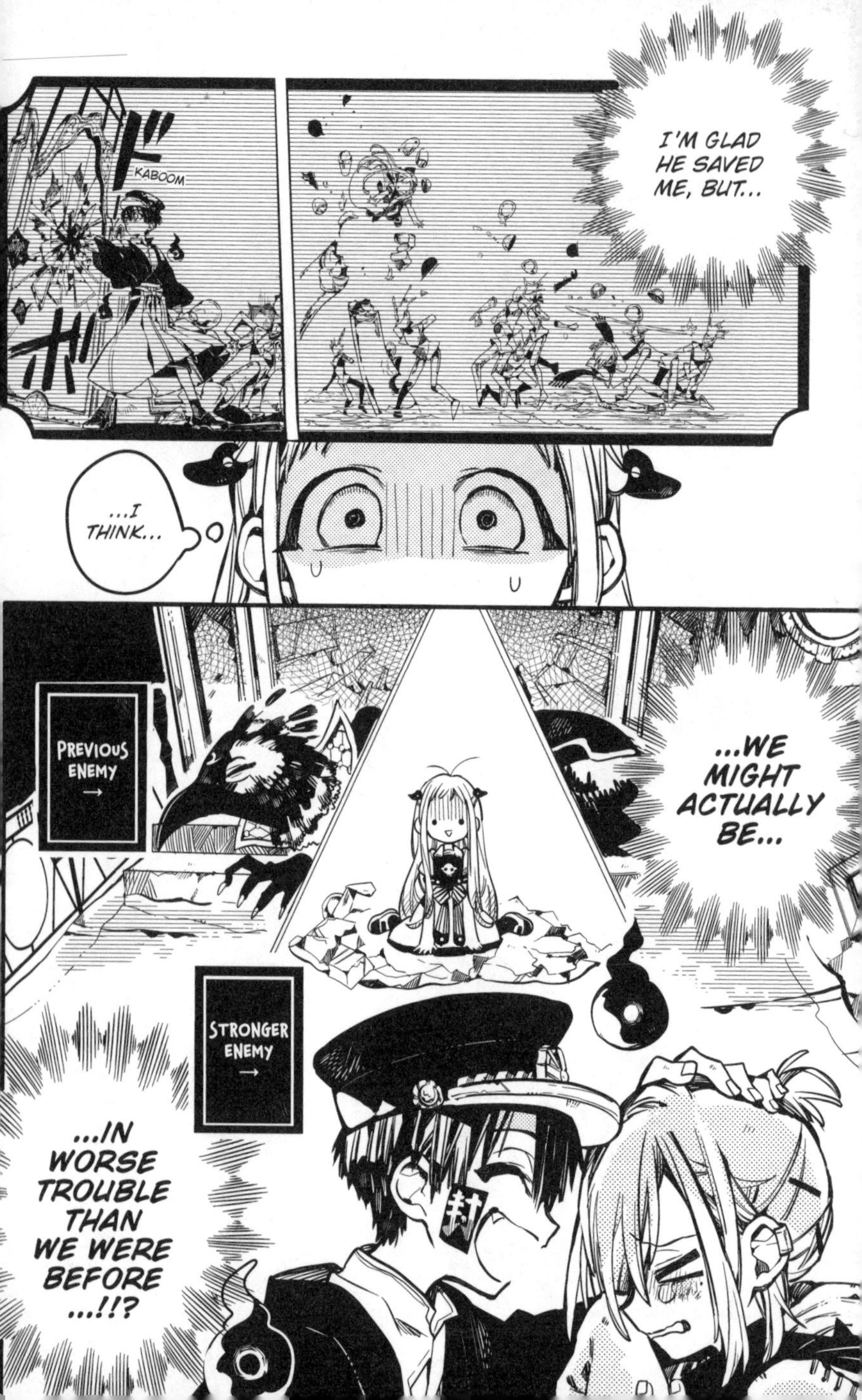
I'M GLAD HE SAVED ME, BUT...
KABOOM
...I THINK...
...WE MIGHT ACTUALLY BE...
PREVIOUS ENEMY →
STRONGER ENEMY →
...IN WORSE TROUBLE THAN WE WERE BEFORE ...!!?

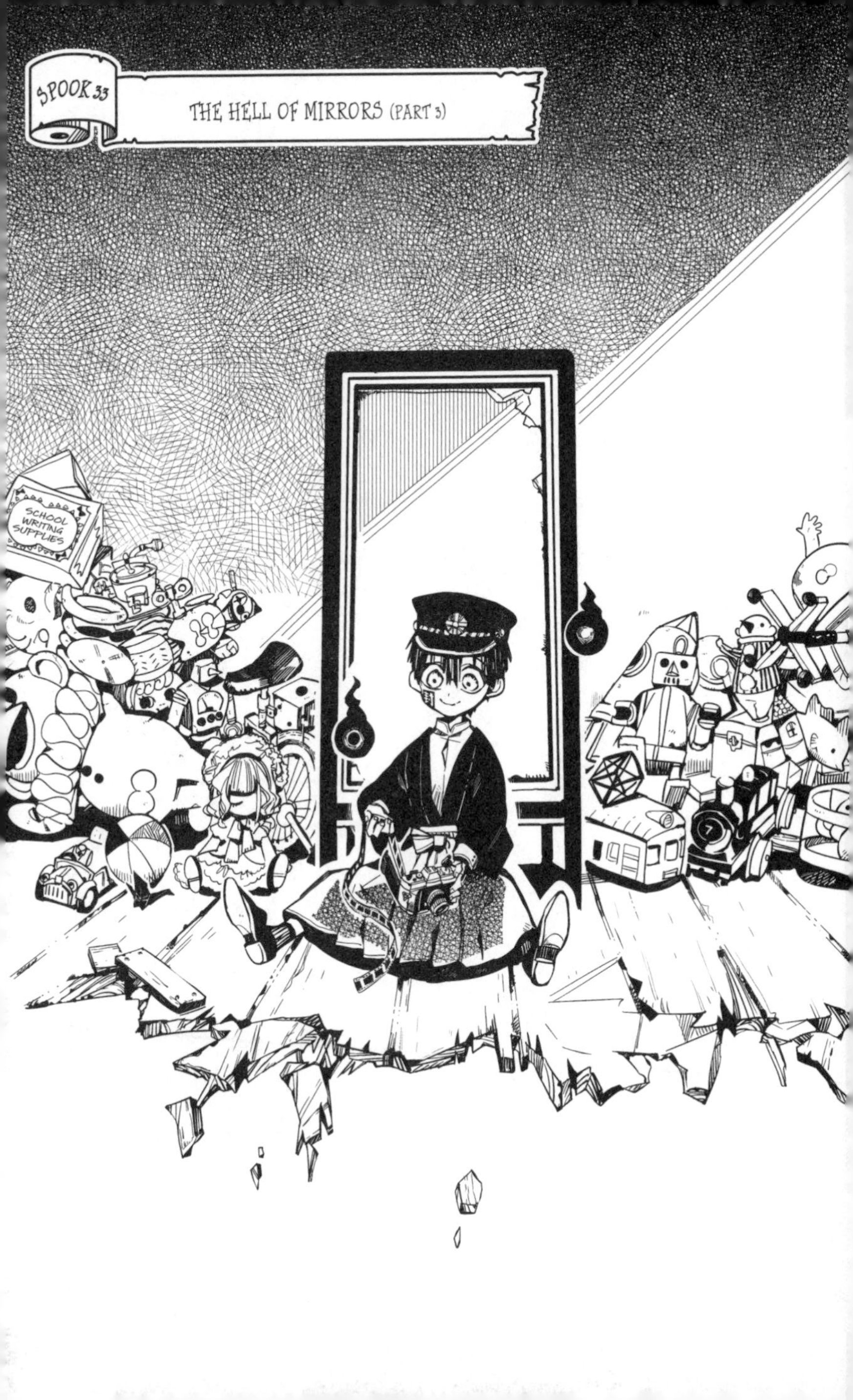
SPOOK 33
THE HELL OF MIRRORS (PART 3)
SCHOOL WRITING SUPPLIES

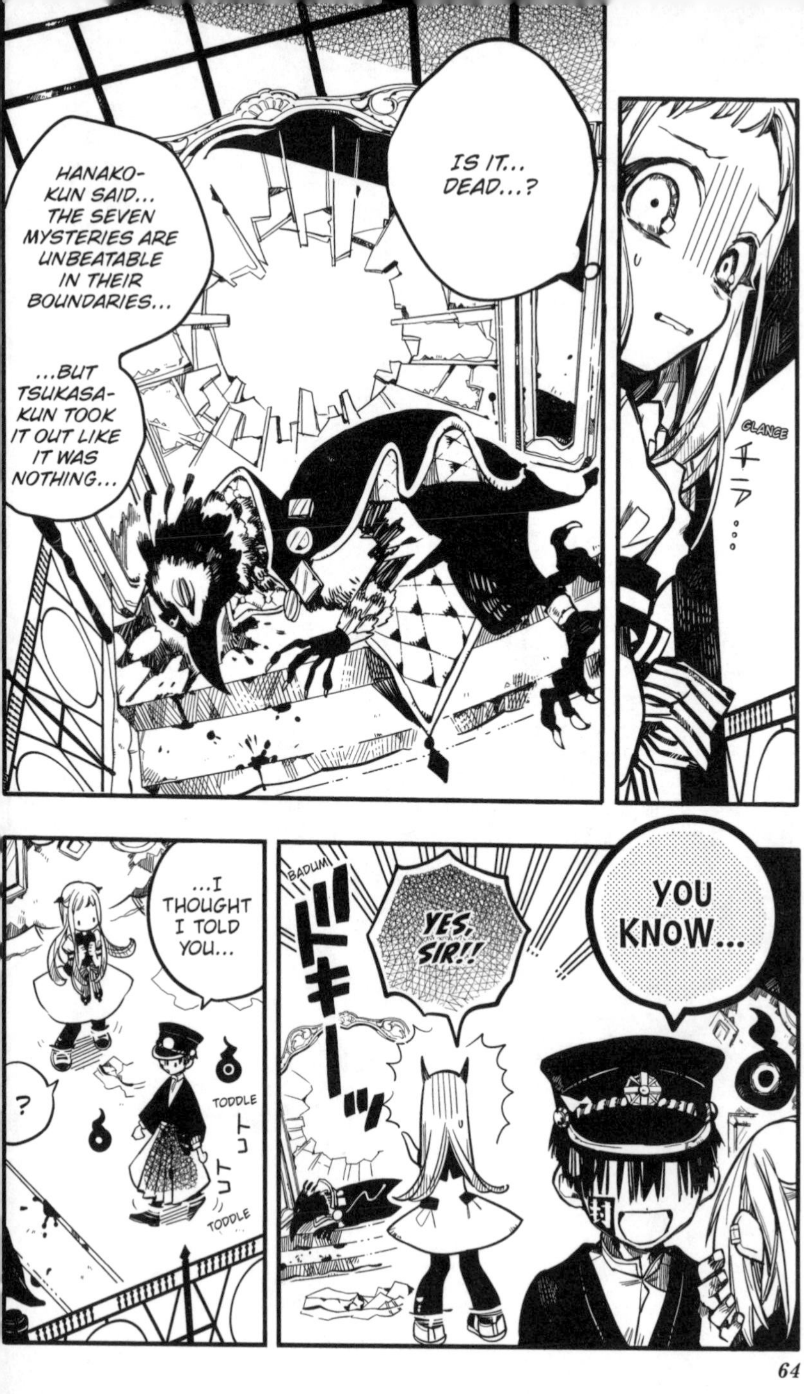
GLANCE
チラ…
IS IT... DEAD...?
HANAKO-KUN SAID... THE SEVEN MYSTERIES ARE UNBEATABLE IN THEIR BOUNDARIES...
...BUT TSUKASA-KUN TOOK IT OUT LIKE IT WAS NOTHING...
YOU KNOW...
BADUM
ドキーッ
YES, SIR!!
...I THOUGHT I TOLD YOU...
?
TODDLE
TODDLE

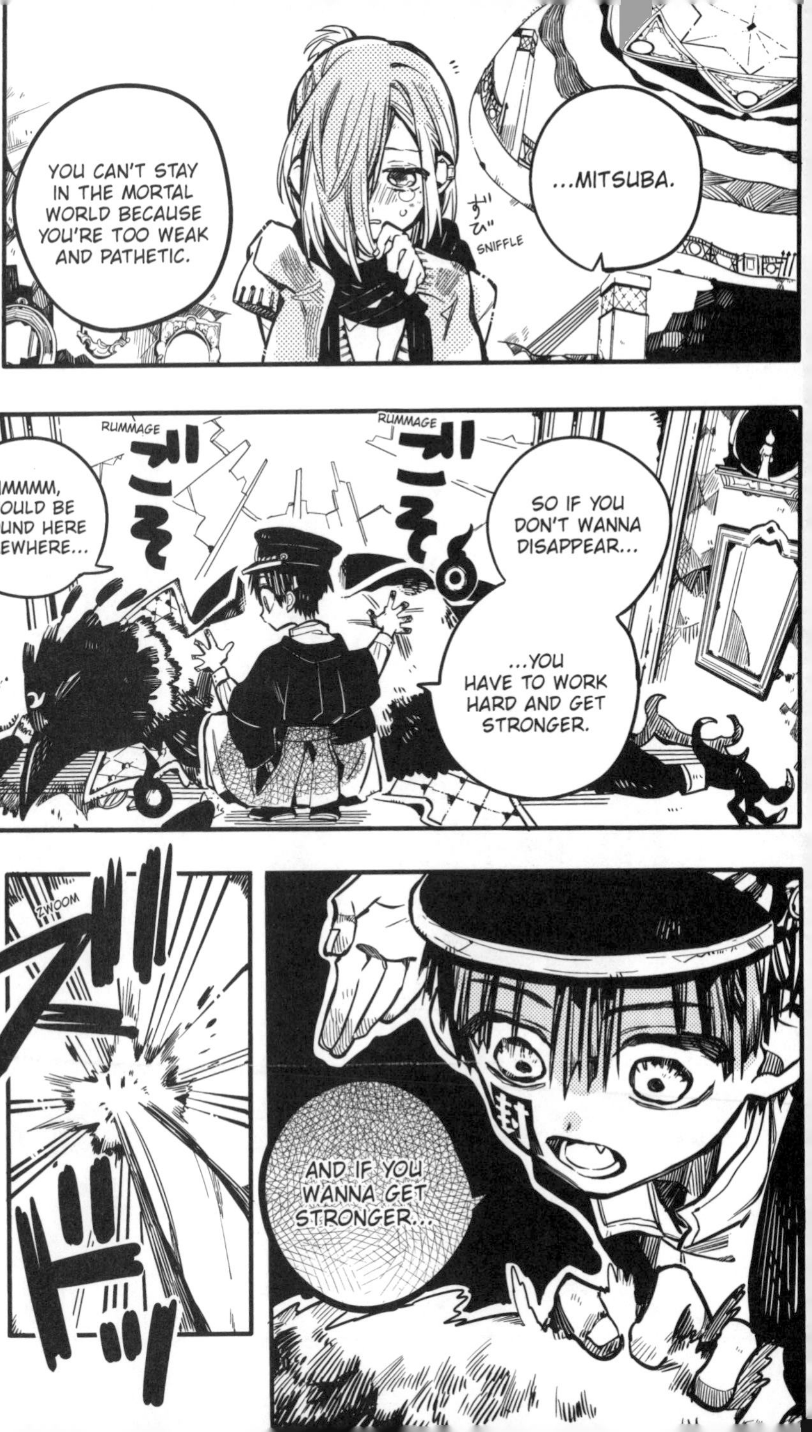
...MITSUBA.
SNIFFLE
YOU CAN'T STAY IN THE MORTAL WORLD BECAUSE YOU'RE TOO WEAK AND PATHETIC.
RUMMAGE
SO IF YOU DON'T WANNA DISAPPEAR...
...YOU HAVE TO WORK HARD AND GET STRONGER.
RUMMAGE
HMMMM, SHOULD BE AROUND HERE SOMEWHERE...
AND IF YOU WANNA GET STRONGER...
ZWOOM

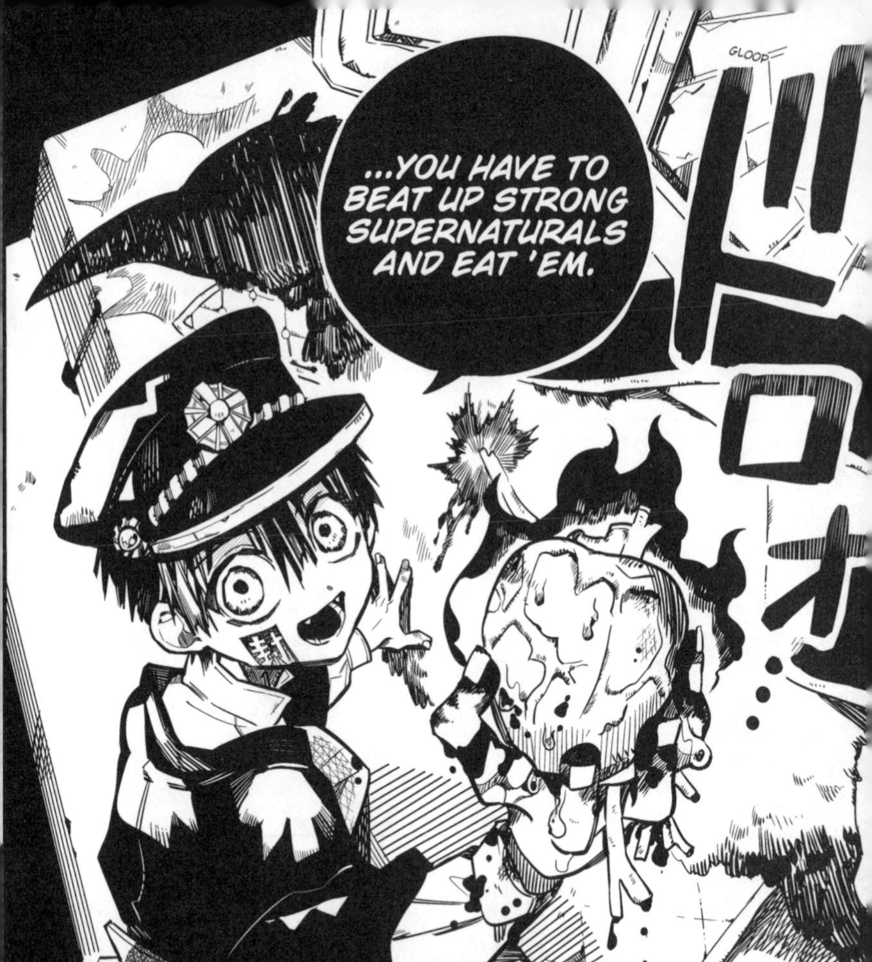
GLOOP
...YOU HAVE TO BEAT UP STRONG SUPERNATURALS AND EAT 'EM.

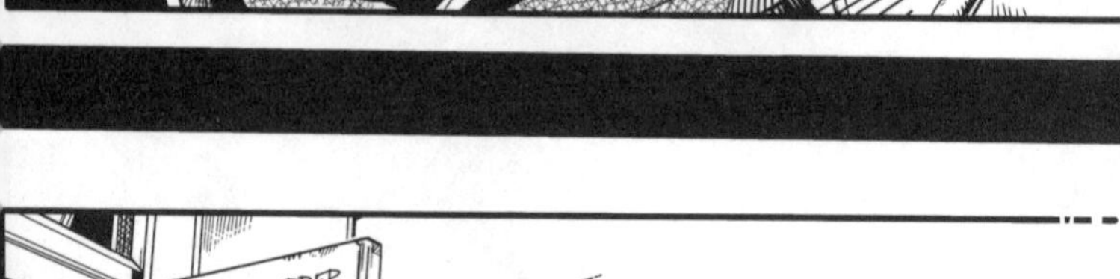
SCIENCE PREP ROOM No. 2

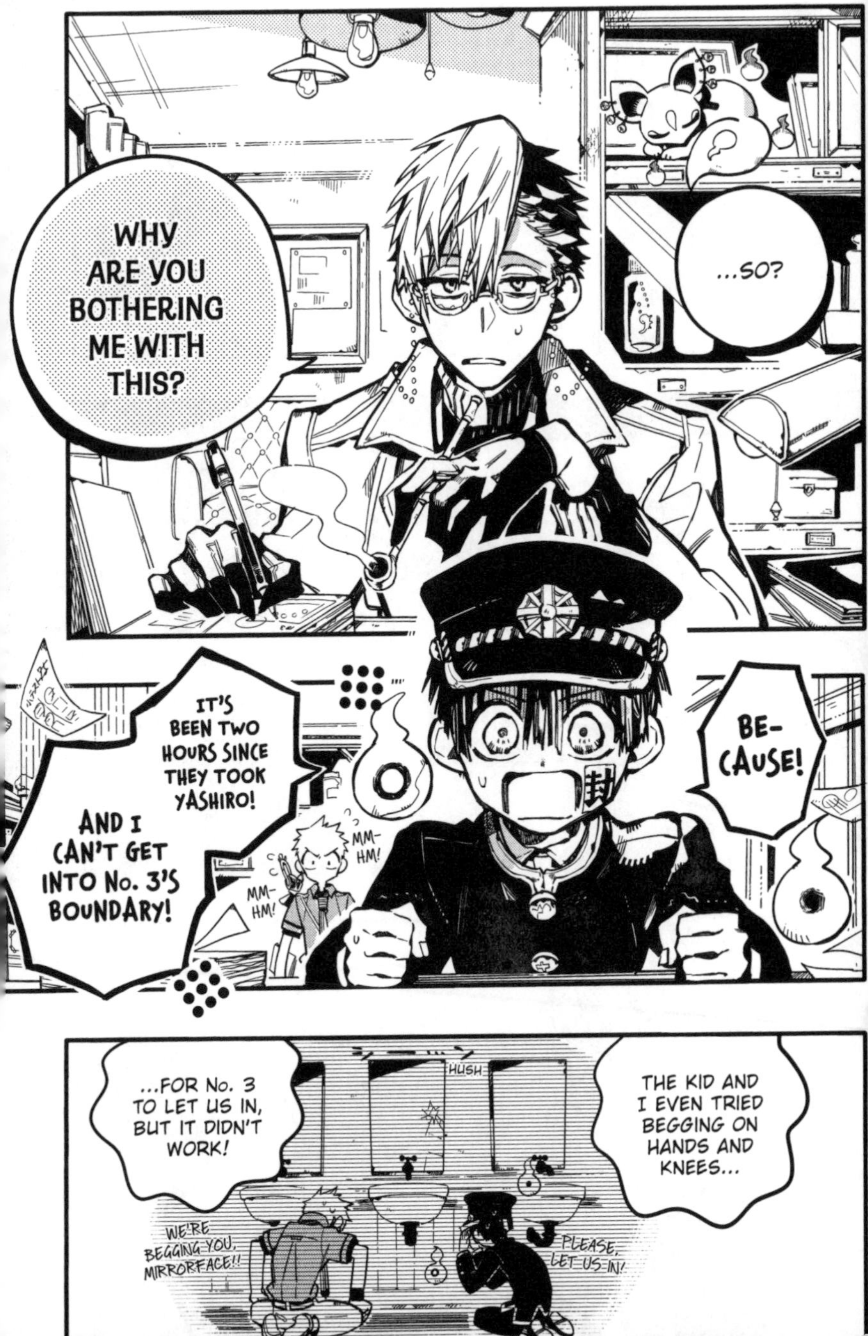
...SO?
WHY ARE YOU BOTHERING ME WITH THIS?
BE-CAUSE!
IT'S BEEN TWO HOURS SINCE THEY TOOK YASHIRO!
AND I CAN'T GET INTO No. 3'S BOUNDARY!
MM-HM!
MM-HM!
THE KID AND I EVEN TRIED BEGGING ON HANDS AND KNEES...
HUSH
...FOR No. 3 TO LET US IN, BUT IT DIDN'T WORK!
PLEASE, LET US IN!
WE'RE BEGGING YOU, MIRRORFACE!!

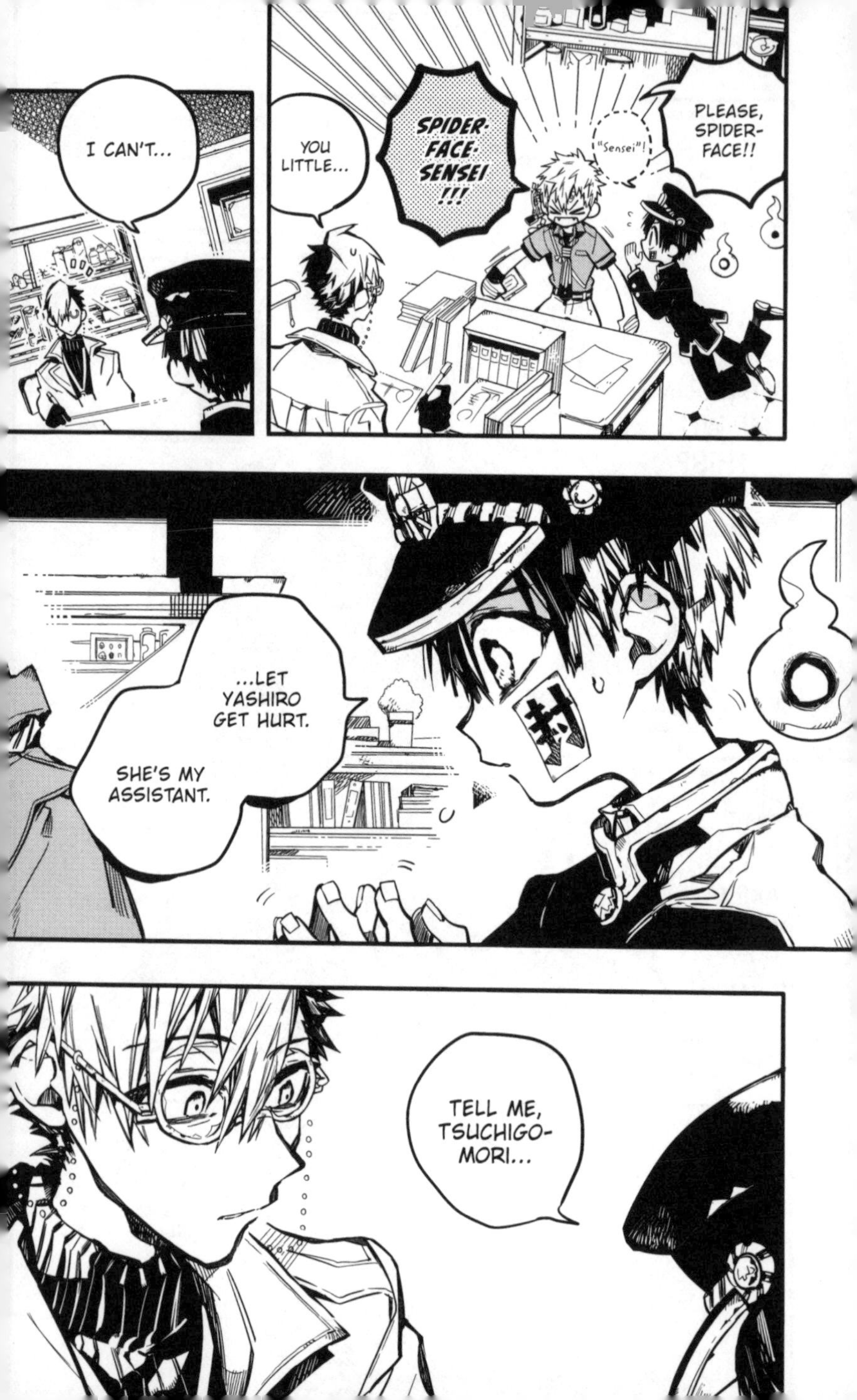
PLEASE, SPIDER-FACE!!
"Sensei"!
SPIDER-FACE-SENSEI!!!
YOU LITTLE...
I CAN'T...
...LET YASHIRO GET HURT.
SHE'S MY ASSISTANT.
TELL ME, TSUCHIGOMORI...

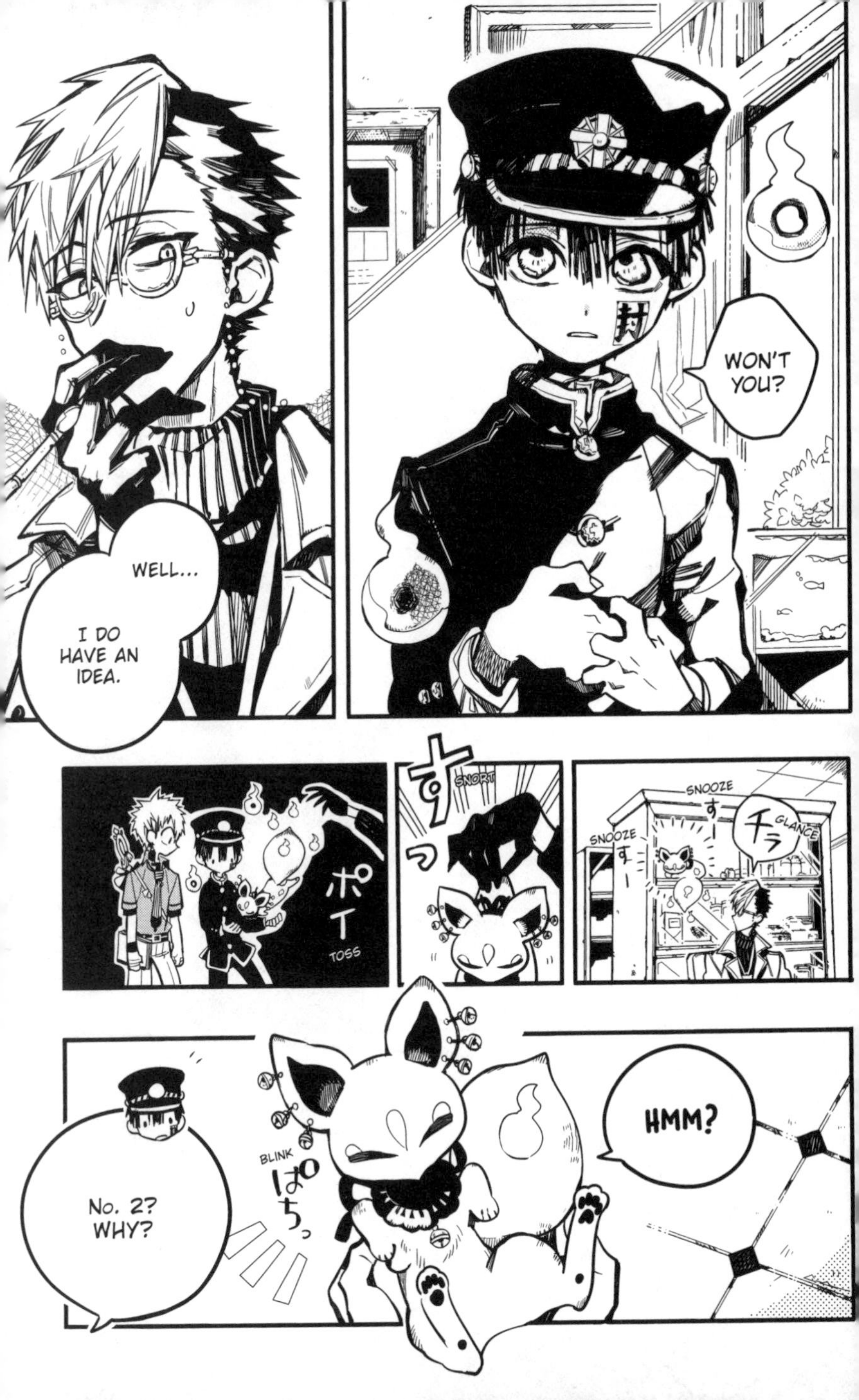
WON'T YOU?
WELL...
I DO HAVE AN IDEA.
SNOOZE
す
チラ
GLANCE
SNOOZE
す
すっ
SNORT
ポイ
TOSS
HMM?
BLINK
ぱちっ
No. 2? WHY?

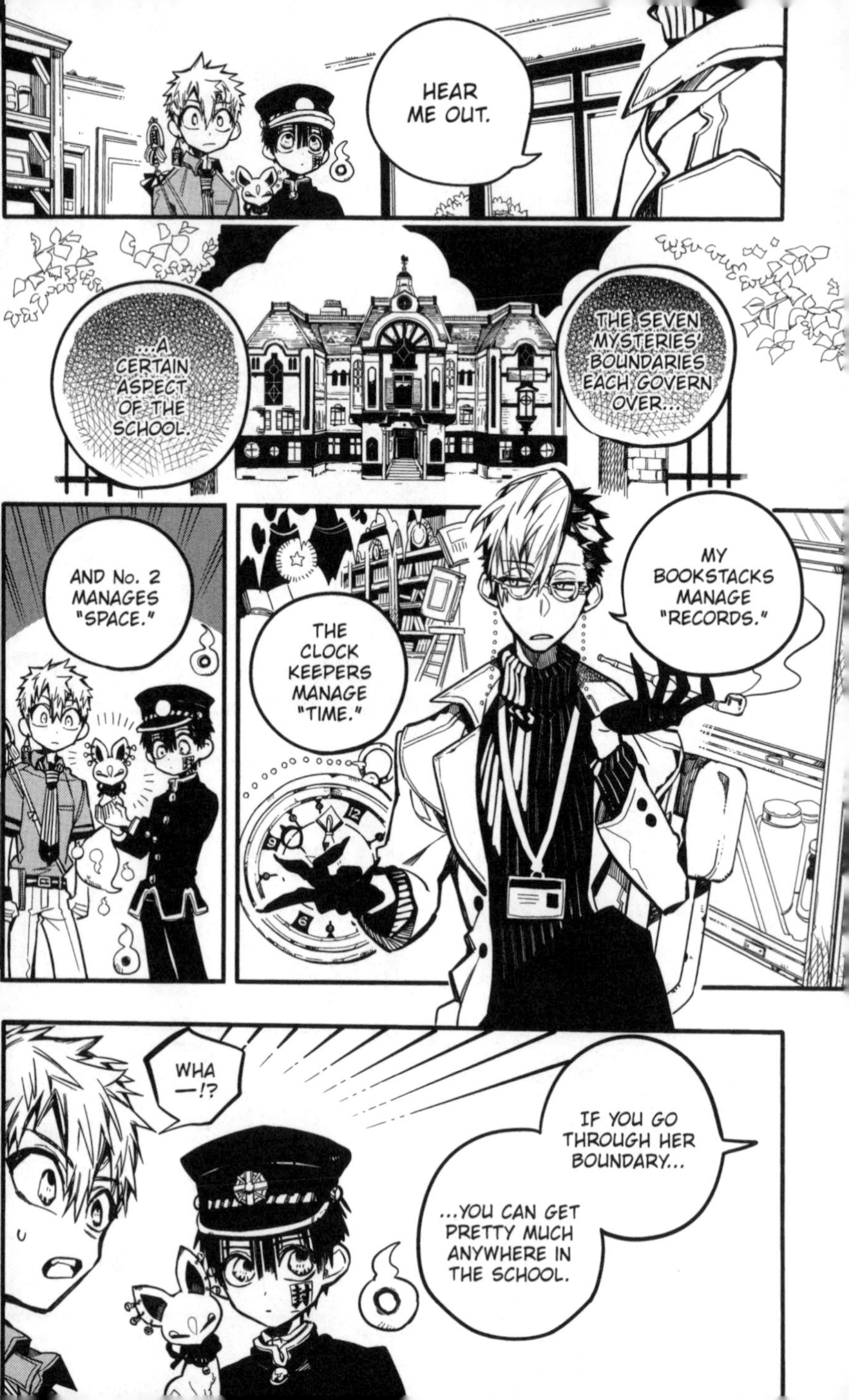
HEAR ME OUT.
THE SEVEN MYSTERIES' BOUNDARIES EACH GOVERN OVER...
...A CERTAIN ASPECT OF THE SCHOOL.
MY BOOKSTACKS MANAGE "RECORDS."
THE CLOCK KEEPERS MANAGE "TIME."
AND No. 2 MANAGES "SPACE."
IF YOU GO THROUGH HER BOUNDARY...
...YOU CAN GET PRETTY MUCH ANYWHERE IN THE SCHOOL.
WHA—!?

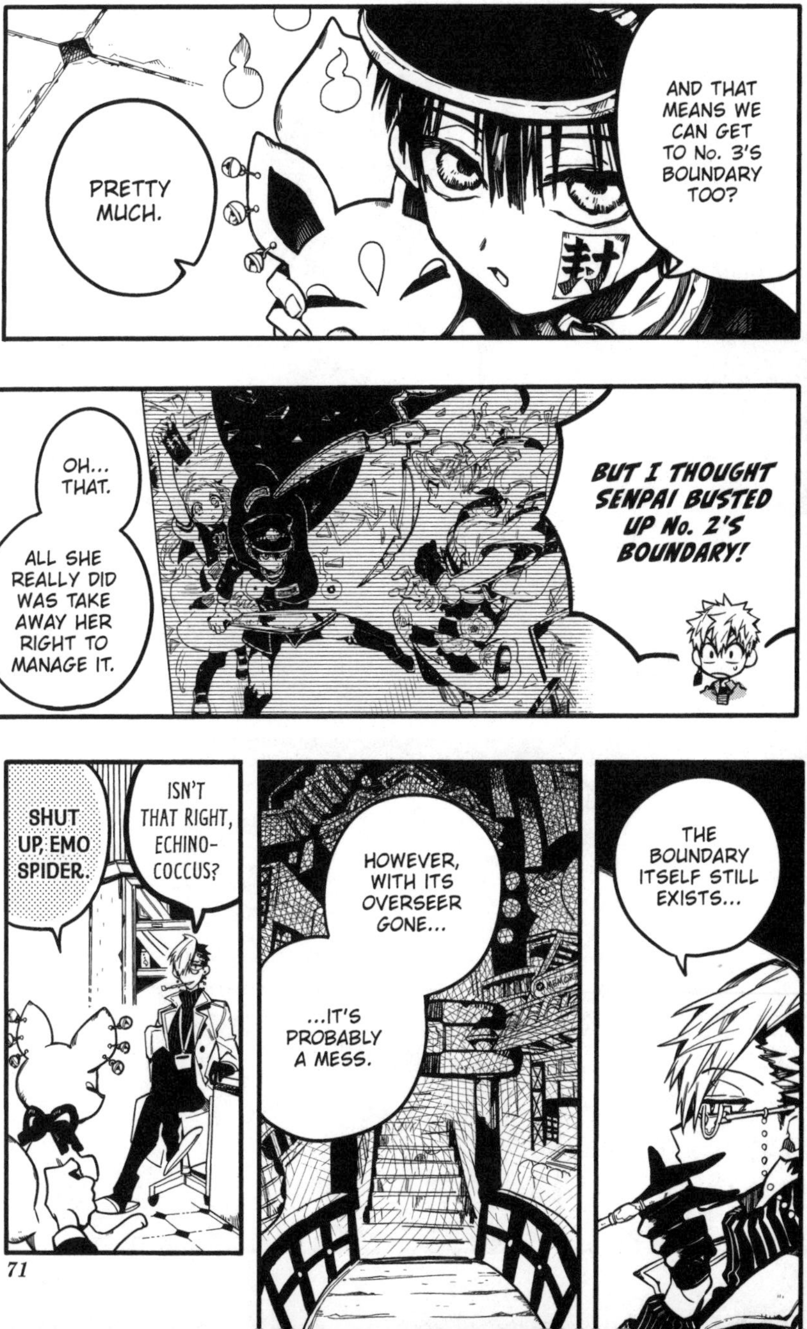
AND THAT MEANS WE CAN GET TO No. 3'S BOUNDARY TOO?
PRETTY MUCH.
BUT I THOUGHT SENPAI BUSTED UP No. 2'S BOUNDARY!
OH... THAT.
ALL SHE REALLY DID WAS TAKE AWAY HER RIGHT TO MANAGE IT.
THE BOUNDARY ITSELF STILL EXISTS...
HOWEVER, WITH ITS OVERSEER GONE...
...IT'S PROBABLY A MESS.
ISN'T THAT RIGHT, ECHINO-COCCUS?
SHUT UP, EMO SPIDER.

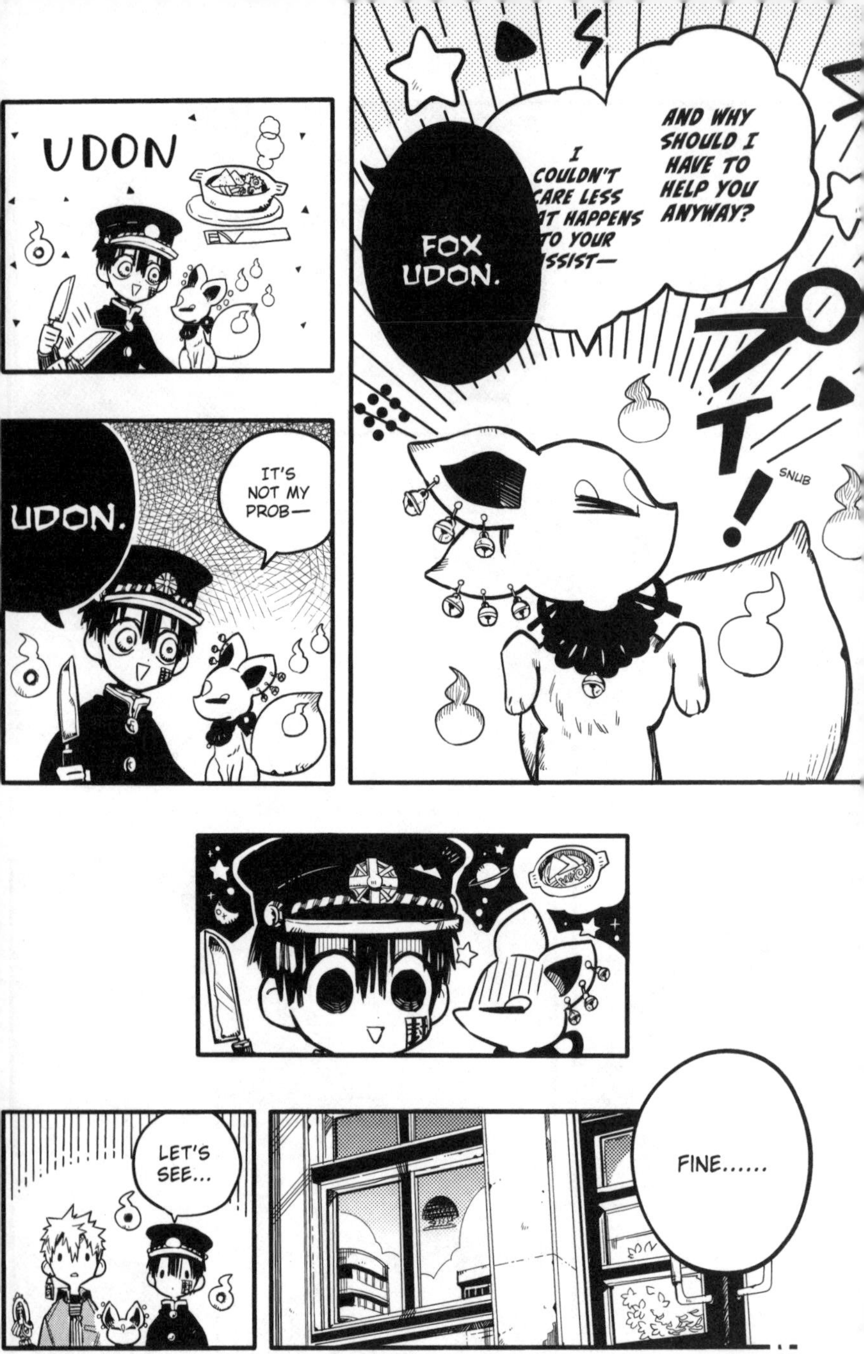

AND WHY SHOULD I HAVE TO HELP YOU ANYWAY?
I COULDN'T CARE LESS AT HAPPENS TO YOUR SSIST—
FOX UDON.
SNUB
UDON
IT'S NOT MY PROB—
UDON.
FINE......
LET'S SEE...

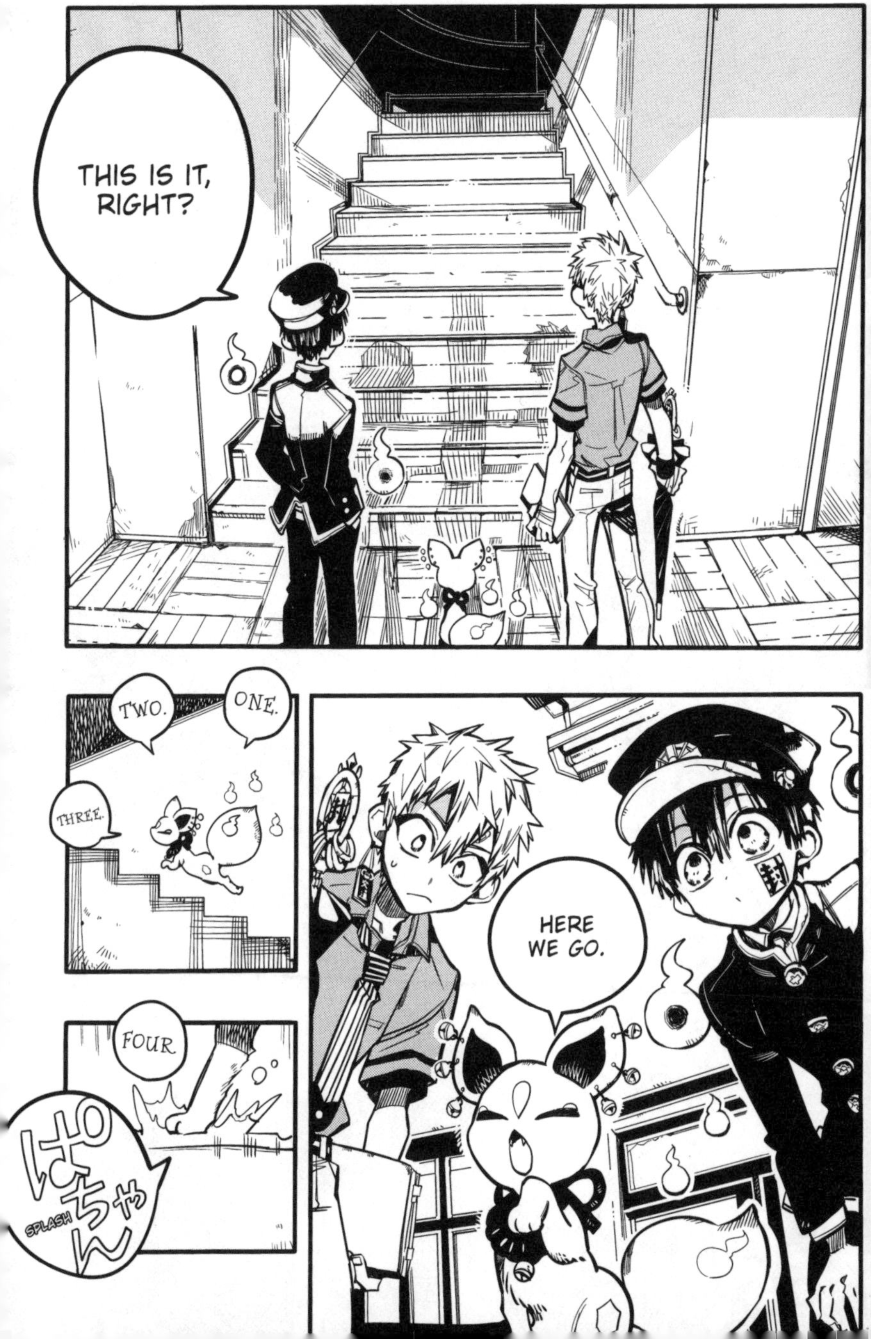
THIS IS IT, RIGHT?
HERE WE GO.
ONE.
TWO.
THREE.
FOUR.
ぱちゃん
SPLASH

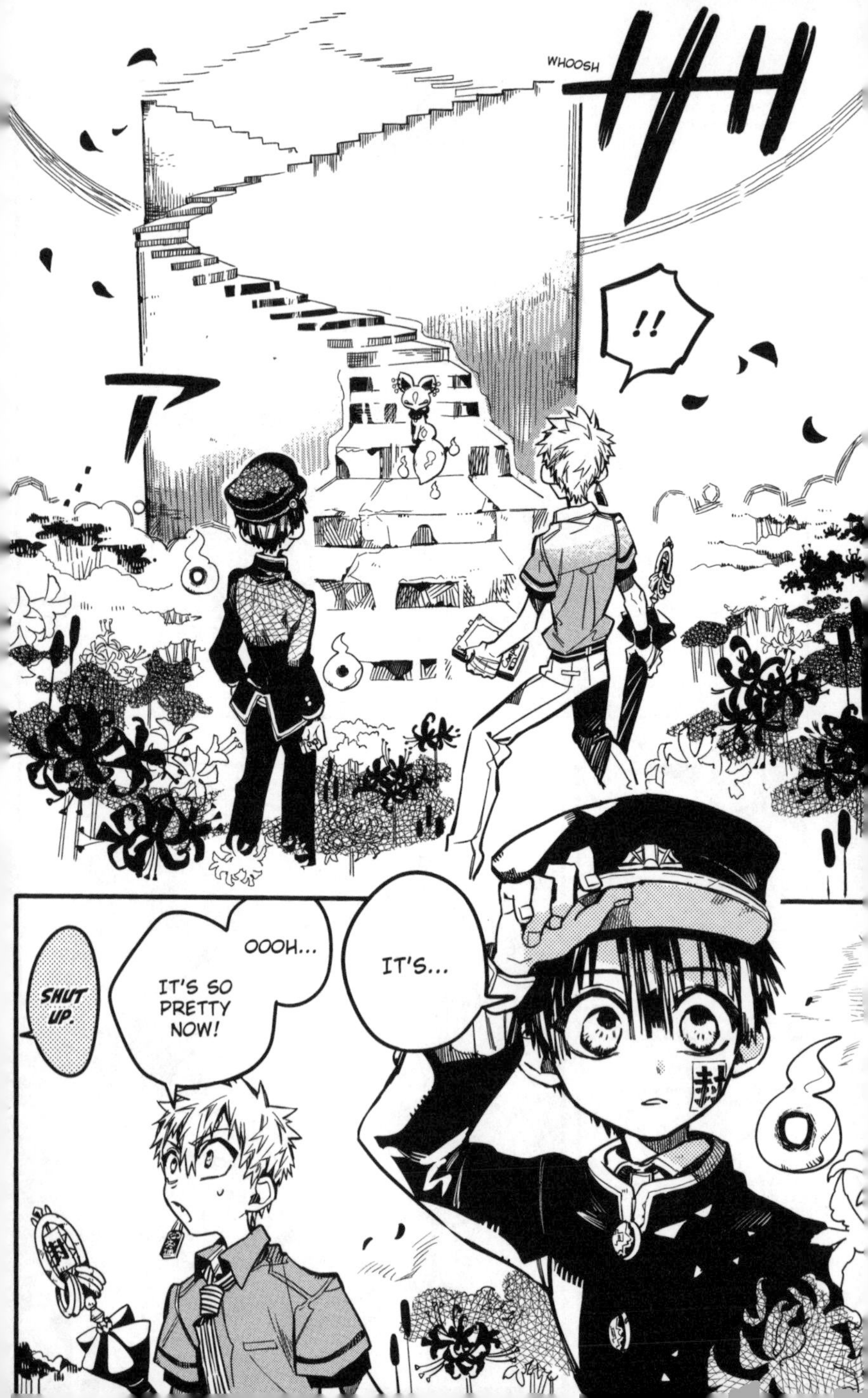
WHOOSH
!!
ア
IT'S...
OOOH...
IT'S SO PRETTY NOW!
SHUT UP.

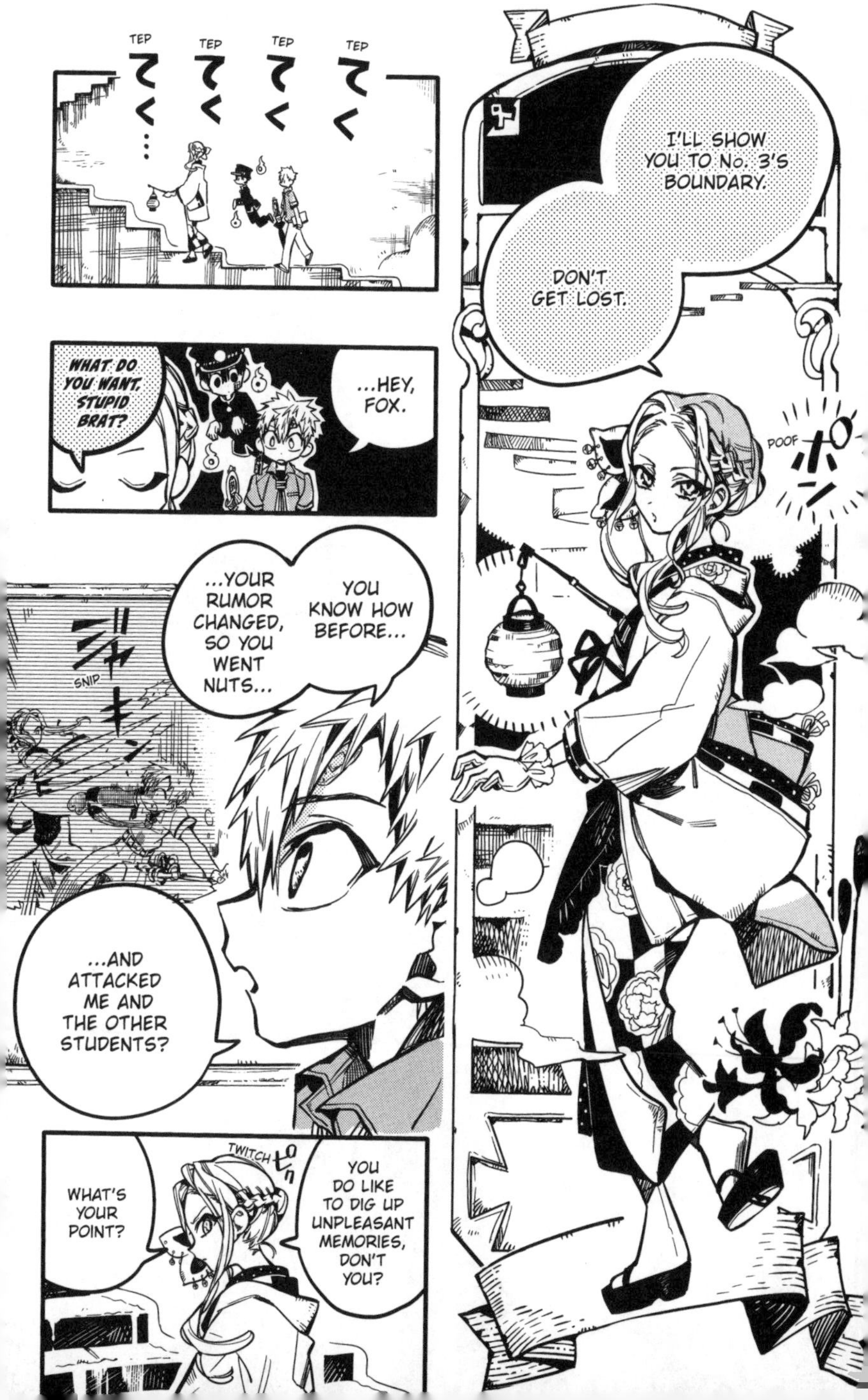
I'LL SHOW YOU TO No. 3'S BOUNDARY.
DON'T GET LOST.
POOF
TEP TEP TEP TEP
...HEY, FOX.
WHAT DO YOU WANT, STUPID BRAT?
YOU KNOW HOW BEFORE...
...YOUR RUMOR CHANGED, SO YOU WENT NUTS...
SNIP
...AND ATTACKED ME AND THE OTHER STUDENTS?
YOU DO LIKE TO DIG UP UNPLEASANT MEMORIES, DON'T YOU?
TWITCH
WHAT'S YOUR POINT?

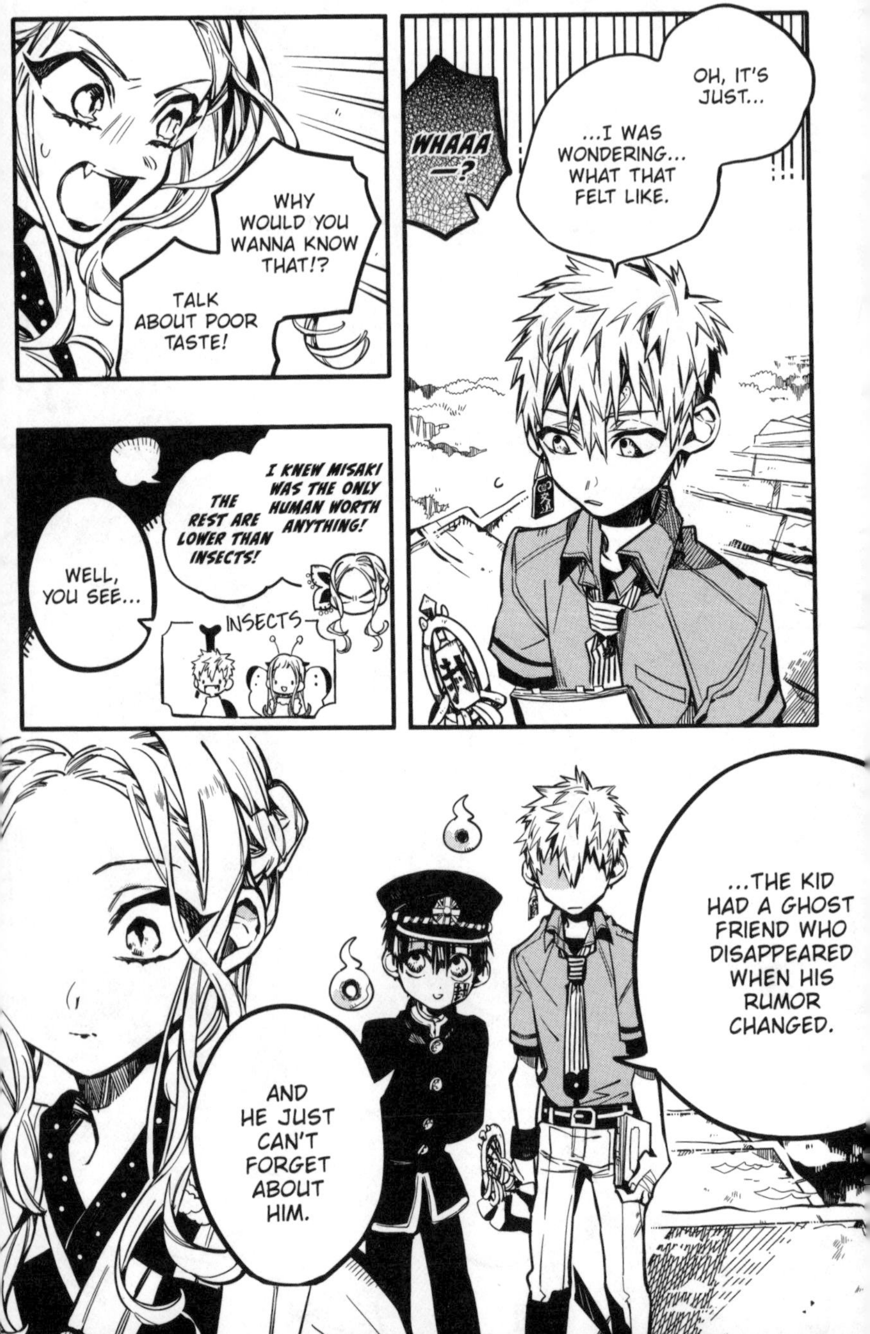
OH, IT'S JUST...
...I WAS WONDERING... WHAT THAT FELT LIKE.
WHAAA—?
WHY WOULD YOU WANNA KNOW THAT!?
TALK ABOUT POOR TASTE!
I KNEW MISAKI WAS THE ONLY HUMAN WORTH ANYTHING!
THE REST ARE LOWER THAN INSECTS!
WELL, YOU SEE...
INSECTS
...THE KID HAD A GHOST FRIEND WHO DISAPPEARED WHEN HIS RUMOR CHANGED.
AND HE JUST CAN'T FORGET ABOUT HIM.

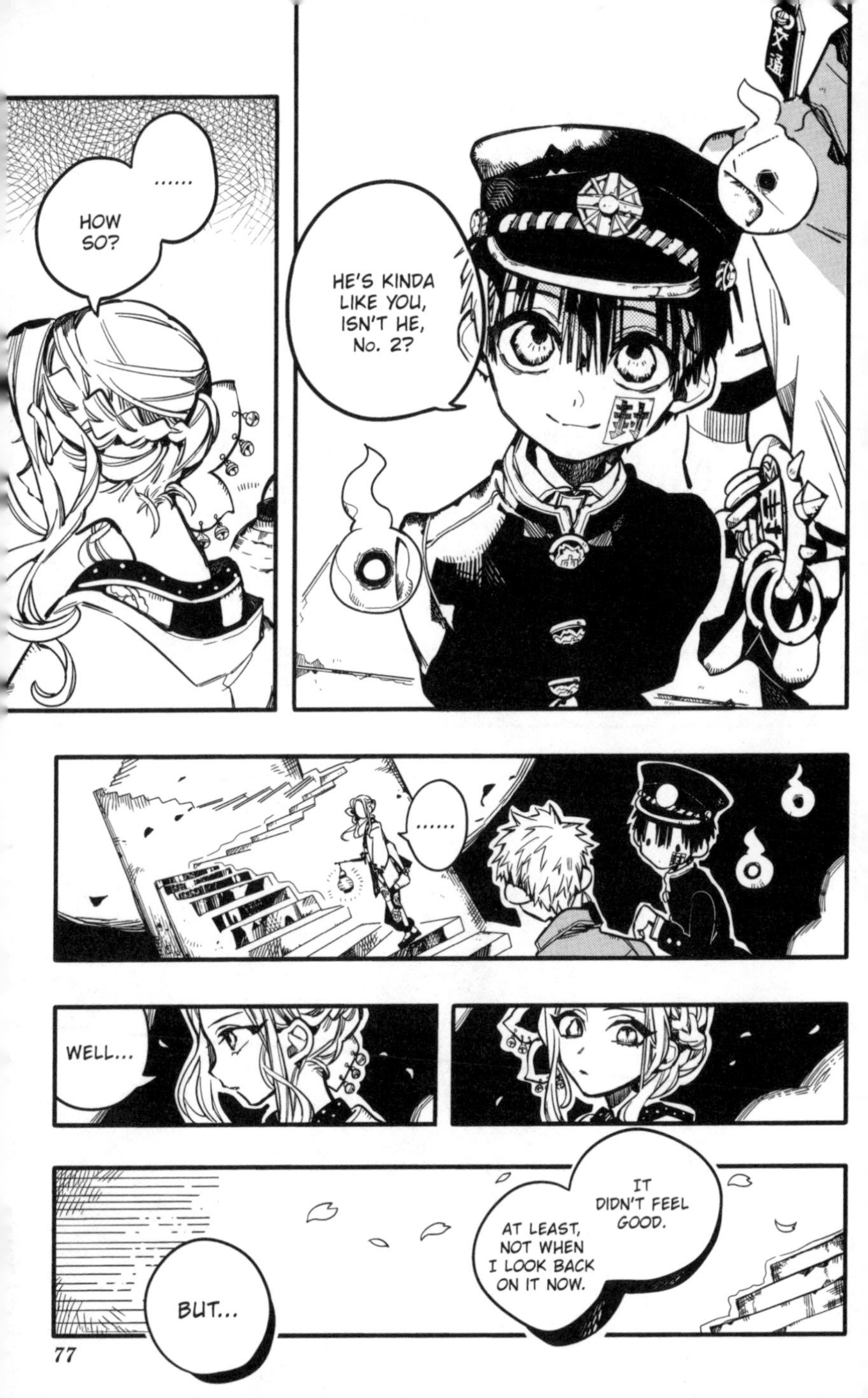
交通
HE'S KINDA LIKE YOU, ISN'T HE, No. 2?
......
HOW SO?
......
WELL...
IT DIDN'T FEEL GOOD.
AT LEAST, NOT WHEN I LOOK BACK ON IT NOW.
BUT...

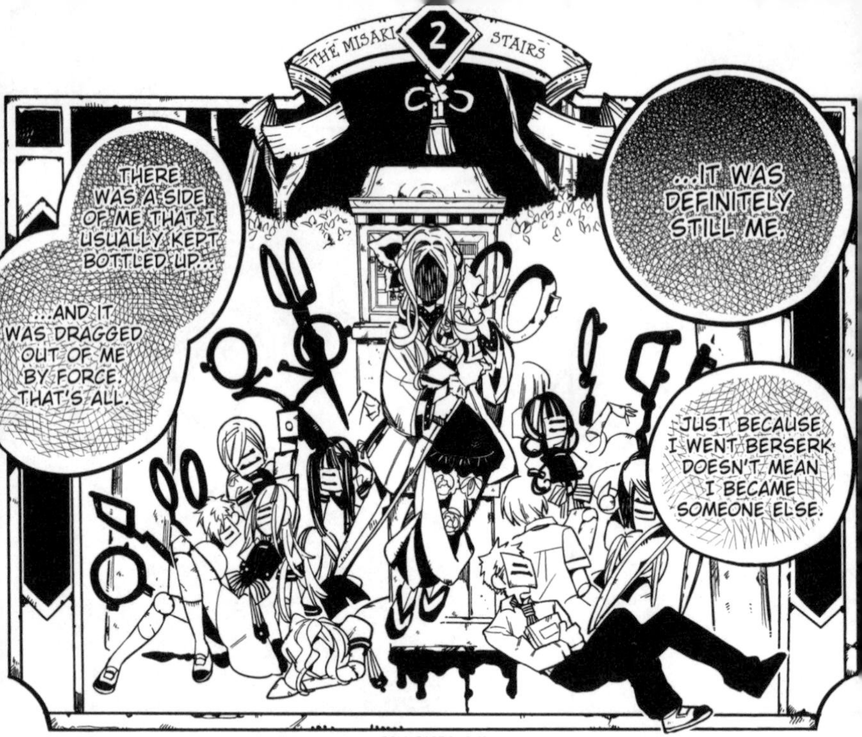
THE MISAKI 2 STAIRS
...IT WAS DEFINITELY STILL ME.
THERE WAS A SIDE OF ME THAT I USUALLY KEPT BOTTLED UP...
...AND IT WAS DRAGGED OUT OF ME BY FORCE. THAT'S ALL.
JUST BECAUSE I WENT BERSERK DOESN'T MEAN I BECAME SOMEONE ELSE.

DOLL FACES: TWO

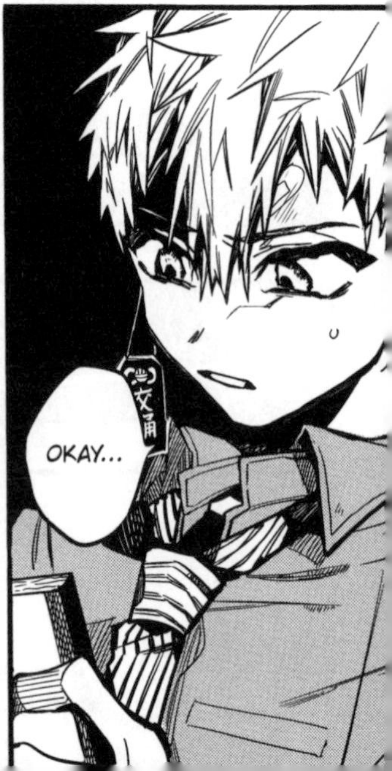
OKAY...

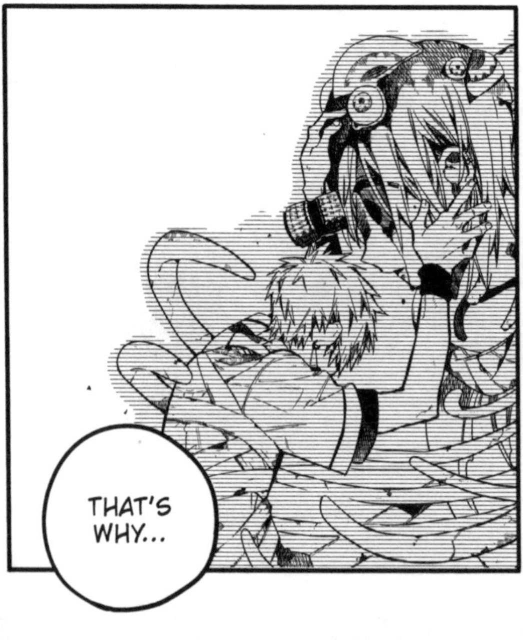
THAT'S WHY...

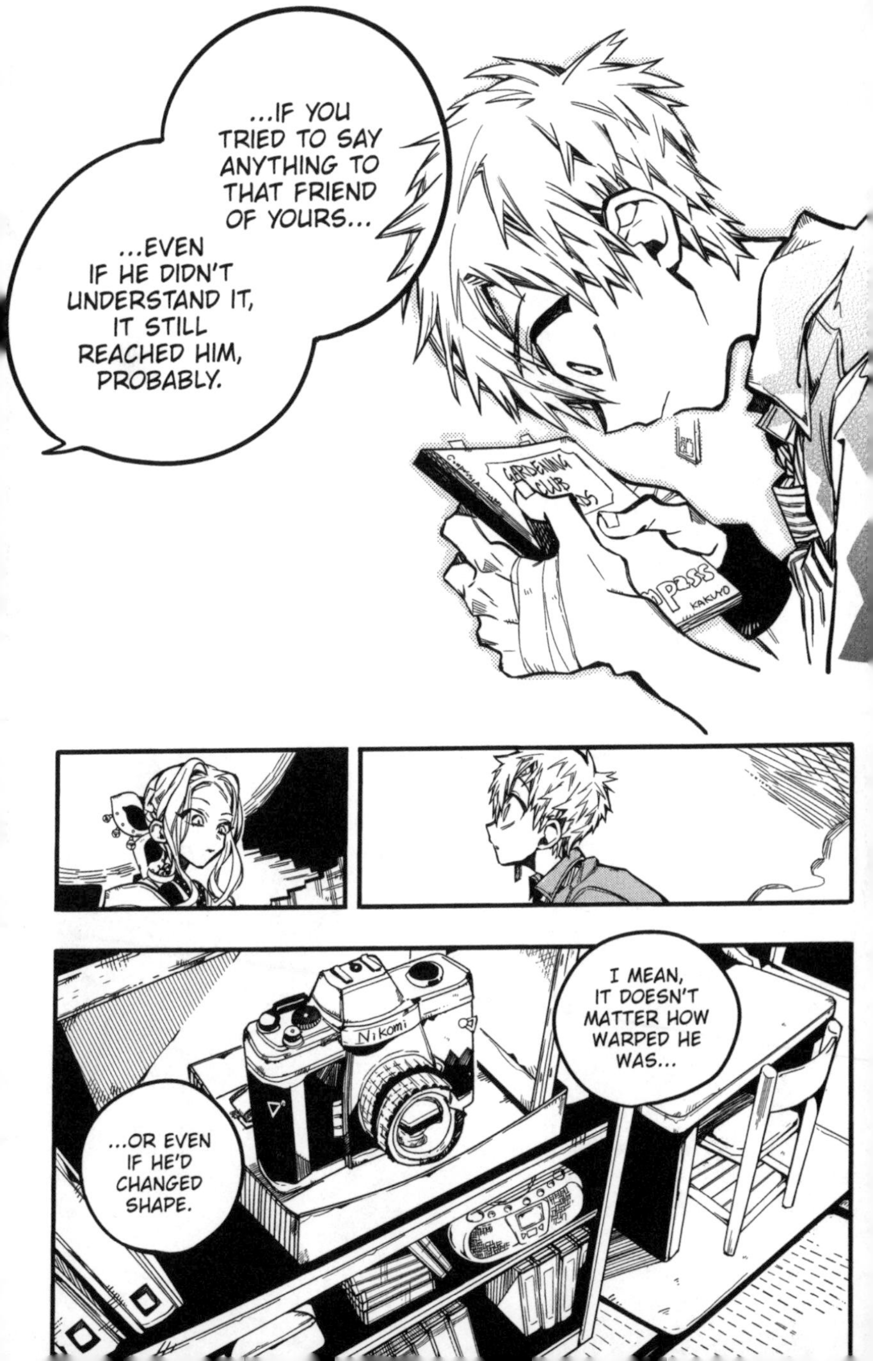
...IF YOU TRIED TO SAY ANYTHING TO THAT FRIEND OF YOURS...
...EVEN IF HE DIDN'T UNDERSTAND IT, IT STILL REACHED HIM, PROBABLY.
GARDENING CLUB
KAKUYO
Nikomi
I MEAN, IT DOESN'T MATTER HOW WARPED HE WAS...
...OR EVEN IF HE'D CHANGED SHAPE.

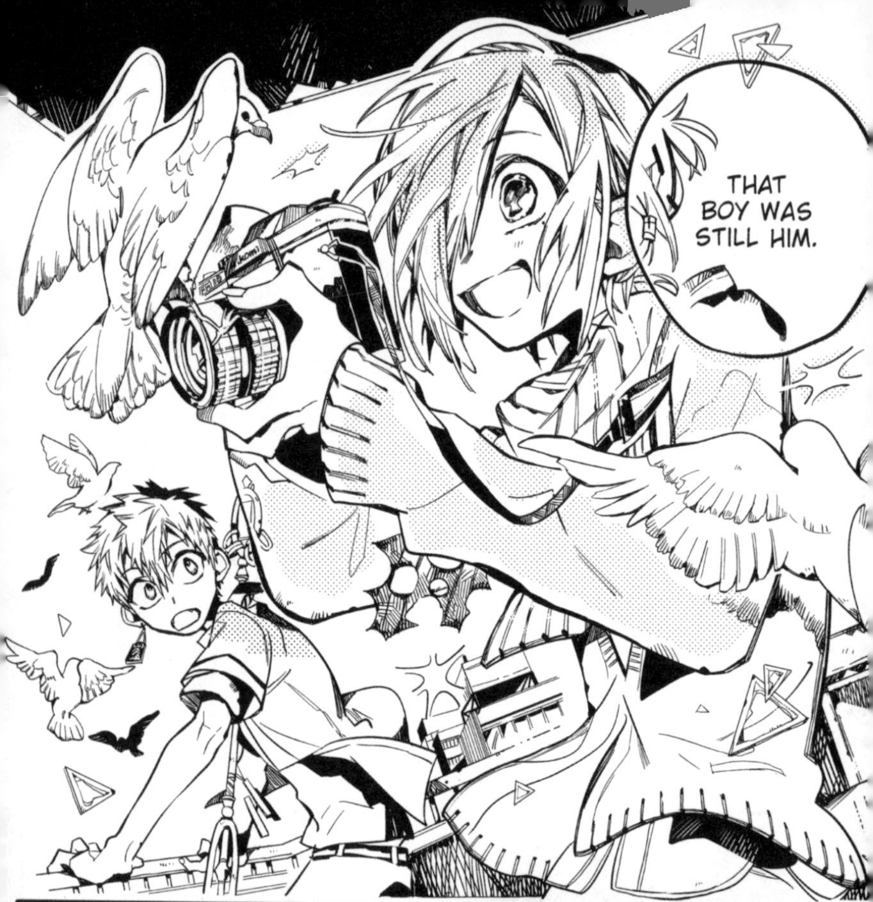
THAT BOY WAS STILL HIM.
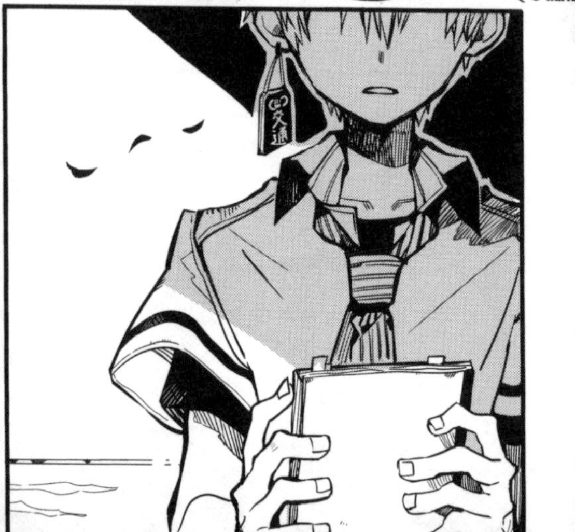
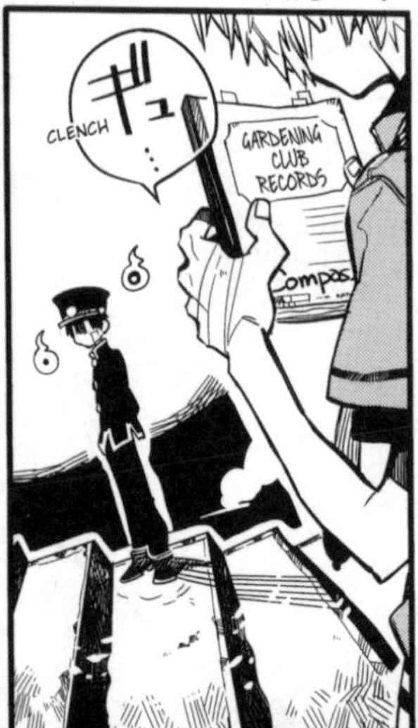
ギュ
CLENCH
...
GARDENING CLUB RECORDS

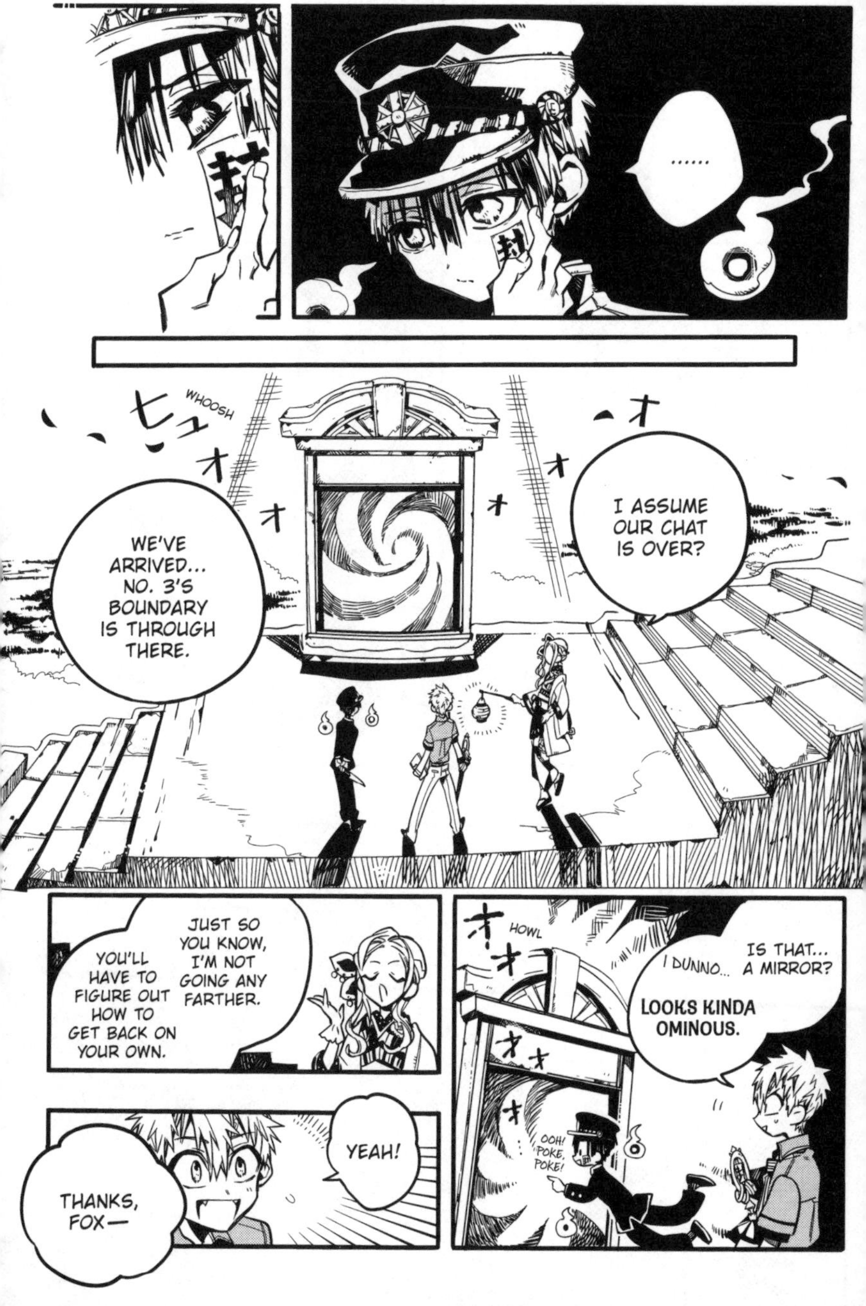
......
WHOOSH
I ASSUME OUR CHAT IS OVER?
WE'VE ARRIVED... NO. 3'S BOUNDARY IS THROUGH THERE.
HOWL
IS THAT... A MIRROR?
I DUNNO...
LOOKS KINDA OMINOUS.
OOH! POKE, POKE!
JUST SO YOU KNOW, I'M NOT GOING ANY FARTHER.
YOU'LL HAVE TO FIGURE OUT HOW TO GET BACK ON YOUR OWN.
YEAH!
THANKS, FOX—

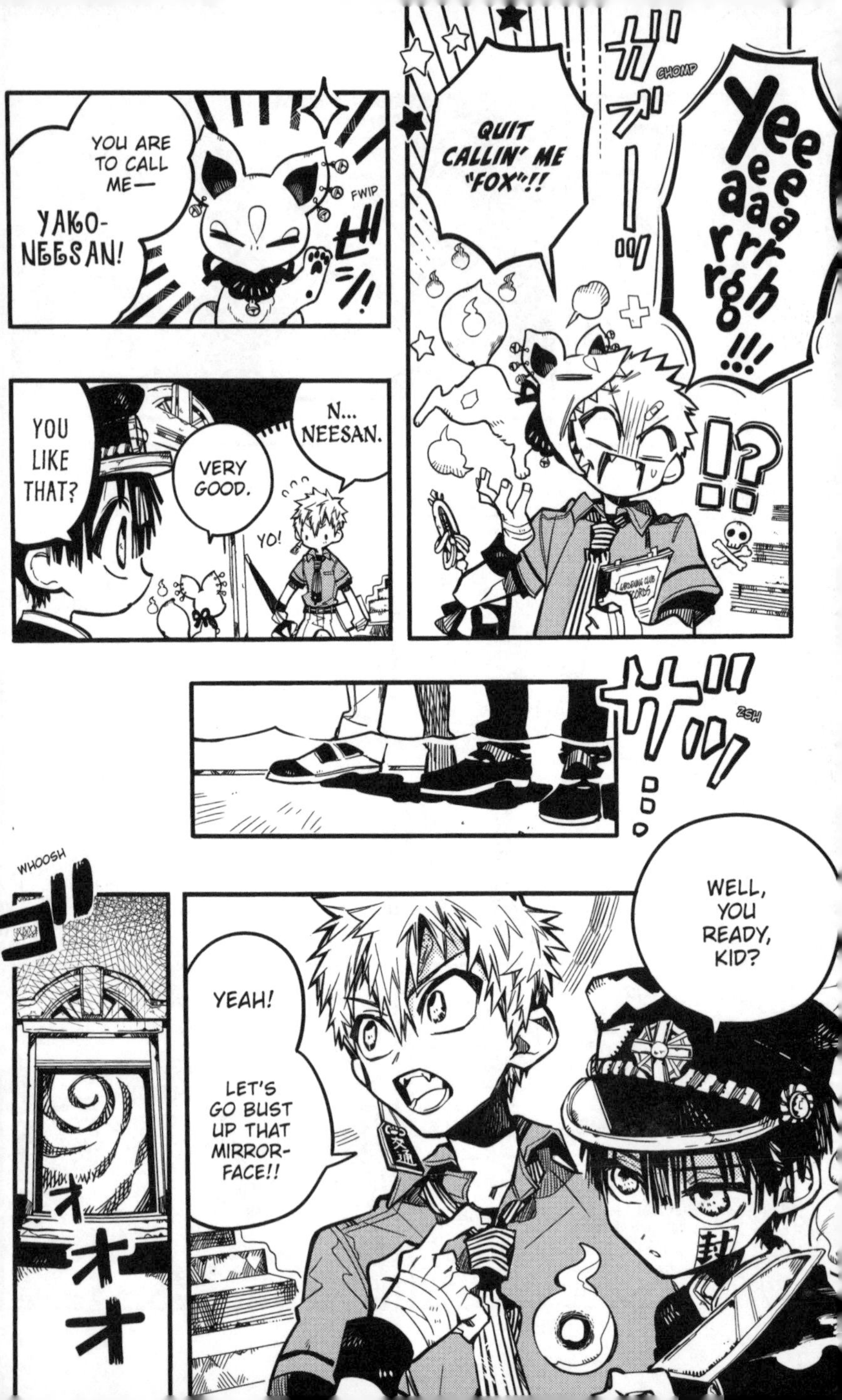

Yeeeeaaarrrrgh!!!
CHOMP
QUIT CALLIN' ME "FOX"!!
!?
YOU ARE TO CALL ME—
YAKO-NEESAN!
FWIP
N... NEESAN.
VERY GOOD.
YO!
YOU LIKE THAT?
ZSH
WELL, YOU READY, KID?
YEAH!
LET'S GO BUST UP THAT MIRROR-FACE!!
WHOOSH

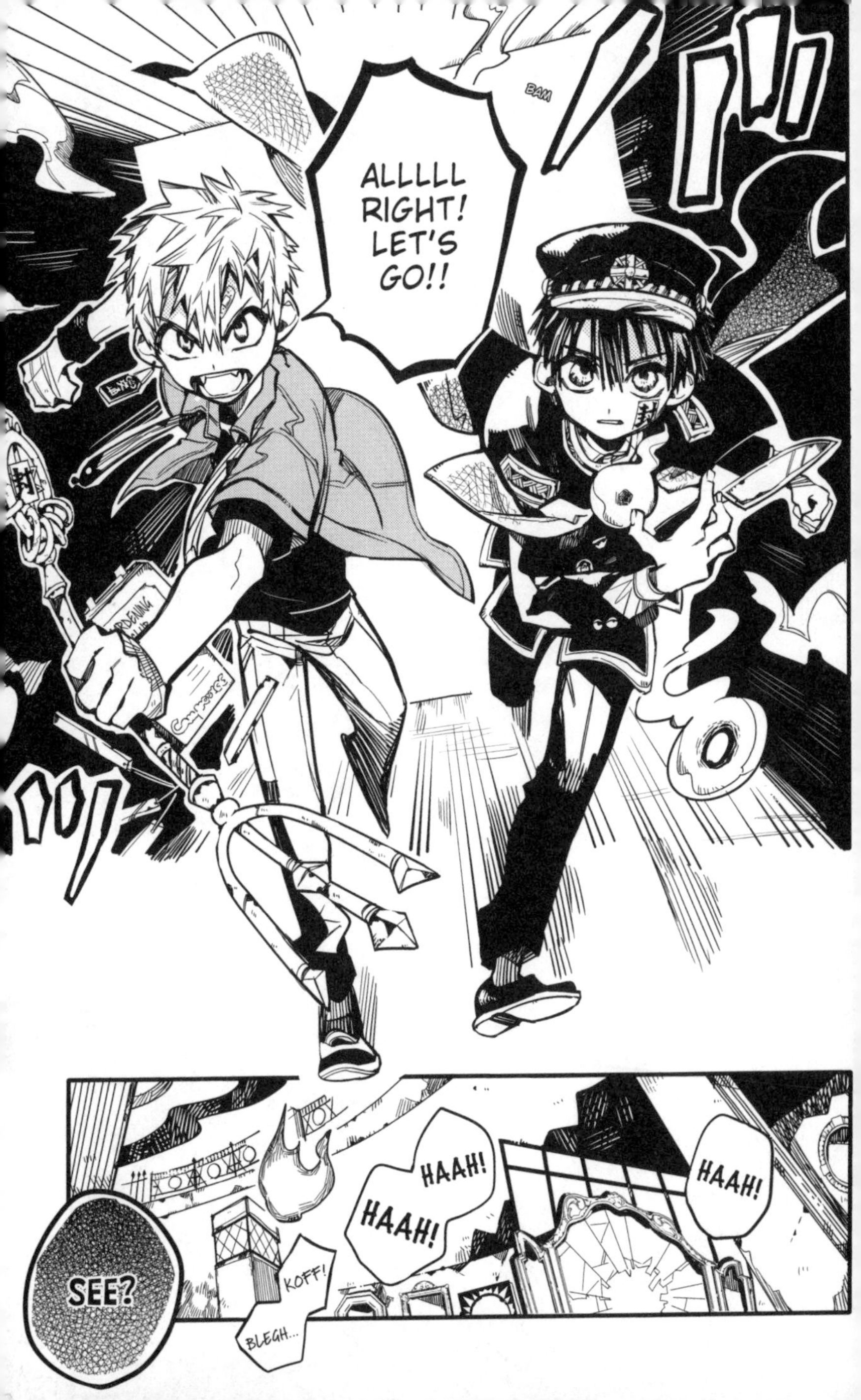
BAM
ALLLLL RIGHT! LET'S GO!!
HAAH!
HAAH!
HAAH!
KOFF!
BLEGH...
SEE?

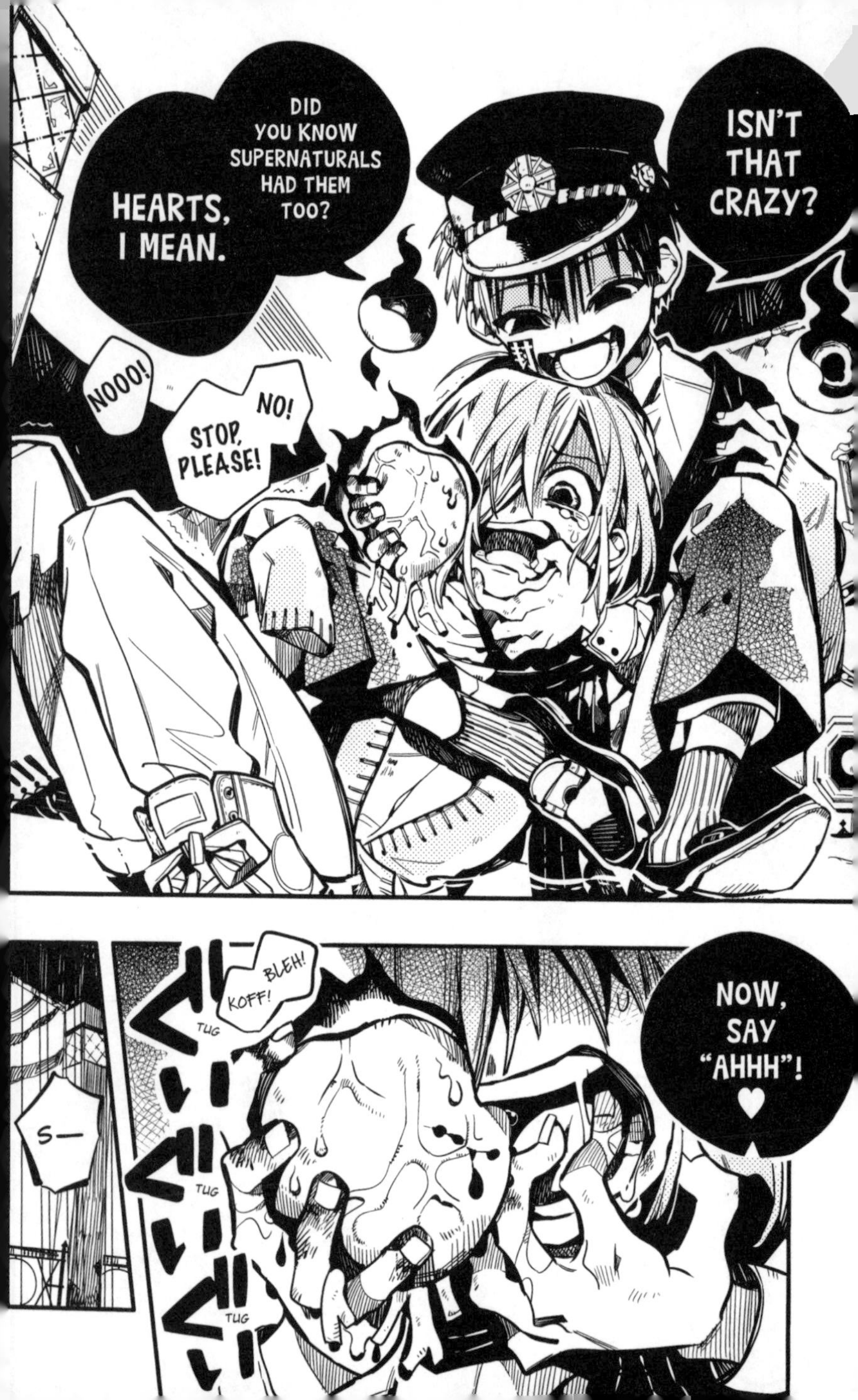
ISN'T THAT CRAZY?
DID YOU KNOW SUPERNATURALS HAD THEM TOO?
HEARTS, I MEAN.
NO!
STOP, PLEASE!
NOOO!
NOW, SAY "AHHH"! ♥
BLEH!
KOFF!
TUG
S—
TUG
TUG

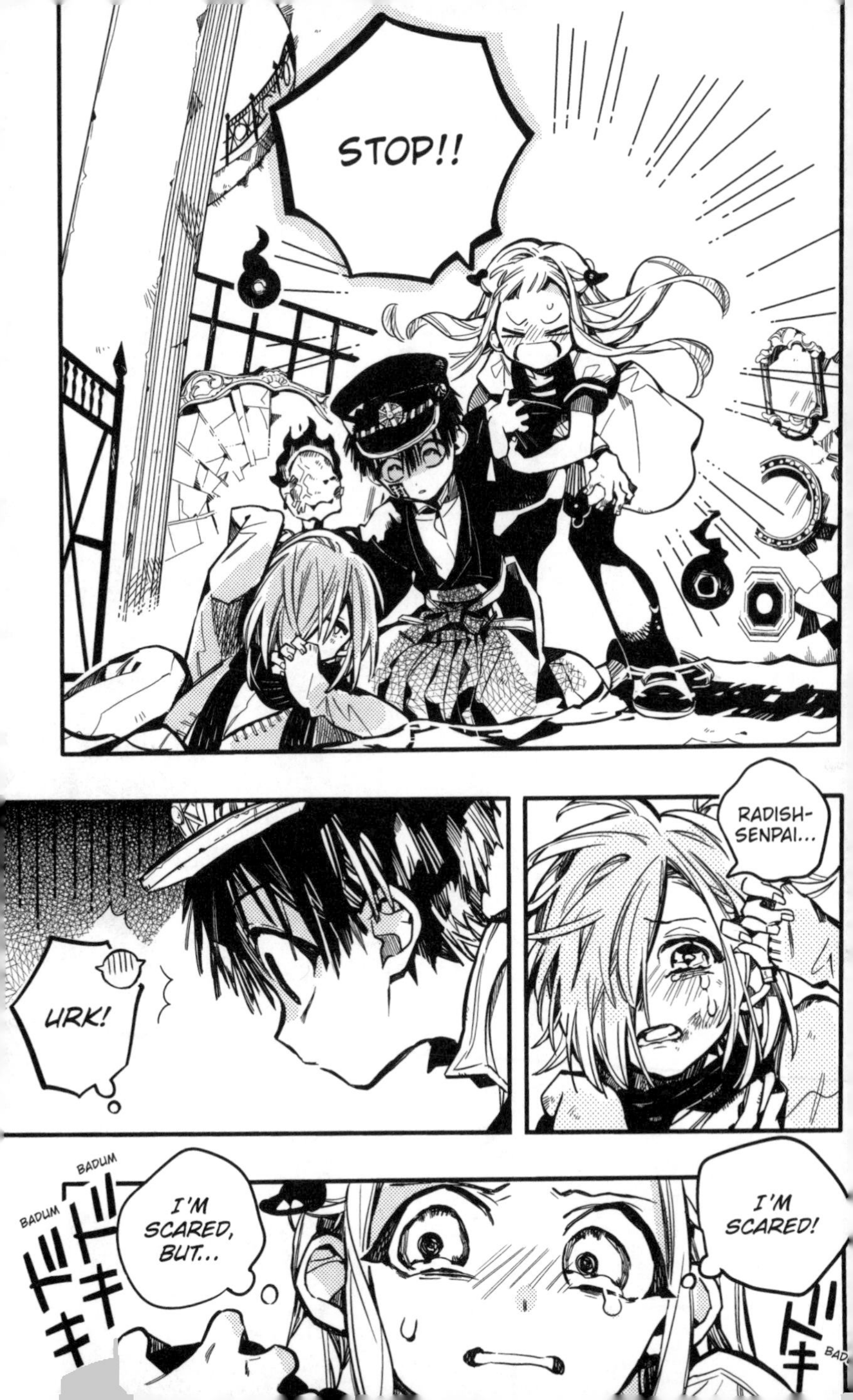
STOP!!
RADISH-SENPAI...
URK!
I'M SCARED!
ドキ
I'M SCARED, BUT...
BADUM
BADUM
ドキドキ

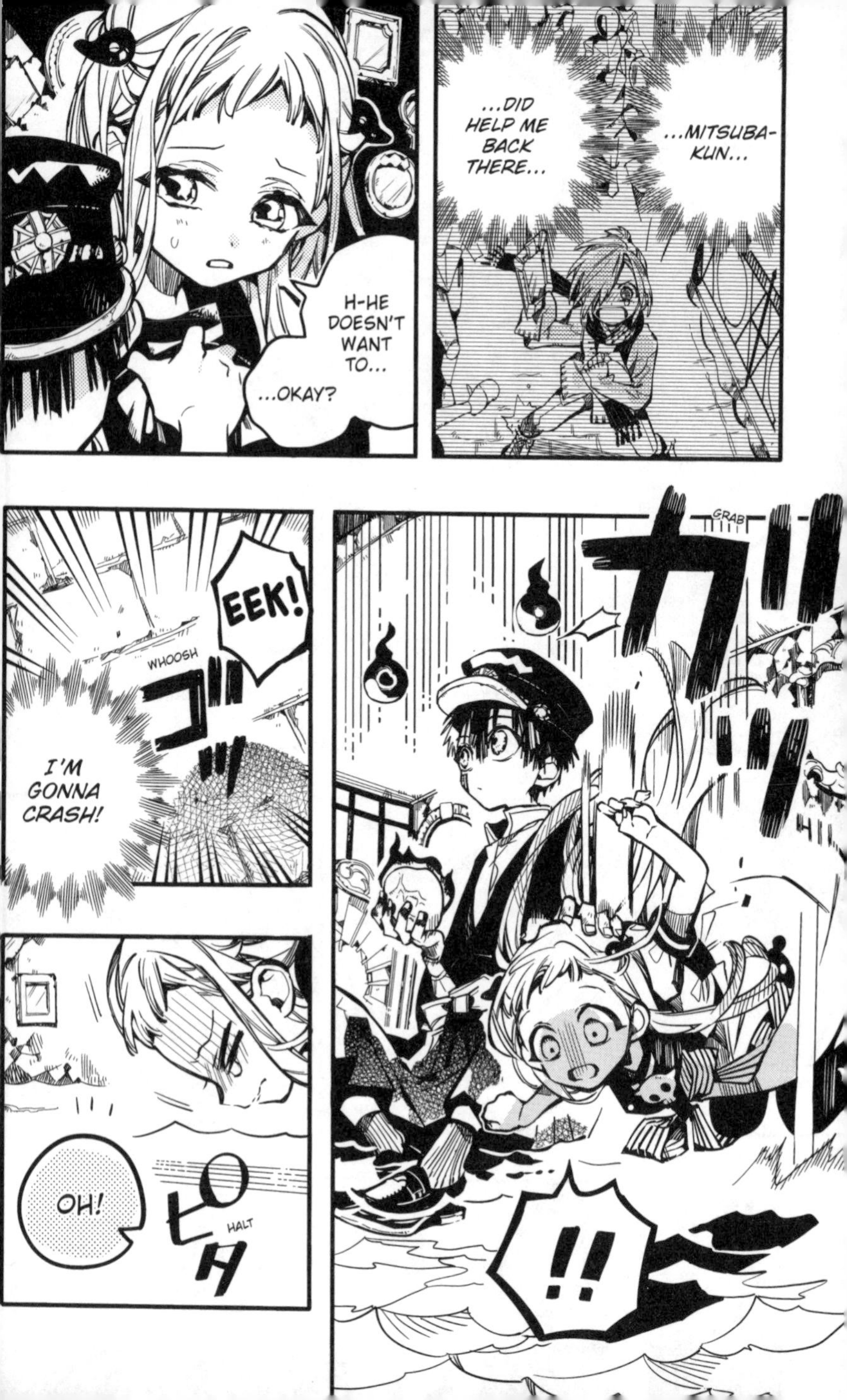
...MITSUBA-KUN...
...DID HELP ME BACK THERE...
H-HE DOESN'T WANT TO...
...OKAY?
GRAB
!!
EEK!
WHOOSH
I'M GONNA CRASH!
OH!
HALT

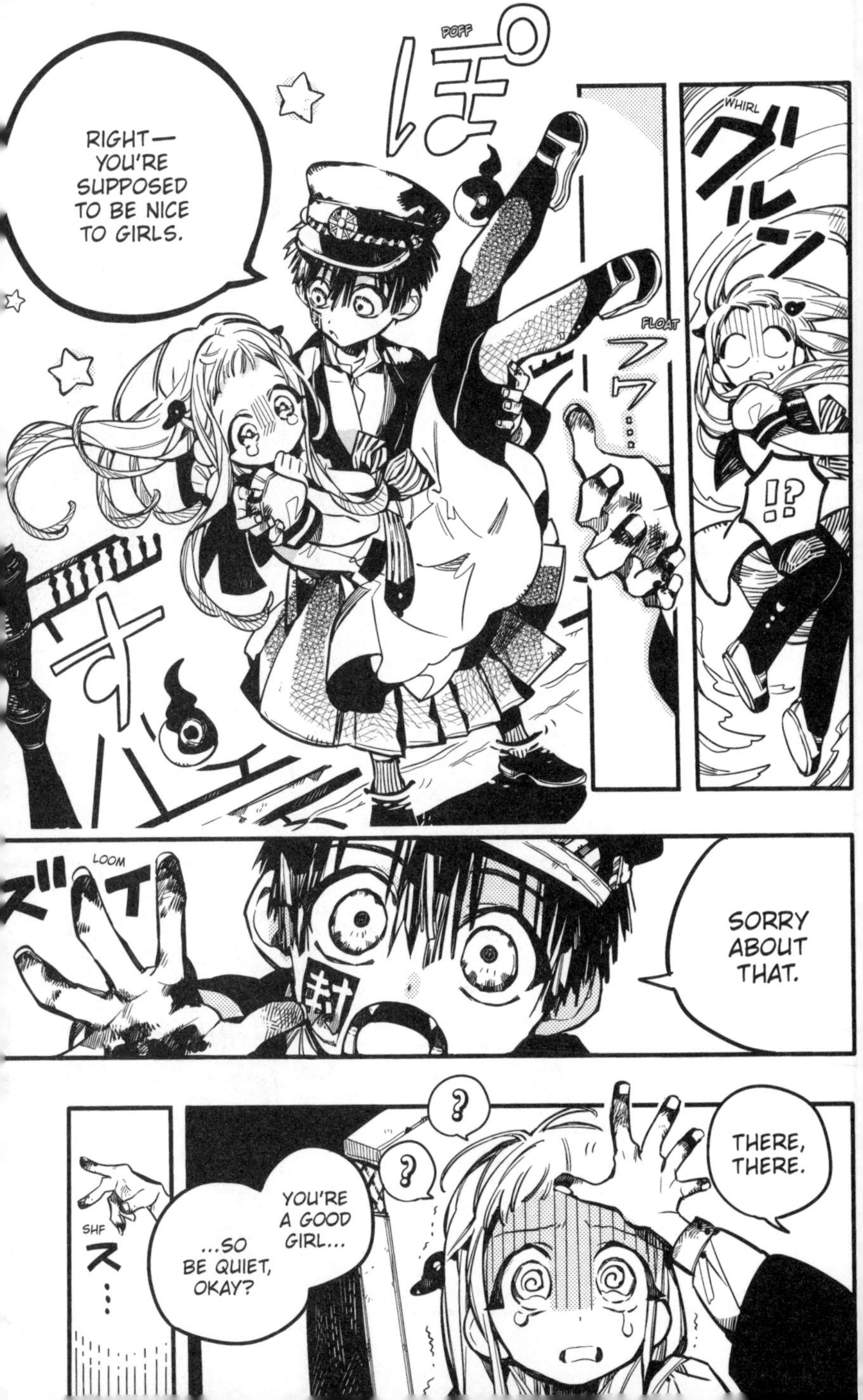
WHIRL
グルン
!?
FLOAT
フワ…
POFF
ぽ
RIGHT— YOU'RE SUPPOSED TO BE NICE TO GIRLS.
LOOM
ズイ
SORRY ABOUT THAT.
THERE, THERE.
?
?
YOU'RE A GOOD GIRL…
…SO BE QUIET, OKAY?
SHF
ス…

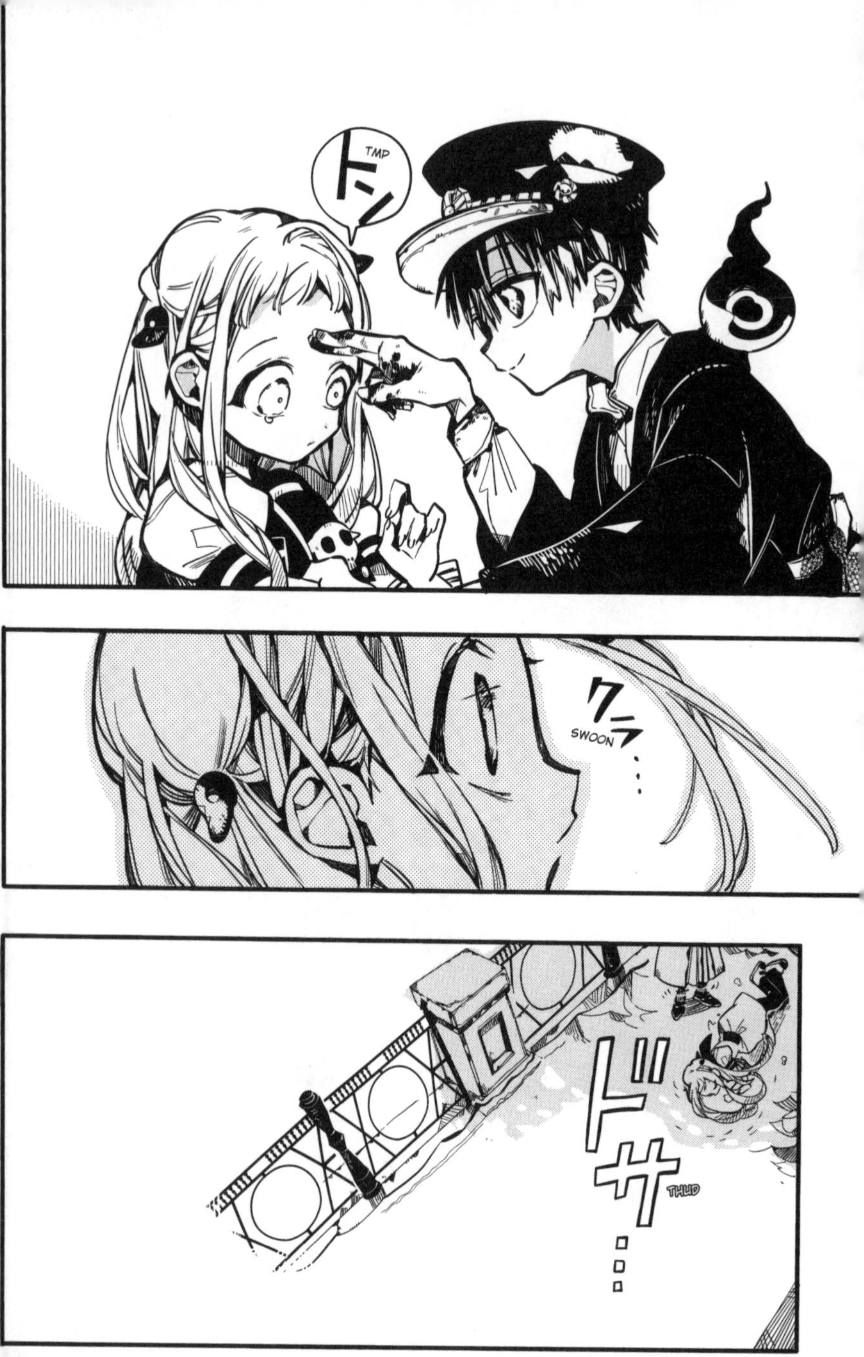
トン
TMP
クラ…
SWOON
ドサ…
THUD

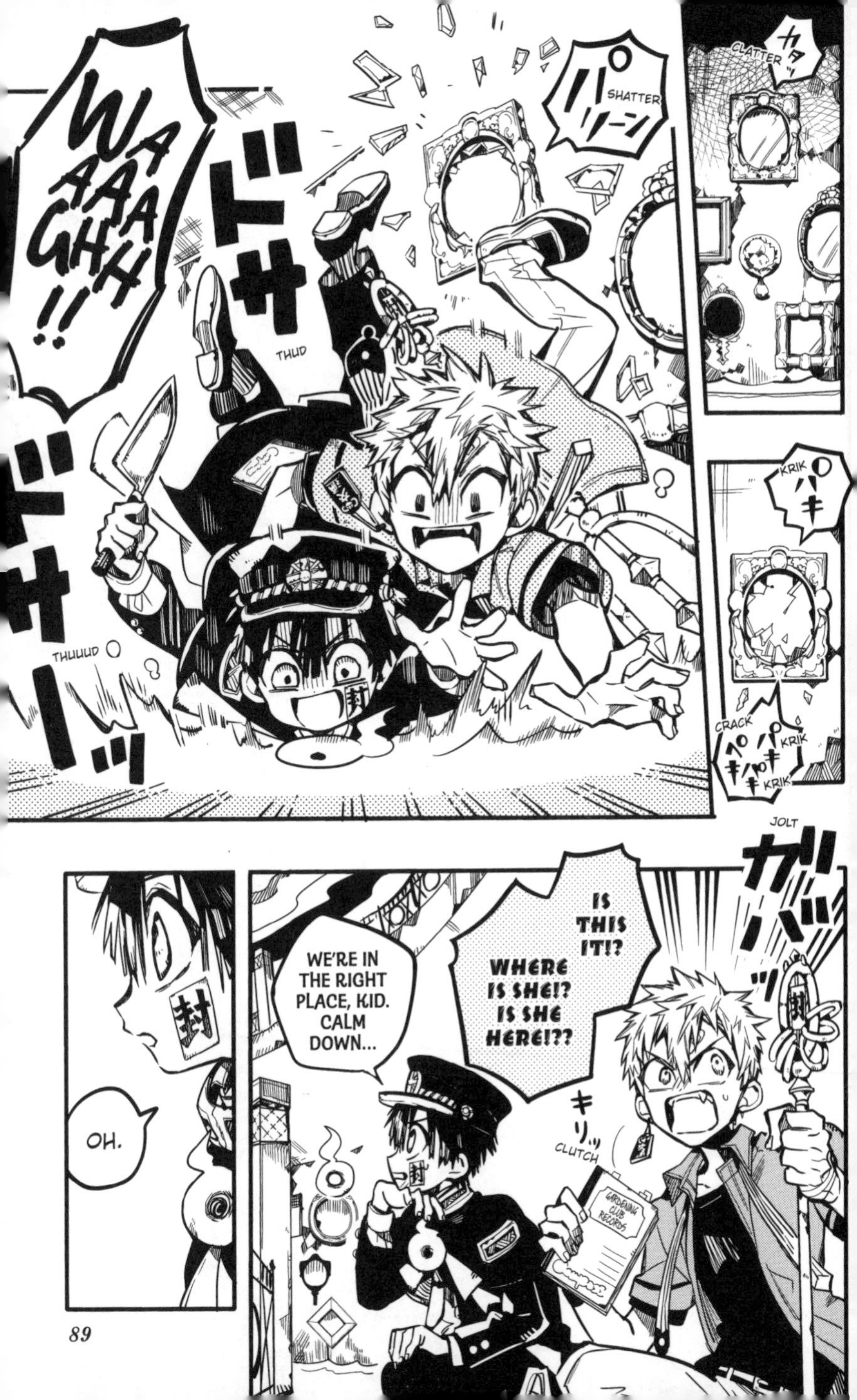
カタッ
CLATTER
パキ
KRIK
パ パキ パキ
CRACK
KRIK
KRIK
パリーン
SHATTER
ドサ
THUD
WAAAAGHH!!
ドサーッ
THUUUD
ガバッ
JOLT
IS THIS IT!?
WHERE IS SHE!? IS SHE HERE!??
キリッ
CLUTCH
WE'RE IN THE RIGHT PLACE, KID. CALM DOWN...
GARDENING CLUB RECORDS
OH.

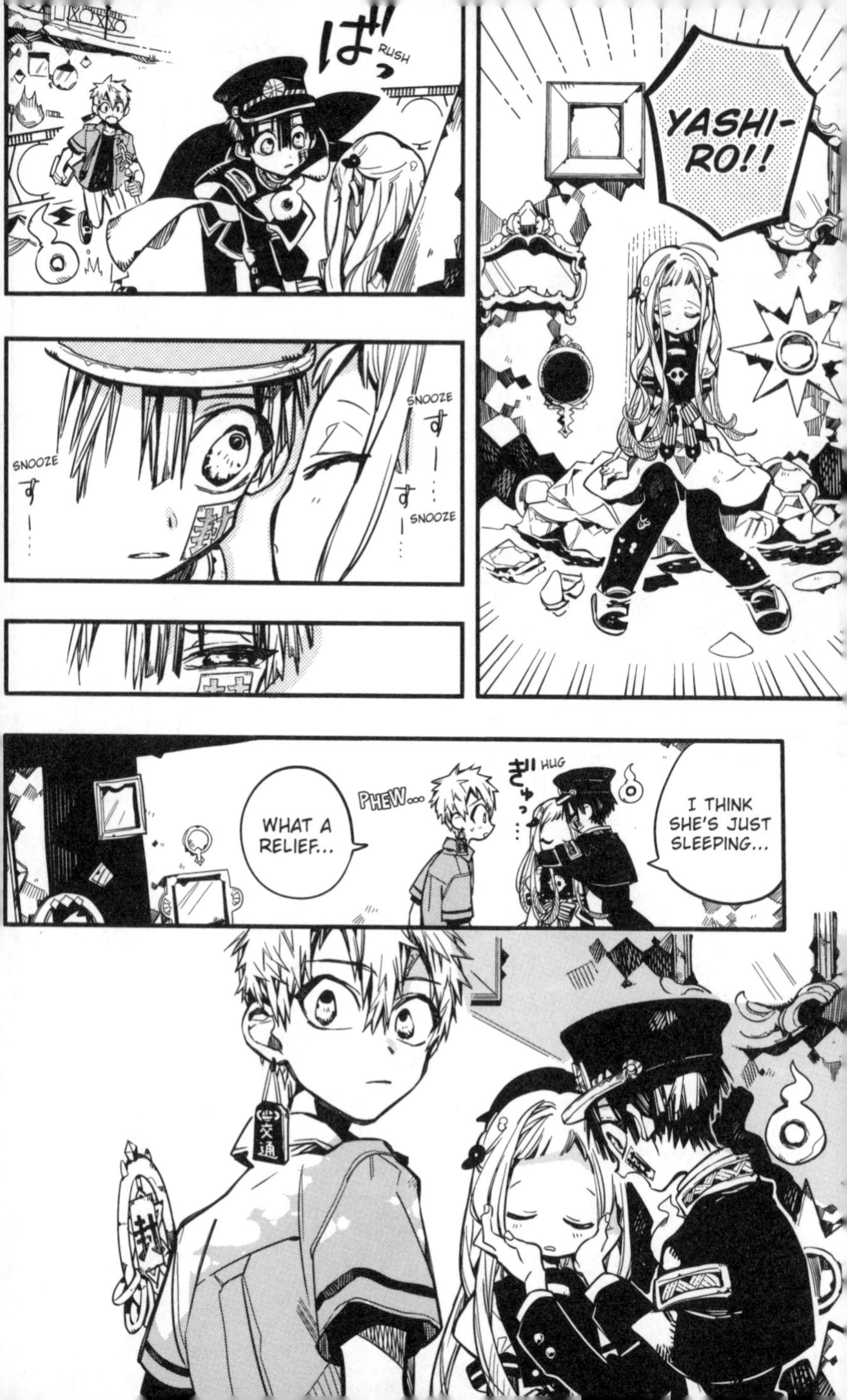
YASHI-RO!!
ばっ
RUSH
SNOOZE
すー…
すー…
SNOOZE
SNOOZE
すー…
I THINK SHE'S JUST SLEEPING...
ぎゅっ…
HUG
PHEW...
WHAT A RELIEF...

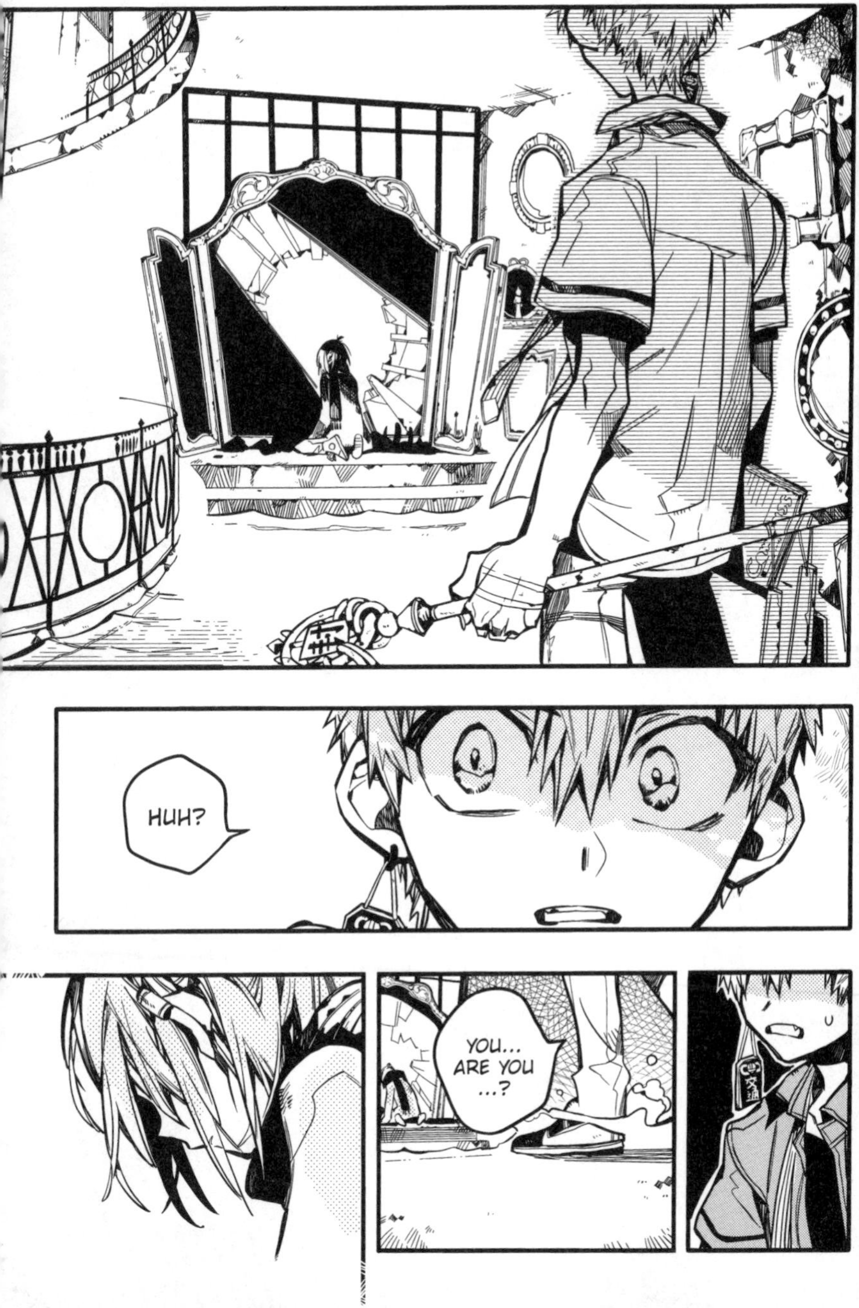
HUH?
YOU... ARE YOU ...?

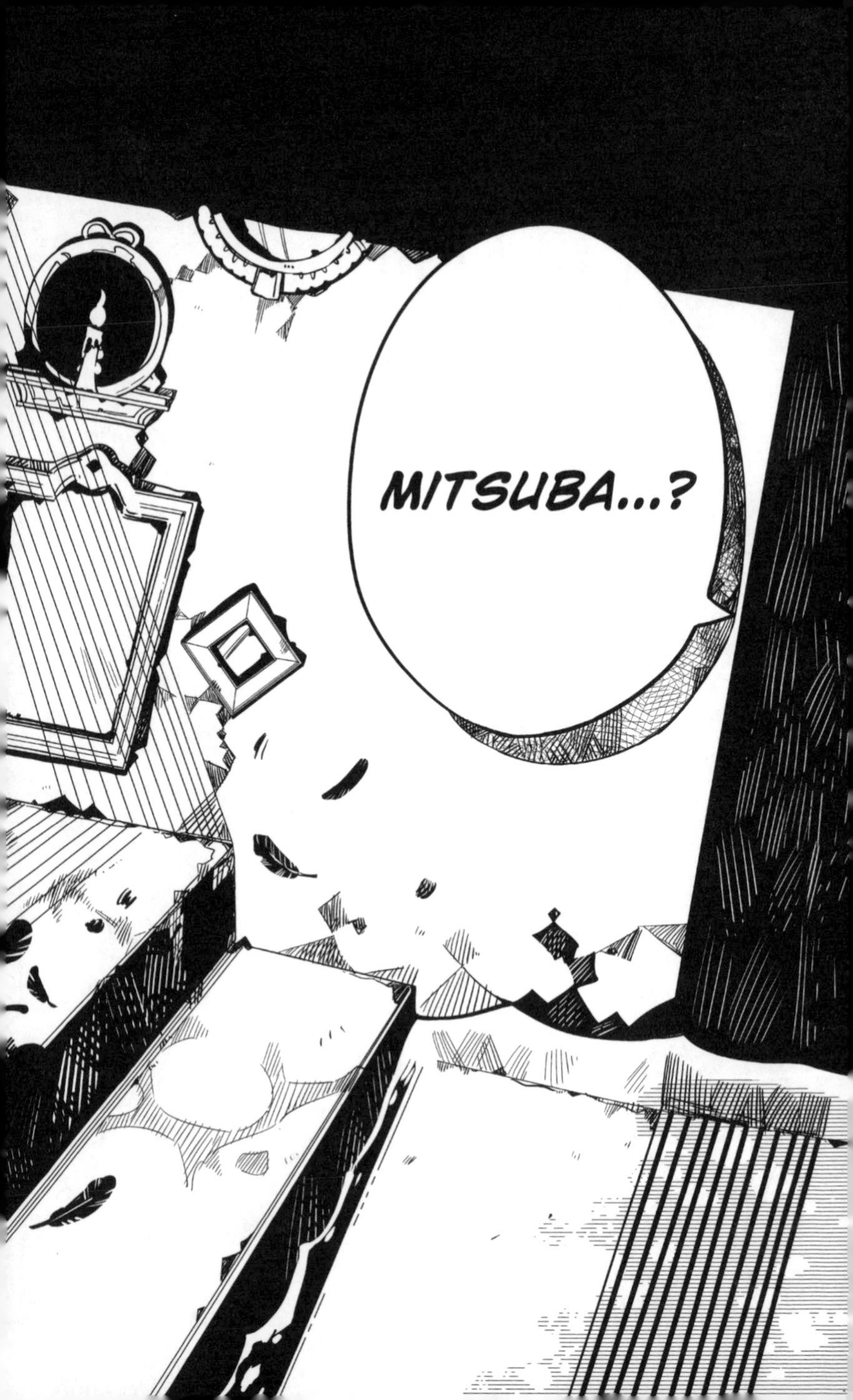
MITSUBA...?

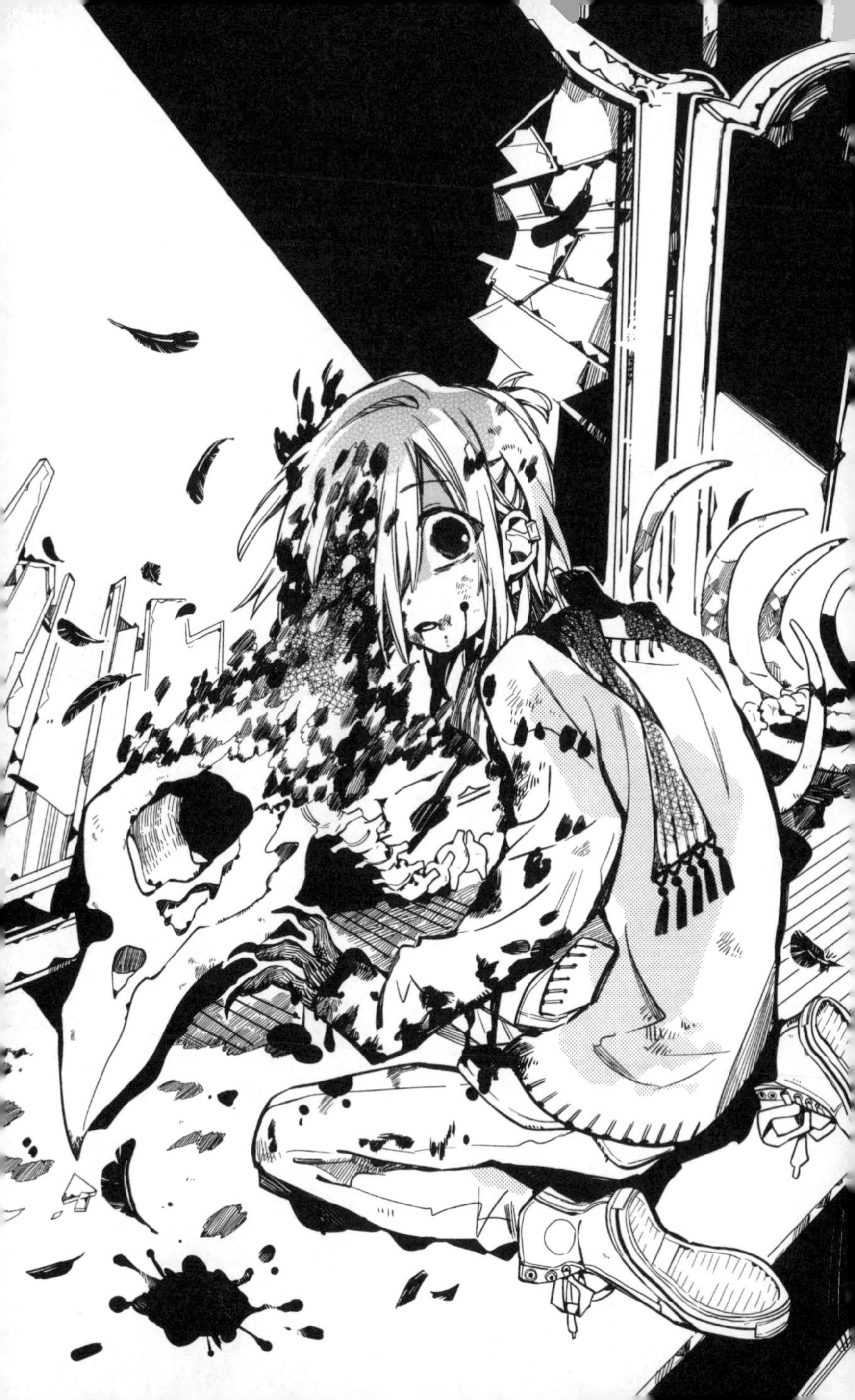

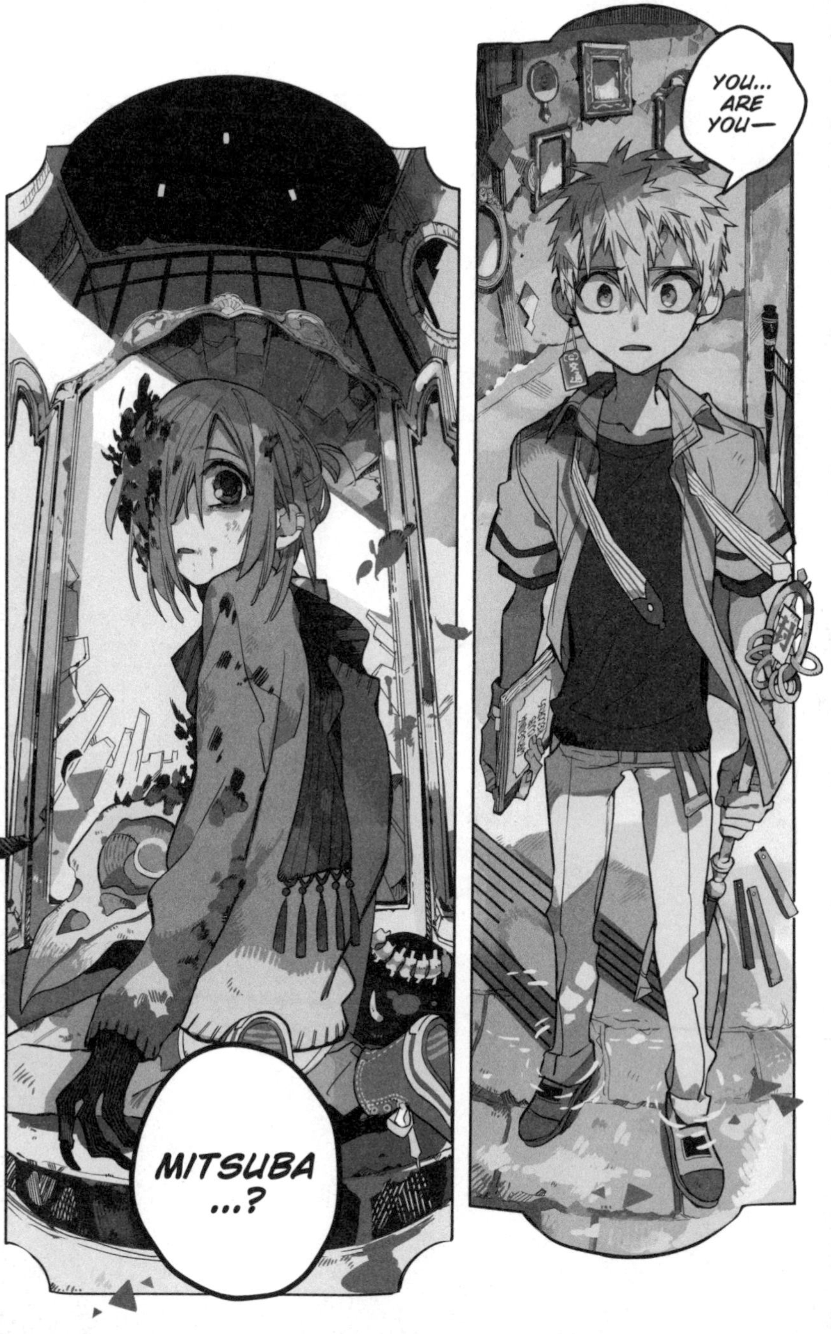
YOU... ARE YOU—
MITSUBA ...?

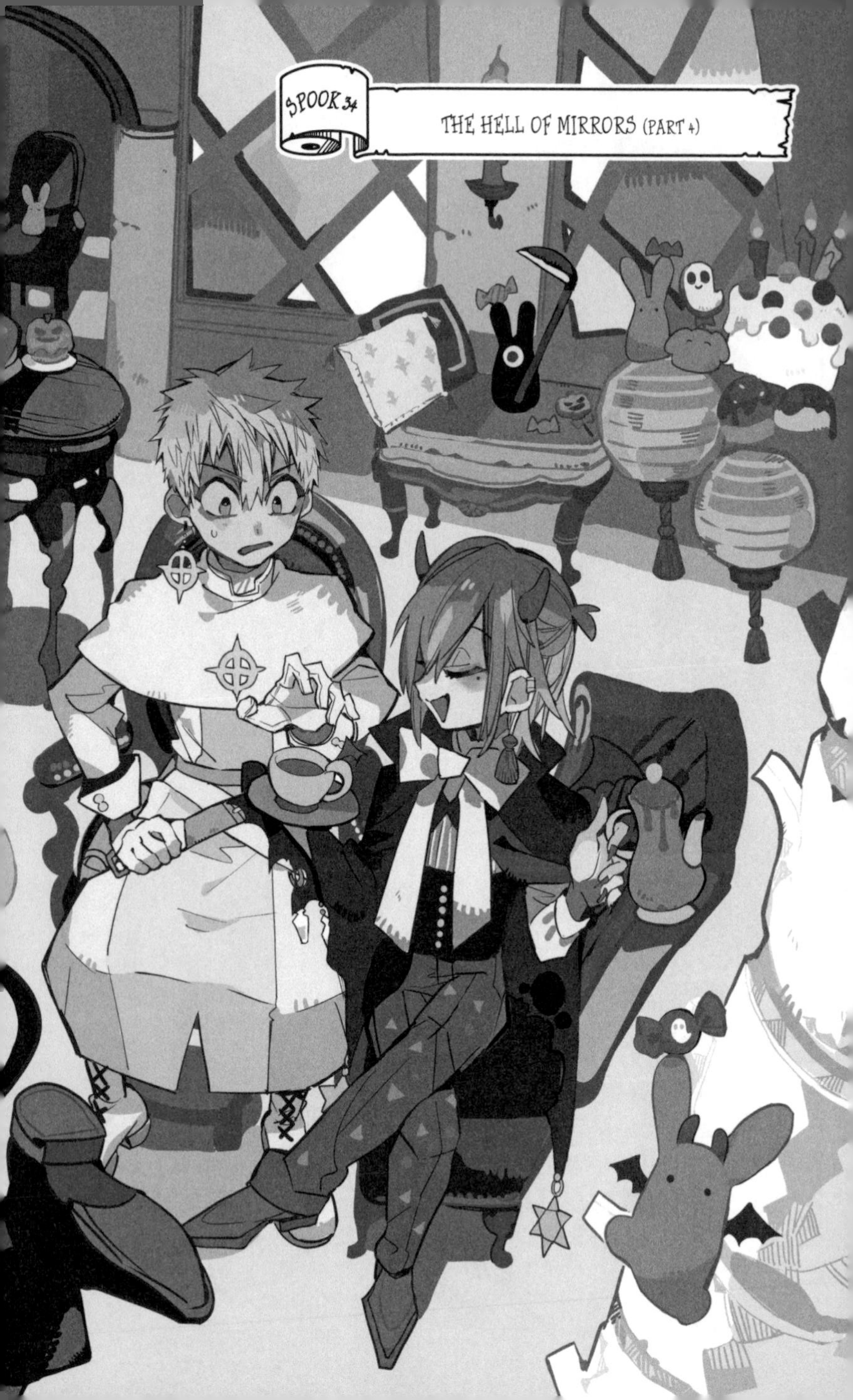
SPOOK 34
THE HELL OF MIRRORS (PART 4)

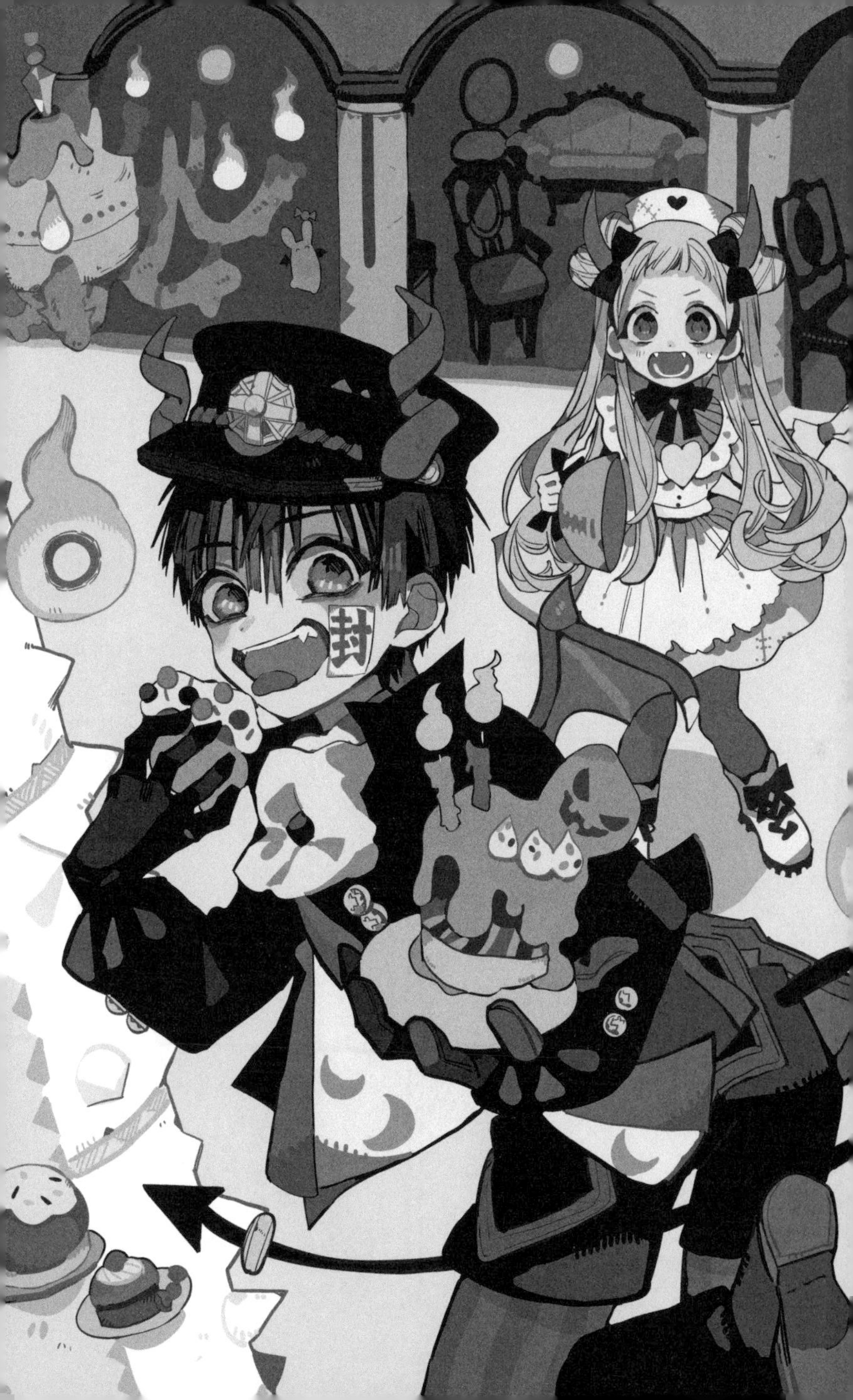
封

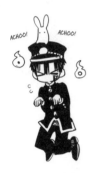

ACHOO!
ACHOO!

THE UGLY-RADISH INCIDENT

—WITH AOI—

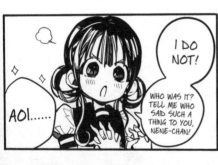

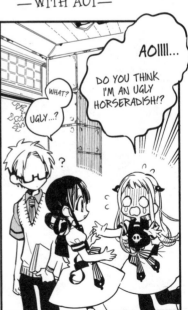

AOIIII...
DO YOU THINK I'M AN UGLY HORSERADISH!?
WHAT?
UGLY...?
I DO NOT!
WHO WAS IT? TELL ME WHO SAID SUCH A THING TO YOU, NENE-CHAN!
AOI......
HIM
WAS IT HIM?
WANT ME TO MAKE HIM DIS-APPEAR?
AKANE-KUN...

IT WASN'T HANAKO-KUN!

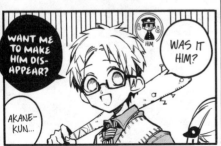

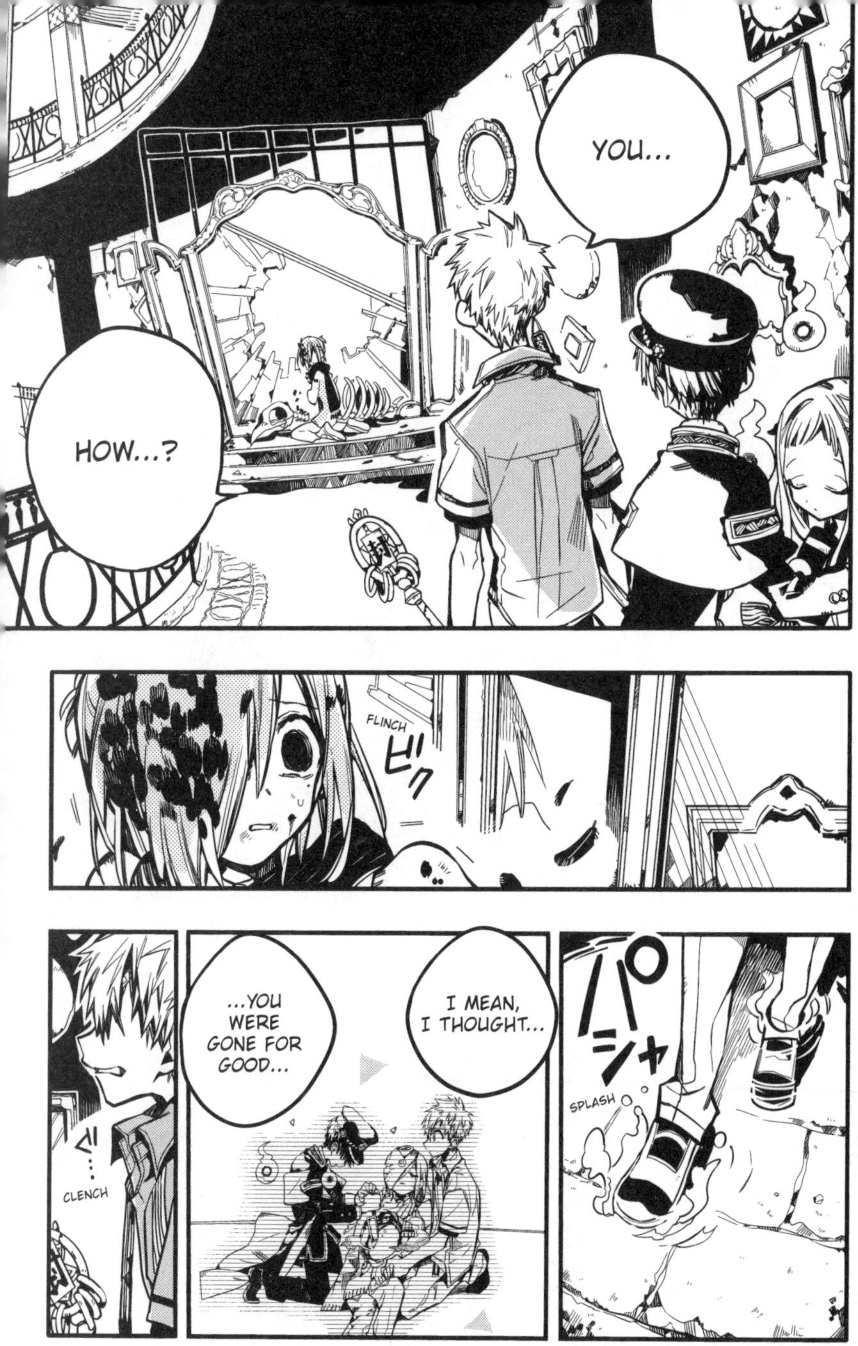
YOU...
HOW...?
FLINCH
ビク
パシャ
SPLASH
I MEAN, I THOUGHT...
...YOU WERE GONE FOR GOOD...
ぐ...
CLENCH

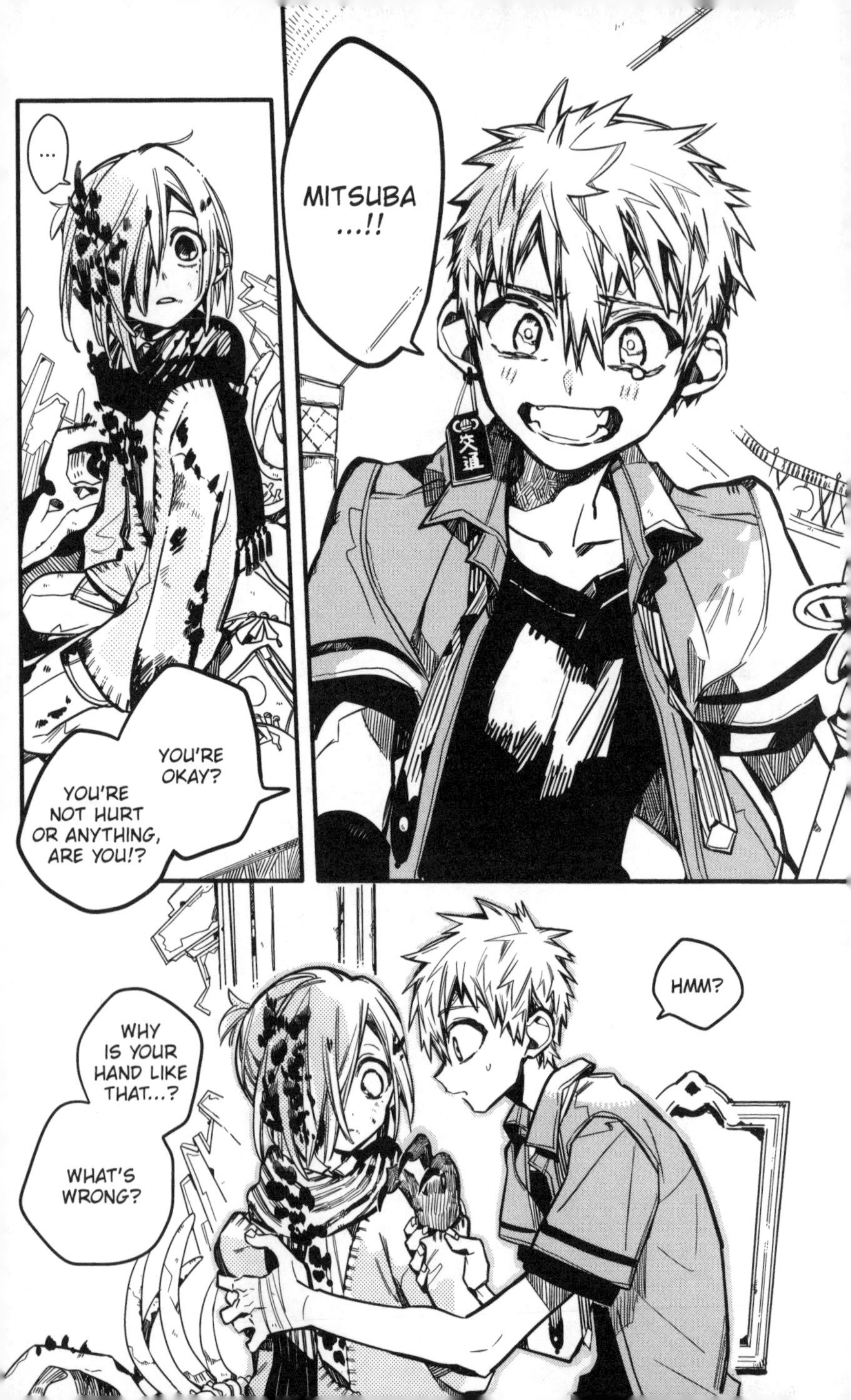
MITSUBA ...!!
交通
...
YOU'RE OKAY?
YOU'RE NOT HURT OR ANYTHING, ARE YOU!?
HMM?
WHY IS YOUR HAND LIKE THAT...?
WHAT'S WRONG?

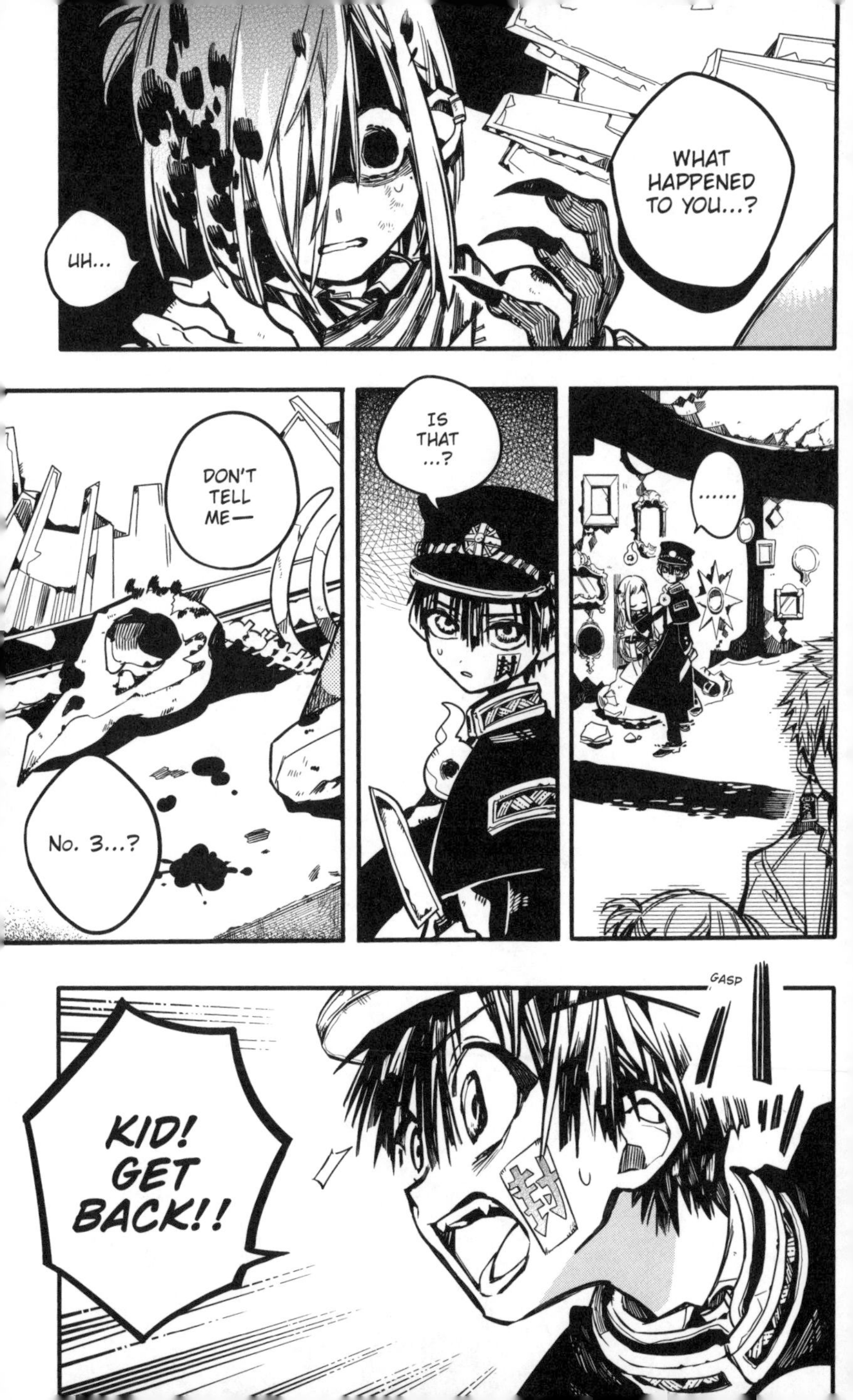
WHAT HAPPENED TO YOU...?
UH...
......
IS THAT ...?
DON'T TELL ME—
No. 3...?
GASP
KID! GET BACK!!

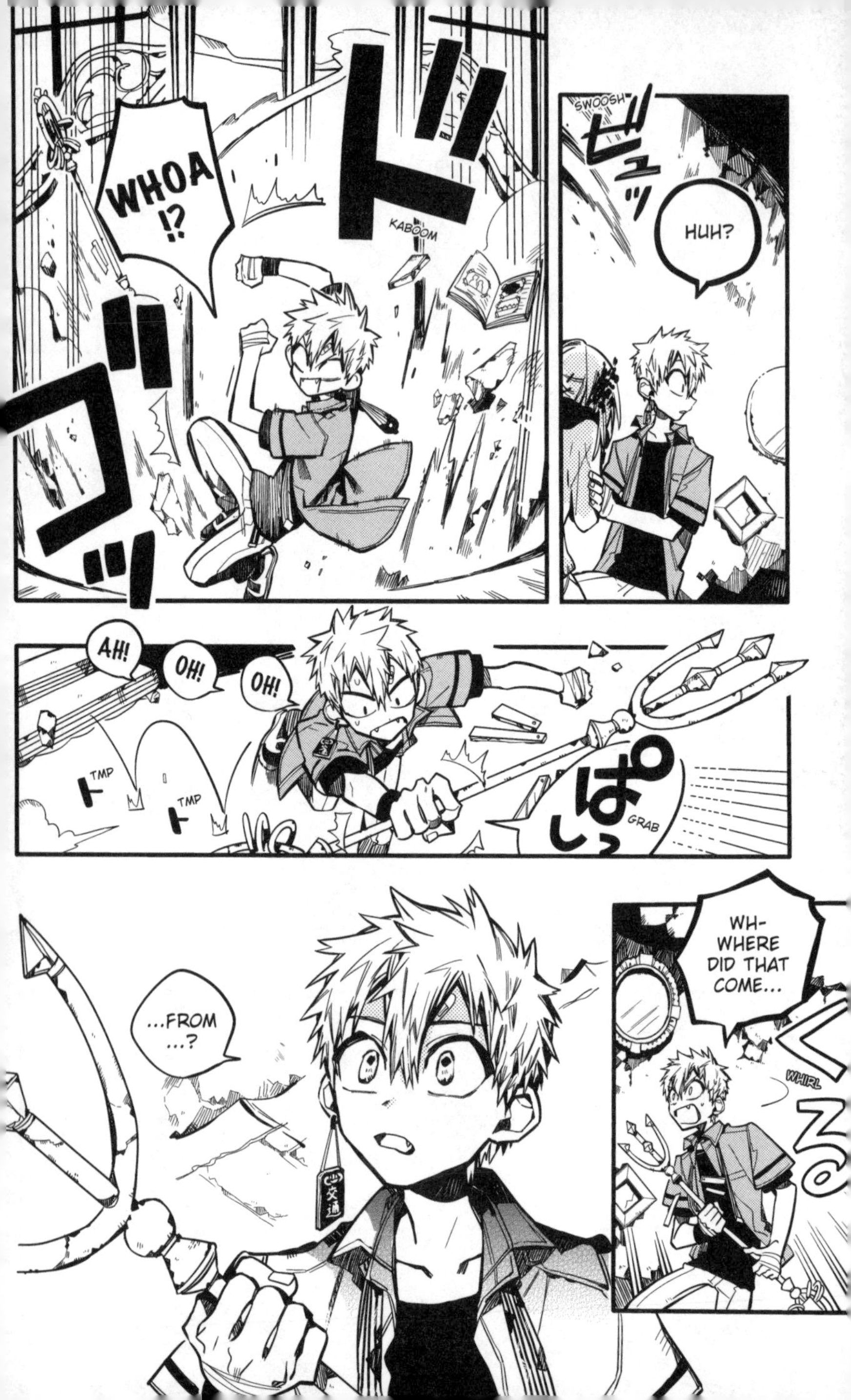
SWOOSH
HUH?
KABOOM
WHOA !?
GRAB
OH!
OH!
AH!
TMP
TMP
WH- WHERE DID THAT COME...
WHIRL
...FROM ...?

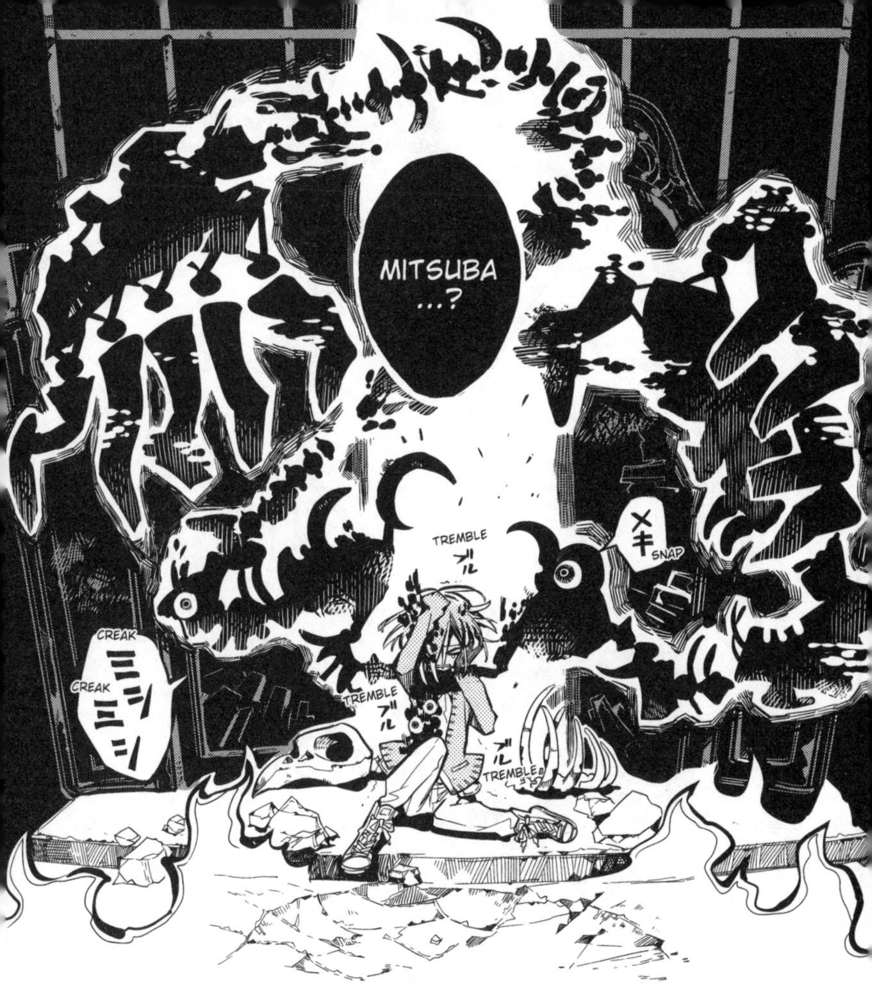
MITSUBA ...?
メキ SNAP
TREMBLE ブル
CREAK ミシ CREAK ミシ
TREMBLE ブル
ブル TREMBLE

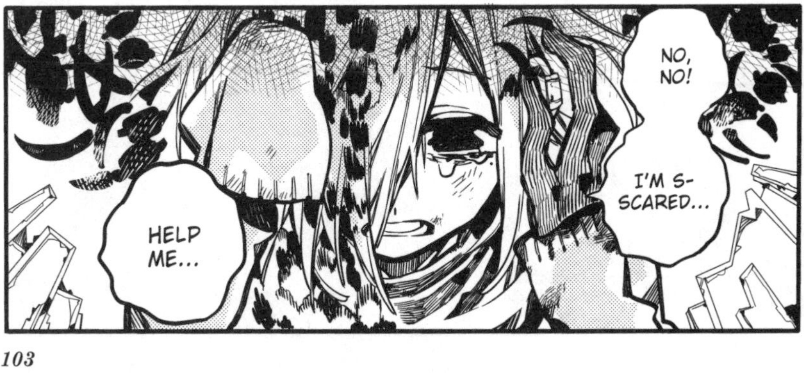
NO, NO!
I'M S-SCARED...
HELP ME...

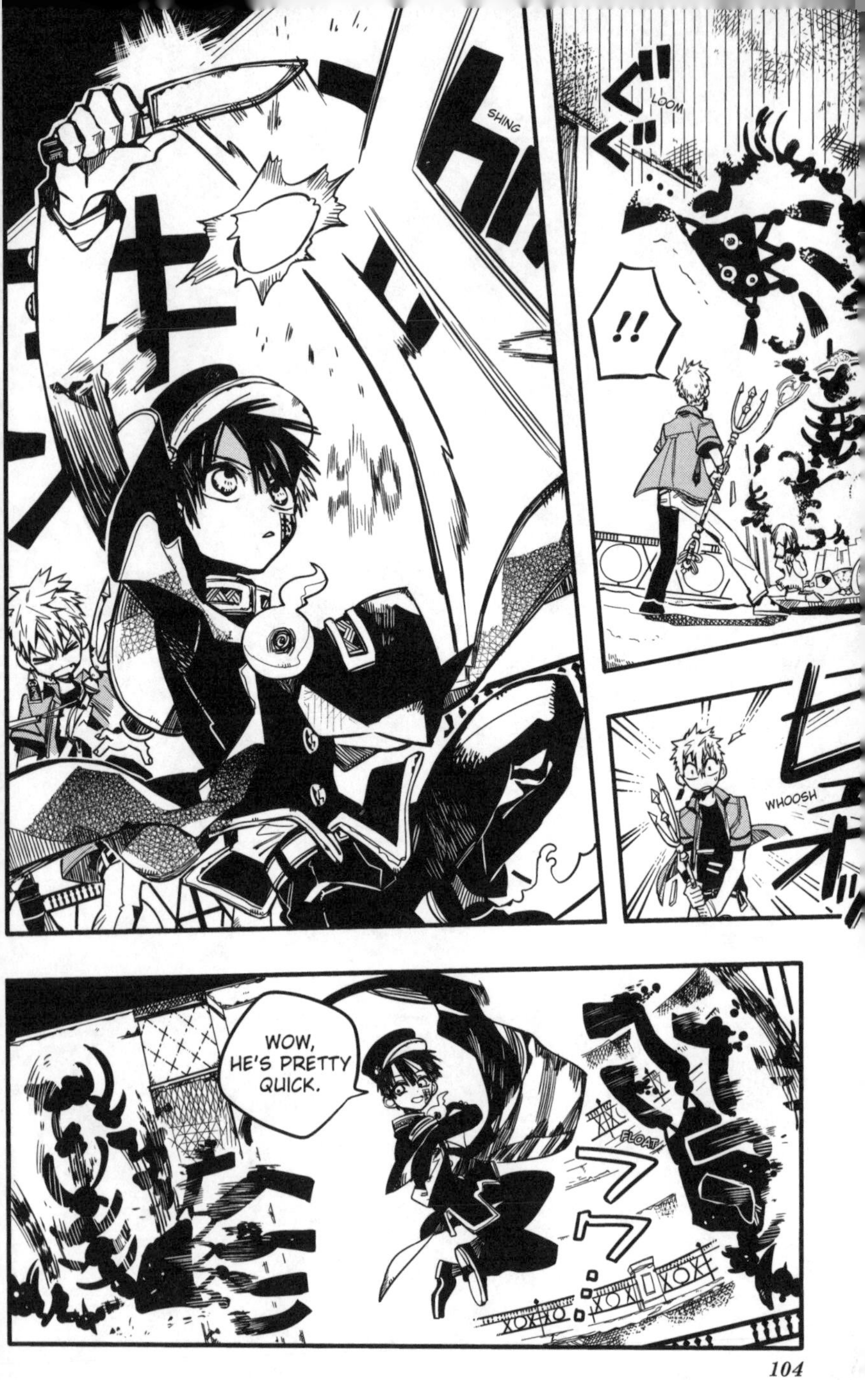
LOOM
!!
WHOOSH
SHING
WOW, HE'S PRETTY QUICK.
FLOAT

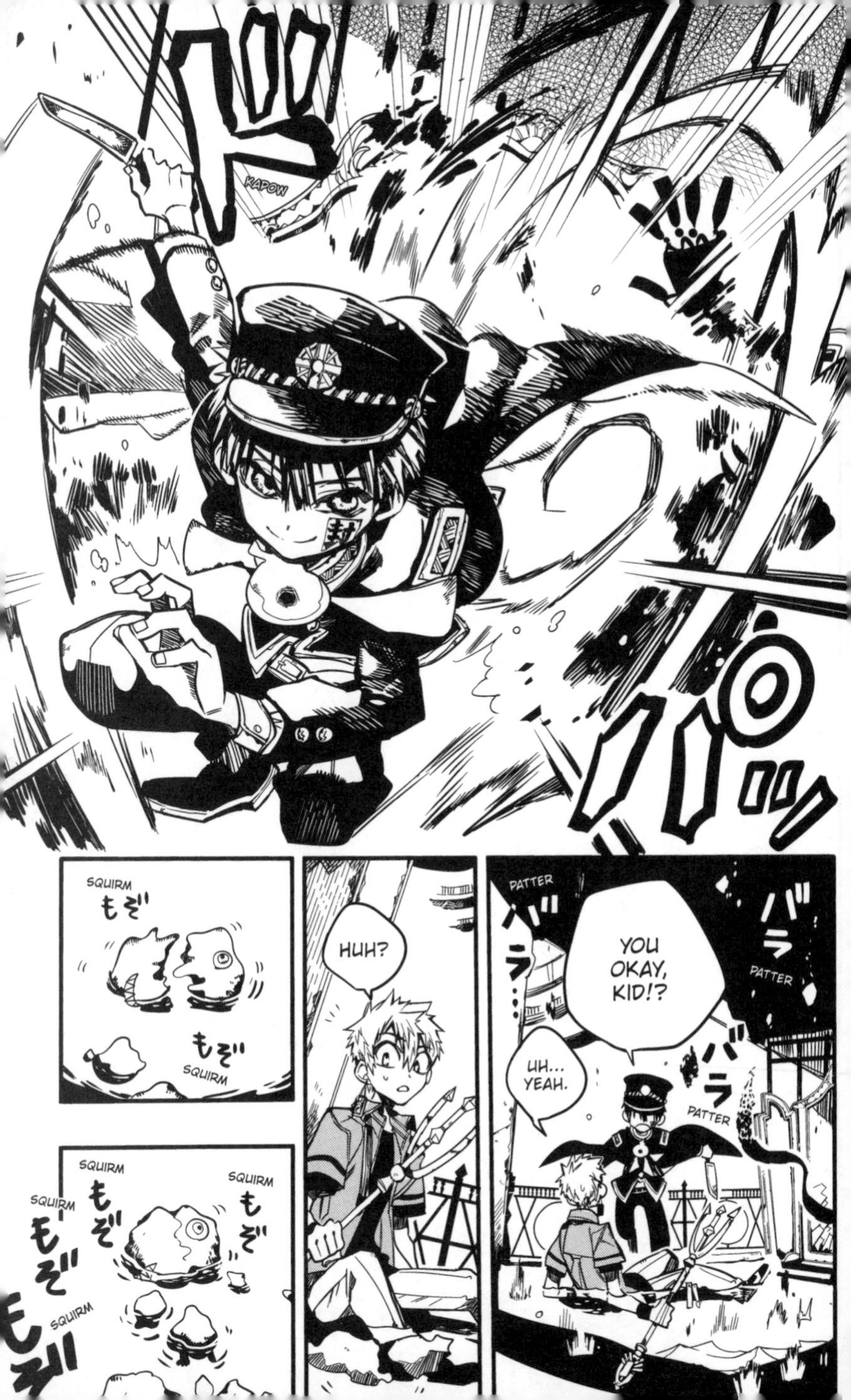
KAPOW
PATTER
バラ
YOU OKAY, KID!?
バラ
PATTER
UH... YEAH.
バラ
PATTER
HUH?
SQUIRM
もぞ
もぞ
SQUIRM
SQUIRM
もぞ
SQUIRM
もぞ
SQUIRM
もぞ
SQUIRM

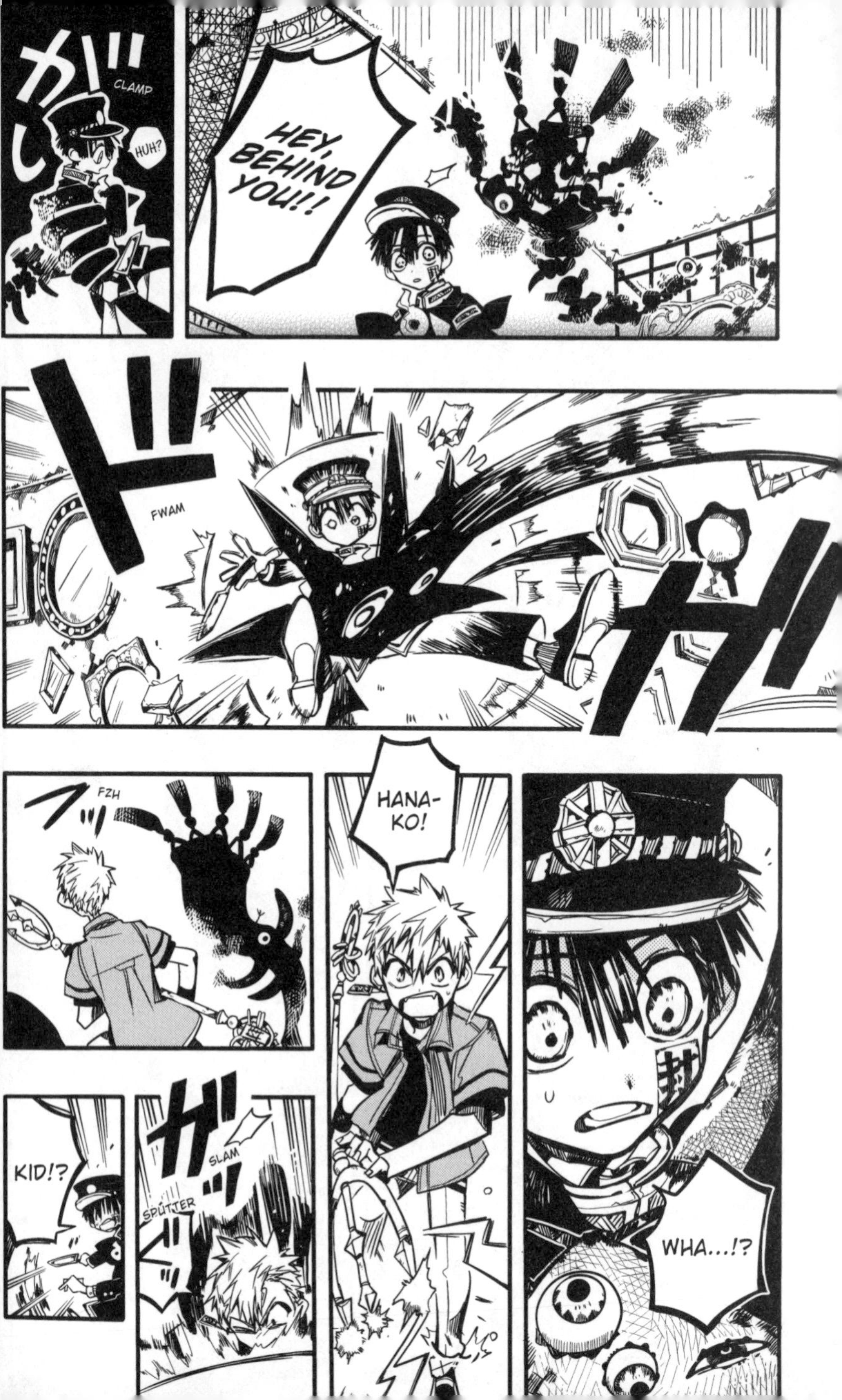
HEY, BEHIND YOU!!!
CLAMP
HUH?
FWAM
WHA...!?
HANA-KO!
FZH
SLAM
SPUTTER
KID!?

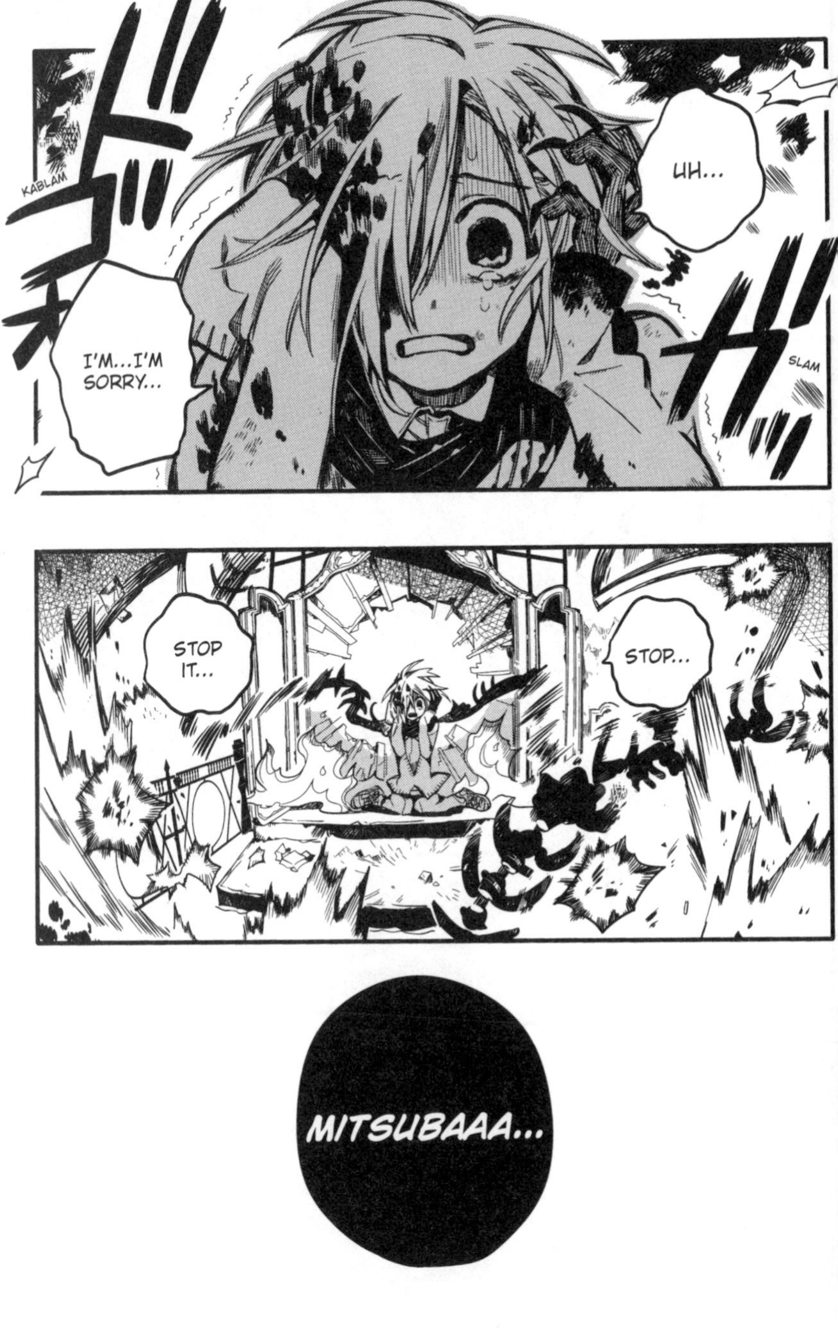
UH...
SLAM
KABLAM
I'M...I'M SORRY...
STOP...
STOP IT...
MITSUBAAA...

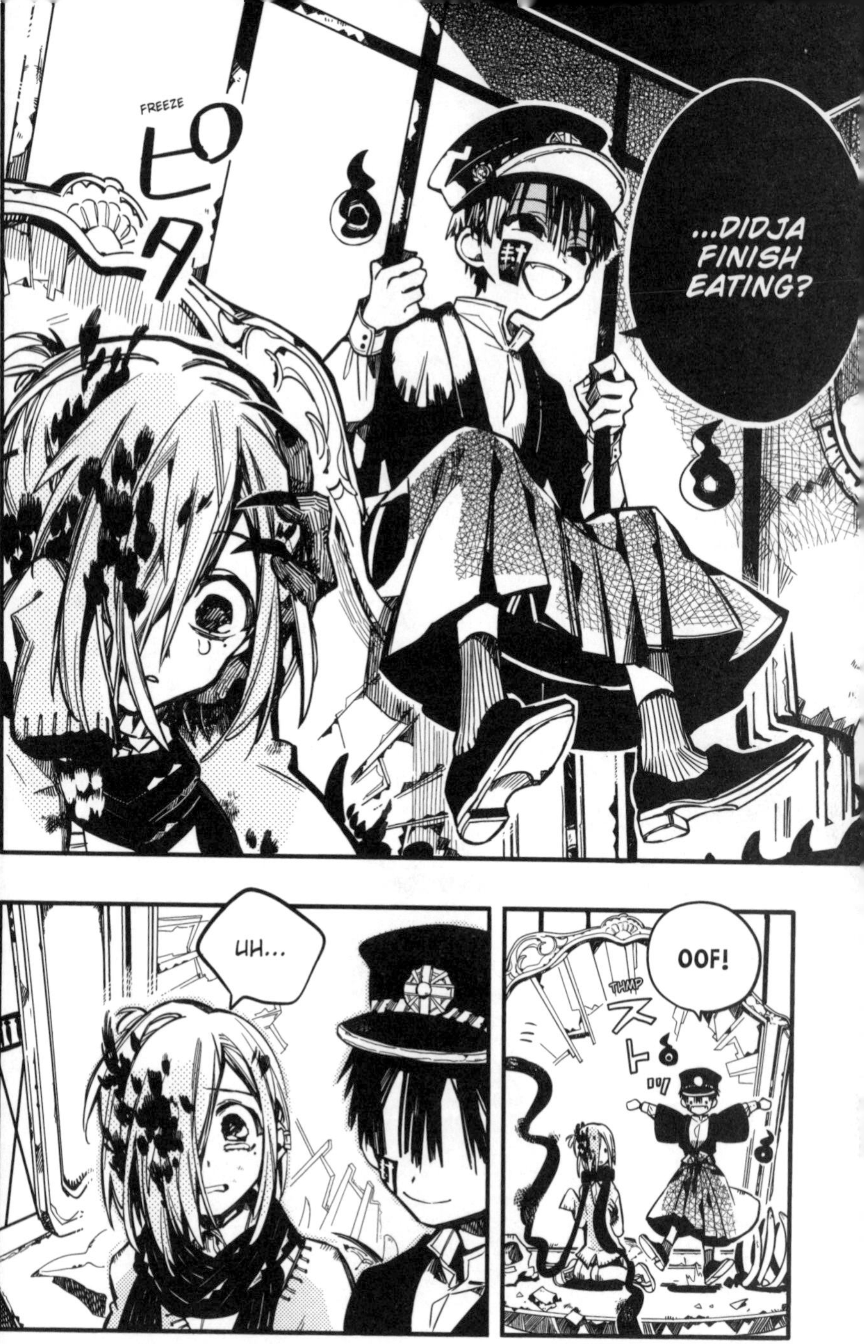
...DIDJA FINISH EATING?
FREEZE
OOF!
THMP
UH...

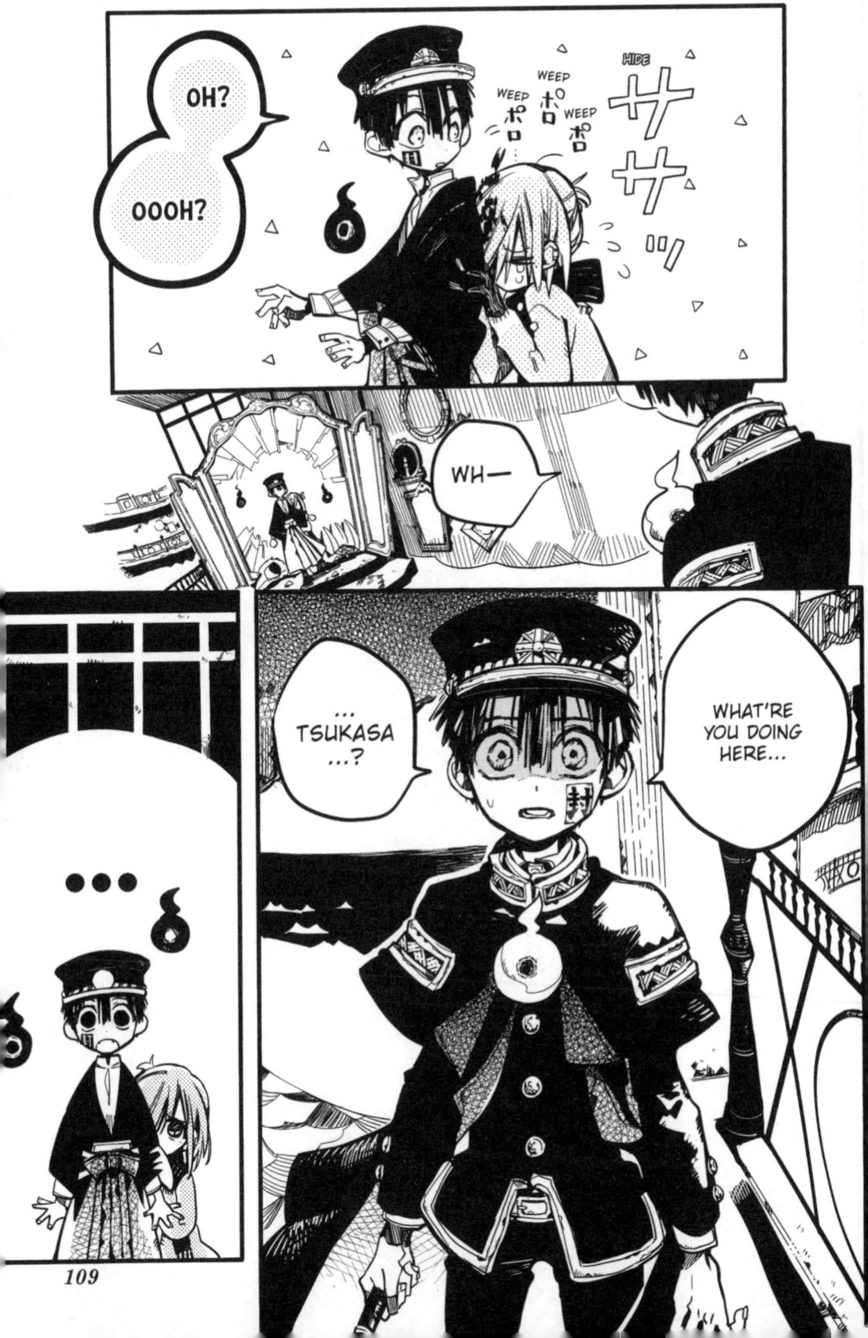
HIDE
WEEP
WEEP
WEEP
OH?
OOOH?
WH—
WHAT'RE YOU DOING HERE...
...TSUKASA ...?
•••

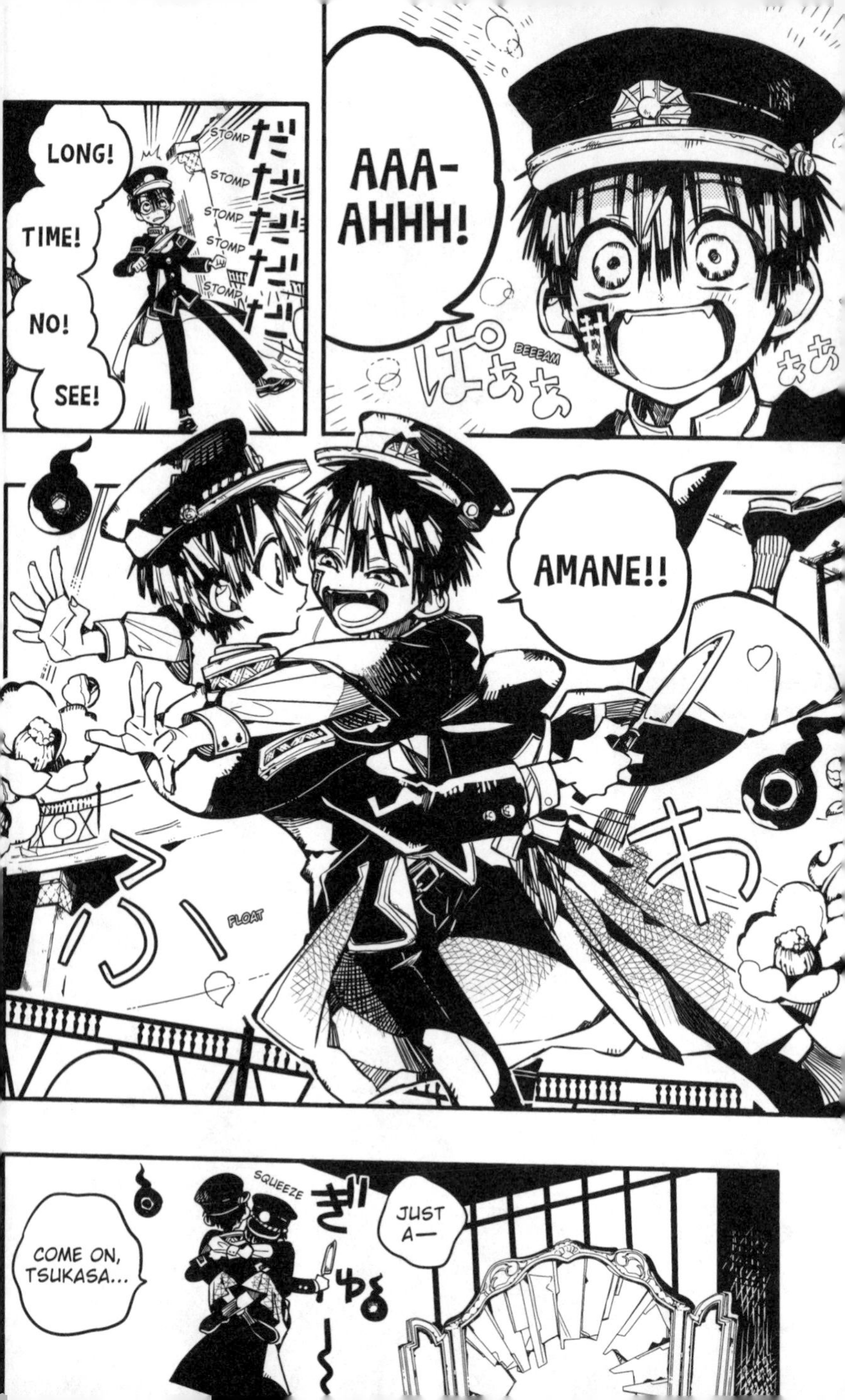
AAA-AHHH!
BEEEAM
LONG! TIME! NO! SEE!
STOMP
STOMP
STOMP
STOMP
STOMP
AMANE!!
FLOAT
JUST A—
SQUEEZE
COME ON, TSUKASA...

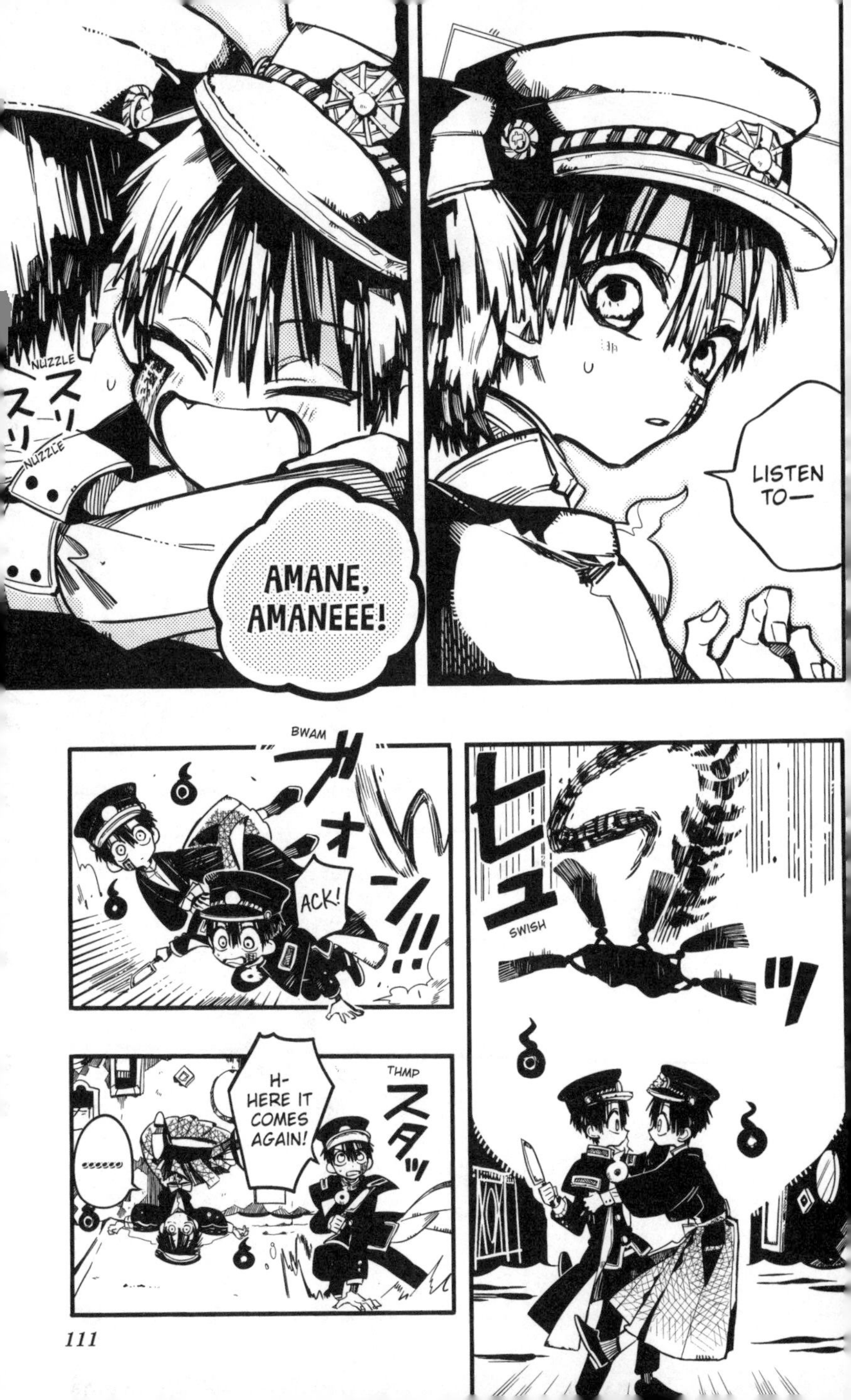
LISTEN TO—
NUZZLE
スリスリ
NUZZLE
AMANE, AMANEEE!
ヒュッ
SWISH
ガォーン!!
BWAM
ACK!
スタッ
THMP
H-HERE IT COMES AGAIN!
......

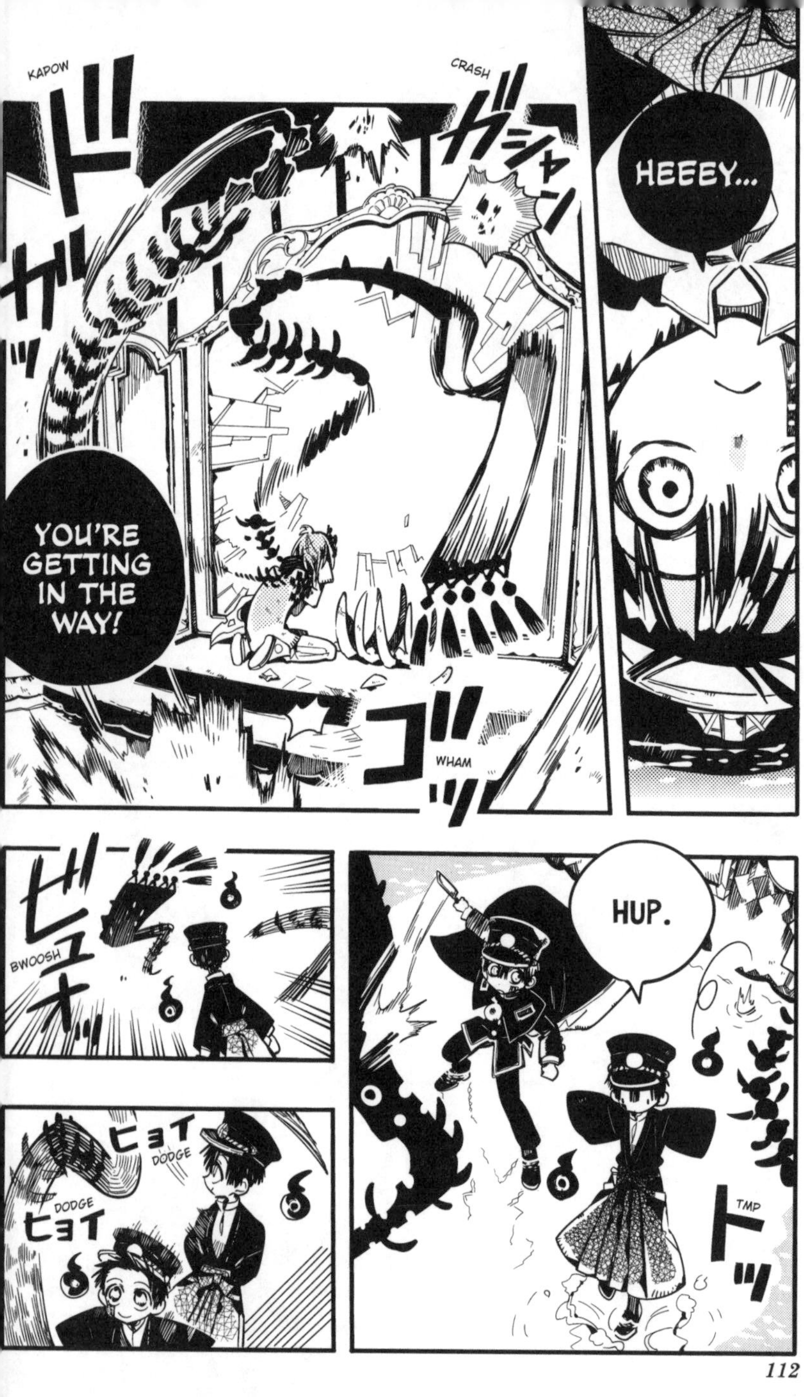
HEEEY...
CRASH
ガシャン
KAPOW
ドガッ
YOU'RE GETTING IN THE WAY!
WHAM
ゴッ
HUP.
TMP
トッ
ビュオ
BWOOSH
ヒョイ
DODGE
DODGE
ヒョイ

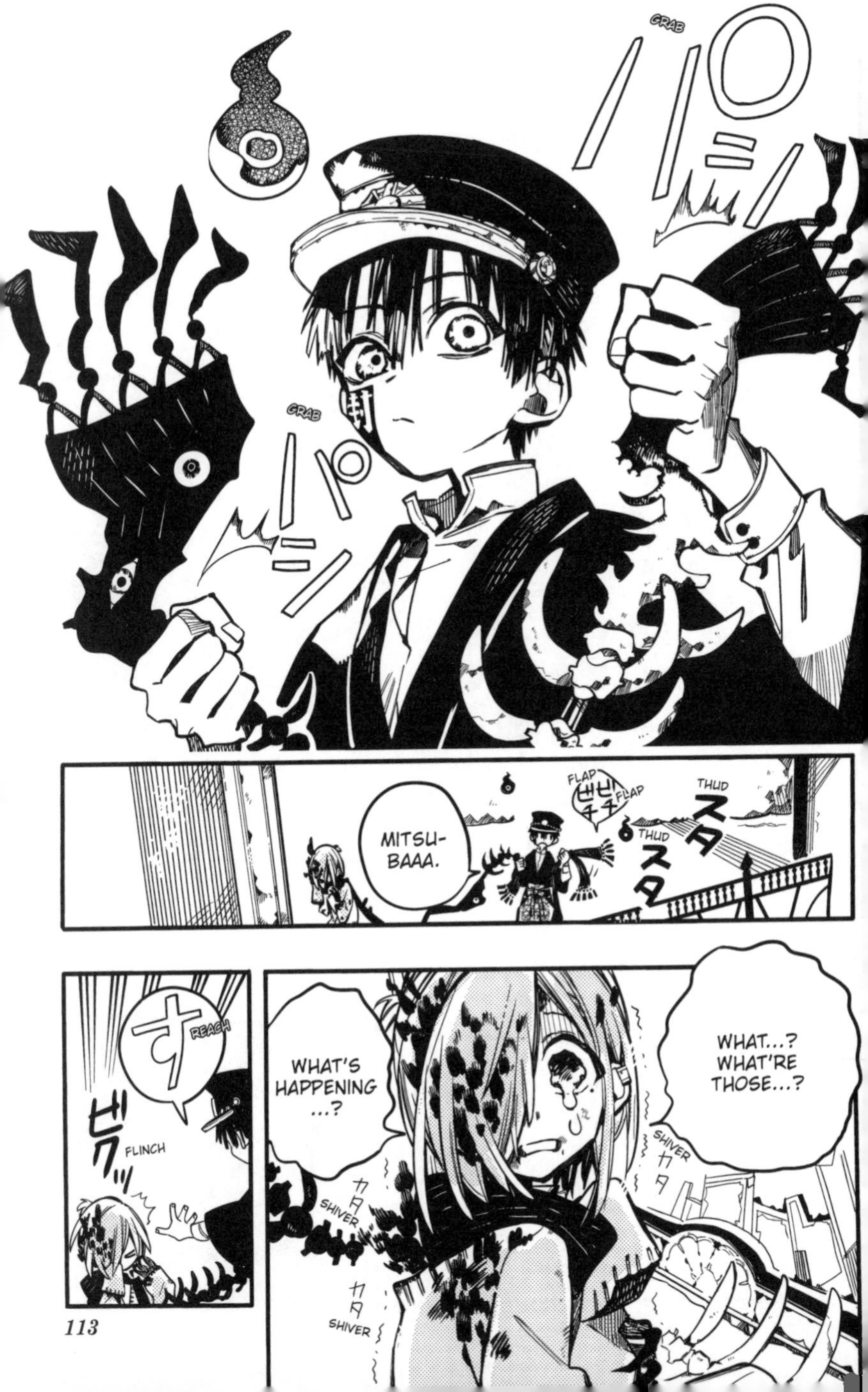
GRAB
GRAB
FLAP FLAP
THUD
THUD
MITSU-BAAA.
WHAT...? WHAT'RE THOSE...?
WHAT'S HAPPENING ...?
SHIVER
SHIVER
SHIVER
REACH
FLINCH

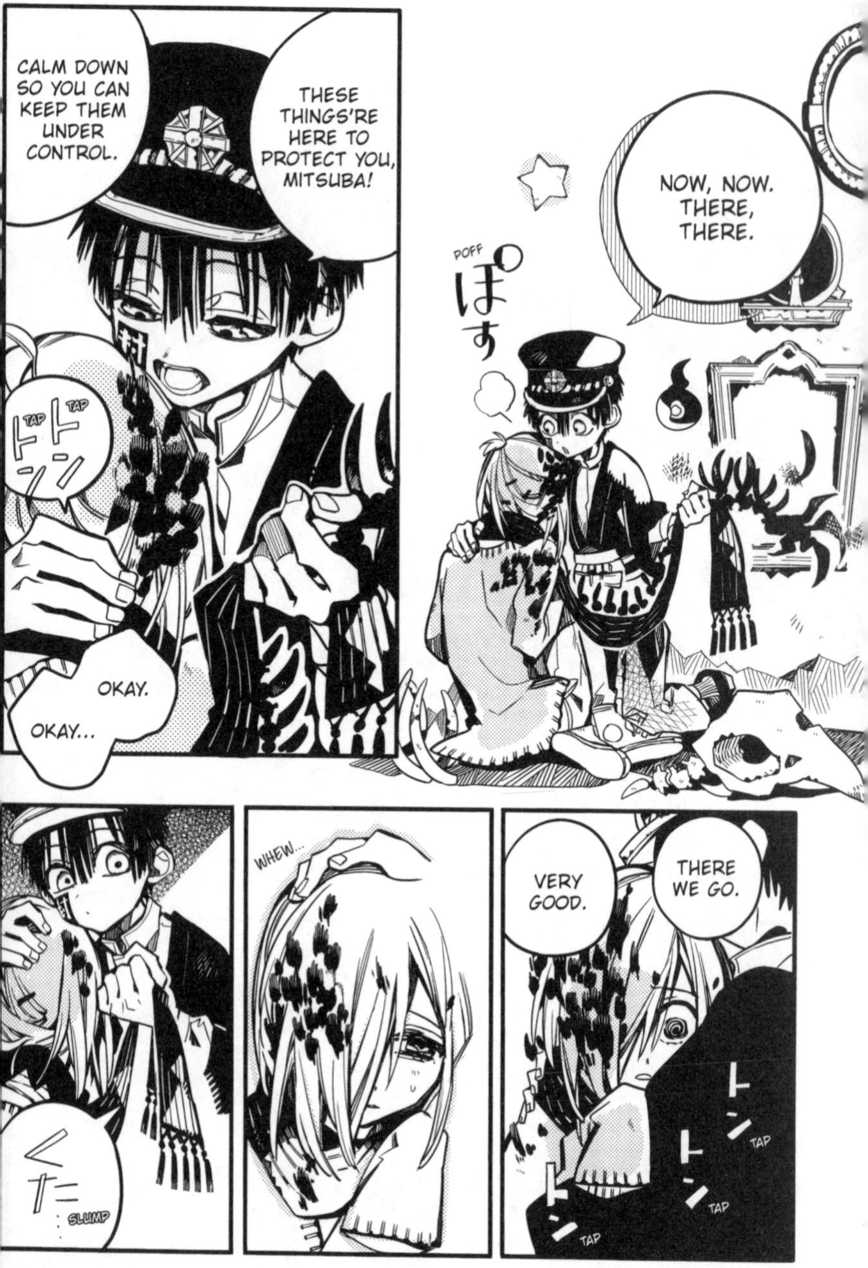
NOW, NOW. THERE, THERE.
POFF
ぽす
THESE THINGS'RE HERE TO PROTECT YOU, MITSUBA!
CALM DOWN SO YOU CAN KEEP THEM UNDER CONTROL.
TAP TAP
ドンドン
OKAY.
OKAY...
THERE WE GO.
VERY GOOD.
トントントン
TAP TAP TAP
WHEW...
くたー
SLUMP

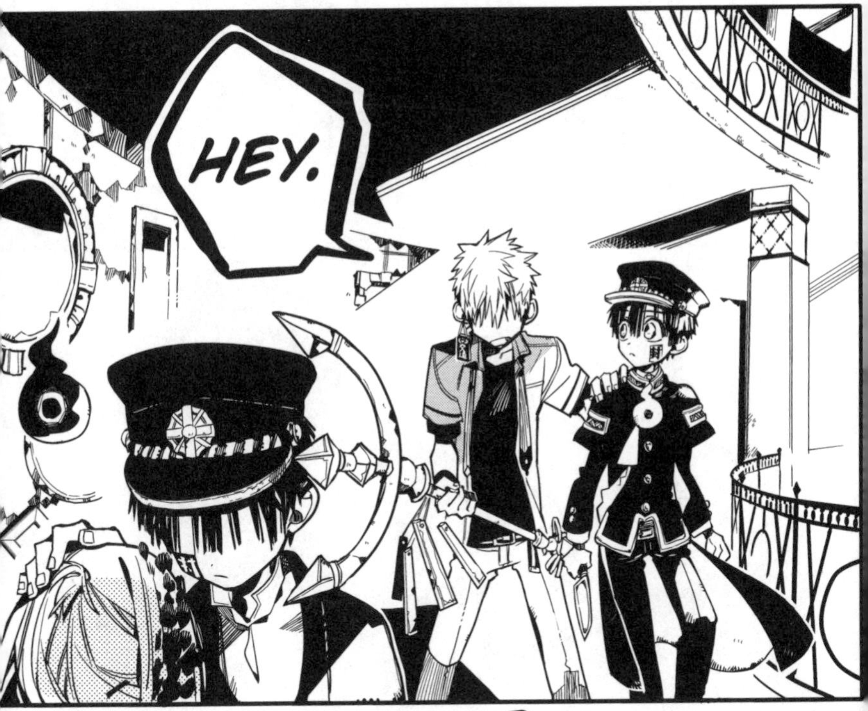
HEY.

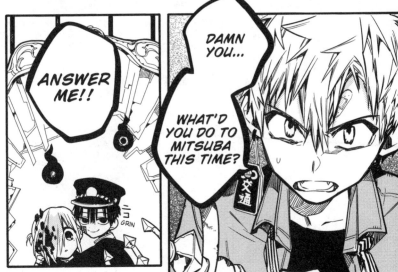

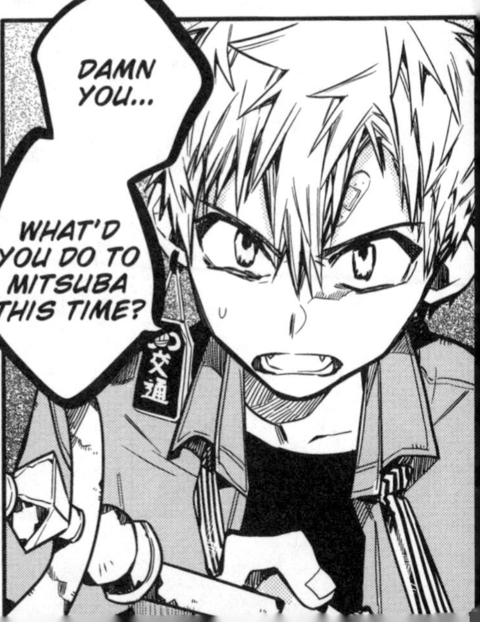
DAMN YOU...
WHAT'D YOU DO TO MITSUBA THIS TIME?

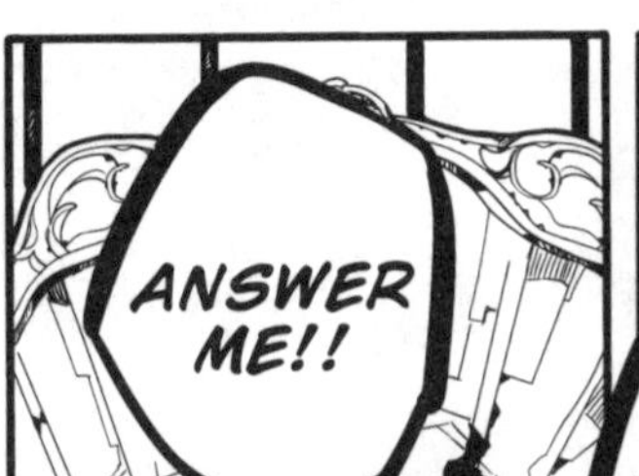
ANSWER ME!!
ニコ
GRIN

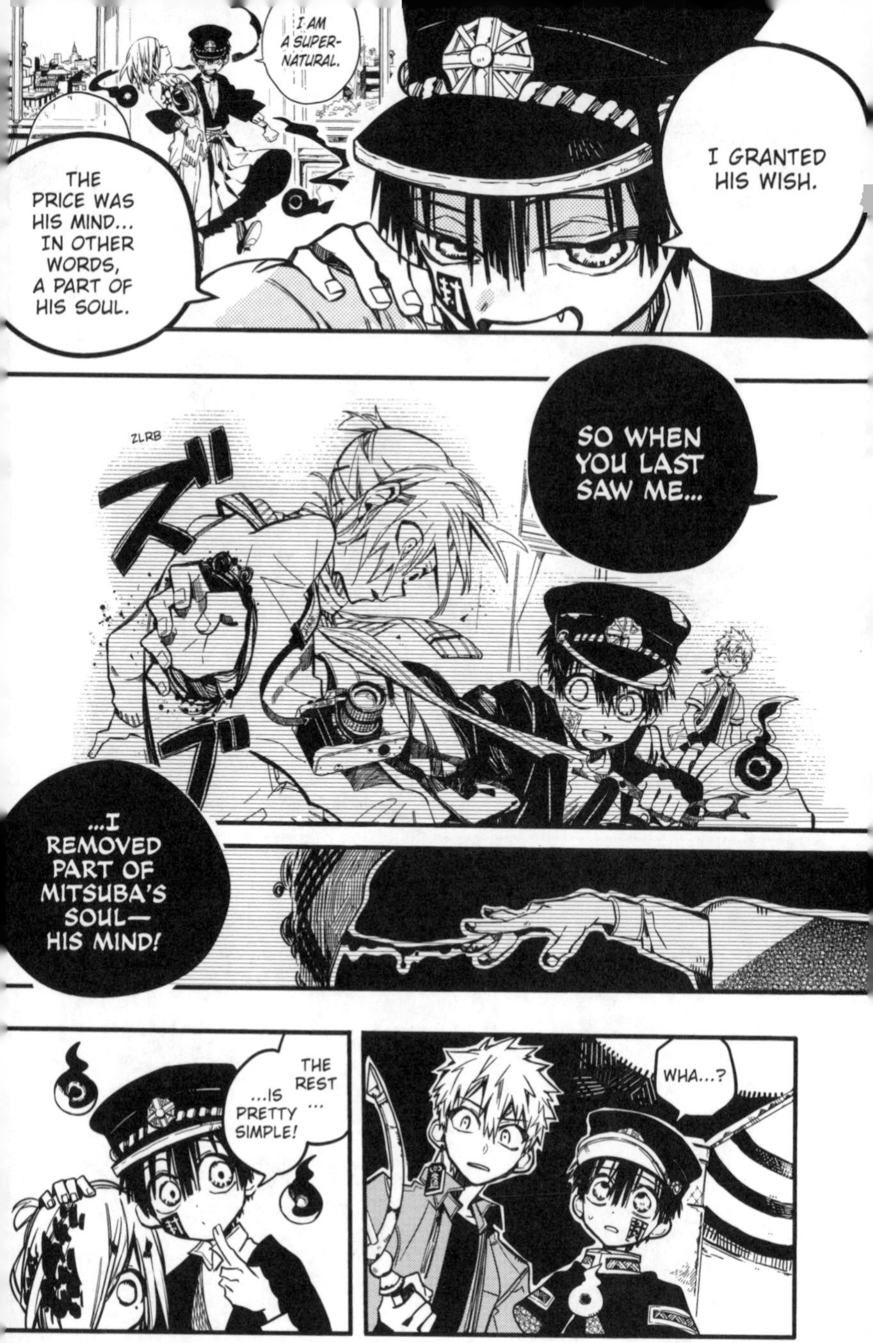
I GRANTED HIS WISH.
I AM A SUPER-NATURAL.
THE PRICE WAS HIS MIND... IN OTHER WORDS, A PART OF HIS SOUL.
SO WHEN YOU LAST SAW ME...
ZLRB
...I REMOVED PART OF MITSUBA'S SOUL—HIS MIND!
WHA...?
THE REST... ...IS PRETTY SIMPLE!

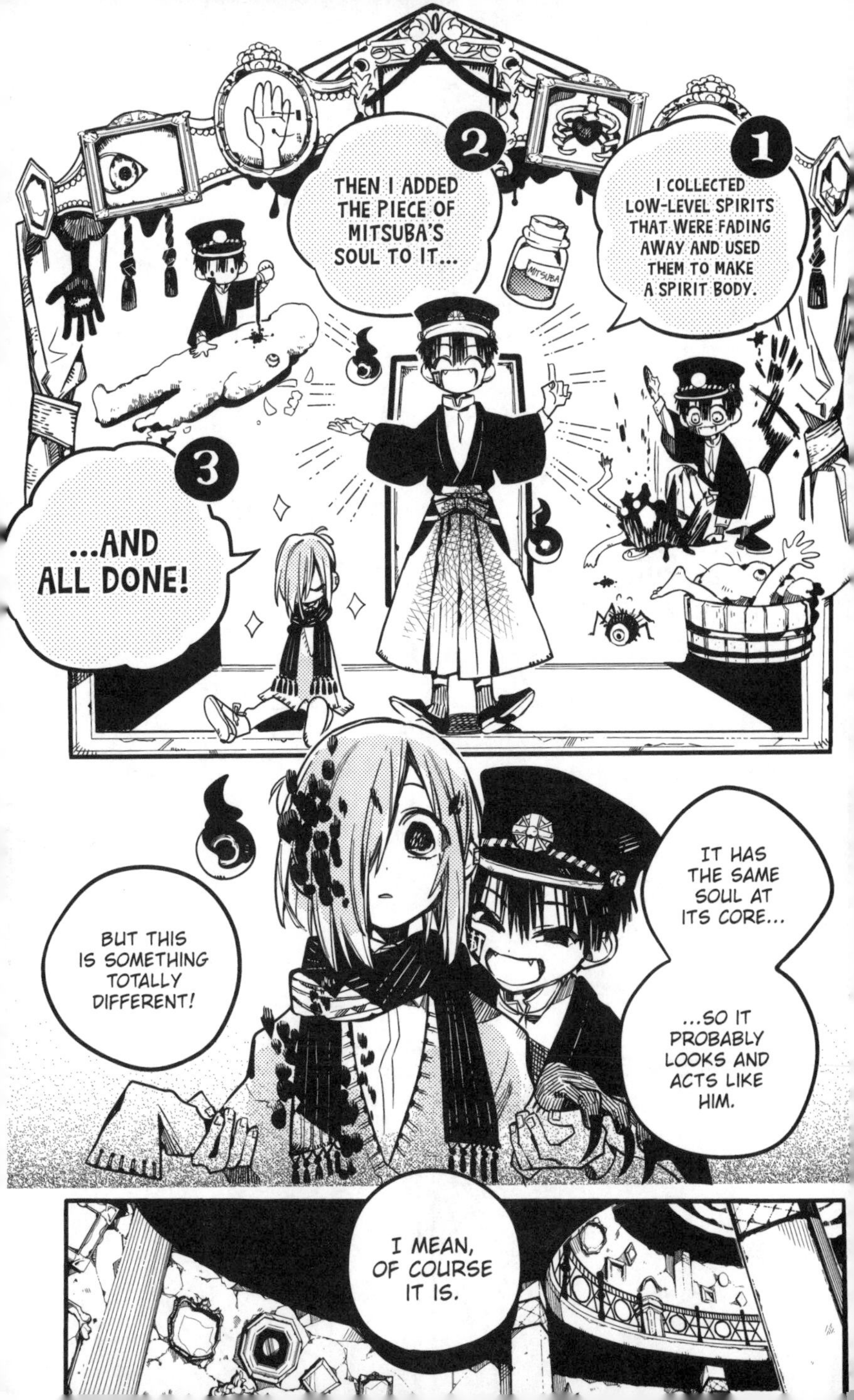
1
I COLLECTED LOW-LEVEL SPIRITS THAT WERE FADING AWAY AND USED THEM TO MAKE A SPIRIT BODY.
MITSUBA
2
THEN I ADDED THE PIECE OF MITSUBA'S SOUL TO IT...
3
...AND ALL DONE!
IT HAS THE SAME SOUL AT ITS CORE...
...SO IT PROBABLY LOOKS AND ACTS LIKE HIM.
BUT THIS IS SOMETHING TOTALLY DIFFERENT!
I MEAN, OF COURSE IT IS.

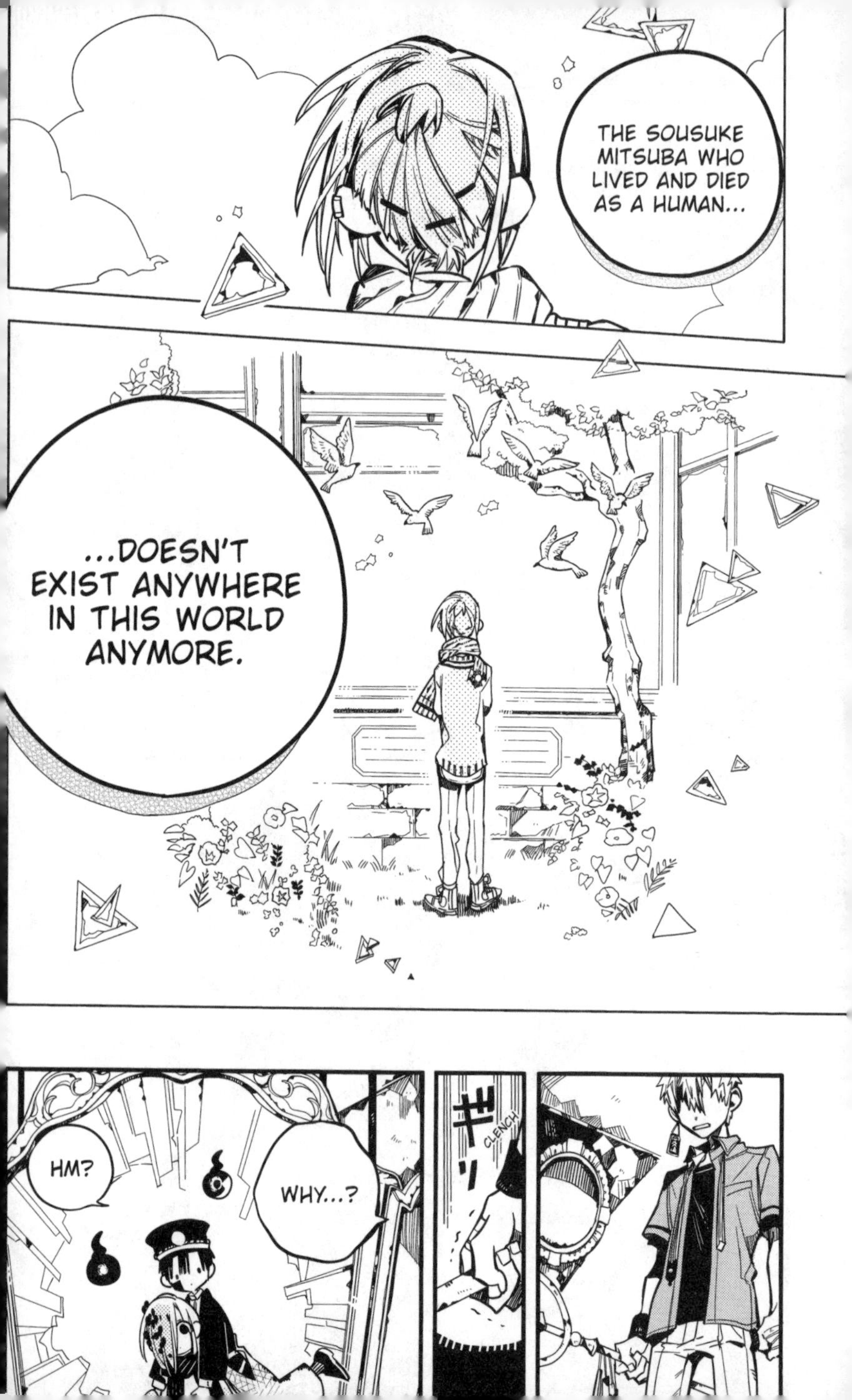
THE SOUSUKE MITSUBA WHO LIVED AND DIED AS A HUMAN...
...DOESN'T EXIST ANYWHERE IN THIS WORLD ANYMORE.
ギリ
CLENCH
WHY...?
HM?

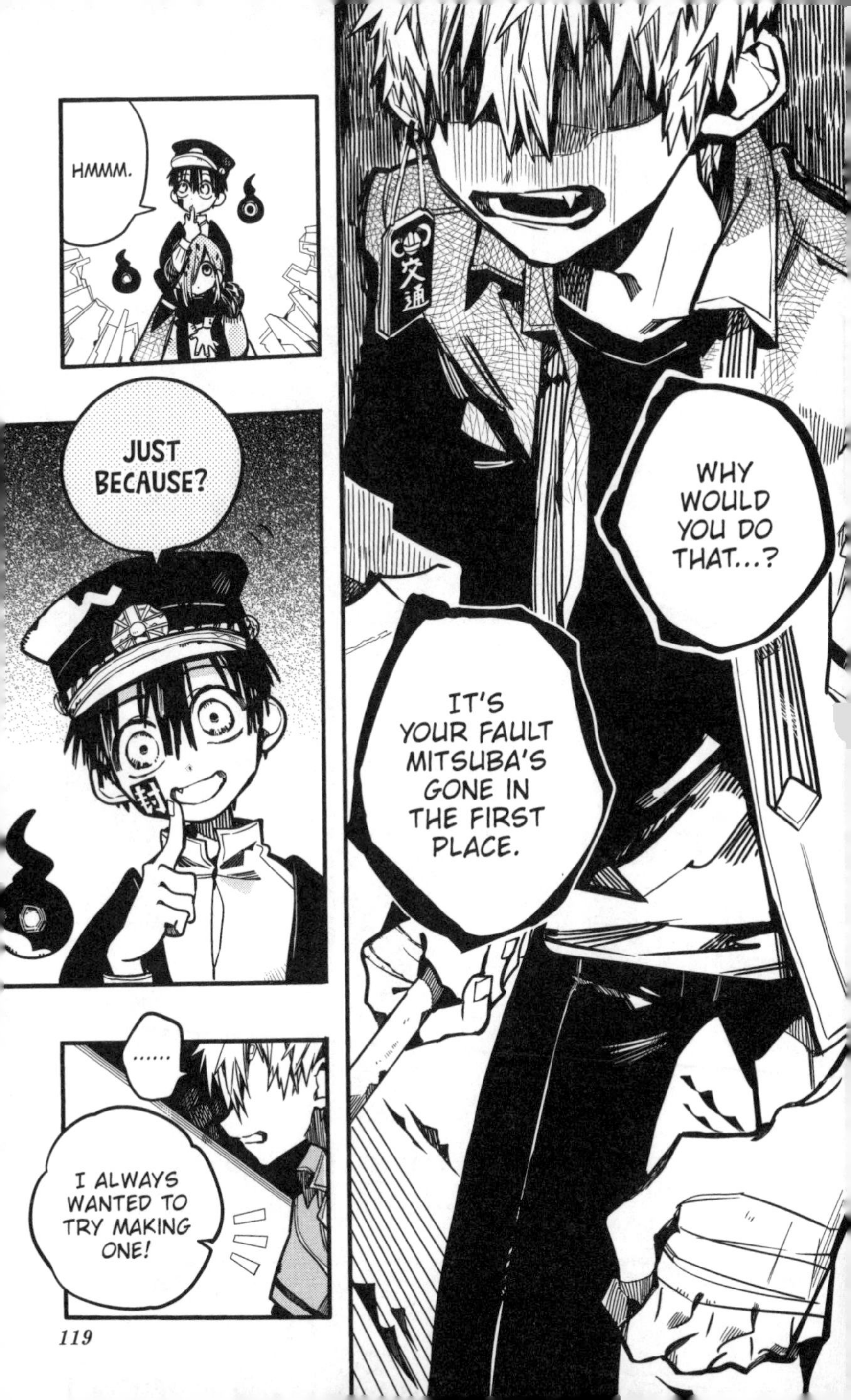
WHY WOULD YOU DO THAT...?
IT'S YOUR FAULT MITSUBA'S GONE IN THE FIRST PLACE.
HMMM.
JUST BECAUSE?
......
I ALWAYS WANTED TO TRY MAKING ONE!

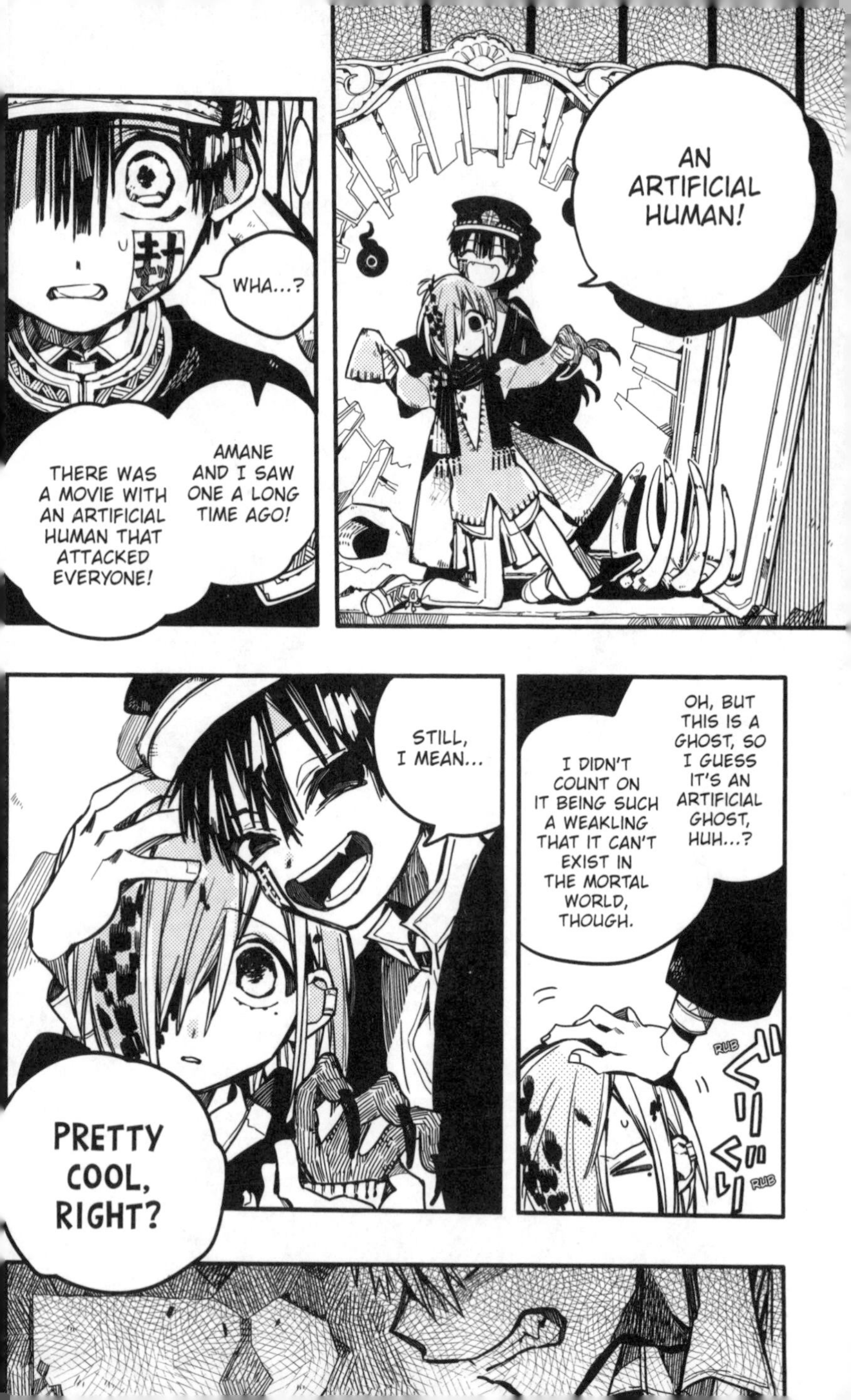
AN ARTIFICIAL HUMAN!
WHA...?
THERE WAS A MOVIE WITH AN ARTIFICIAL HUMAN THAT ATTACKED EVERYONE!
AMANE AND I SAW ONE A LONG TIME AGO!
I DIDN'T COUNT ON IT BEING SUCH A WEAKLING THAT IT CAN'T EXIST IN THE MORTAL WORLD, THOUGH.
OH, BUT THIS IS A GHOST, SO I GUESS IT'S AN ARTIFICIAL GHOST, HUH...?
RUB
RUB
STILL, I MEAN...
PRETTY COOL, RIGHT?

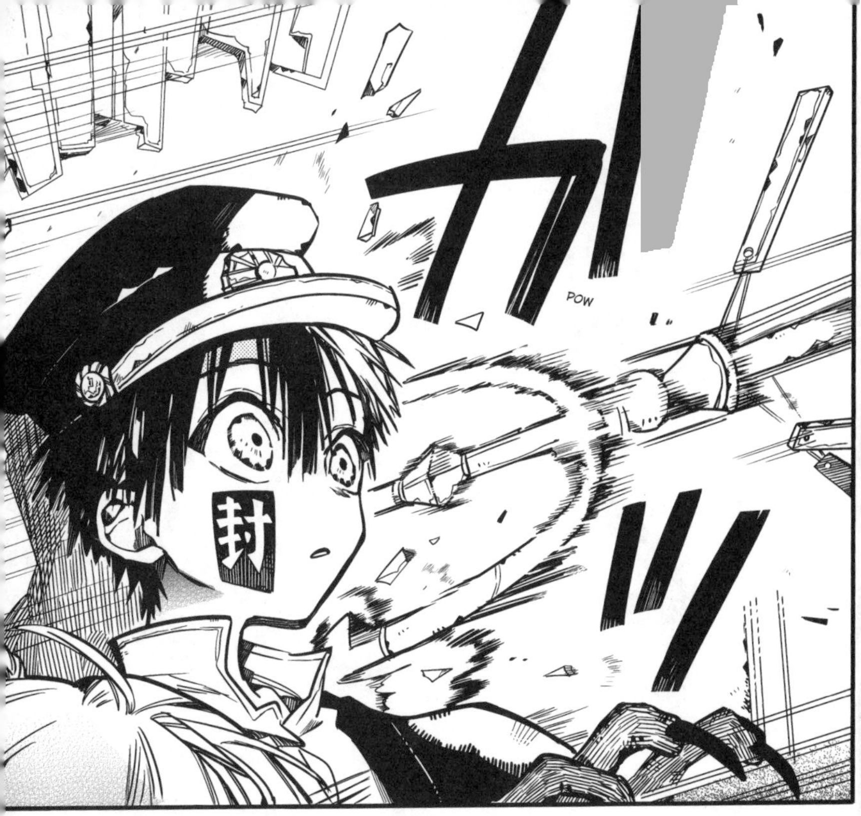
POW

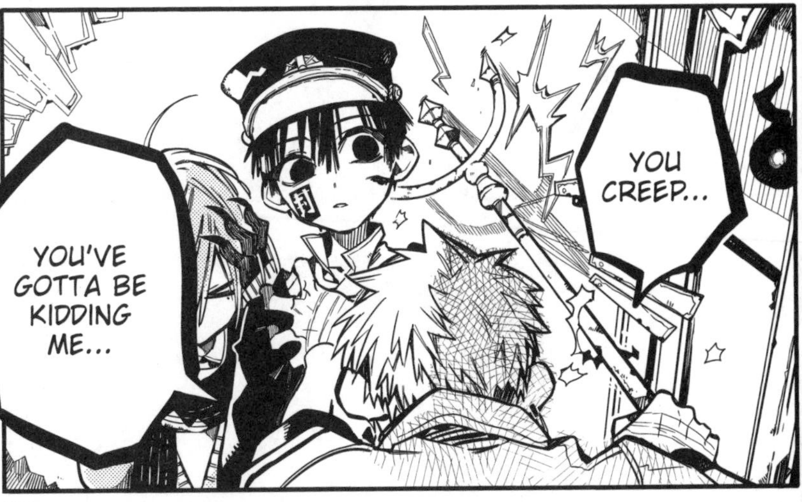
YOU CREEP...
YOU'VE GOTTA BE KIDDING ME...

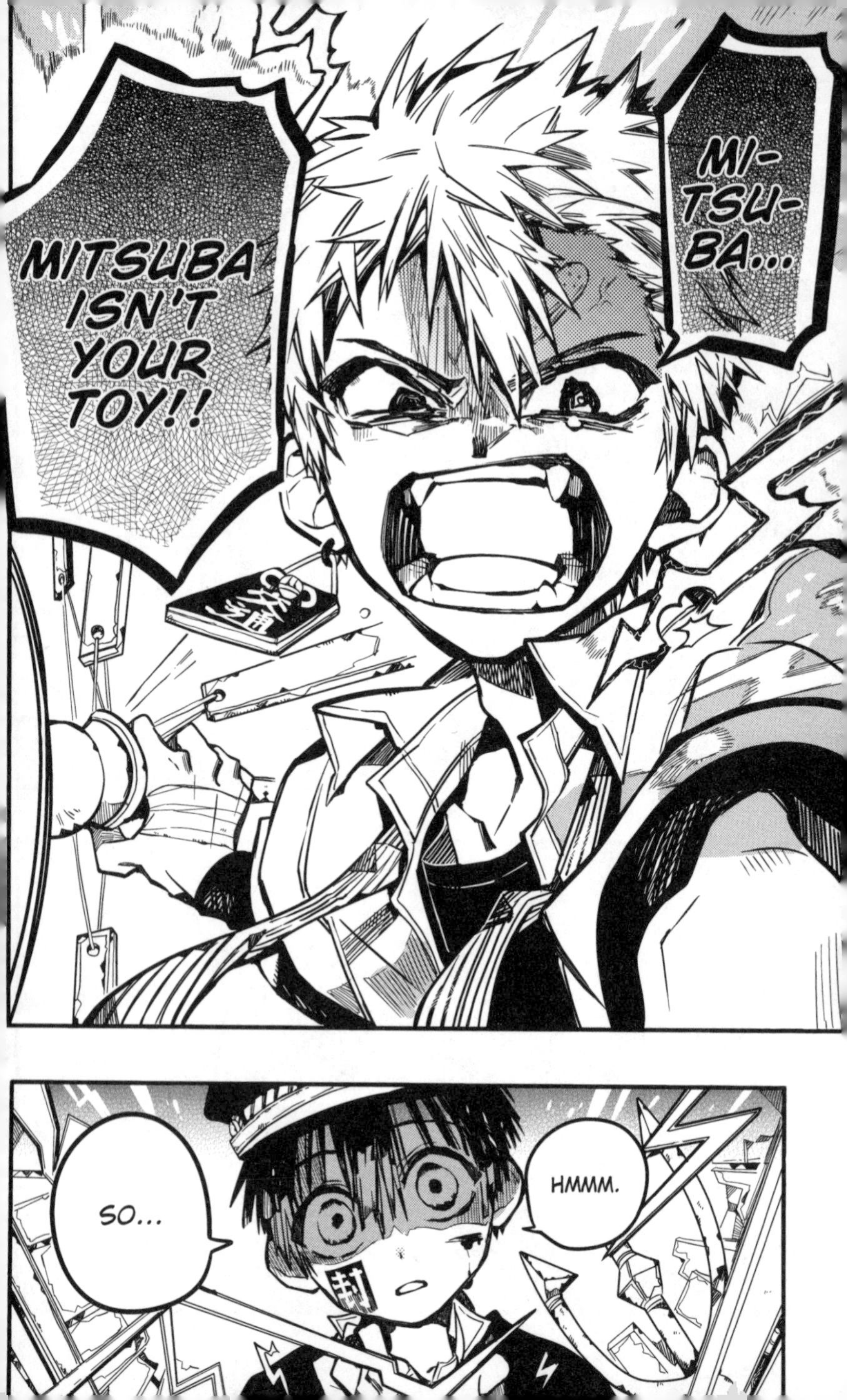
MI-TSU-BA...
MITSUBA ISN'T YOUR TOY!!
HMMM.
SO...

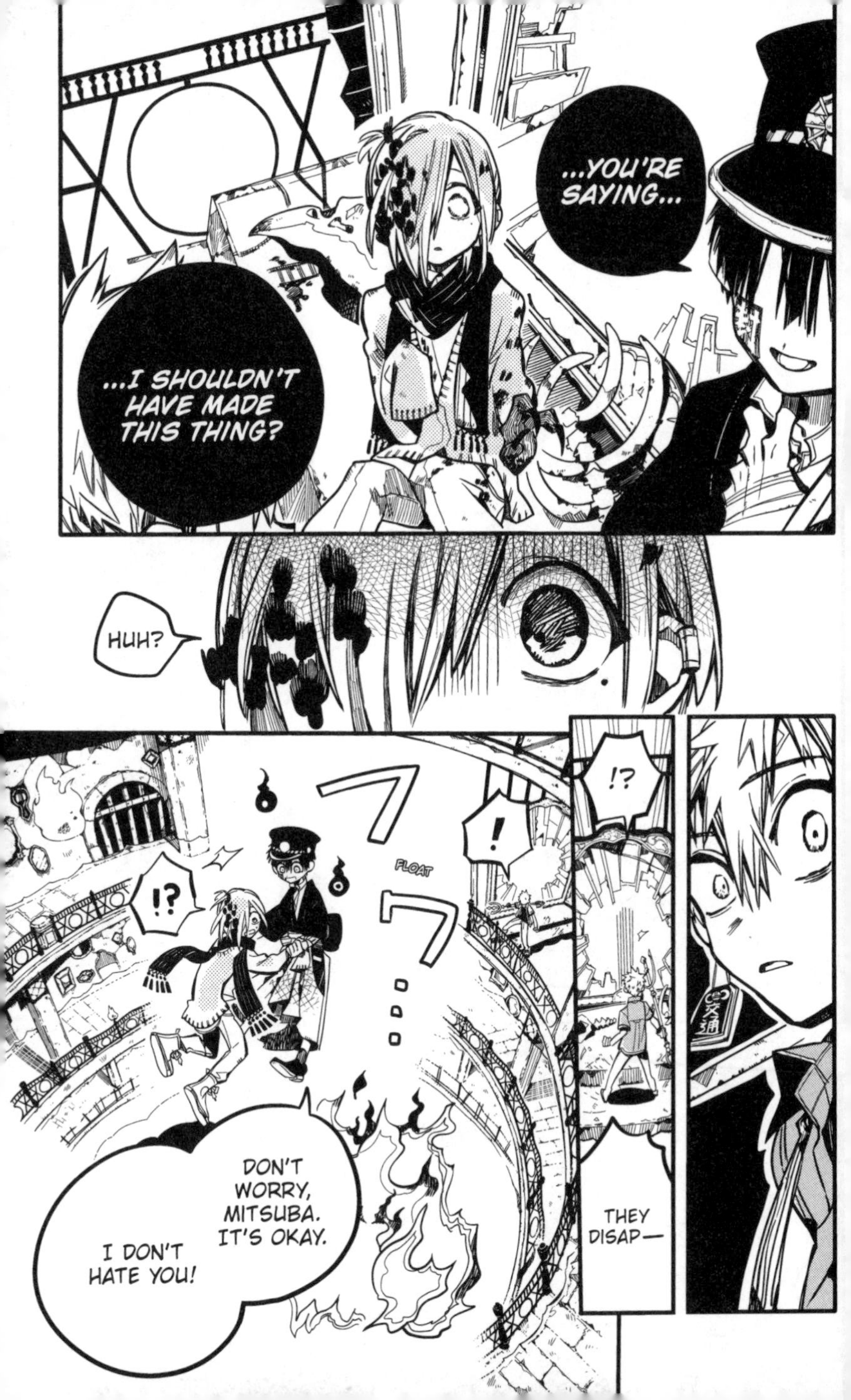
...YOU'RE SAYING...
...I SHOULDN'T HAVE MADE THIS THING?
HUH?
!?
THEY DISAP—
!
FLOAT
!?
DON'T WORRY, MITSUBA. IT'S OKAY.
I DON'T HATE YOU!

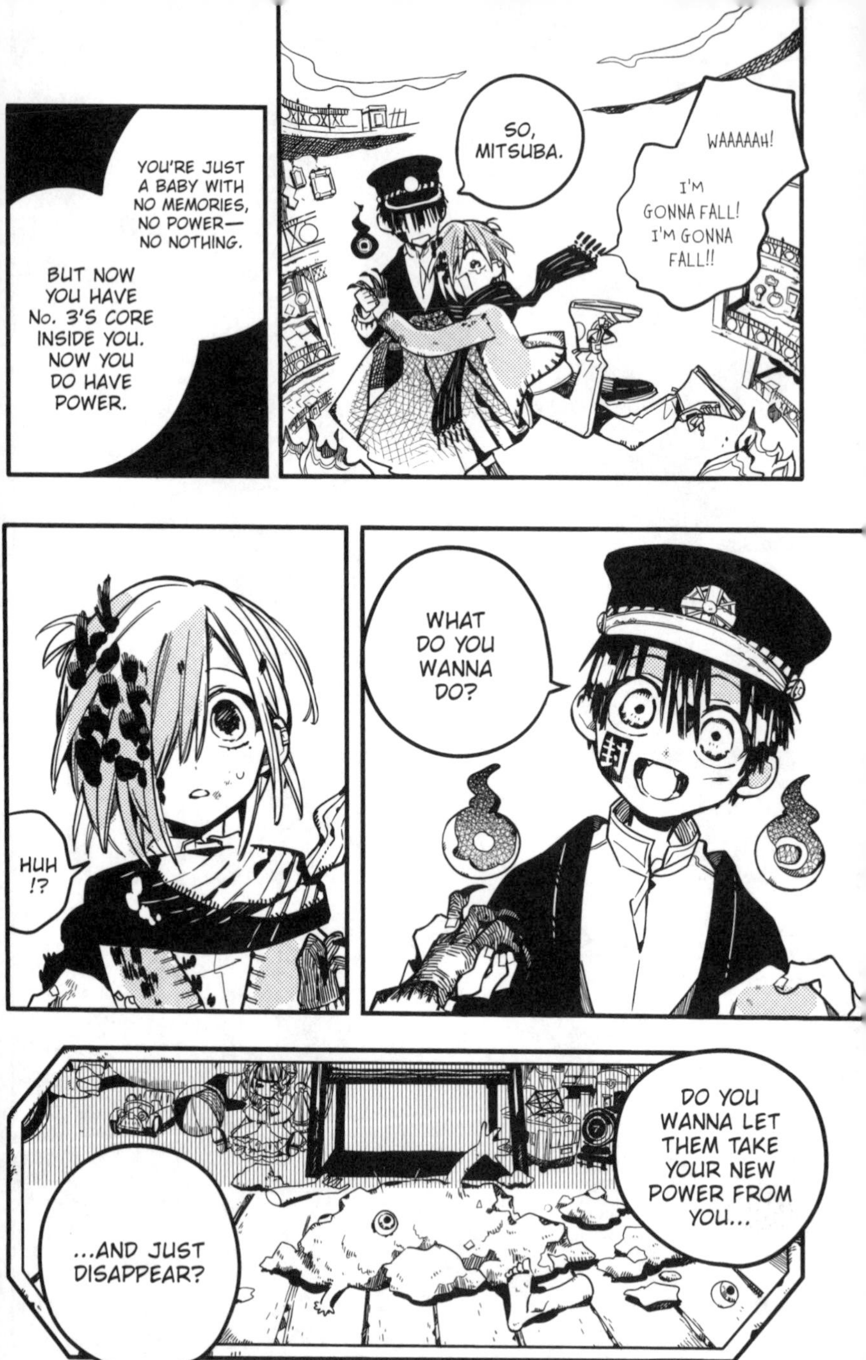
WAAAAAH!
I'M GONNA FALL! I'M GONNA FALL!!
SO, MITSUBA.
YOU'RE JUST A BABY WITH NO MEMORIES, NO POWER—NO NOTHING.
BUT NOW YOU HAVE No. 3'S CORE INSIDE YOU. NOW YOU DO HAVE POWER.
WHAT DO YOU WANNA DO?
HUH!?
DO YOU WANNA LET THEM TAKE YOUR NEW POWER FROM YOU...
...AND JUST DISAPPEAR?

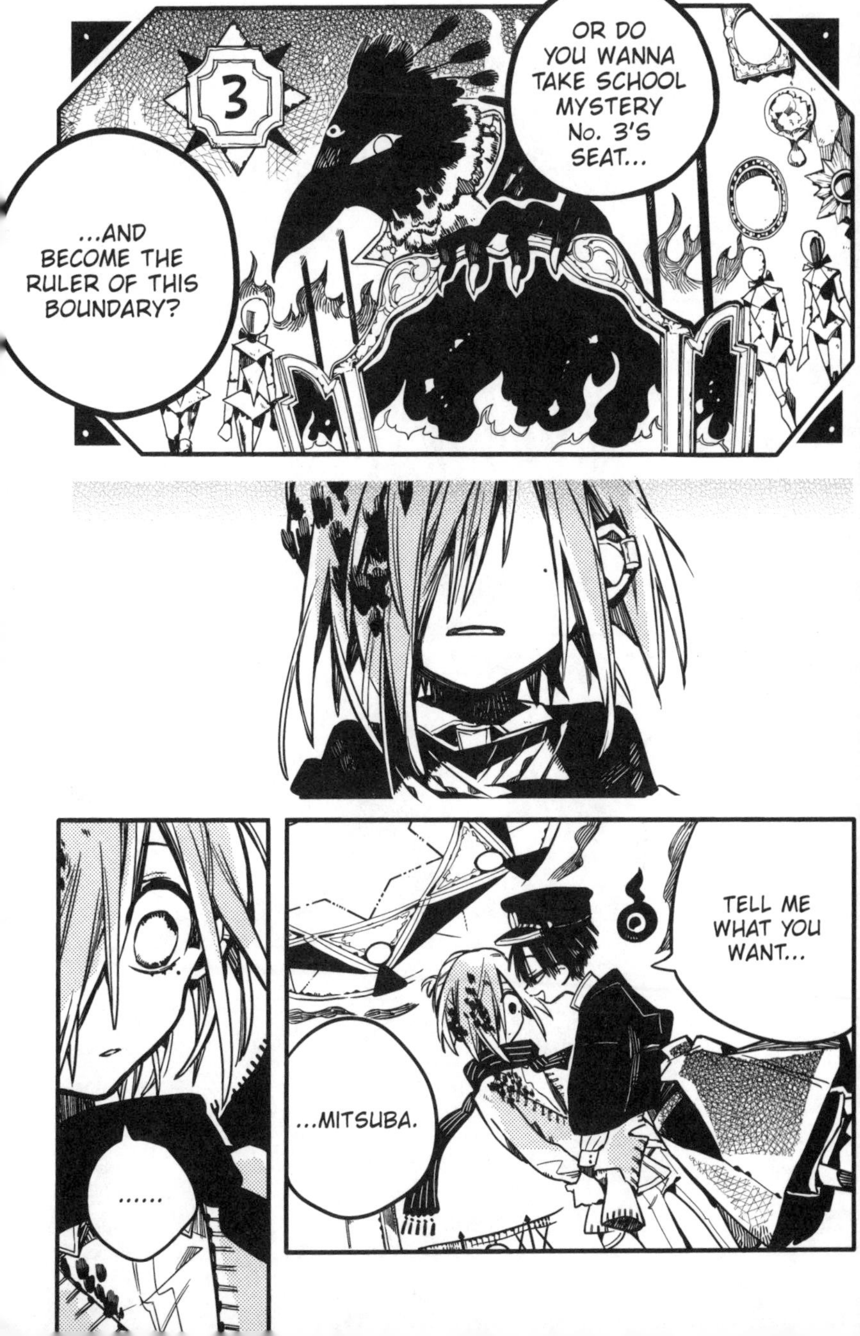
OR DO YOU WANNA TAKE SCHOOL MYSTERY No. 3'S SEAT...
...AND BECOME THE RULER OF THIS BOUNDARY?
TELL ME WHAT YOU WANT...
...MITSUBA.
......

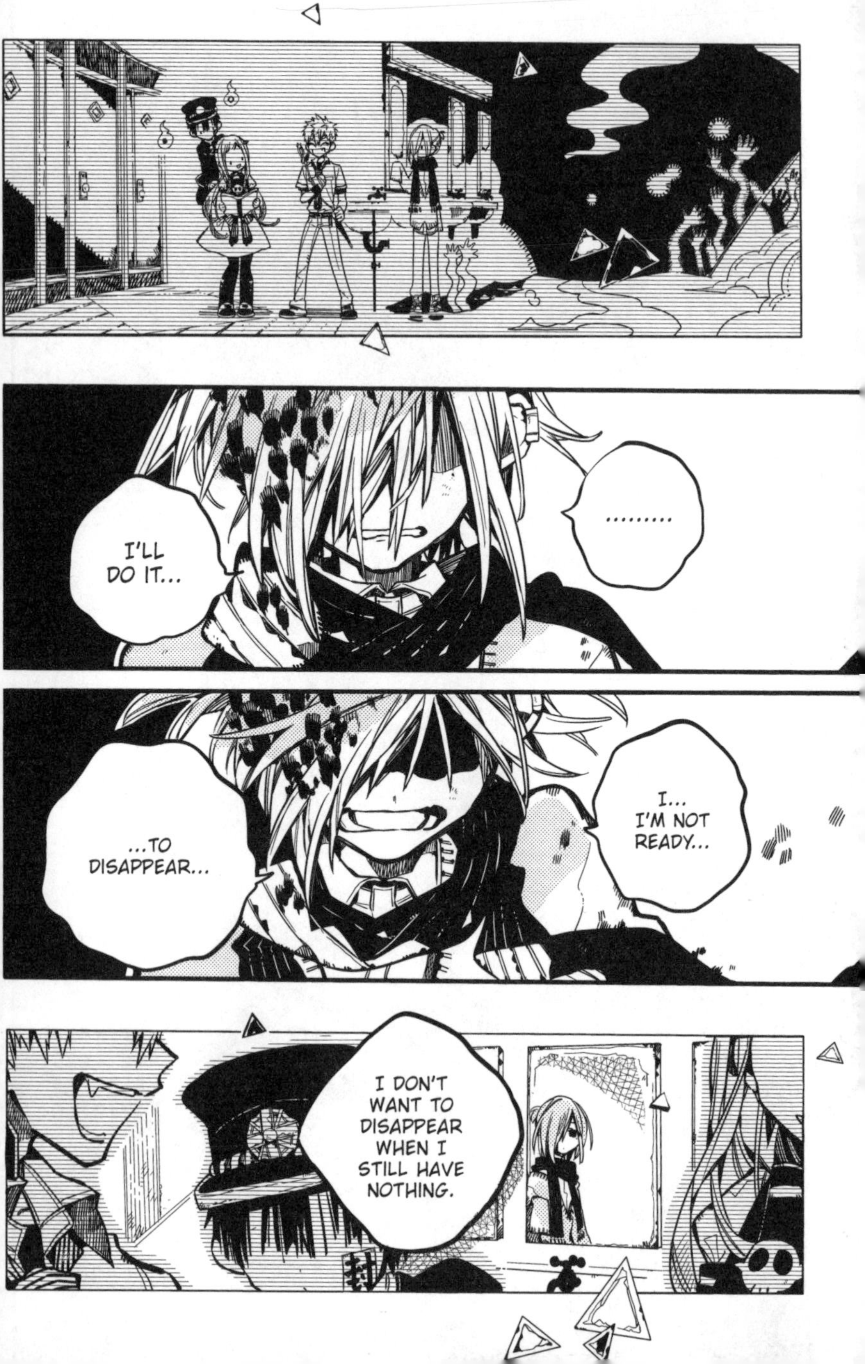
.........
I'LL DO IT...
I... I'M NOT READY...
...TO DISAPPEAR...
I DON'T WANT TO DISAPPEAR WHEN I STILL HAVE NOTHING.

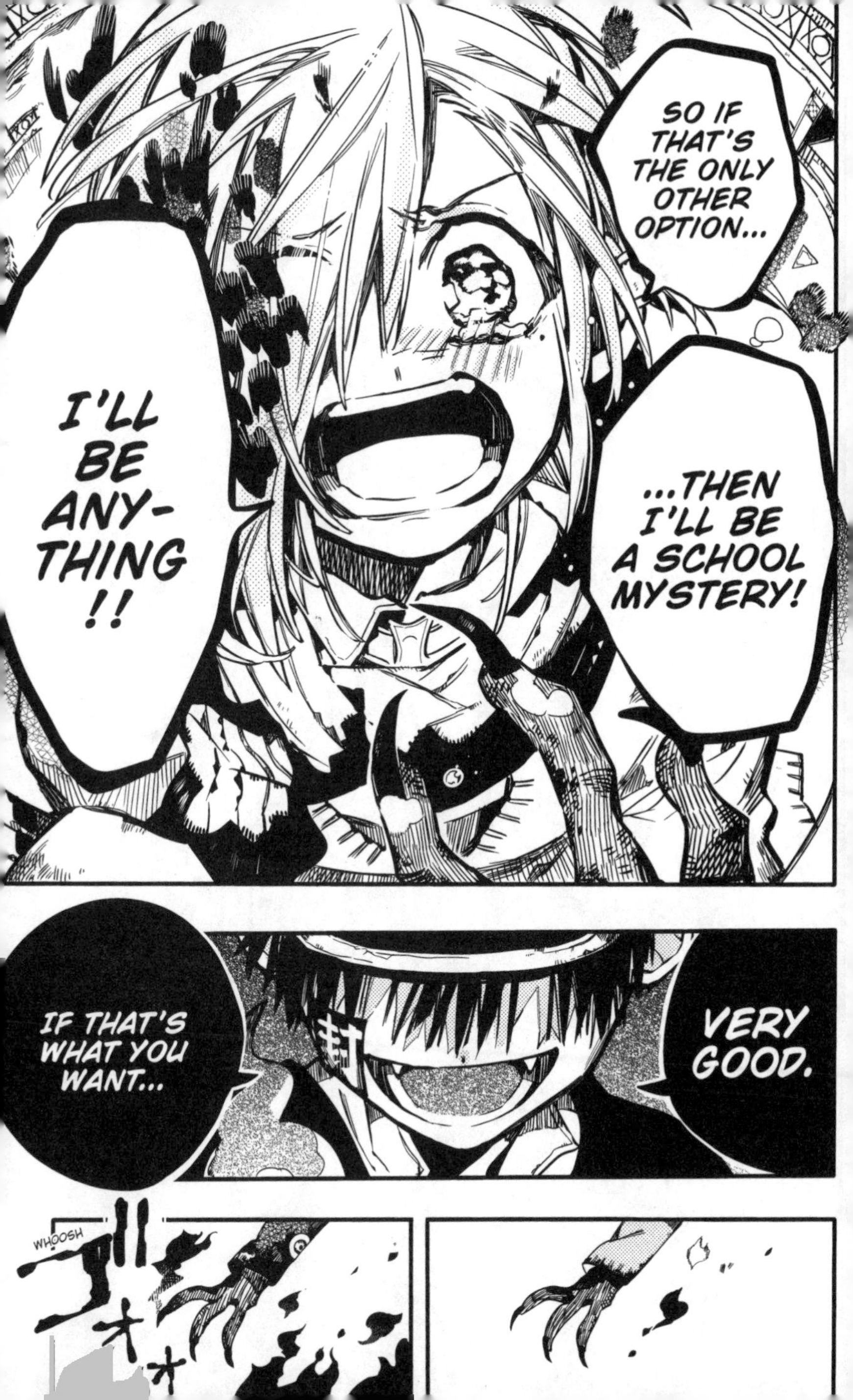
SO IF THAT'S THE ONLY OTHER OPTION...
...THEN I'LL BE A SCHOOL MYSTERY!
I'LL BE ANY-THING!!
VERY GOOD.
IF THAT'S WHAT YOU WANT...
WHOOSH

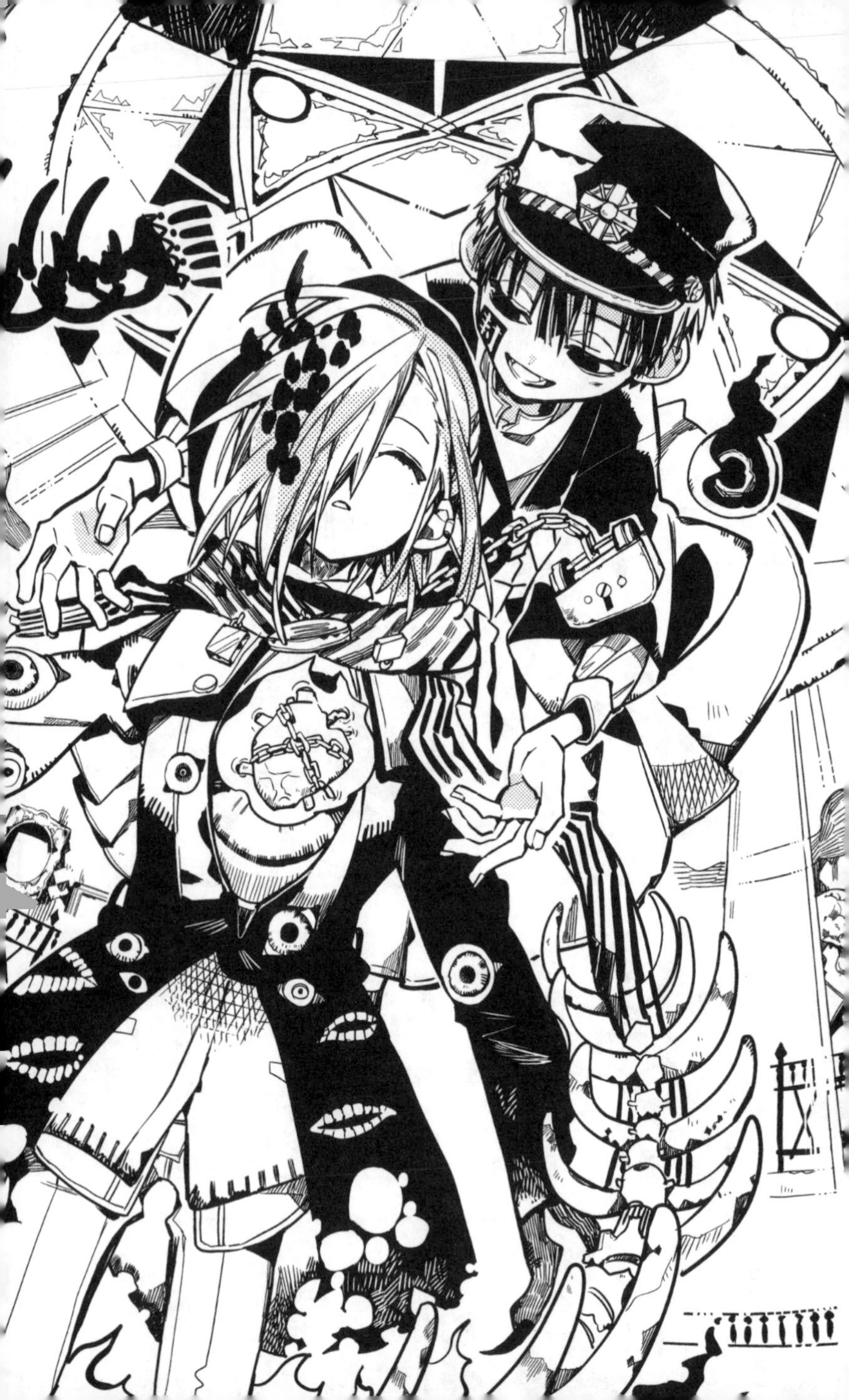

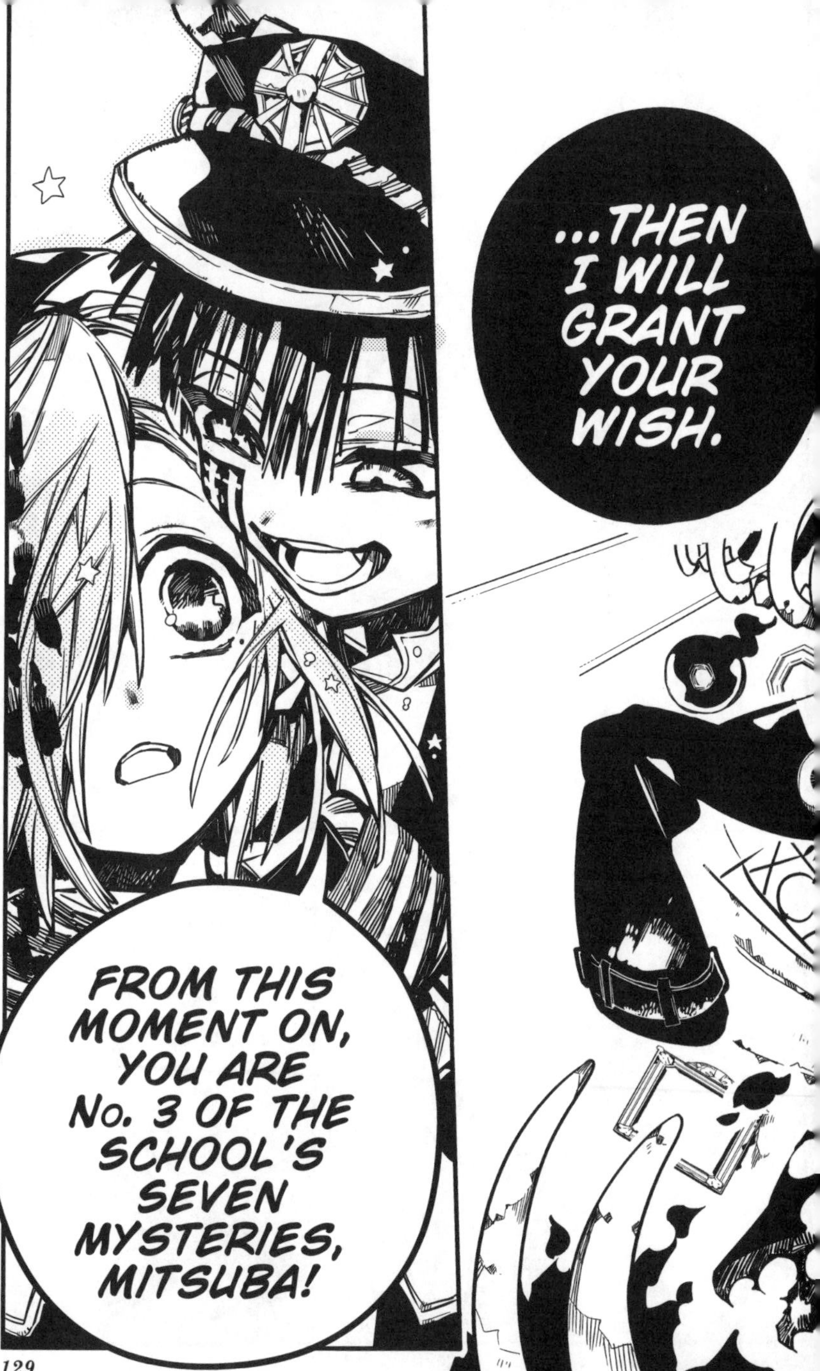
...THEN I WILL GRANT YOUR WISH.
FROM THIS MOMENT ON, YOU ARE No. 3 OF THE SCHOOL'S SEVEN MYSTERIES, MITSUBA!

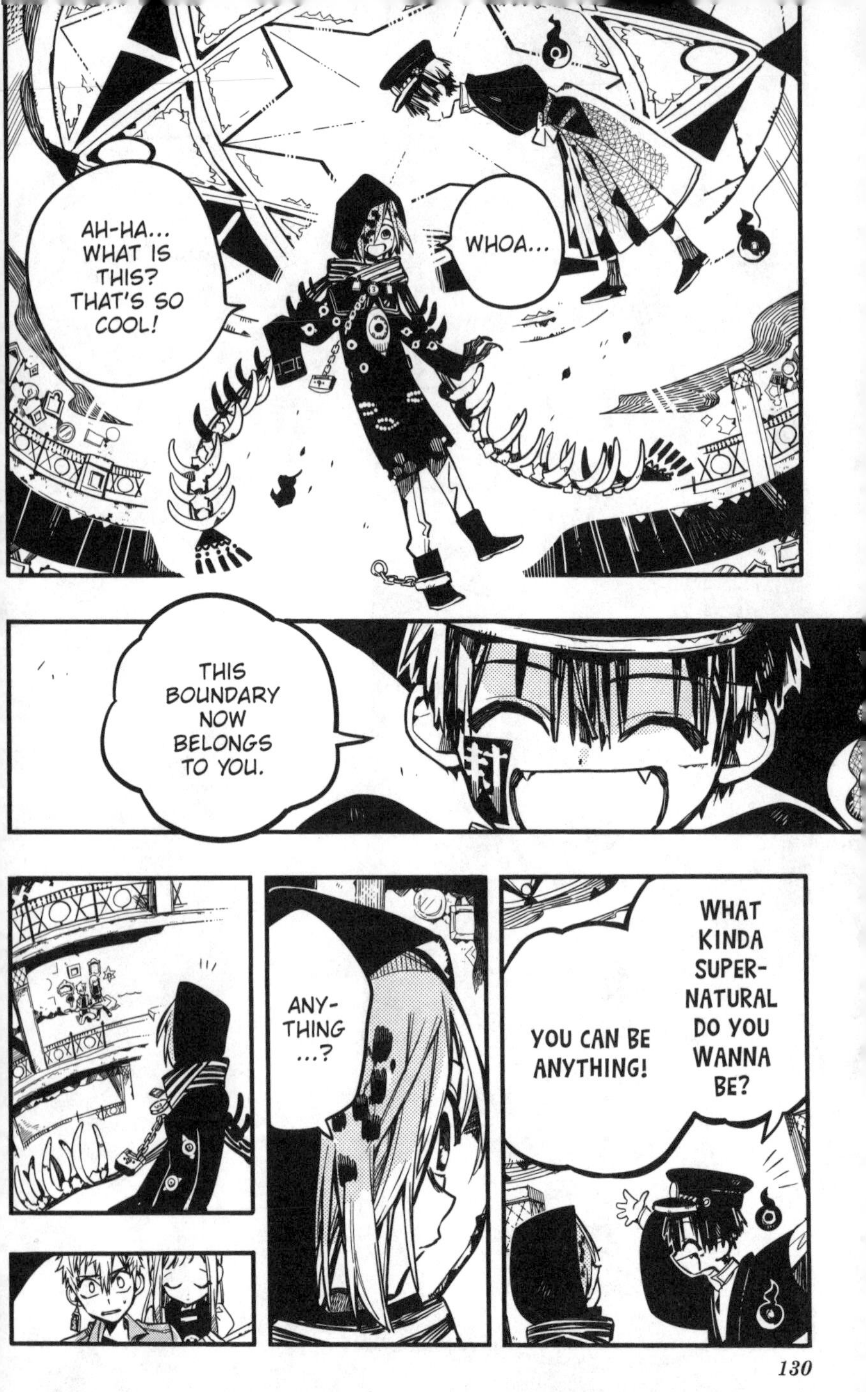
WHOA...
AH-HA... WHAT IS THIS? THAT'S SO COOL!
THIS BOUNDARY NOW BELONGS TO YOU.
WHAT KINDA SUPER-NATURAL DO YOU WANNA BE?
YOU CAN BE ANYTHING!
ANY-THING ...?

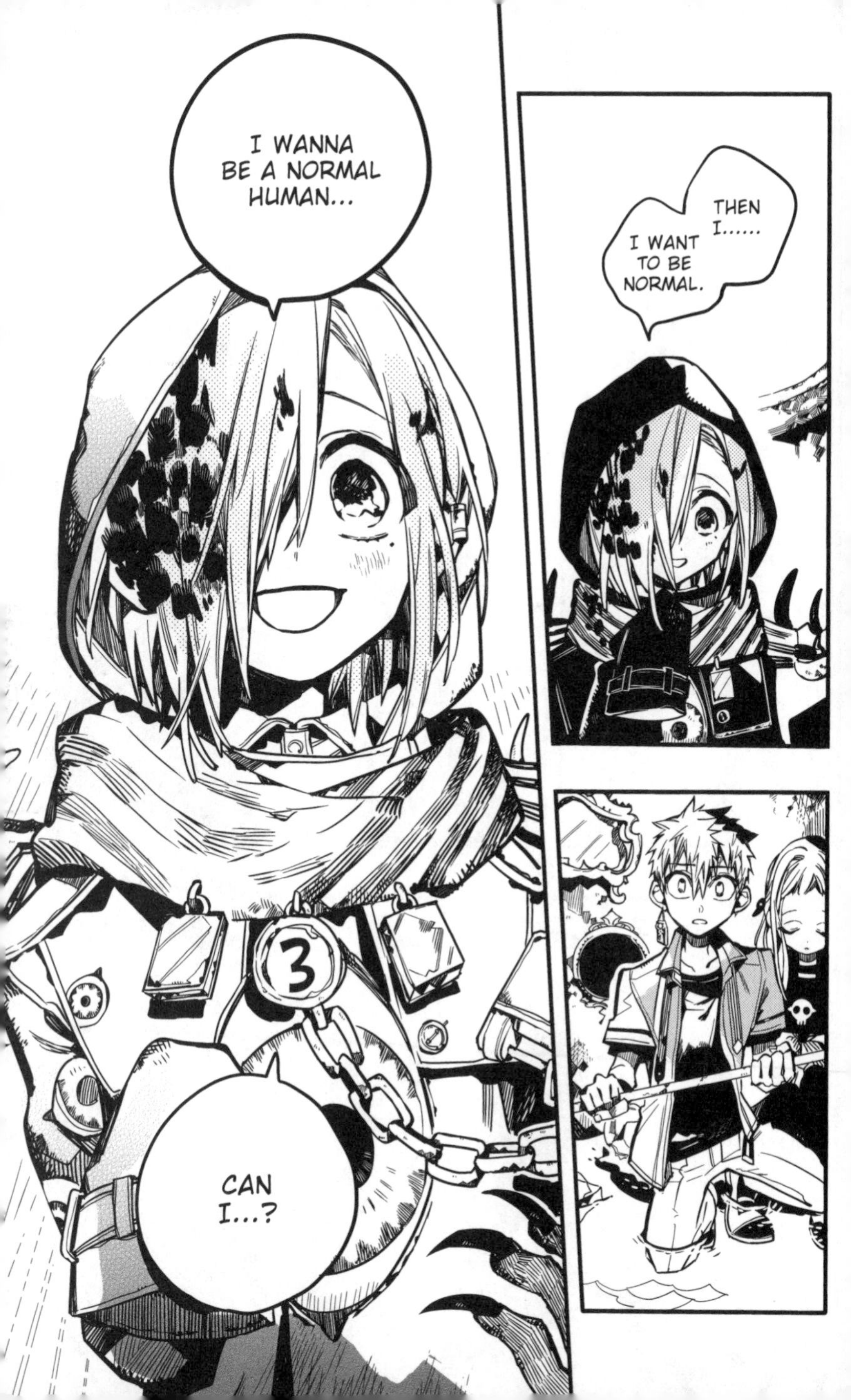
THEN I......
I WANT TO BE NORMAL.
I WANNA BE A NORMAL HUMAN...
CAN I...?

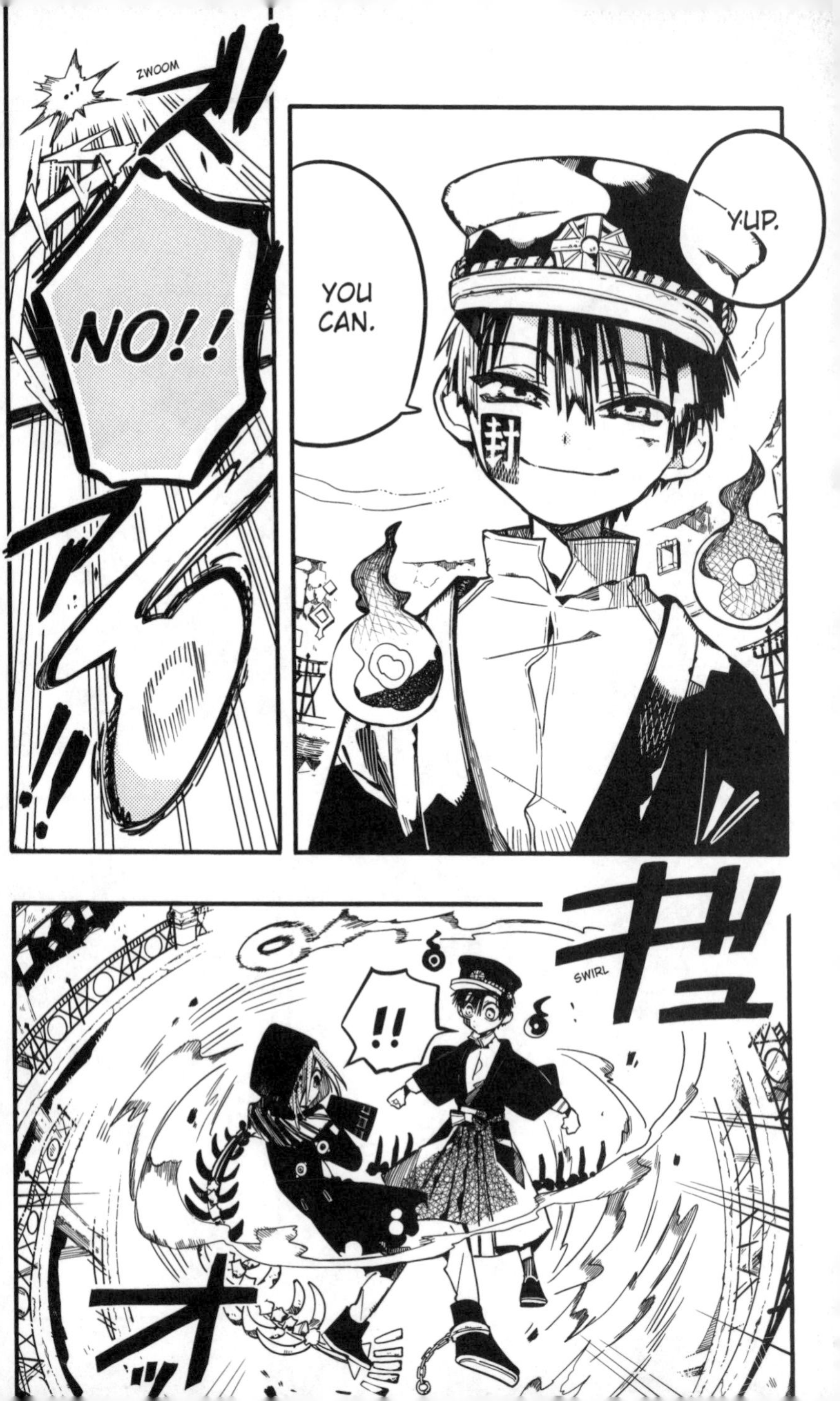
YUP.
YOU CAN.
ZWOOM
NO!!
SWIRL
!!

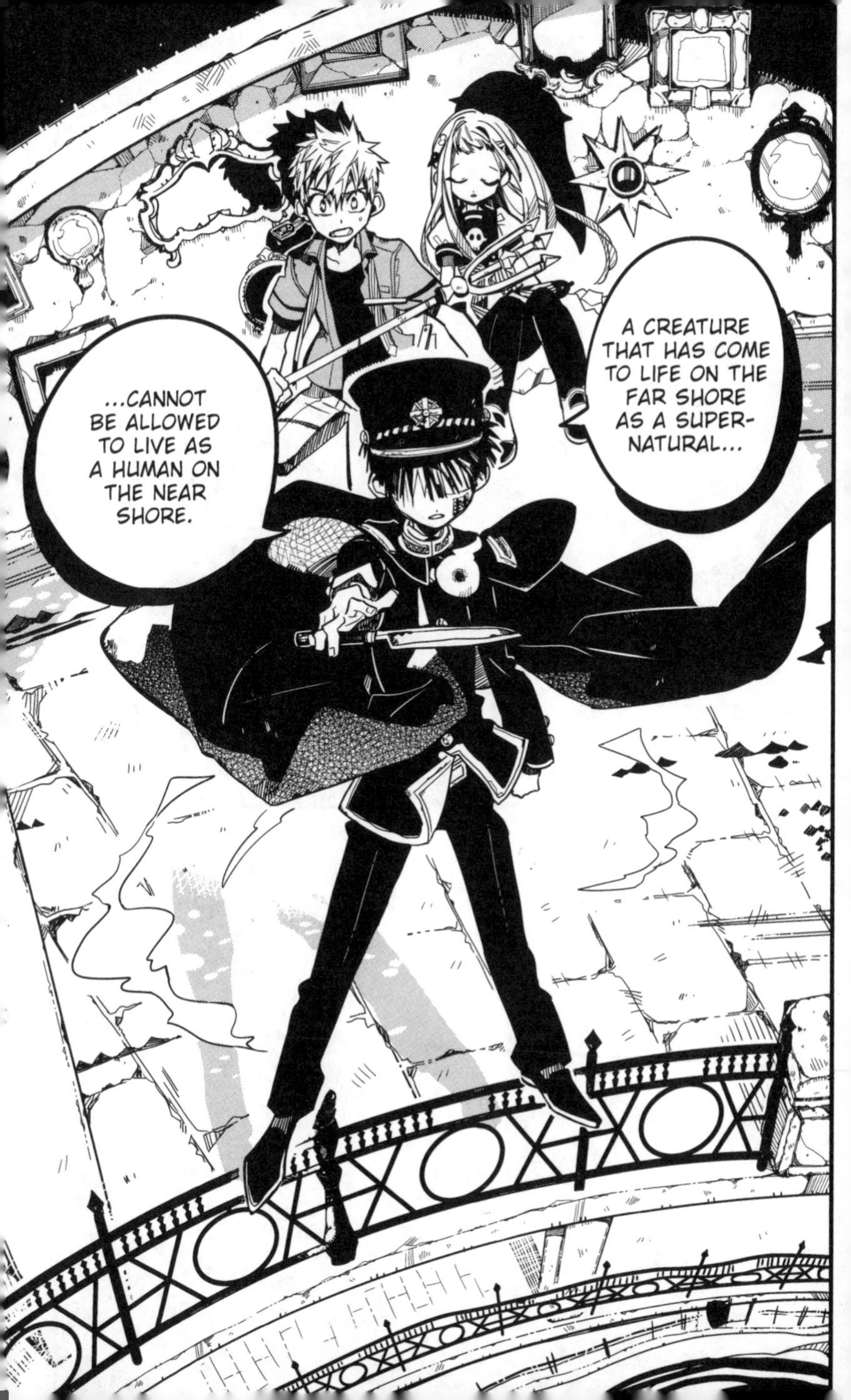
A CREATURE THAT HAS COME TO LIFE ON THE FAR SHORE AS A SUPER-NATURAL...
...CANNOT BE ALLOWED TO LIVE AS A HUMAN ON THE NEAR SHORE.

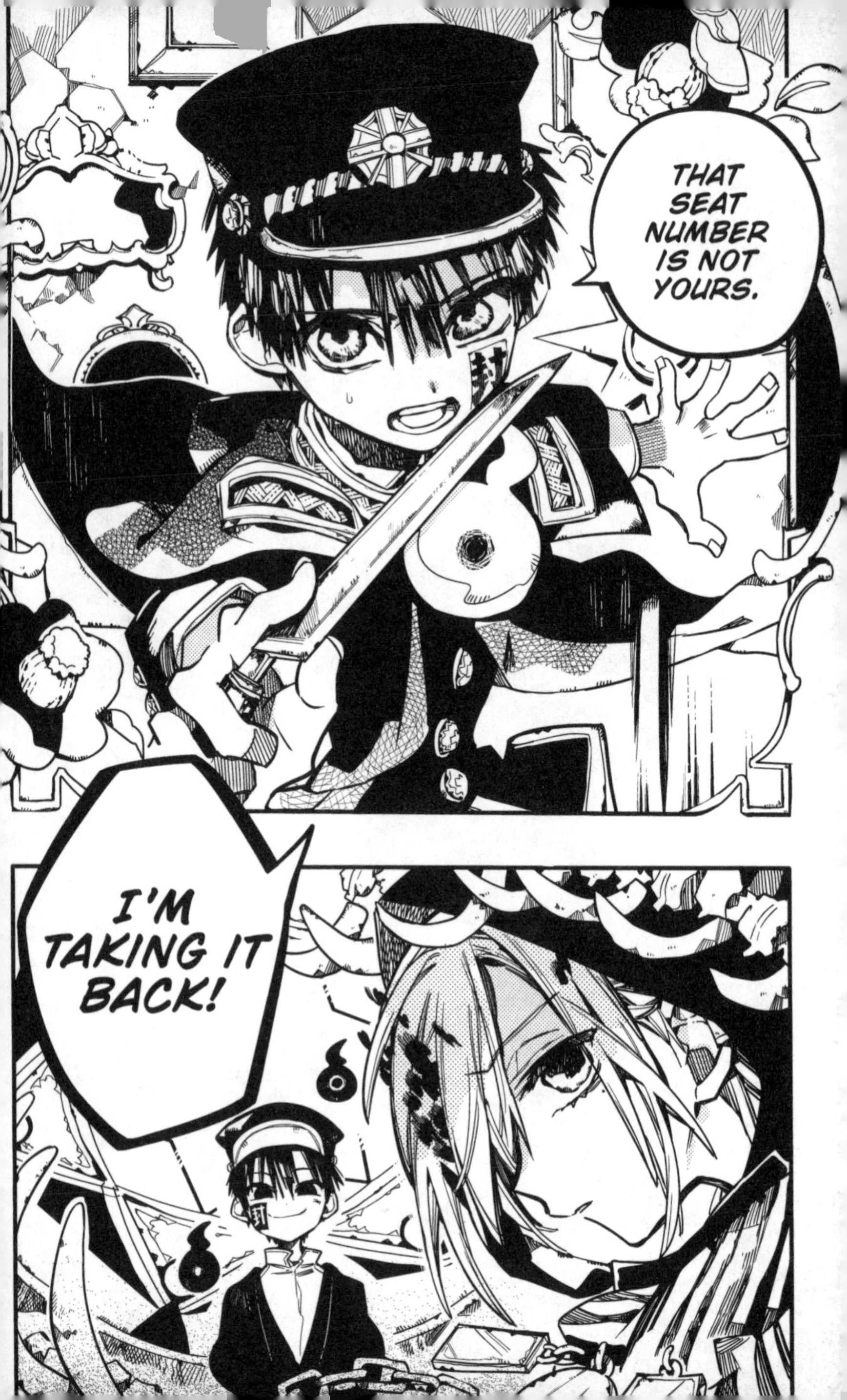
THAT SEAT NUMBER IS NOT YOURS.
I'M TAKING IT BACK!

# SPOOK 35 THE HELL OF MIRRORS (PART 5)

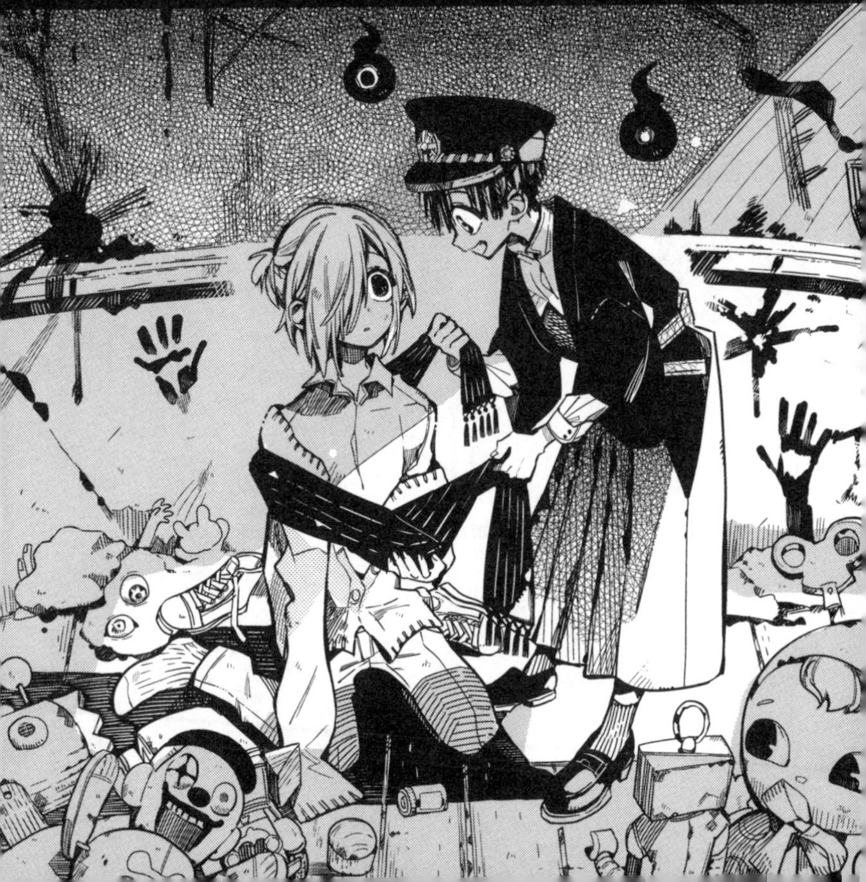

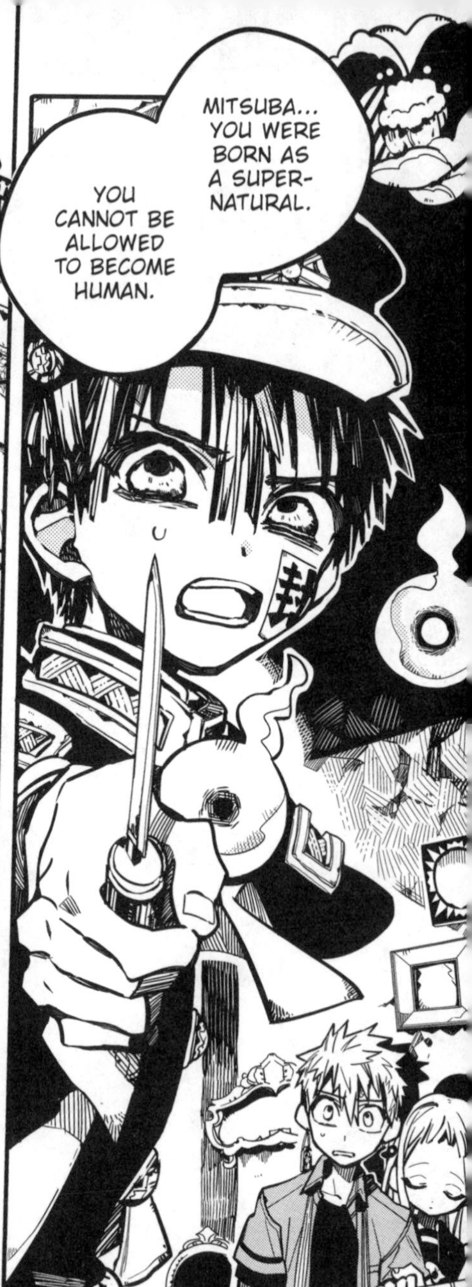
MITSUBA... YOU WERE BORN AS A SUPER-NATURAL.
YOU CANNOT BE ALLOWED TO BECOME HUMAN.

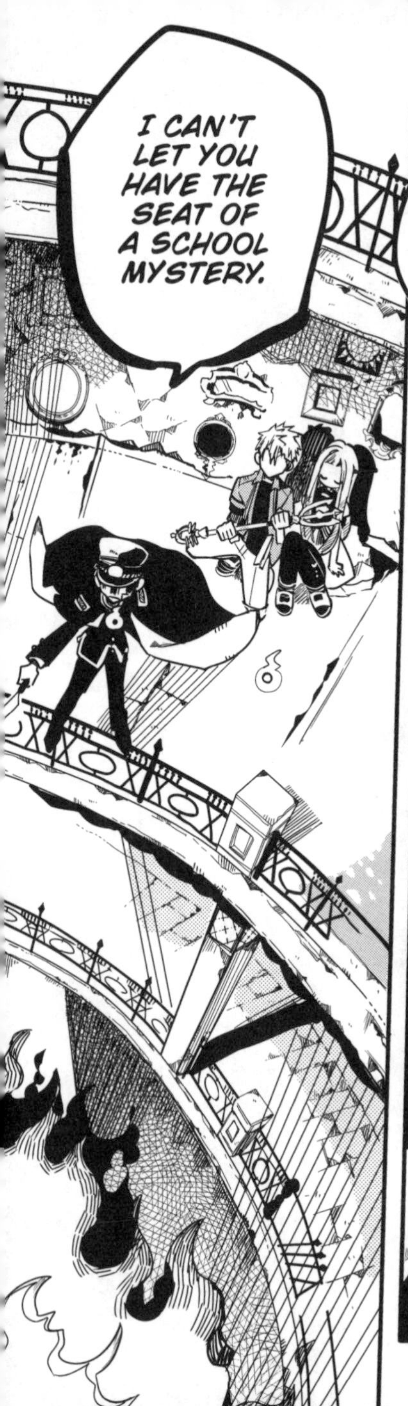
I CAN'T LET YOU HAVE THE SEAT OF A SCHOOL MYSTERY.

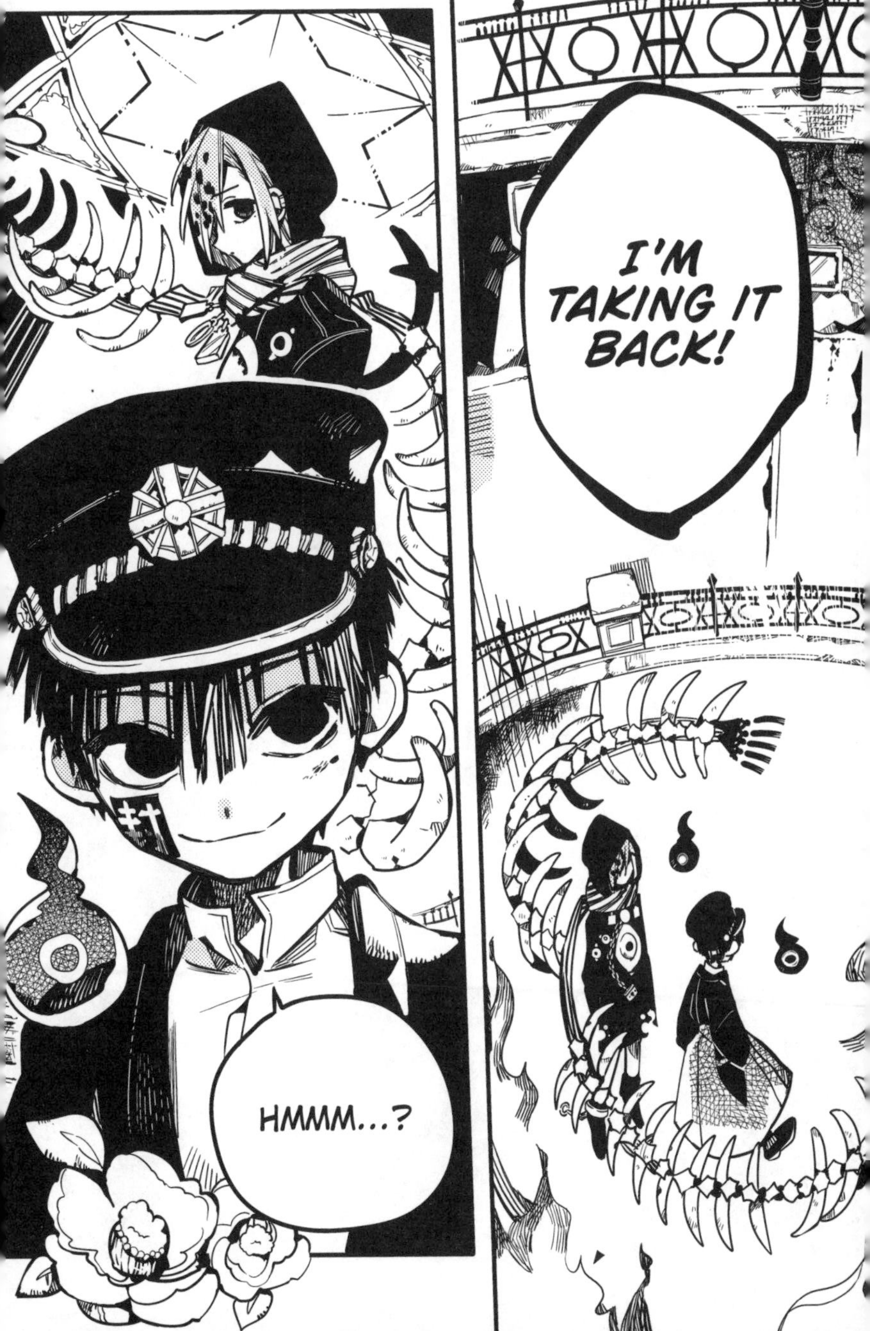
I'M TAKING IT BACK!
HMMM...?

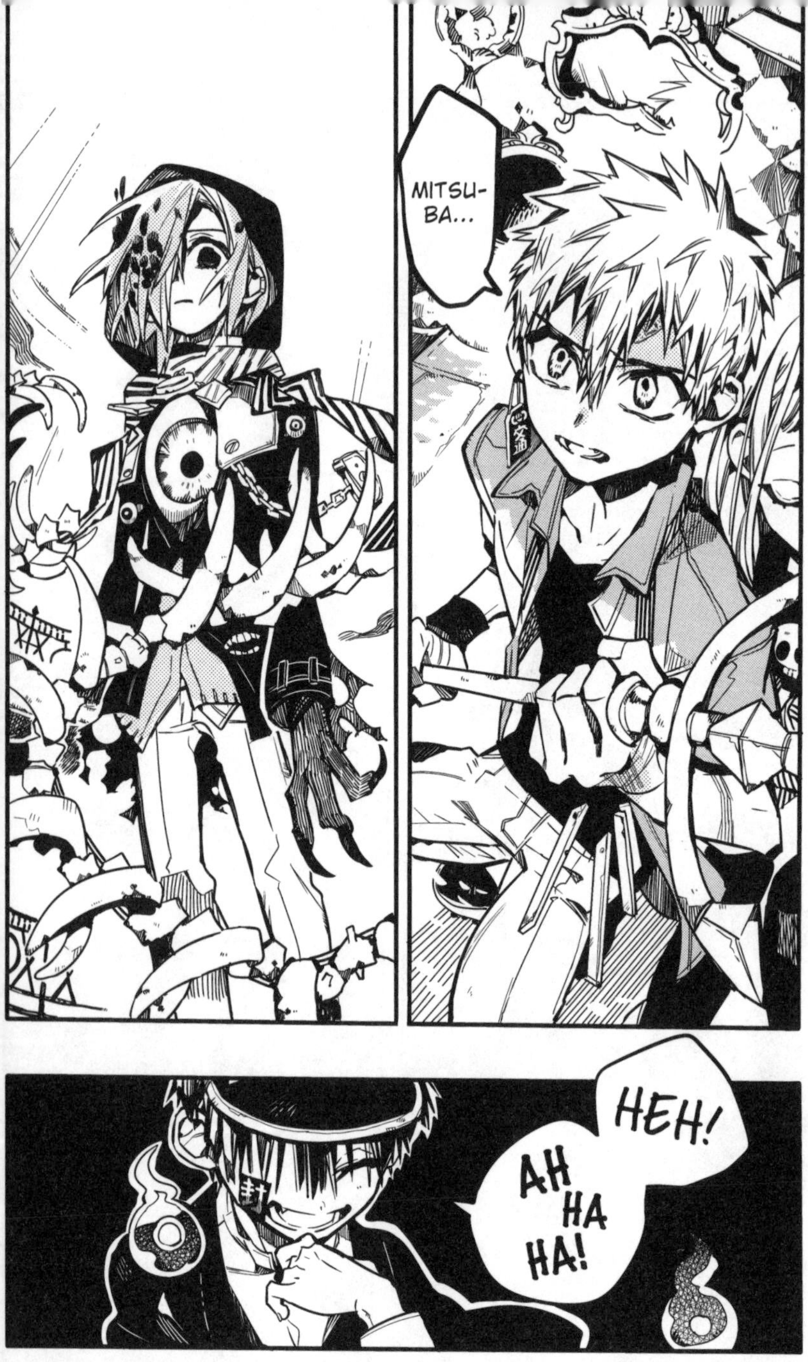
MITSU-BA...
HEH!
AH HA HA HA!

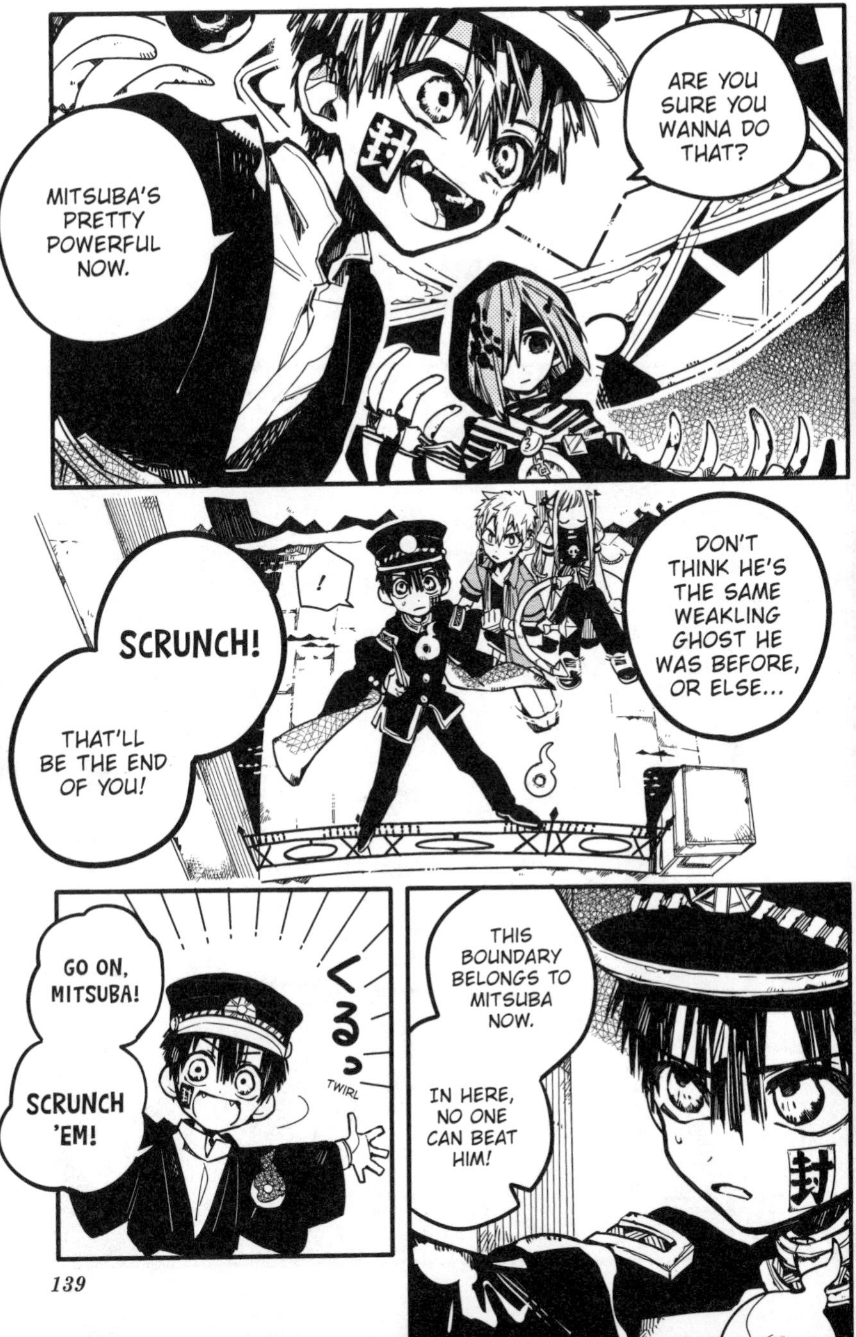
ARE YOU SURE YOU WANNA DO THAT?
MITSUBA'S PRETTY POWERFUL NOW.
DON'T THINK HE'S THE SAME WEAKLING GHOST HE WAS BEFORE, OR ELSE...
!
SCRUNCH!
THAT'LL BE THE END OF YOU!
THIS BOUNDARY BELONGS TO MITSUBA NOW.
IN HERE, NO ONE CAN BEAT HIM!
くるっ
TWIRL
GO ON, MITSUBA!
SCRUNCH 'EM!

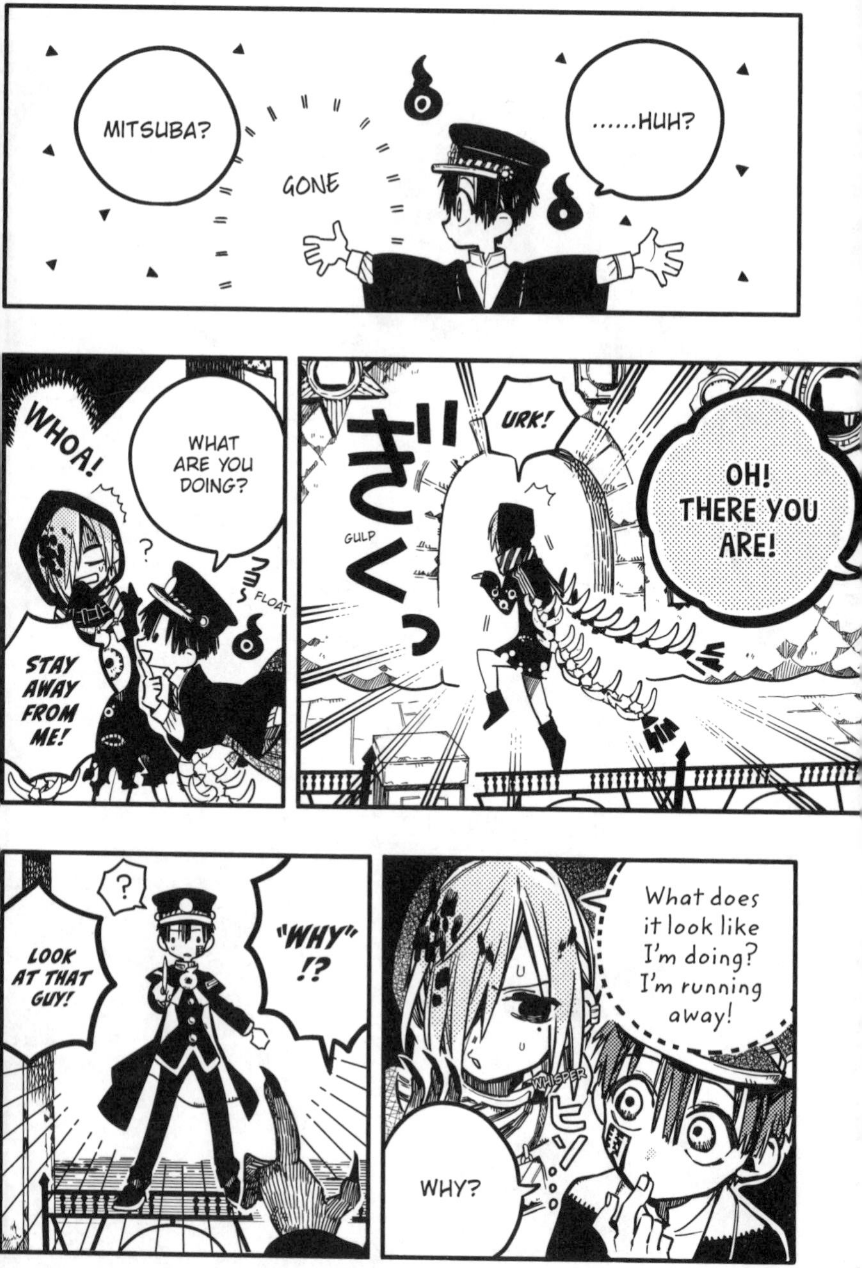

......HUH?
MITSUBA?
GONE
OH! THERE YOU ARE!
URK!
ぎくっ
GULP
WHAT ARE YOU DOING?
WHOA!
FLOAT
STAY AWAY FROM ME!
What does it look like I'm doing? I'm running away!
WHISPER
WHY?
?
"WHY" !?
LOOK AT THAT GUY!

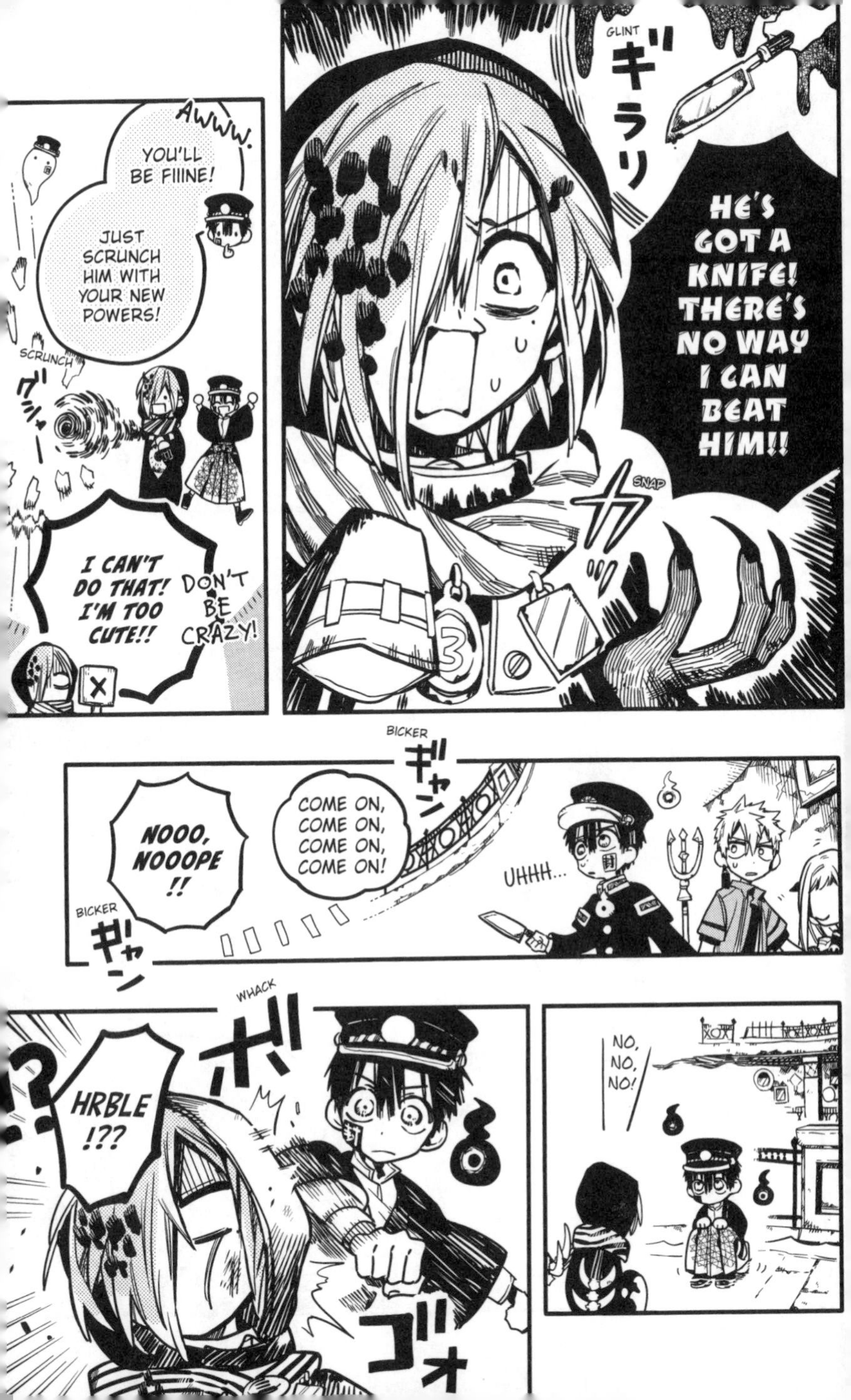
GLINT
ギラリ
HE'S GOT A KNIFE! THERE'S NO WAY I CAN BEAT HIM!!
SNAP
カ
AWWW.
YOU'LL BE FIIINE!
JUST SCRUNCH HIM WITH YOUR NEW POWERS!
SCRUNCH
グシャー
I CAN'T DO THAT! I'M TOO CUTE!!
DON'T BE CRAZY!
BICKER
ギャン
UHHH...
COME ON, COME ON, COME ON, COME ON!
NOOO, NOOOPE!!
BICKER
ギャン
NO, NO, NO!
WHACK
ボ
HRBLE!??
ゴォ

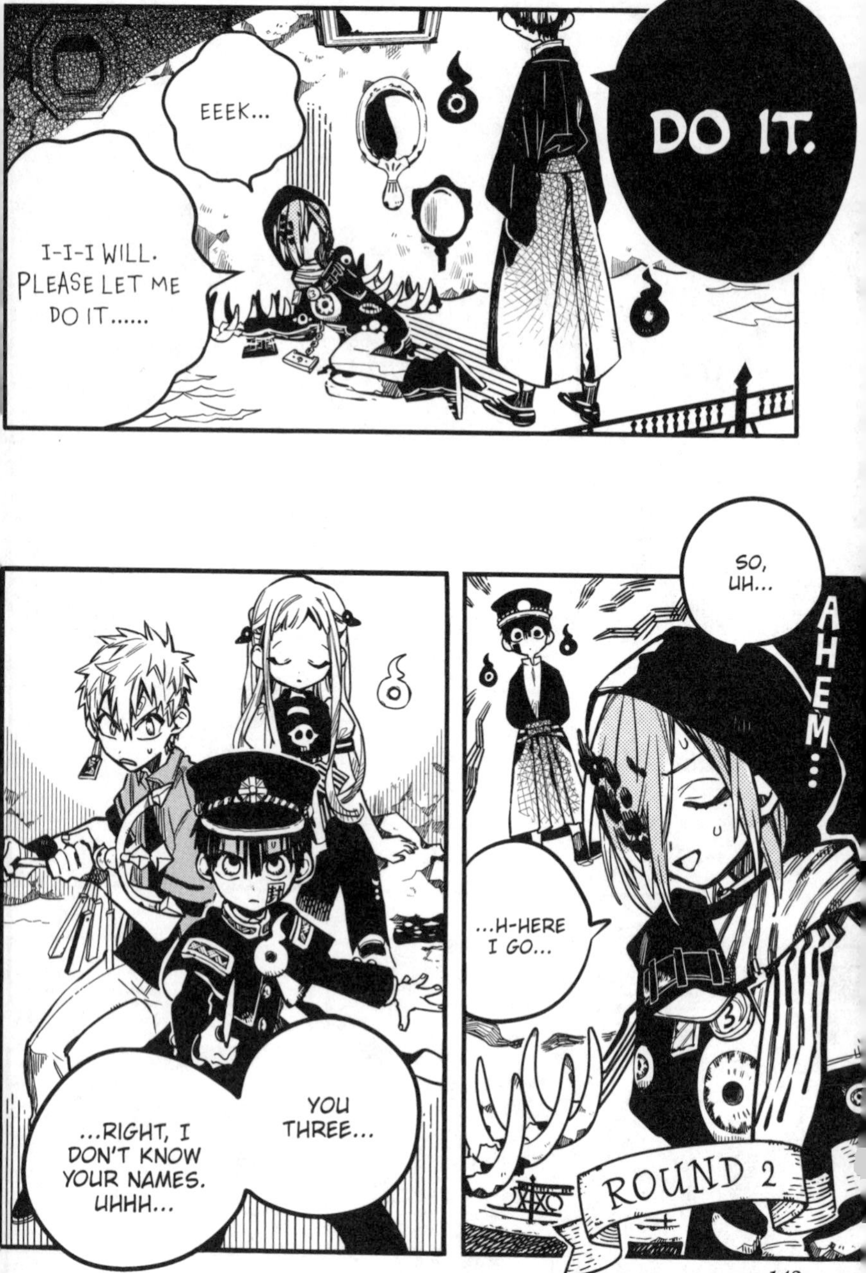
DO IT.
EEEK...
I-I-I WILL. PLEASE LET ME DO IT......
SO, UH...
AHEM...
...H-HERE I GO...
ROUND 2
YOU THREE...
...RIGHT, I DON'T KNOW YOUR NAMES. UHHH...

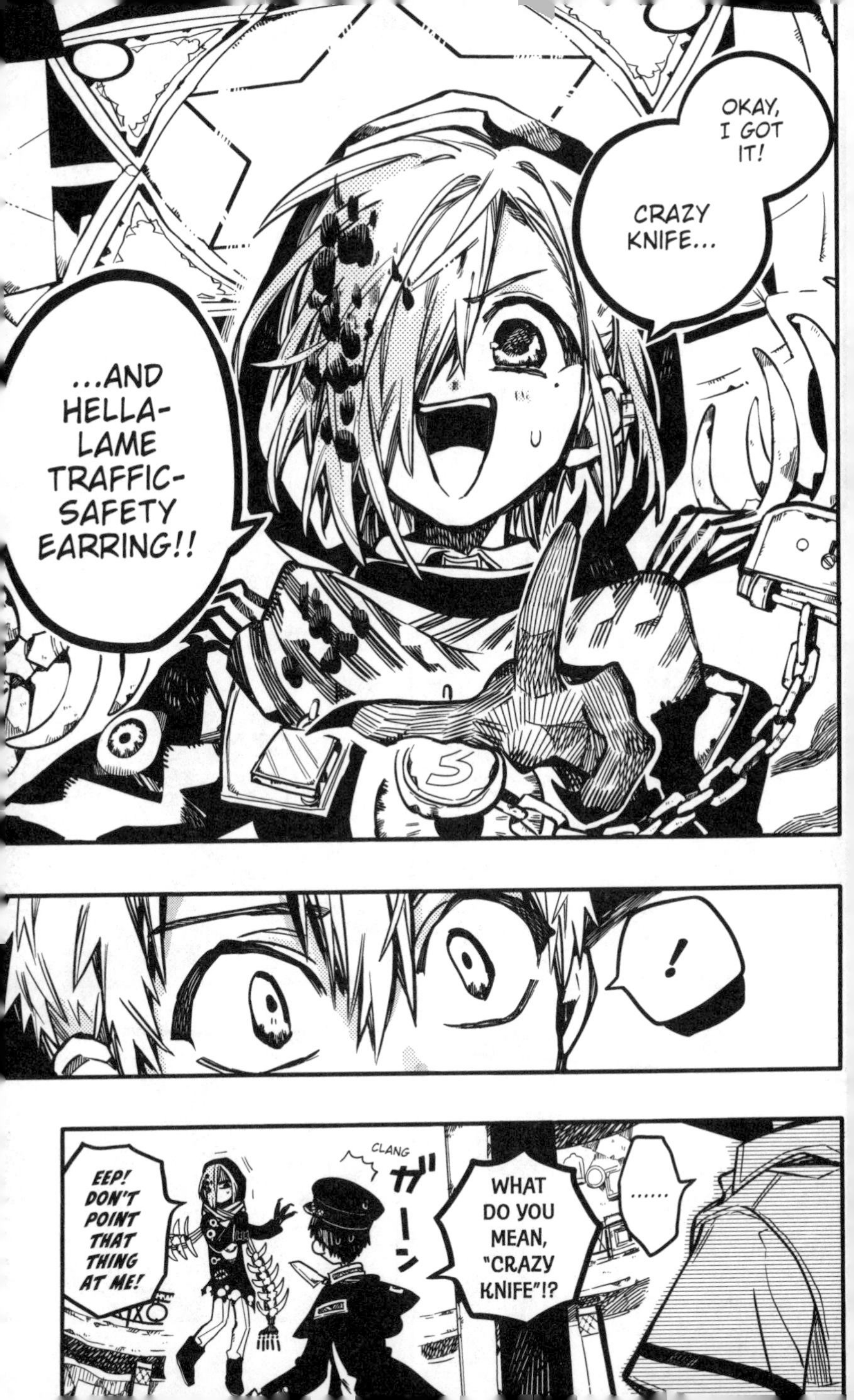
OKAY, I GOT IT!
CRAZY KNIFE...
...AND HELLA-LAME TRAFFIC-SAFETY EARRING!!
!
......
WHAT DO YOU MEAN, "CRAZY KNIFE"!?
CLANG
ガーン
EEP! DON'T POINT THAT THING AT ME!

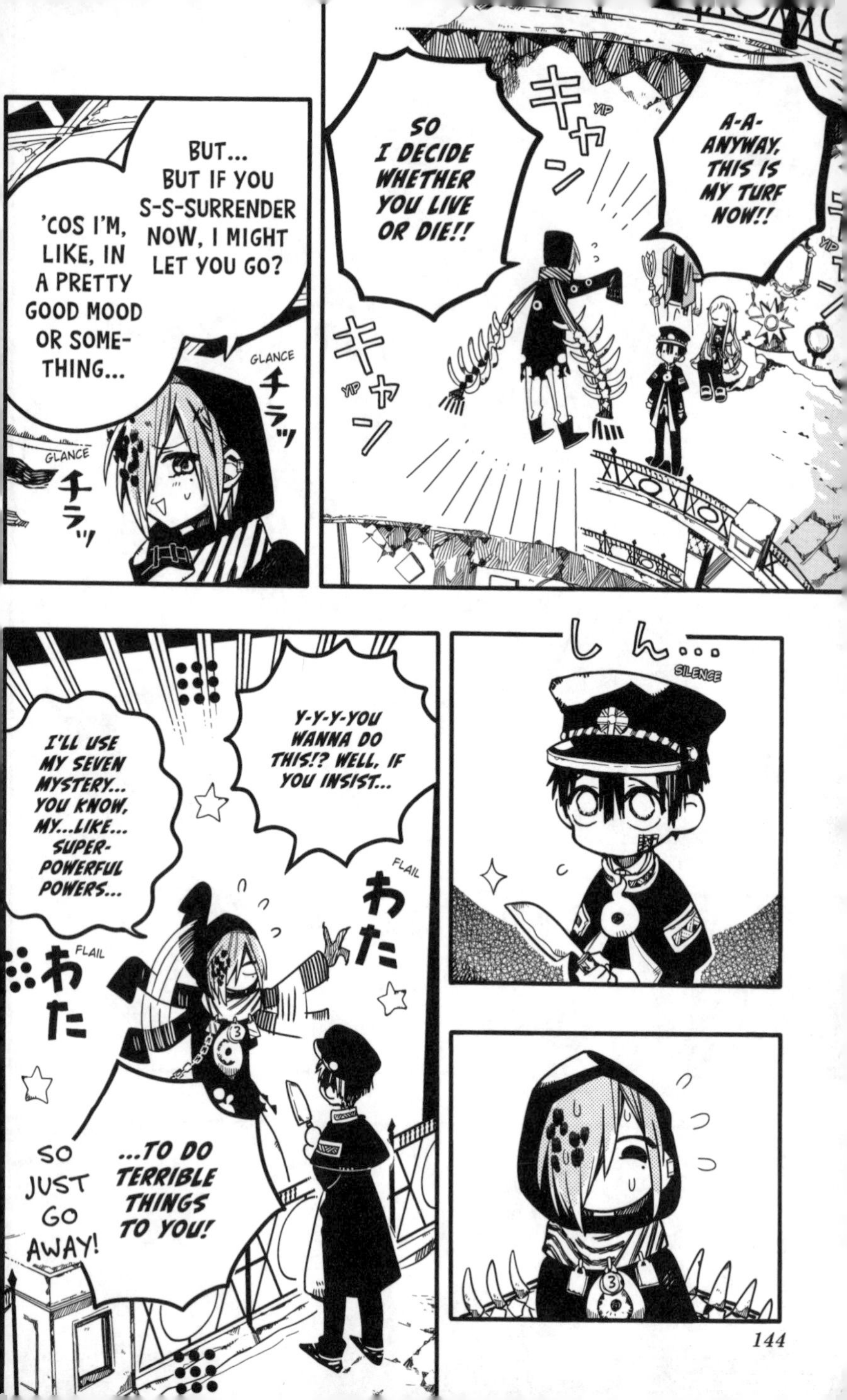
A-A-ANYWAY, THIS IS MY TURF NOW!!
キャン
YIP
SO I DECIDE WHETHER YOU LIVE OR DIE!!
キャン
YIP
キャン
YIP
BUT... BUT IF YOU S-S-SURRENDER NOW, I MIGHT LET YOU GO?
'COS I'M, LIKE, IN A PRETTY GOOD MOOD OR SOME-THING...
チラッ
GLANCE
チラッ
GLANCE
しん...
SILENCE
Y-Y-Y-YOU WANNA DO THIS!? WELL, IF YOU INSIST...
わた
FLAIL
I'LL USE MY SEVEN MYSTERY... YOU KNOW, MY...LIKE... SUPER-POWERFUL POWERS...
わた
FLAIL
...TO DO TERRIBLE THINGS TO YOU!
SO JUST GO AWAY!

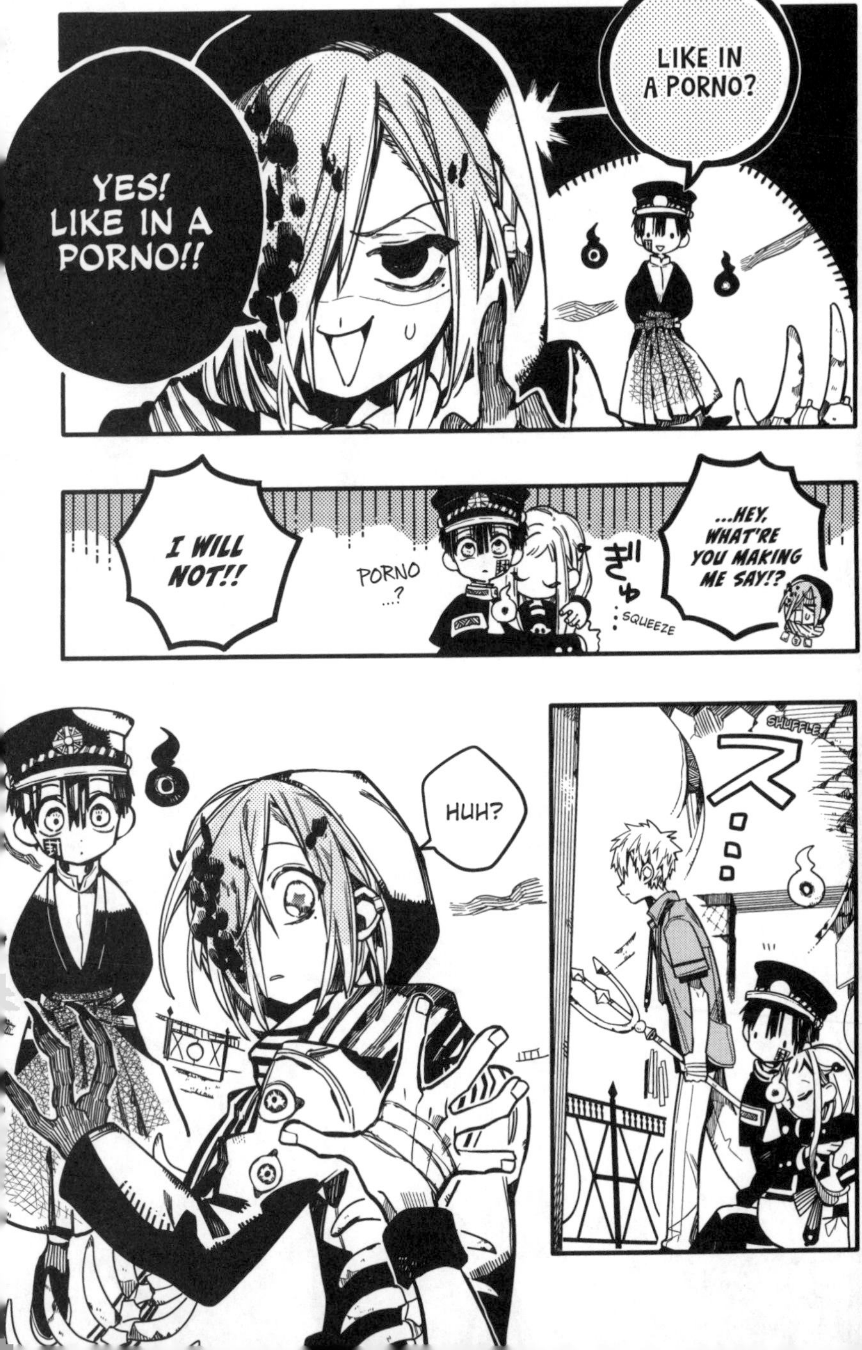
LIKE IN A PORNO?
YES! LIKE IN A PORNO!!
...HEY, WHAT'RE YOU MAKING ME SAY!?
ぎゅ
SQUEEZE
PORNO ...?
I WILL NOT!!
SHUFFLE
ス
HUH?

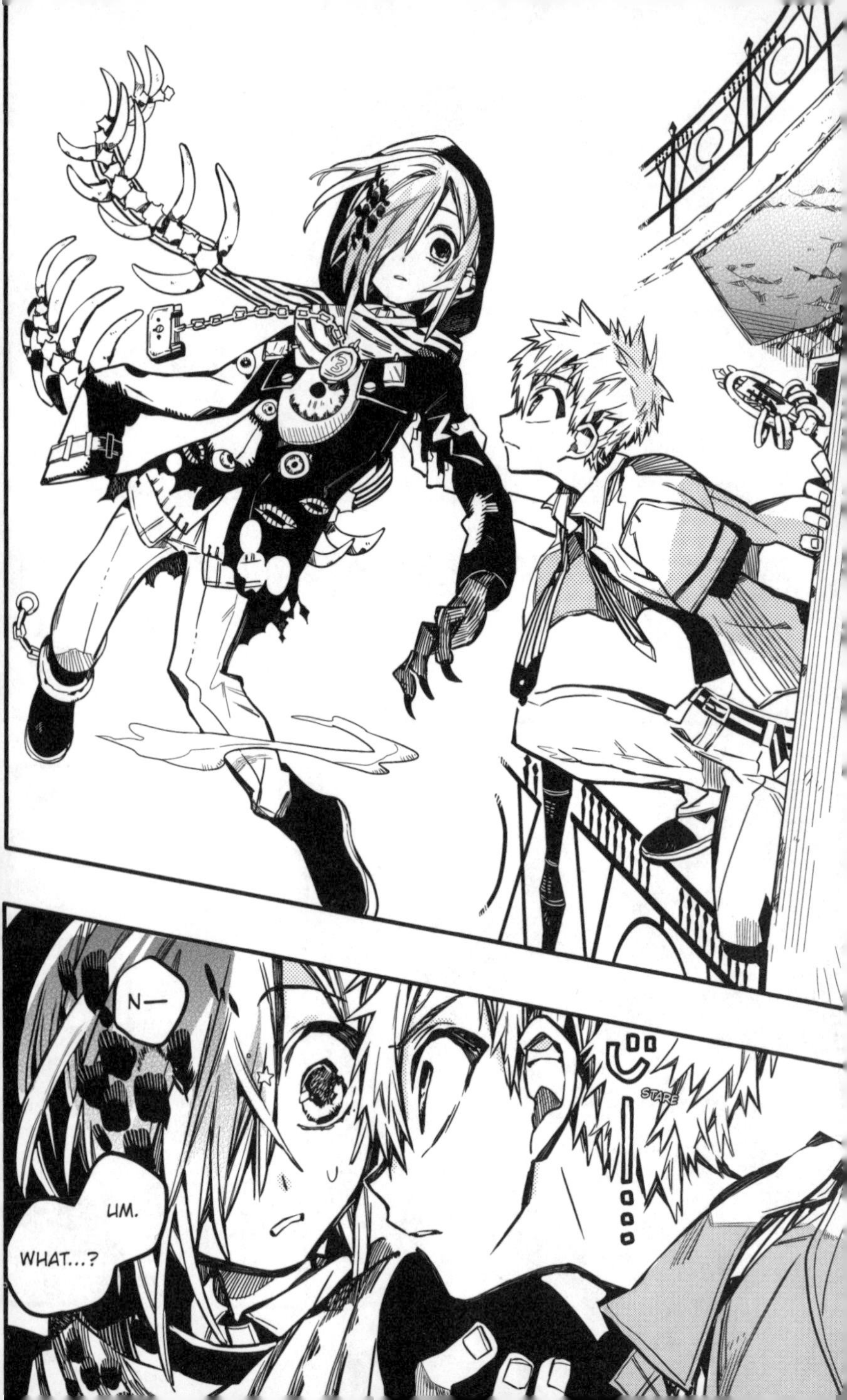
N—
STARE
UM.
WHAT...?

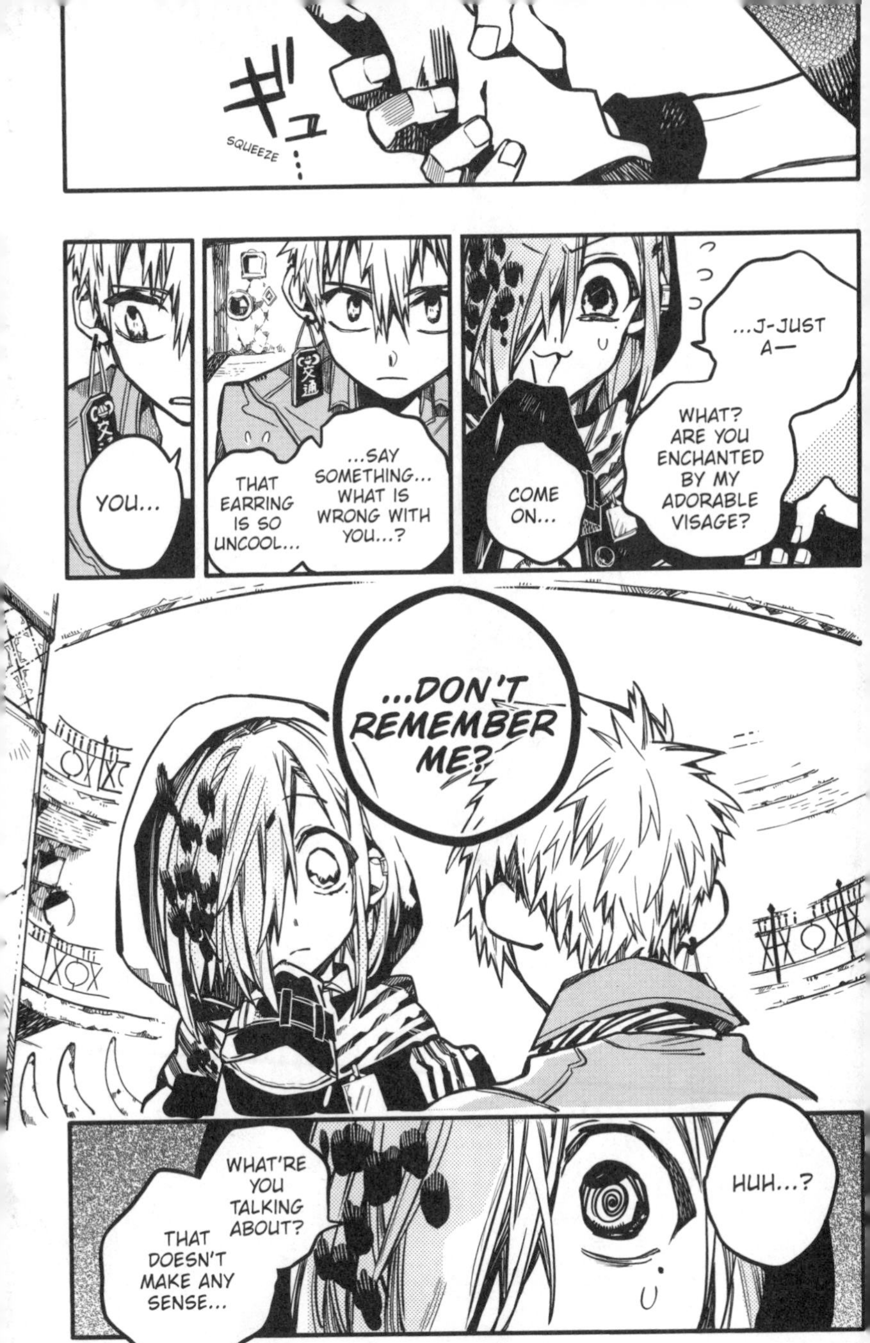
ギュ
SQUEEZE
...J-JUST A—
WHAT? ARE YOU ENCHANTED BY MY ADORABLE VISAGE?
COME ON...
...SAY SOMETHING... WHAT IS WRONG WITH YOU...?
THAT EARRING IS SO UNCOOL...
YOU...
...DON'T REMEMBER ME?
HUH...?
WHAT'RE YOU TALKING ABOUT?
THAT DOESN'T MAKE ANY SENSE...

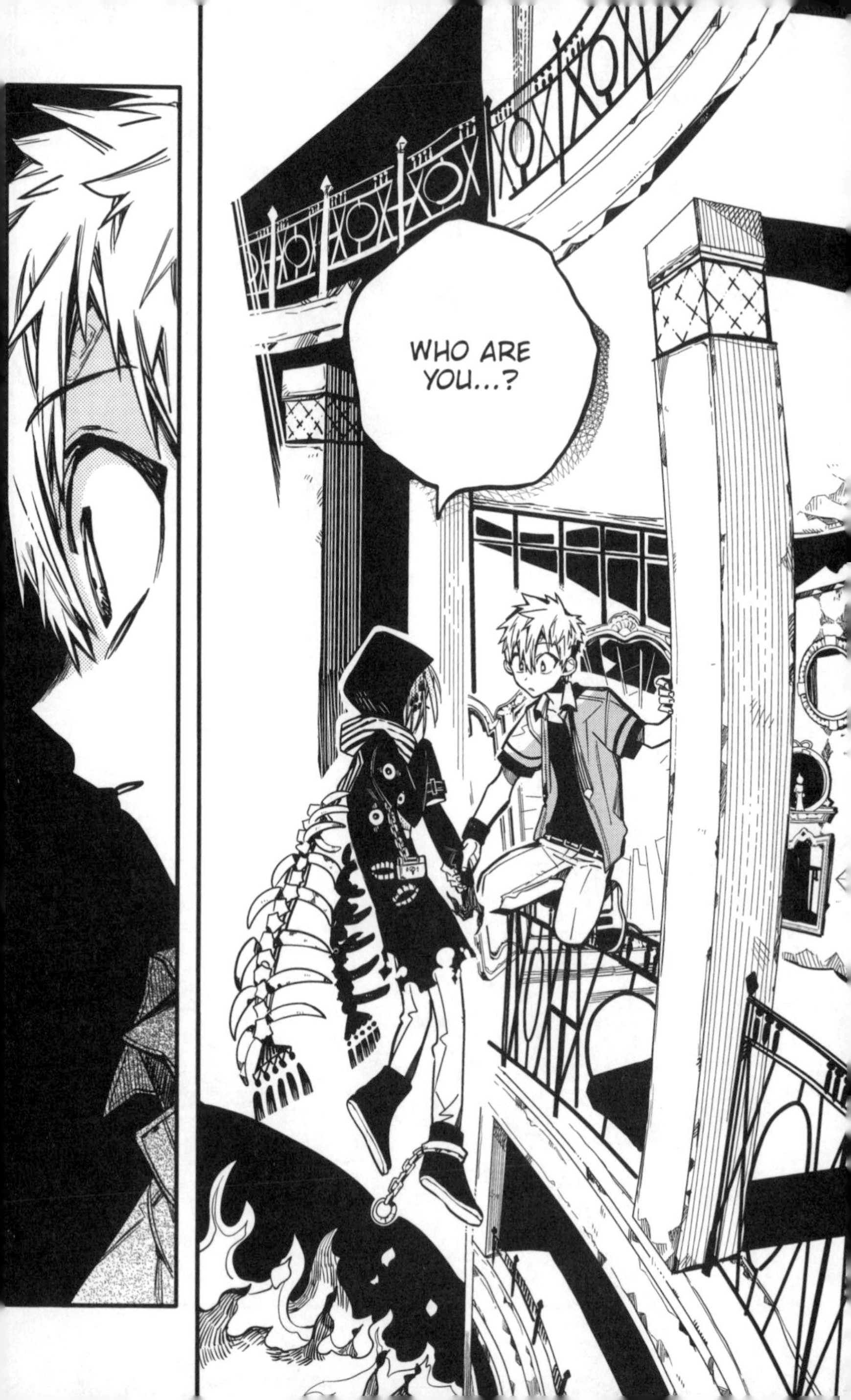
WHO ARE YOU...?

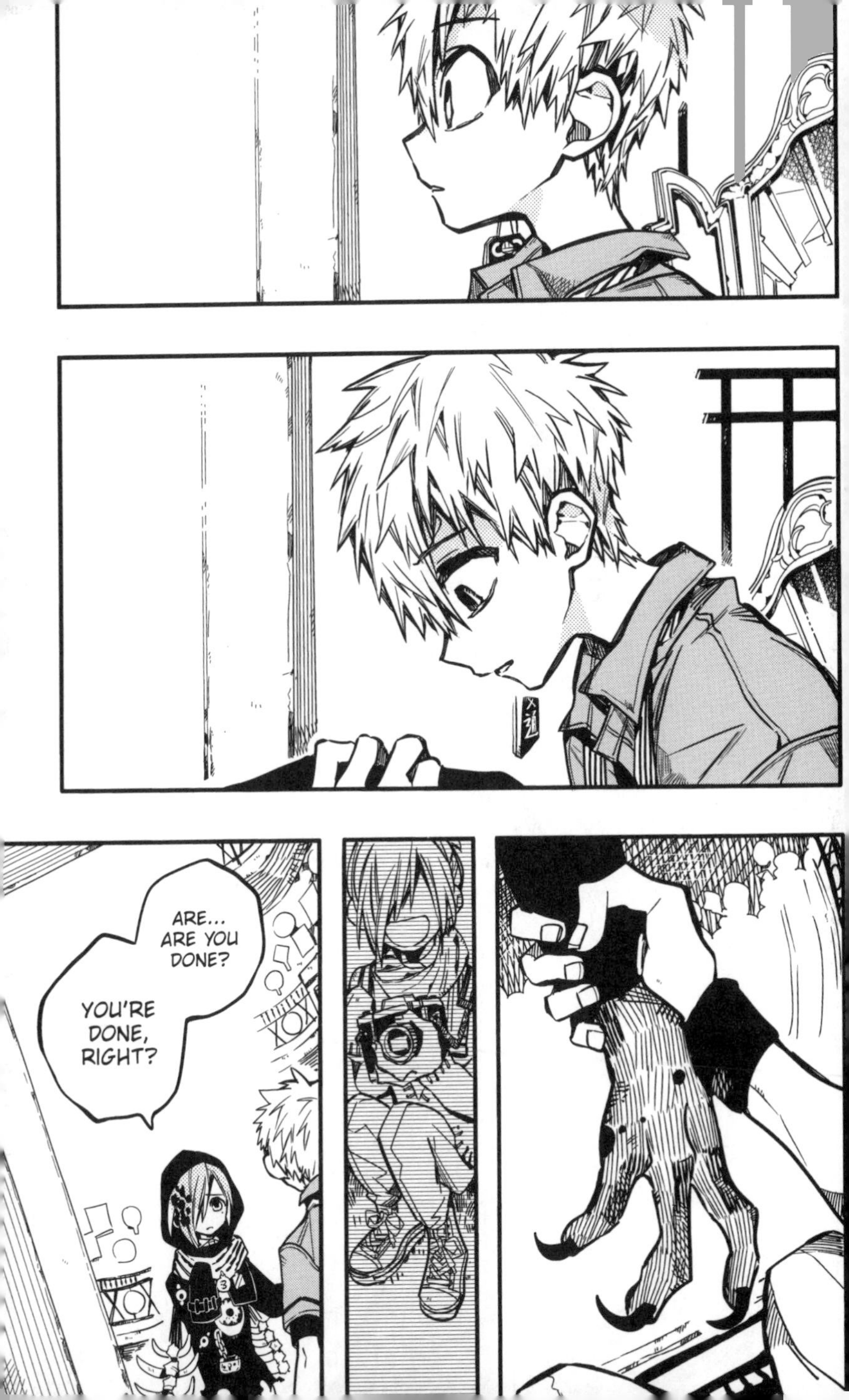
ARE... ARE YOU DONE?
YOU'RE DONE, RIGHT?

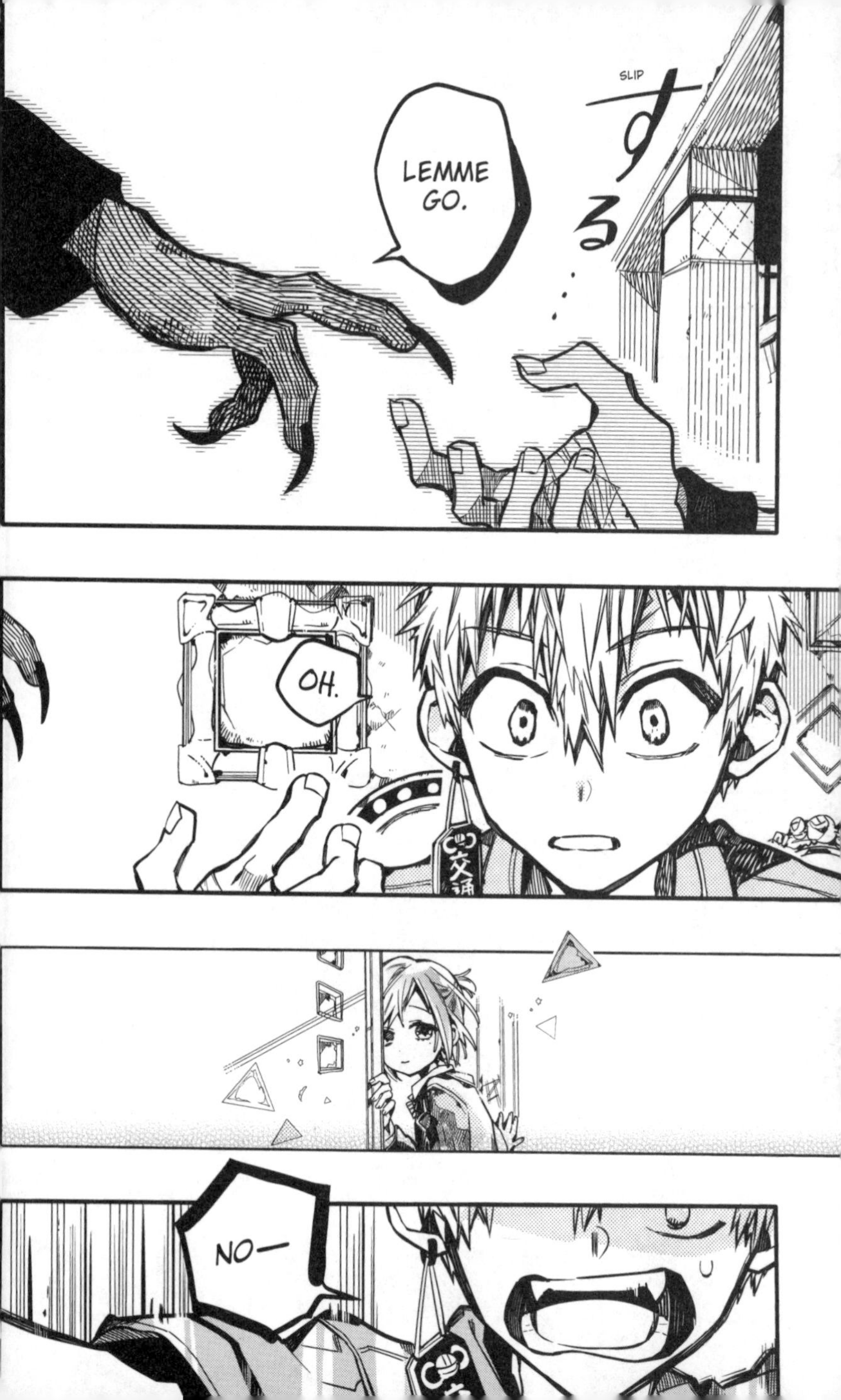
SLIP
する・・・
LEMME GO.
OH.
NO—

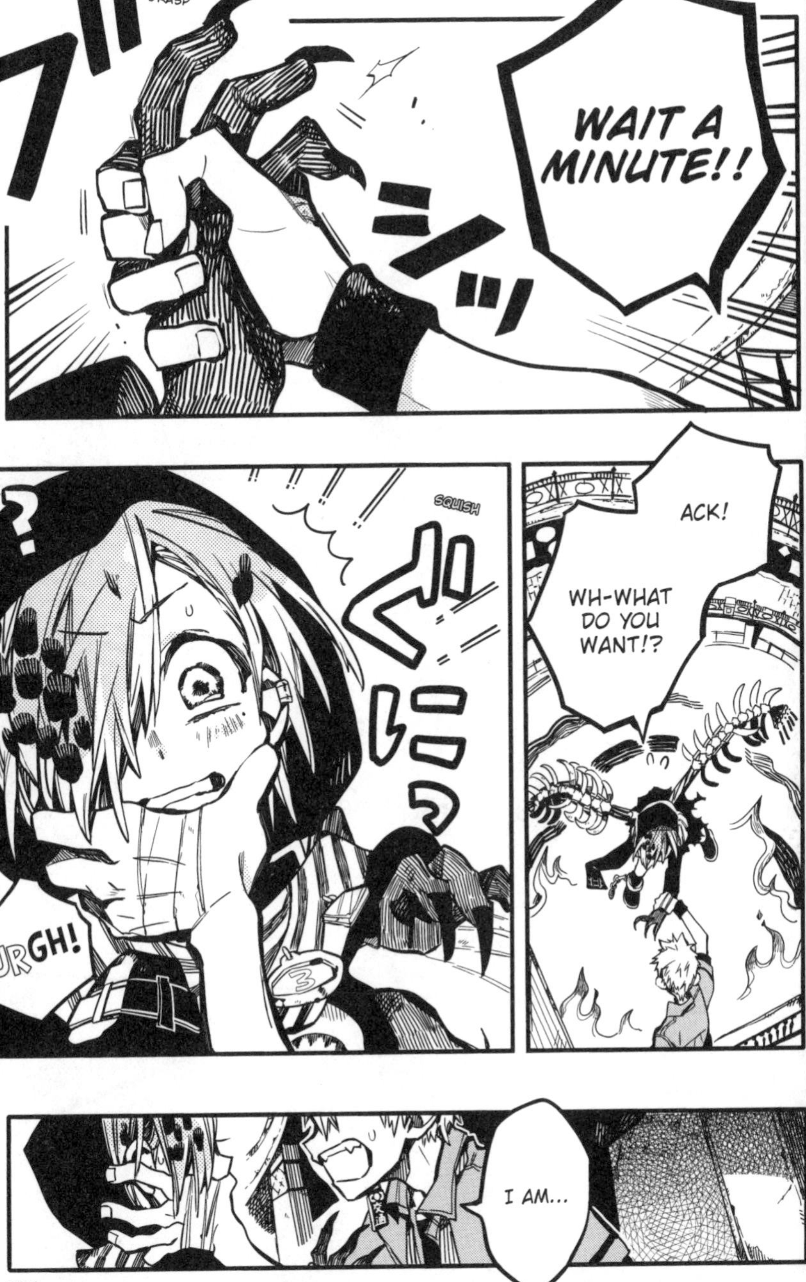
GRASP
WAIT A MINUTE!!
ACK!
WH-WHAT DO YOU WANT!?
!?
SQUISH
URGH!
I AM...

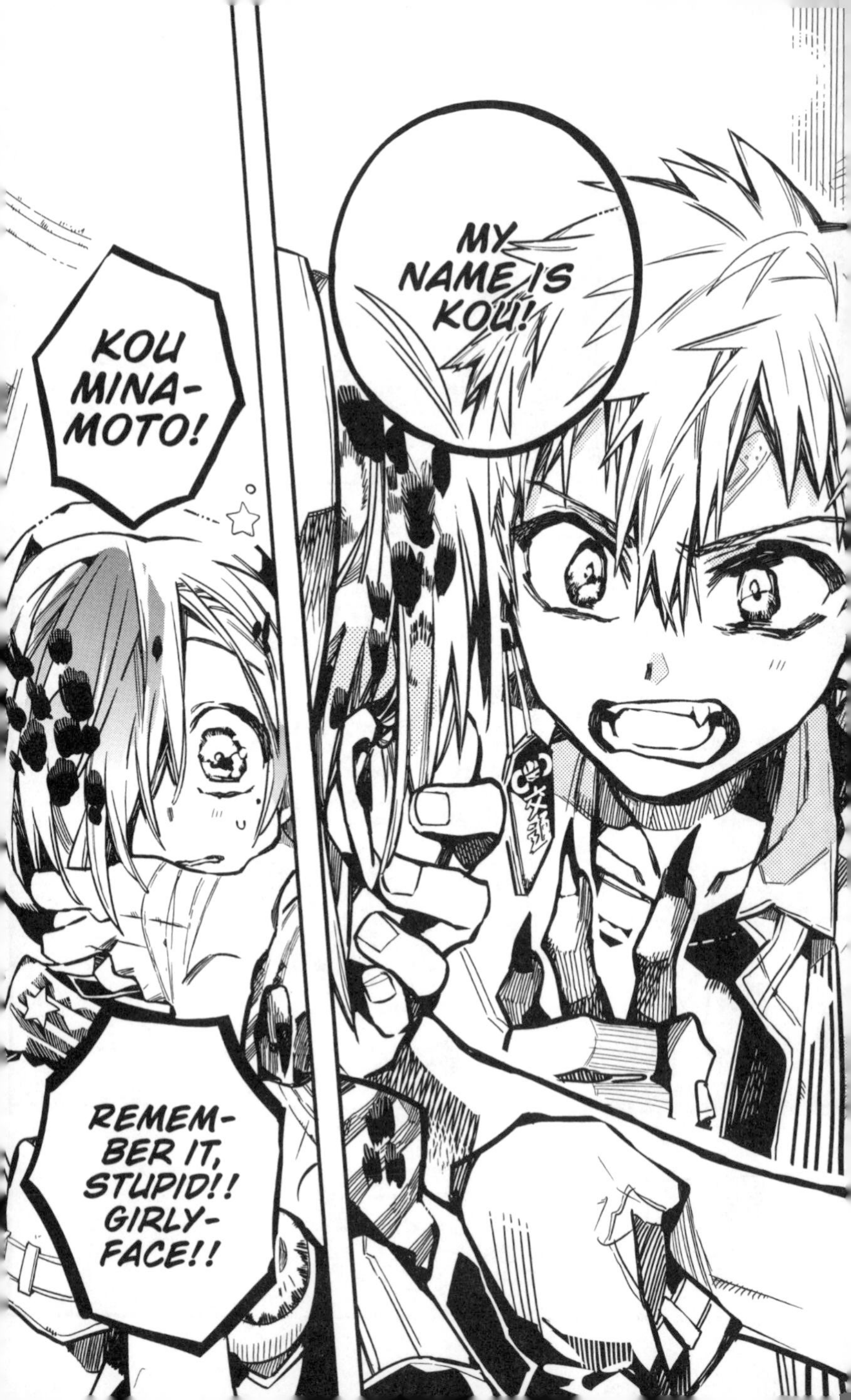
MY NAME IS KOU!
KOU MINA-MOTO!
REMEM-BER IT, STUPID!! GIRLY-FACE!!

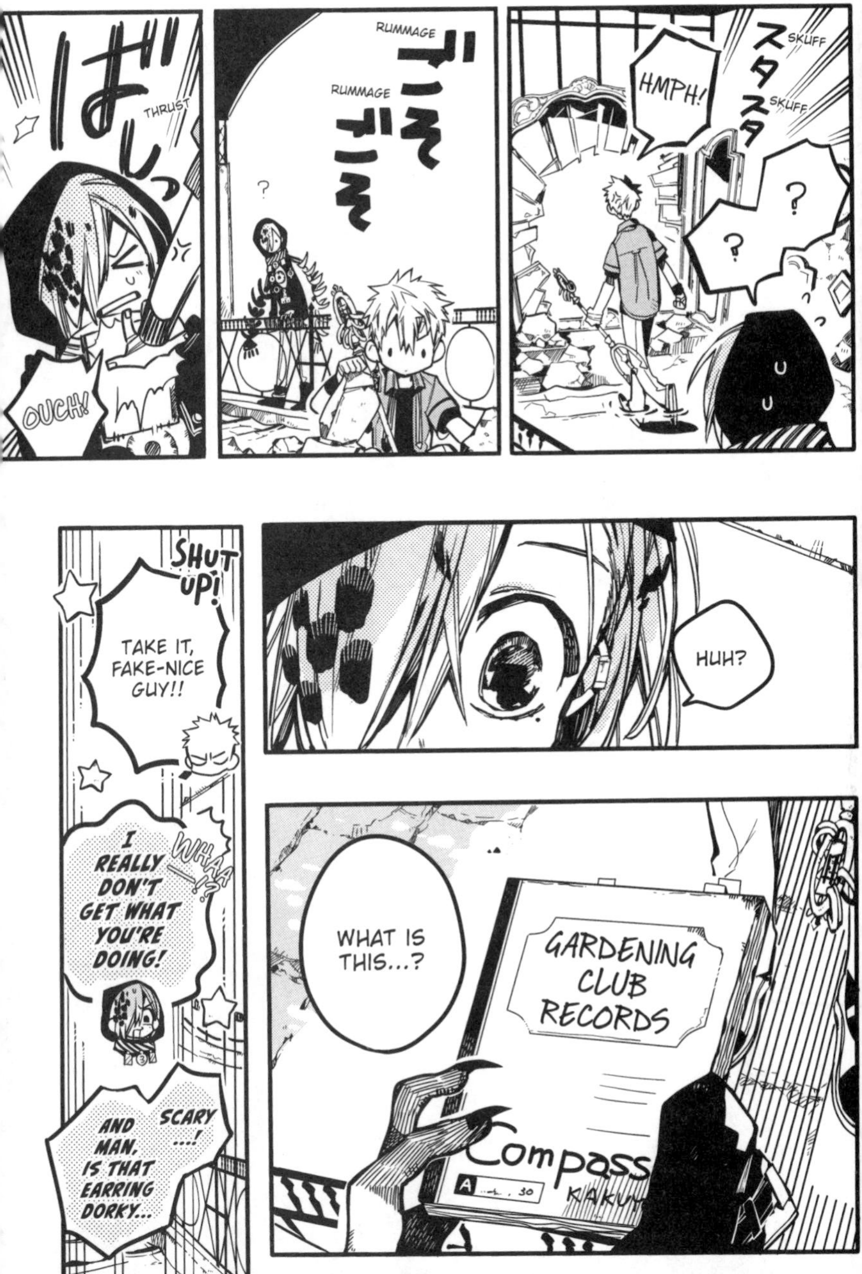
スタ
SKUFF
スタ
SKUFF
HMPH!
?
?
ごそ
RUMMAGE
ごそ
RUMMAGE
?
ばしっ
THRUST
OUCH!
HUH?
WHAT IS THIS...?
GARDENING CLUB RECORDS
Compass
SHUT UP!
TAKE IT, FAKE-NICE GUY!!
WHAA...!?
I REALLY DON'T GET WHAT YOU'RE DOING!
SCARY...!
AND MAN, IS THAT EARRING DORKY...

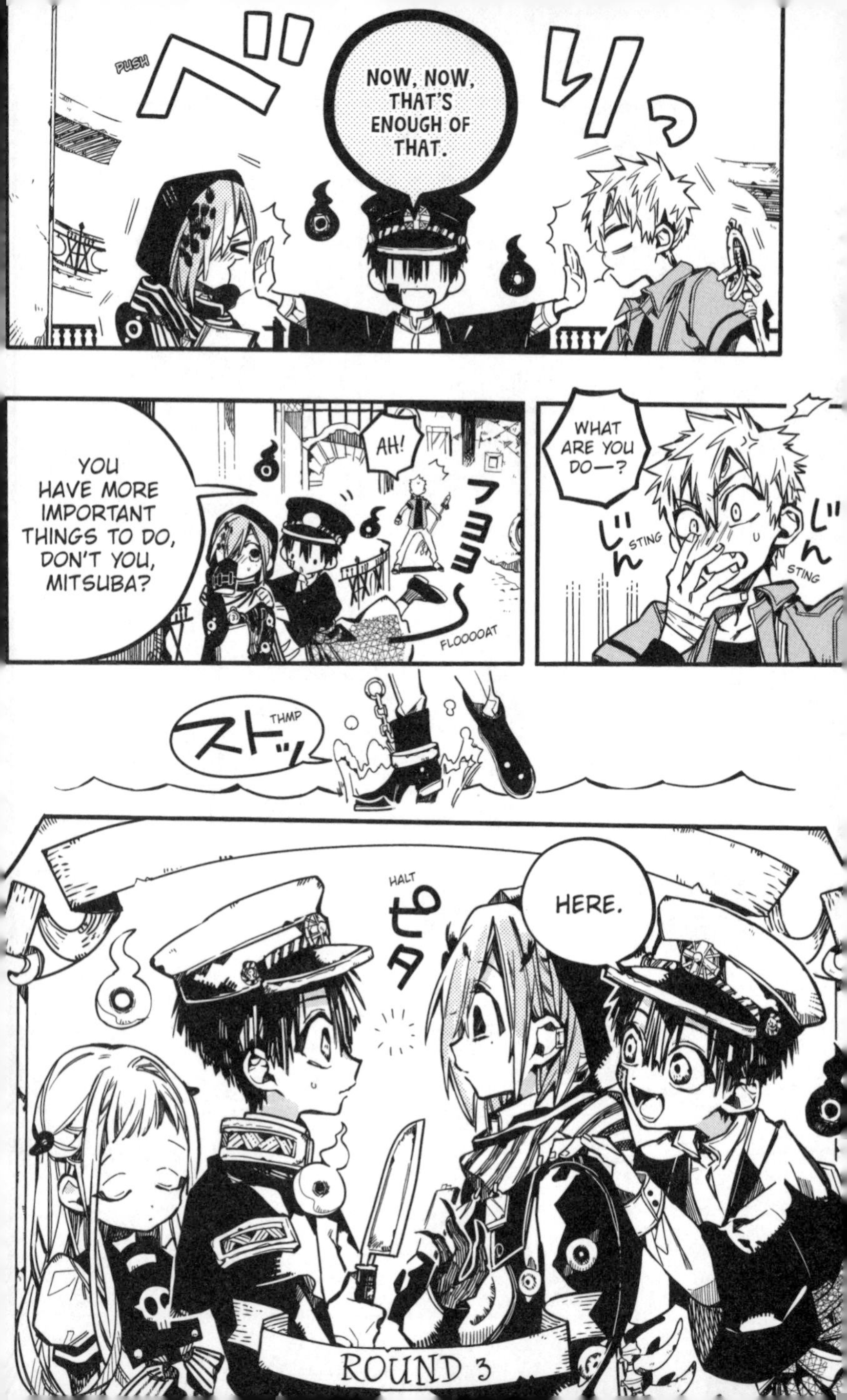
ベリッ
PUSH
NOW, NOW, THAT'S ENOUGH OF THAT.
WHAT ARE YOU DO—?
じん
STING
じん
STING
AH!
フヨヨ
FLOOOOAT
YOU HAVE MORE IMPORTANT THINGS TO DO, DON'T YOU, MITSUBA?
ストッ
THMP
HERE.
ピタ
HALT
ROUND 3

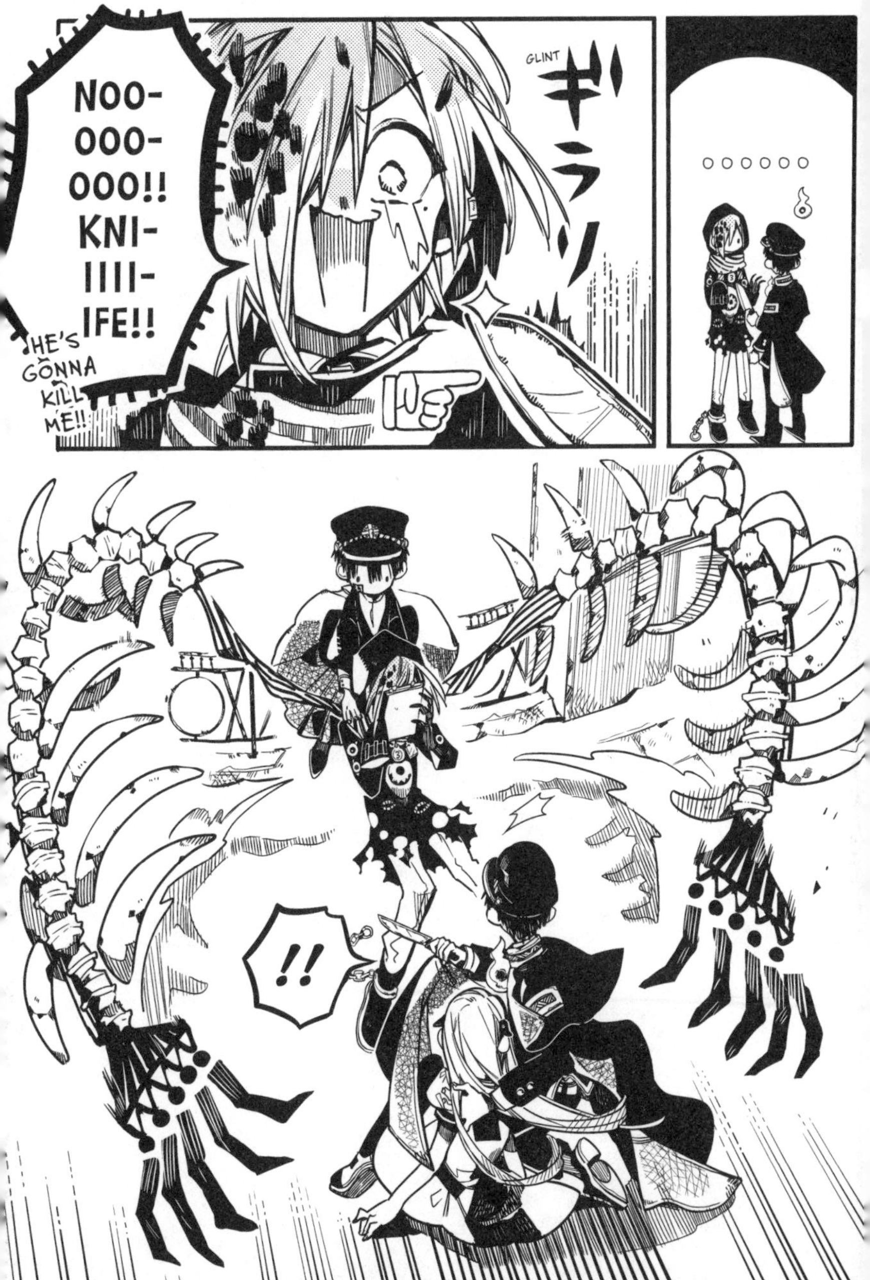
NOO-
OOO-
OOO!!
KNI-
IIII-
IFE!!
GLINT
ギラリ
HE'S GONNA KILL ME!!
!!

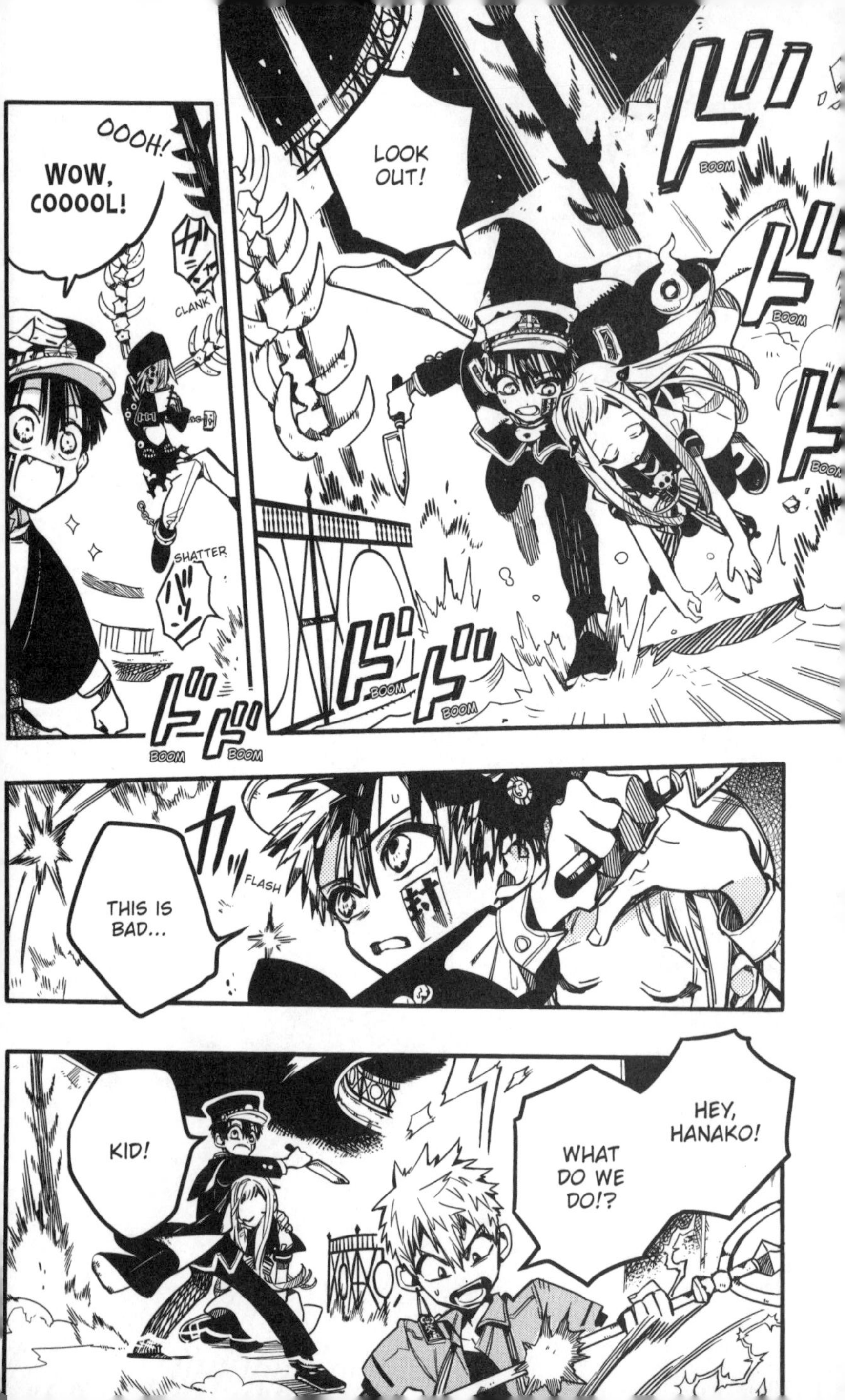
LOOK OUT!
BOOM
BOOM
BOOM
BOOM
BOOM
OOOH!
WOW, COOOOL!
CLANK
SHATTER
BOOM
BOOM
FLASH
THIS IS BAD...
HEY, HANAKO!
WHAT DO WE DO!?
KID!

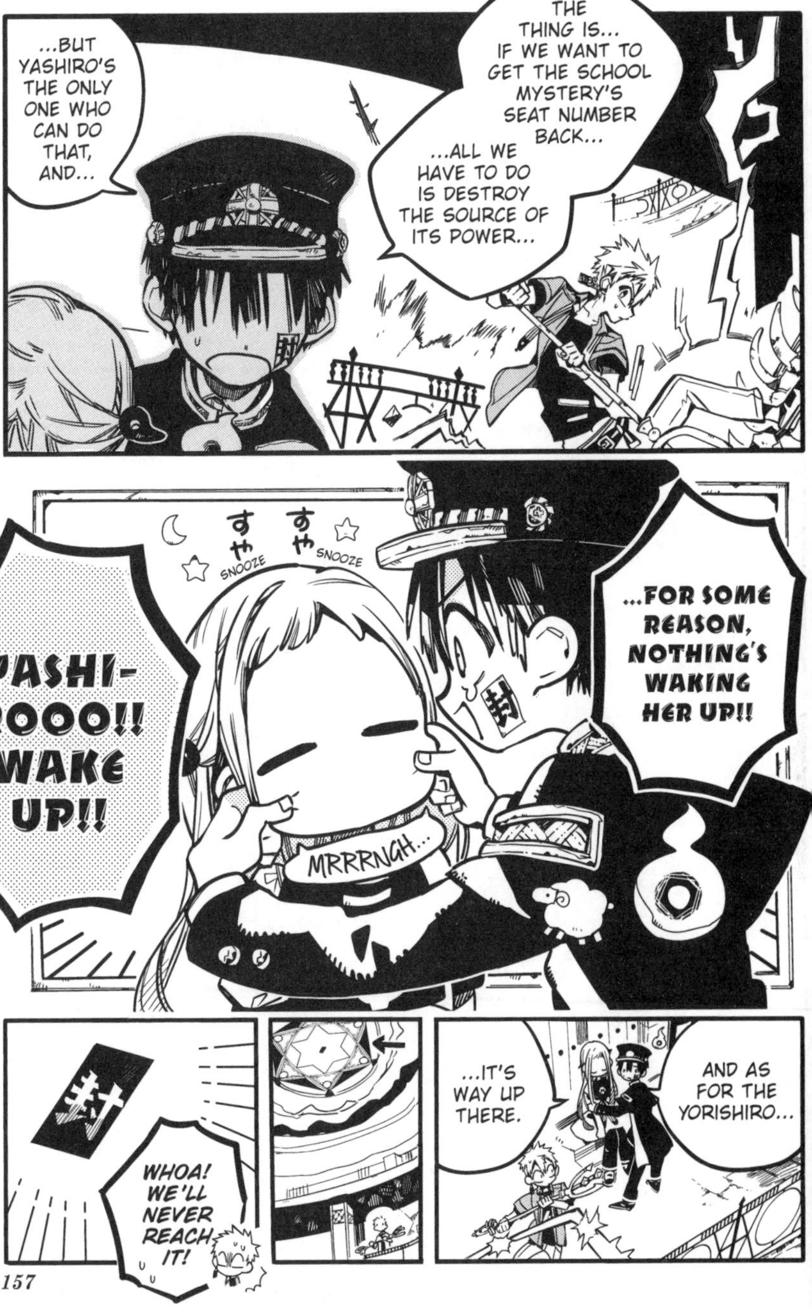
THE THING IS... IF WE WANT TO GET THE SCHOOL MYSTERY'S SEAT NUMBER BACK...
...ALL WE HAVE TO DO IS DESTROY THE SOURCE OF ITS POWER...
...BUT YASHIRO'S THE ONLY ONE WHO CAN DO THAT, AND...
...FOR SOME REASON, NOTHING'S WAKING HER UP!!
すや SNOOZE
すや SNOOZE
YASHI-ROOO!! WAKE UP!!
MRRRNGH...
AND AS FOR THE YORISHIRO...
...IT'S WAY UP THERE.
WHOA! WE'LL NEVER REACH IT!

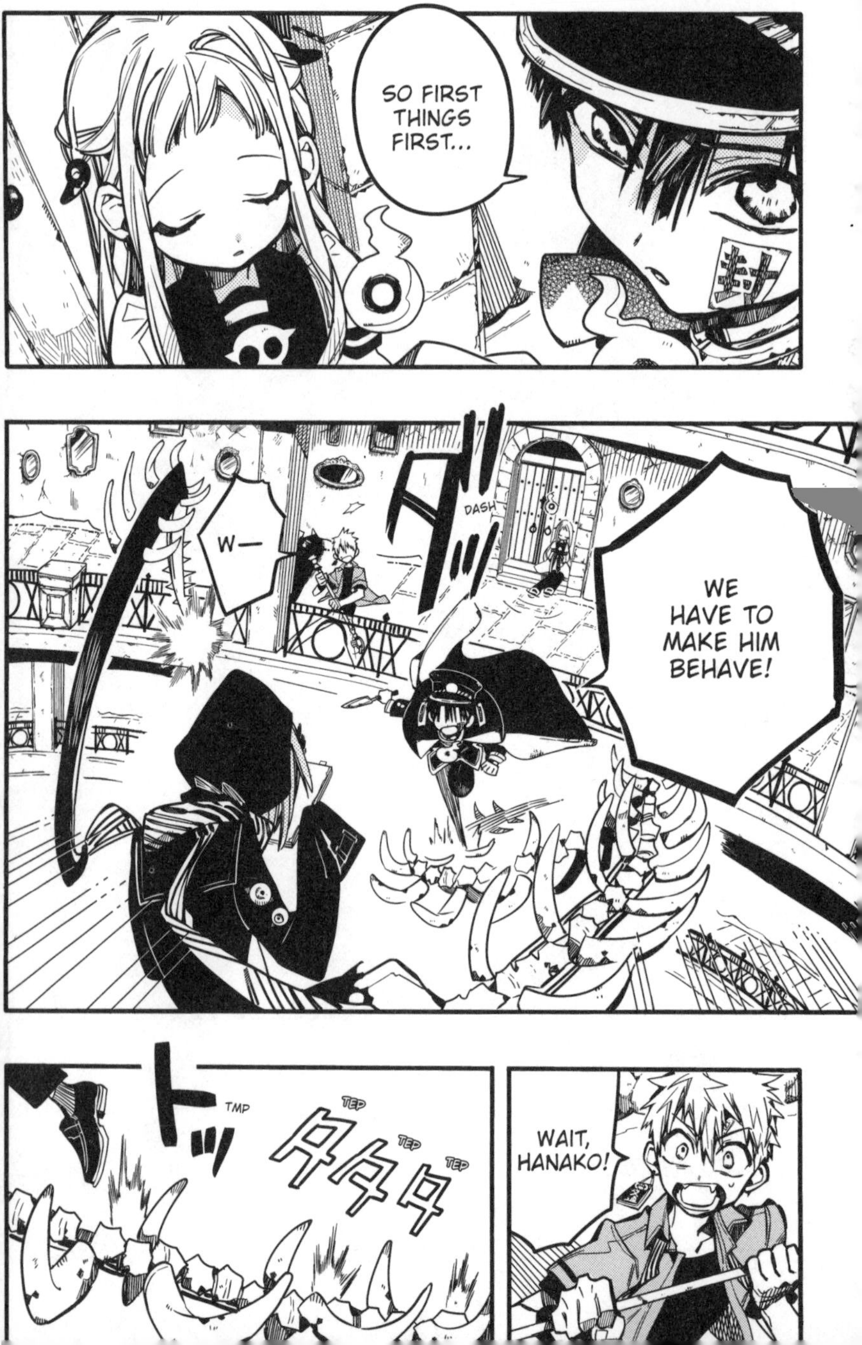
SO FIRST THINGS FIRST...
WE HAVE TO MAKE HIM BEHAVE!
DASH
W—
WAIT, HANAKO!
TMP
TEP
TEP
TEP

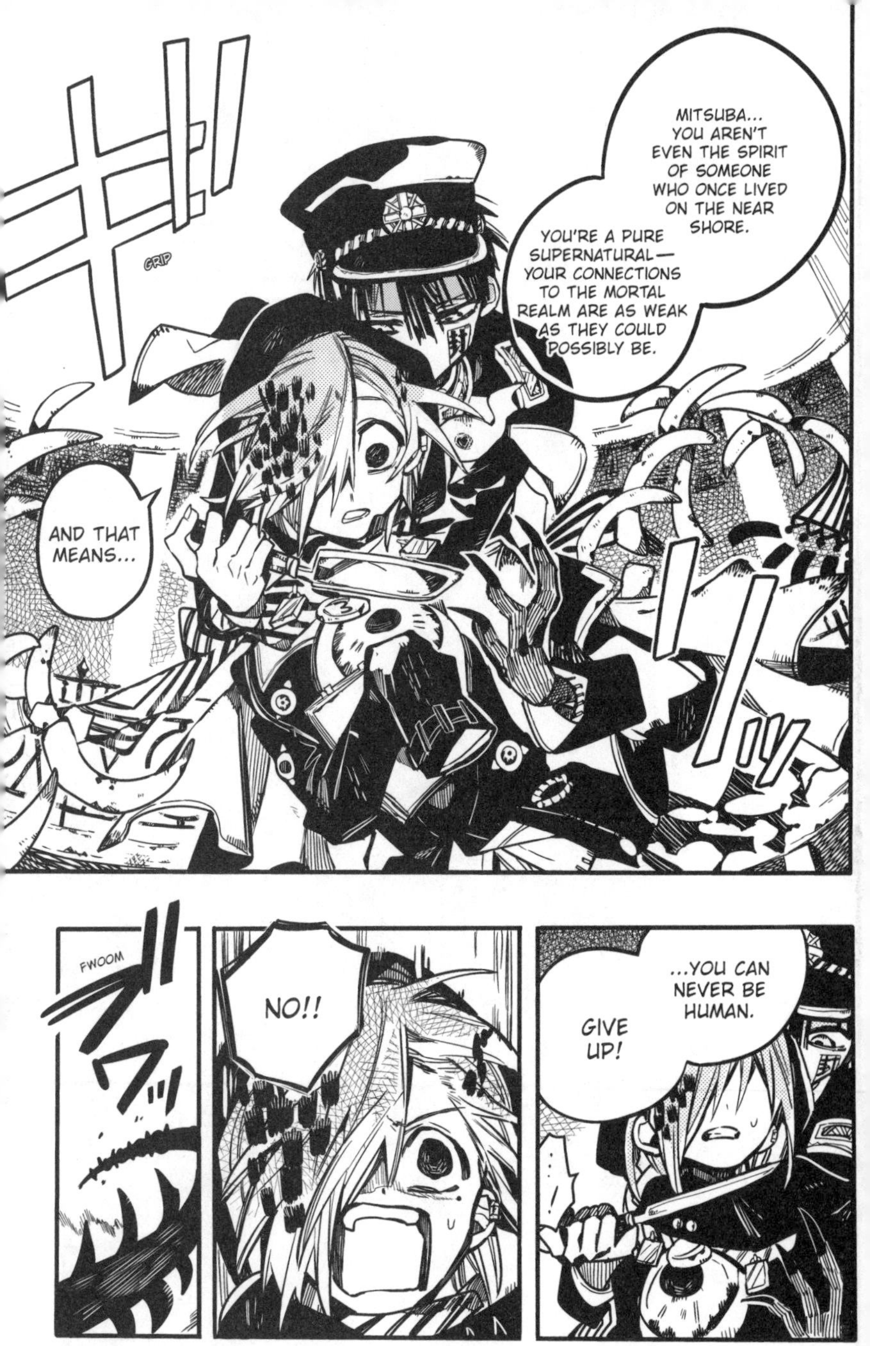
MITSUBA... YOU AREN'T EVEN THE SPIRIT OF SOMEONE WHO ONCE LIVED ON THE NEAR SHORE.
YOU'RE A PURE SUPERNATURAL— YOUR CONNECTIONS TO THE MORTAL REALM ARE AS WEAK AS THEY COULD POSSIBLY BE.
GRIP
AND THAT MEANS...
...YOU CAN NEVER BE HUMAN.
GIVE UP!
NO!!
FWOOM

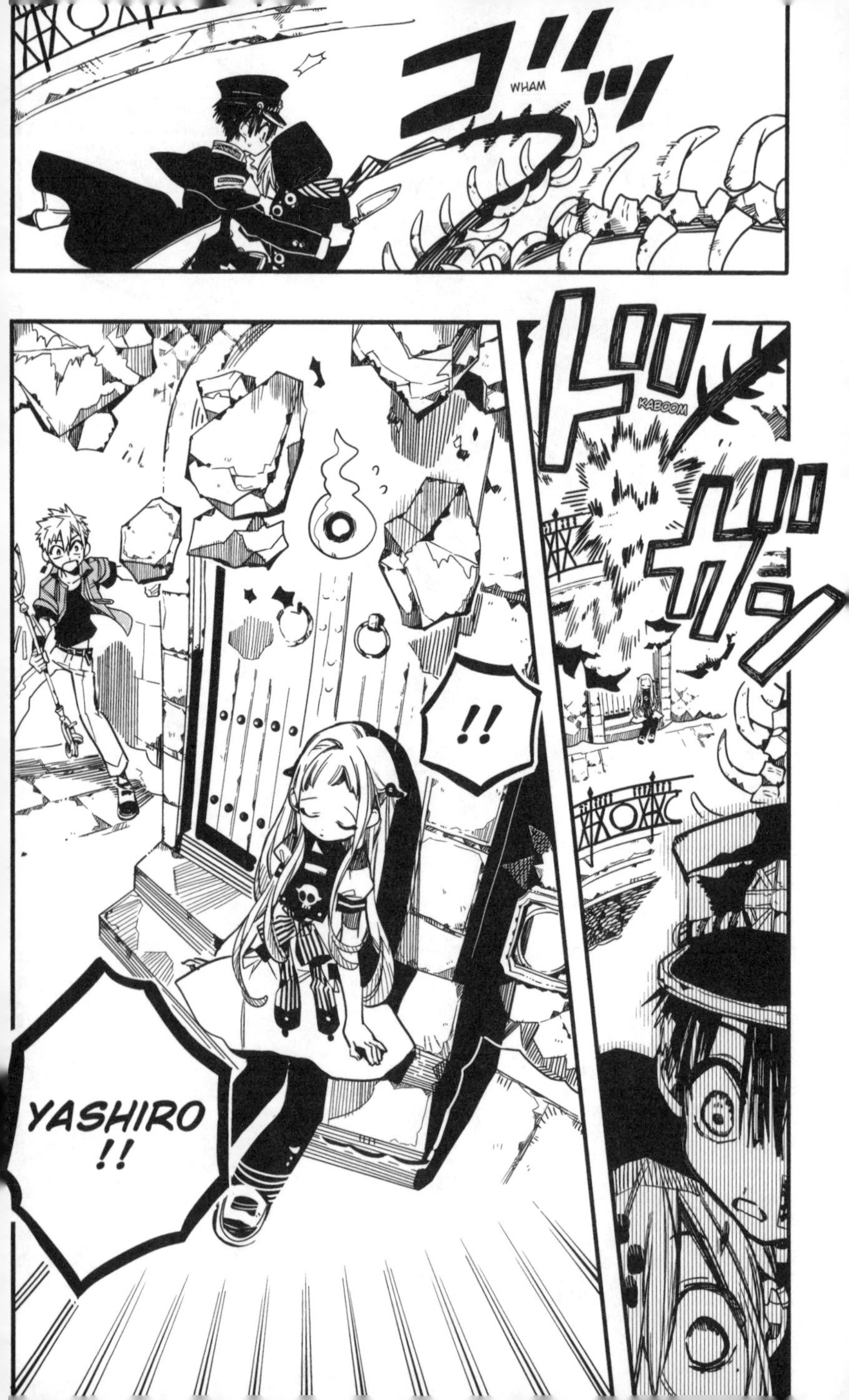
WHAM
KABOOM
!!
YASHIRO !!

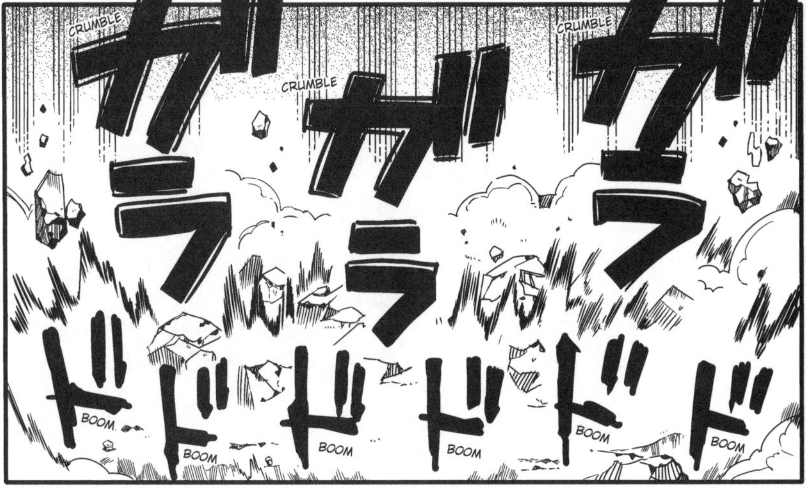
ガラ
CRUMBLE
ガラ
CRUMBLE
ガラ
CRUMBLE
ドドドドドド
BOOM
BOOM
BOOM
BOOM
BOOM
BOOM

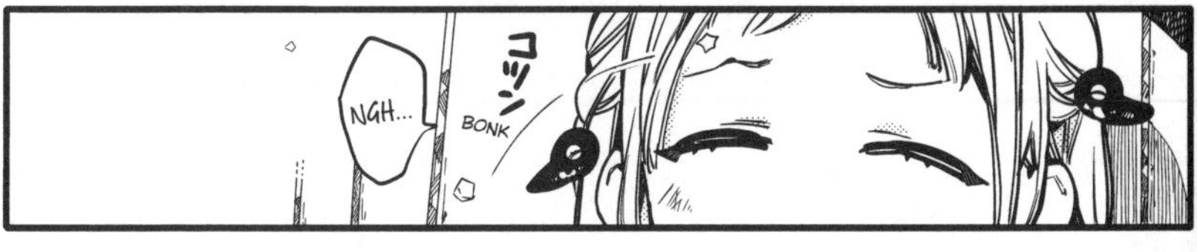
コツン
BONK
NGH...

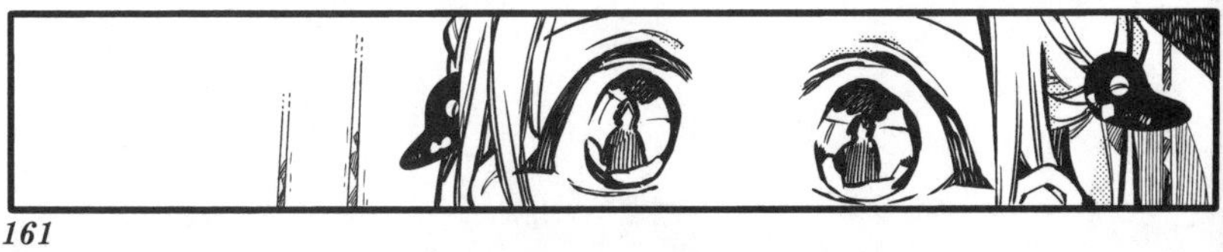

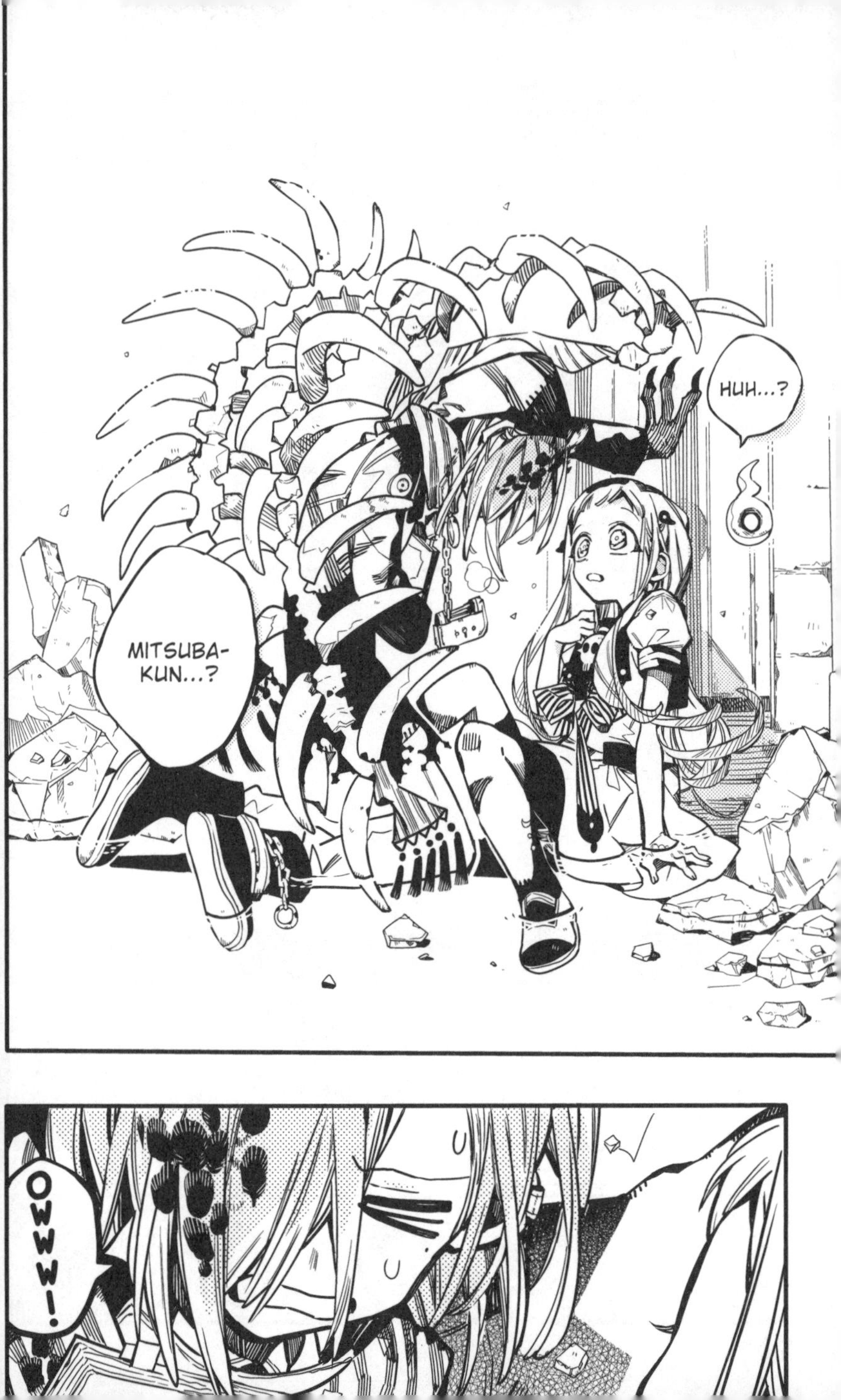
HUH...?
MITSUBA-KUN...?
OWWW!

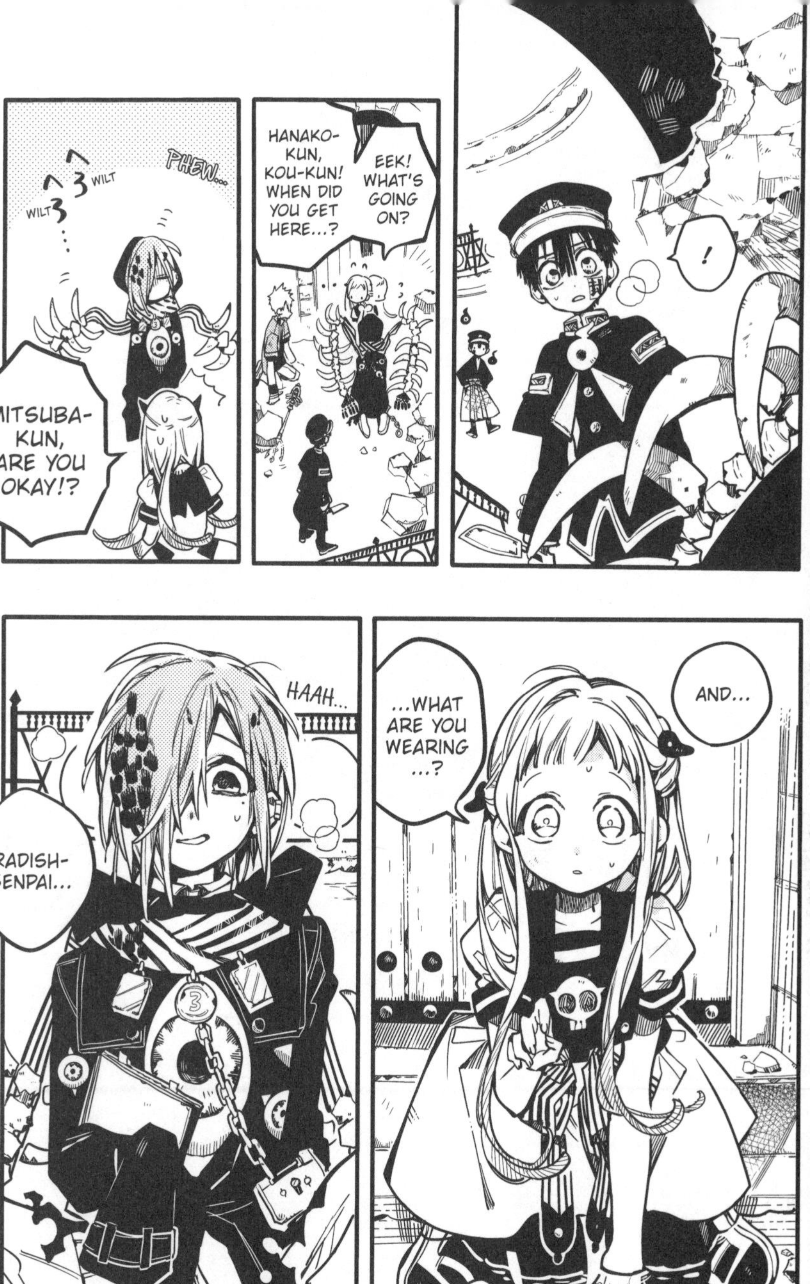
!
EEK! WHAT'S GOING ON?
HANAKO-KUN, KOU-KUN! WHEN DID YOU GET HERE...?
PHEW...
WILT
WILT
MITSUBA-KUN, ARE YOU OKAY!?
AND...
...WHAT ARE YOU WEARING ...?
HAAH...
RADISH-SENPAI...

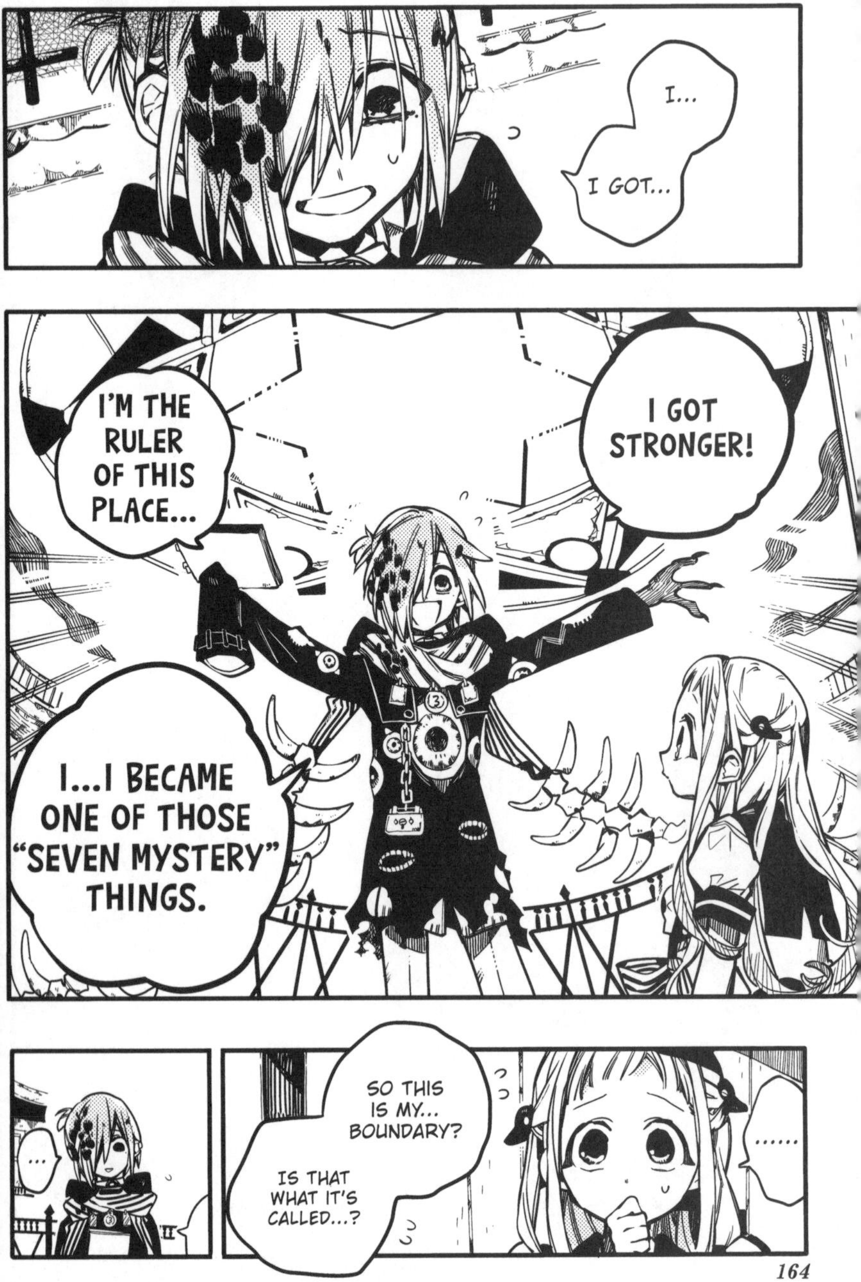
I...
I GOT...
I GOT STRONGER!
I'M THE RULER OF THIS PLACE...
I...I BECAME ONE OF THOSE "SEVEN MYSTERY" THINGS.
......
SO THIS IS MY... BOUNDARY?
IS THAT WHAT IT'S CALLED...?
...

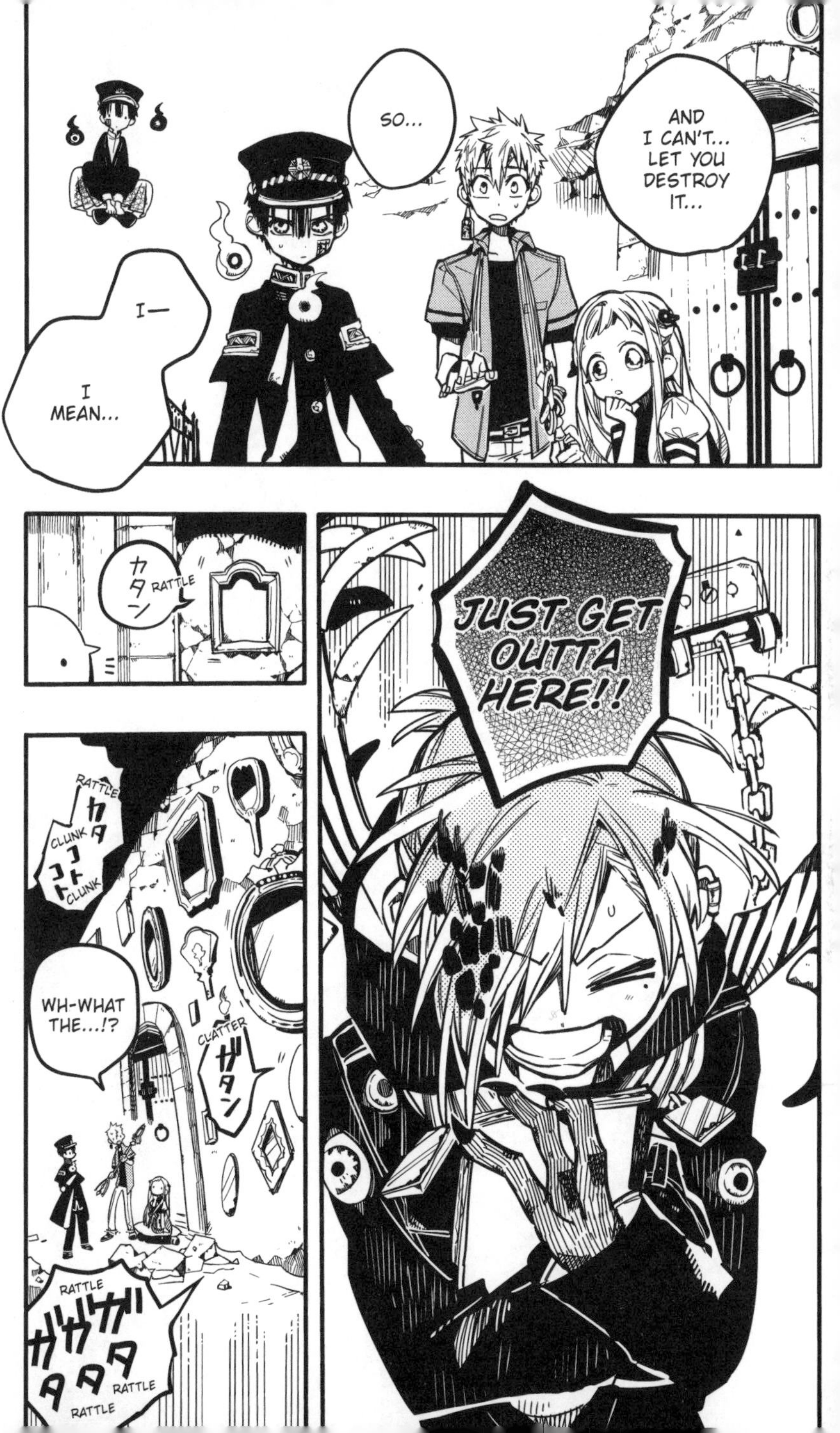
AND I CAN'T... LET YOU DESTROY IT...
SO...
I—
I MEAN...
JUST GET OUTTA HERE!!
カタン
RATTLE
RATTLE
カタ
CLUNK
コトコト
CLUNK
CLATTER
ガタン
WH-WHAT THE...!?
RATTLE
ガガガタタタ
RATTLE
RATTLE

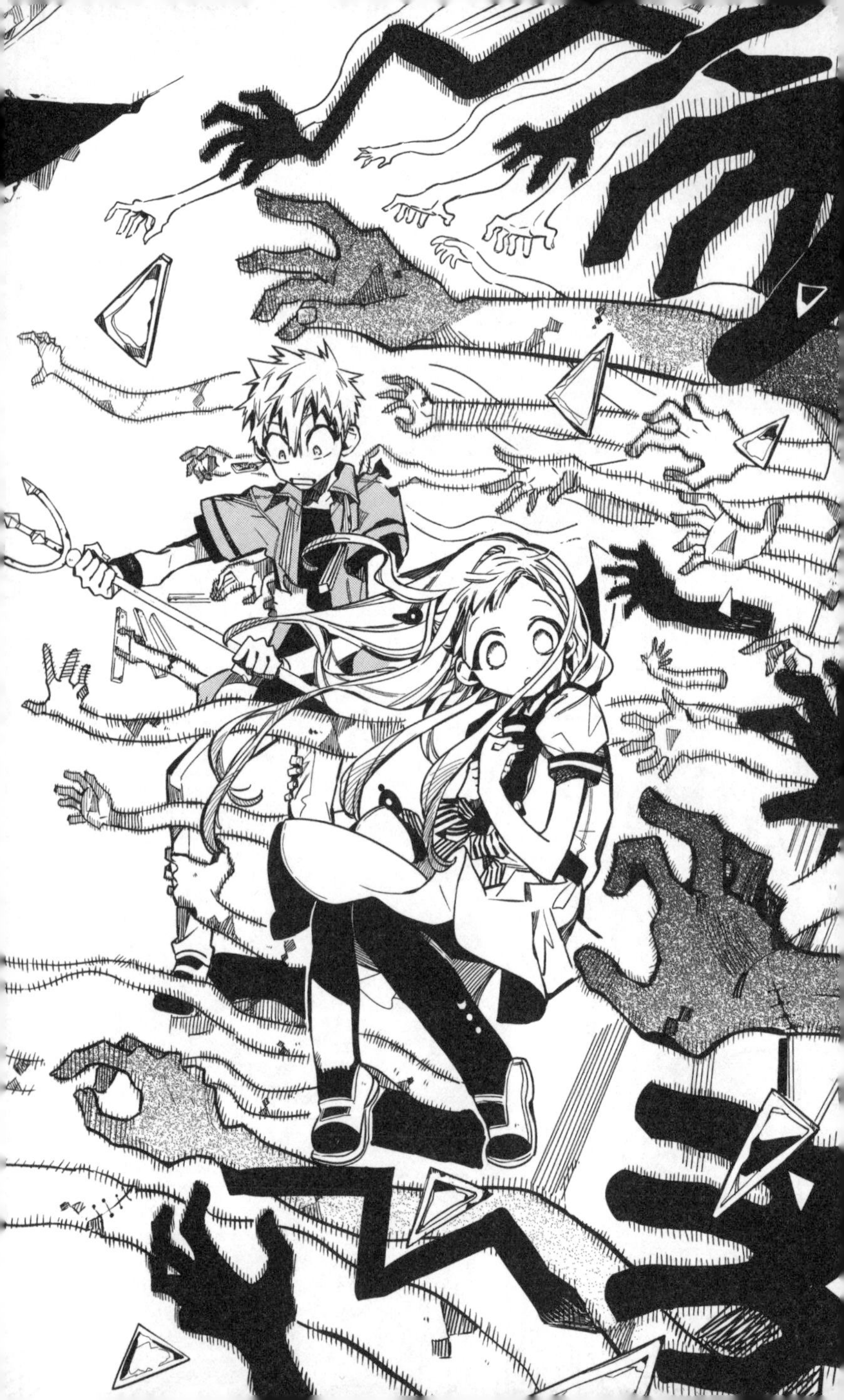

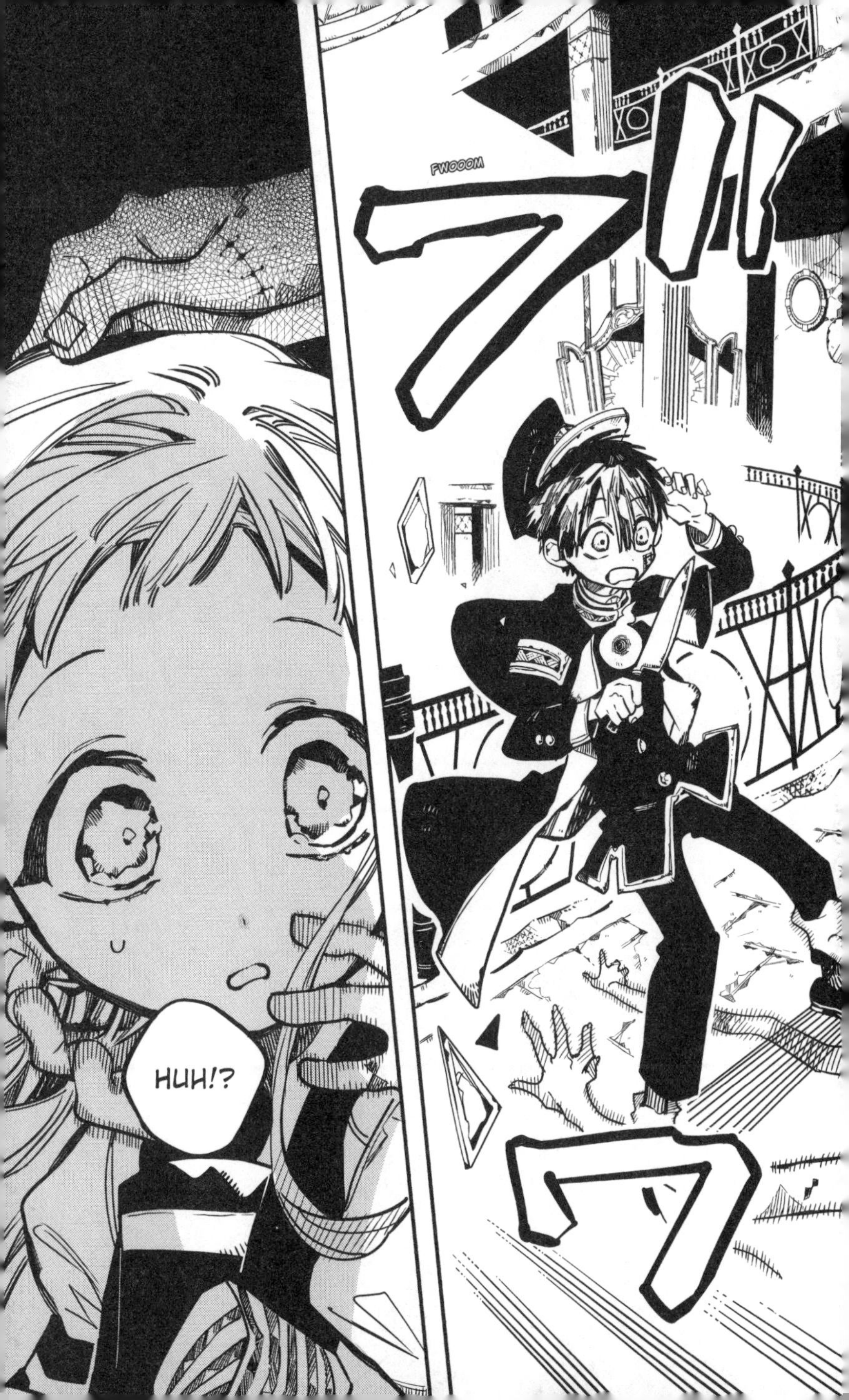
FWOOOM
HUH!?

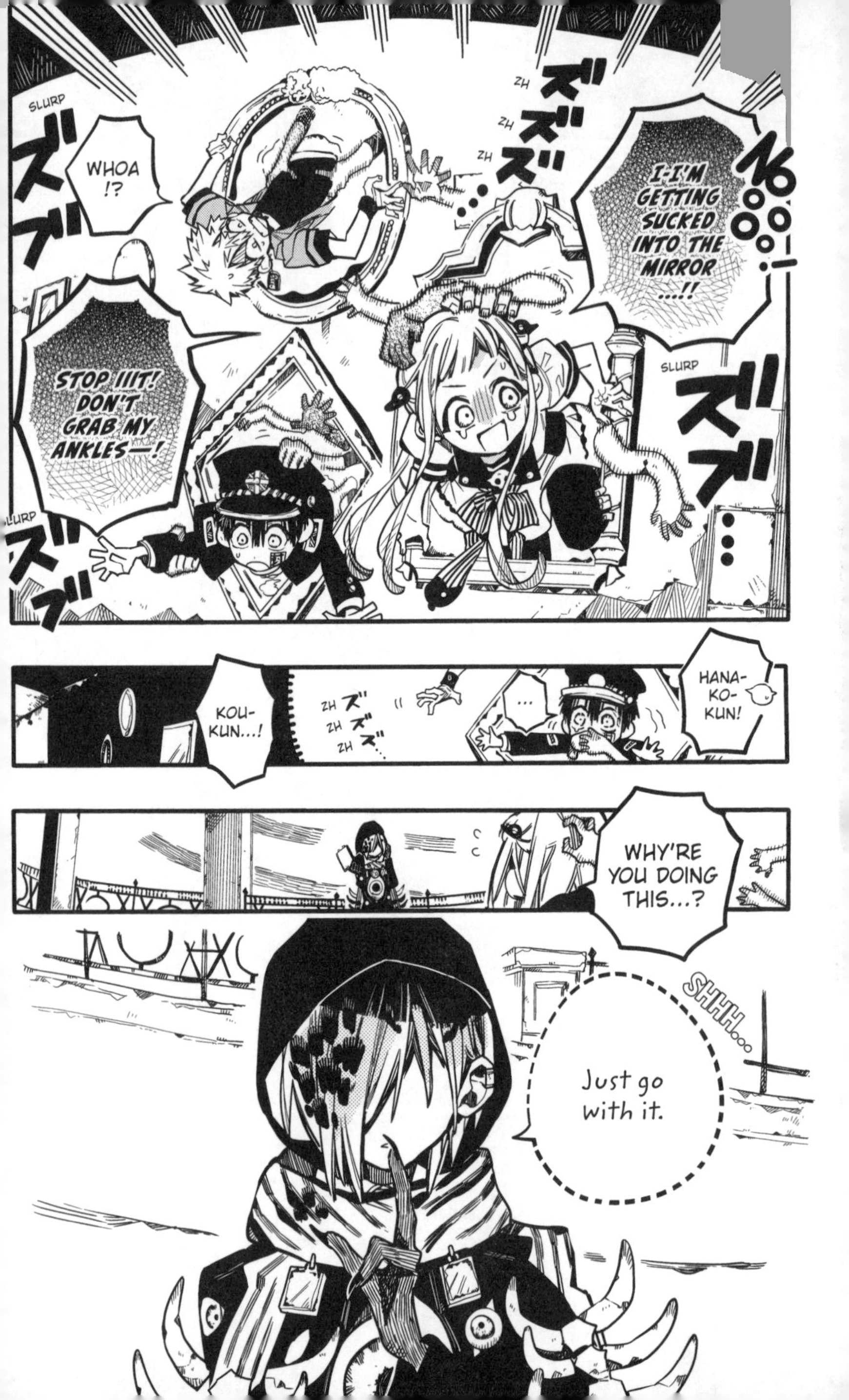
NOOOO—!
I-I'M GETTING SUCKED INTO THE MIRROR ....!!
ZH
ZH
ZH
WHOA !?
SLURP
SLURP
STOP IIIT! DON'T GRAB MY ANKLES—!
SLURP
HANA-KO-KUN!
...
ZH
ZH
ZH
KOU-KUN...!
WHY'RE YOU DOING THIS...?
SHHH...
Just go with it.

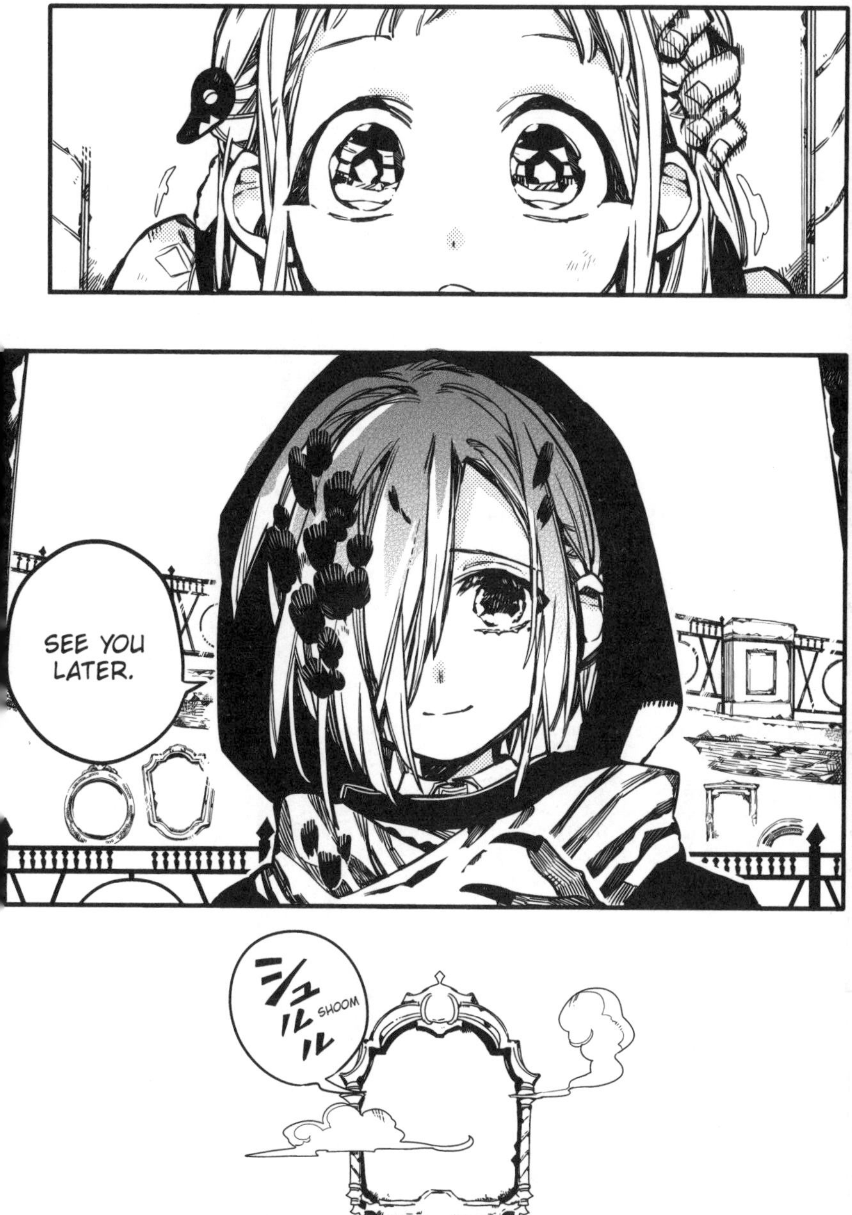
SEE YOU LATER.
シュルル
SHOOM

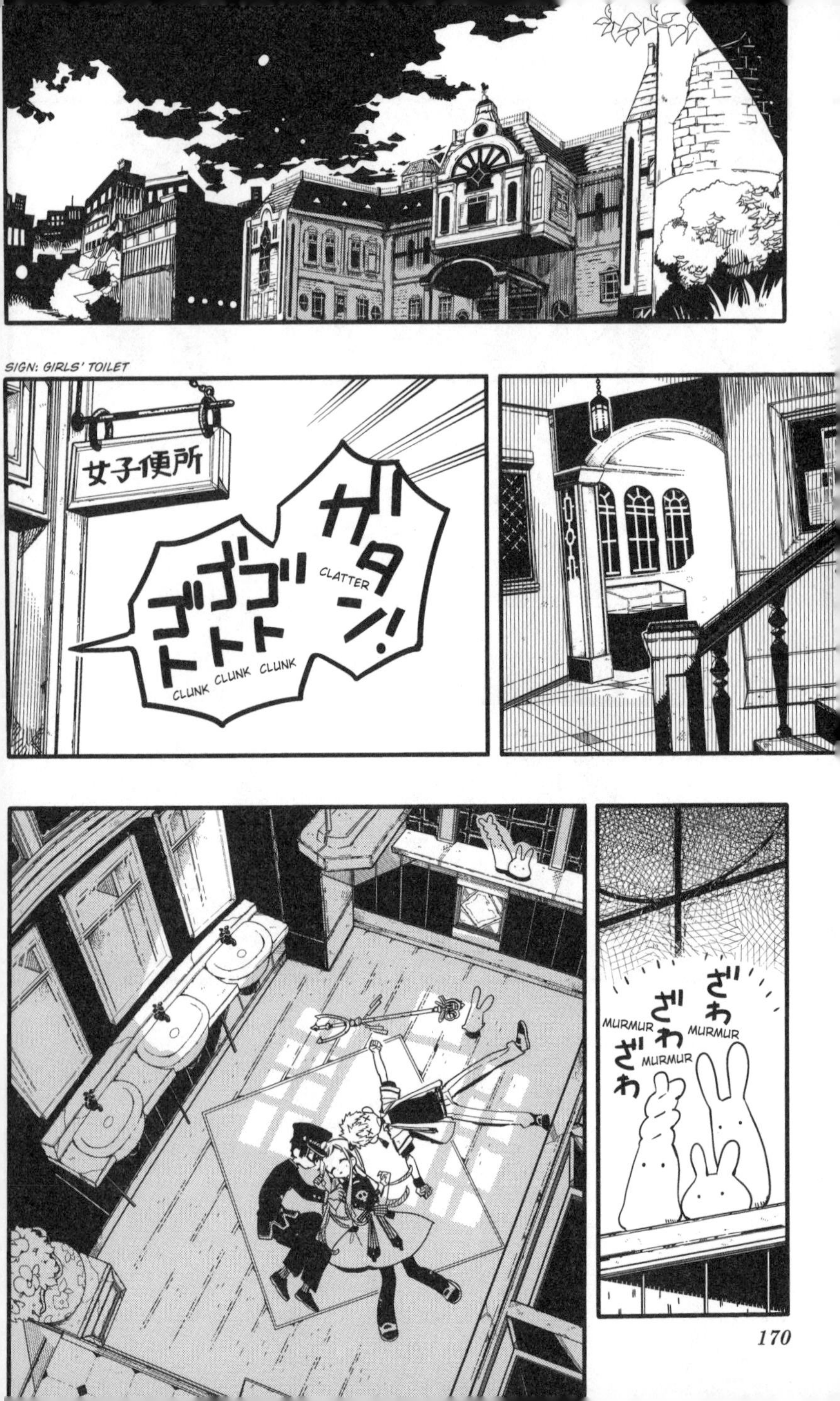
SIGN: GIRLS' TOILET
女子便所
ガターン!
CLATTER
ゴトゴトゴト
CLUNK CLUNK CLUNK
ざわざわざわ
MURMUR MURMUR MURMUR

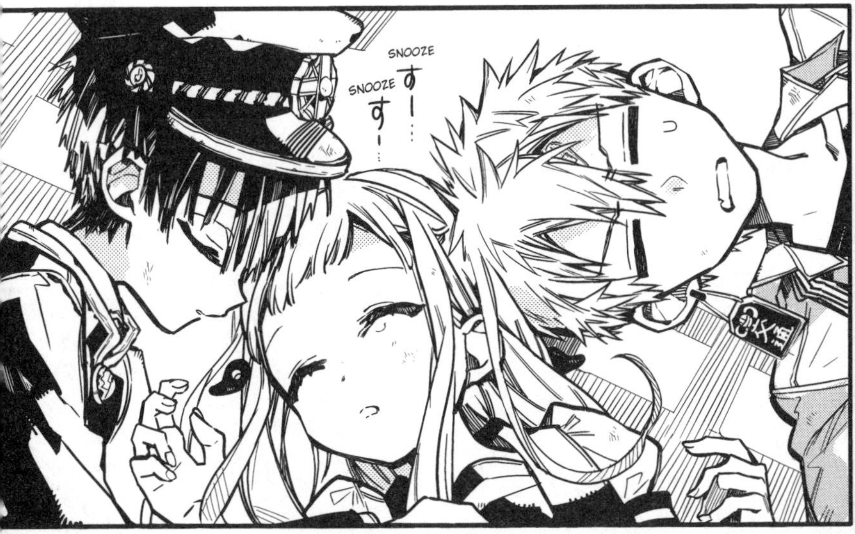
SNOOZE すー…
SNOOZE すー…

MEANWHILE...

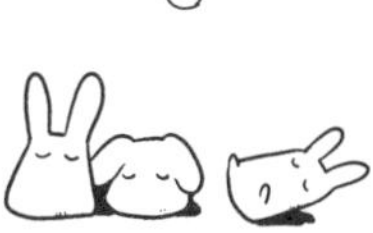

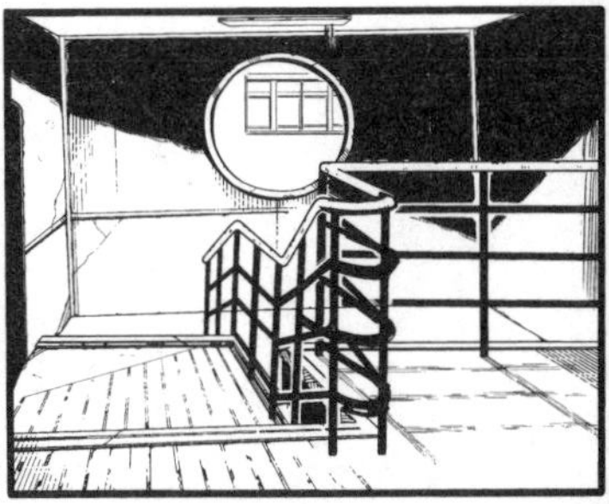

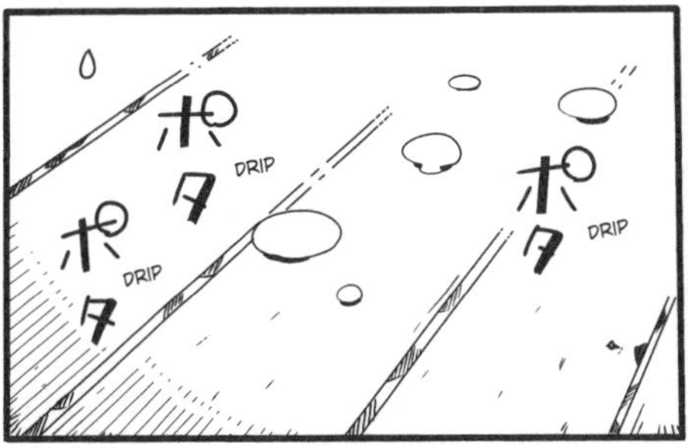
ポタ DRIP
ポタ DRIP
ポタ DRIP

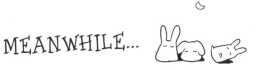

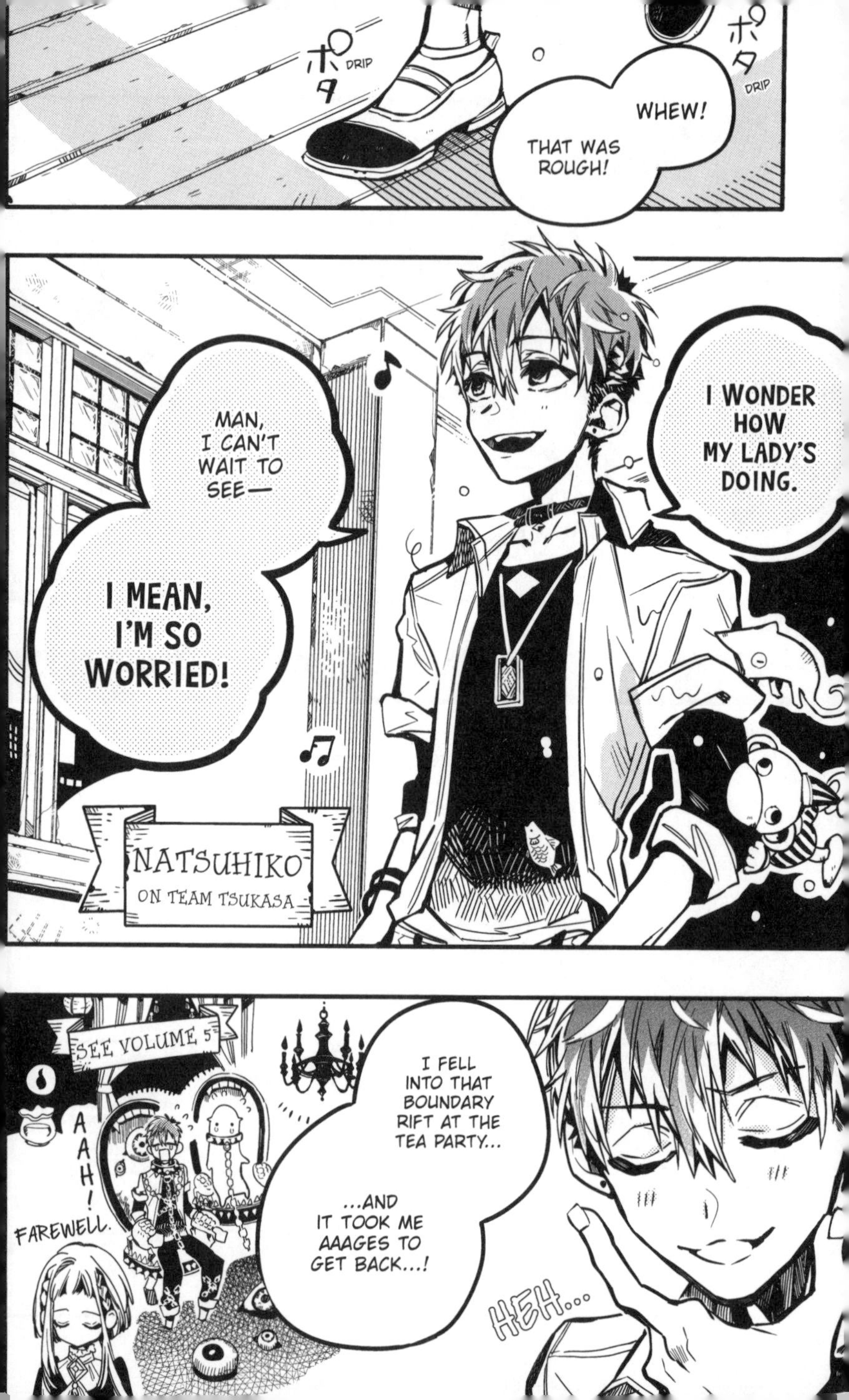
ポタ DRIP
WHEW!
THAT WAS ROUGH!
ポタ DRIP
I WONDER HOW MY LADY'S DOING.
MAN, I CAN'T WAIT TO SEE—
I MEAN, I'M SO WORRIED!
NATSUHIKO
ON TEAM TSUKASA
I FELL INTO THAT BOUNDARY RIFT AT THE TEA PARTY...
...AND IT TOOK ME AAAGES TO GET BACK...!
HEH...
SEE VOLUME 5
AAH!
FAREWELL.

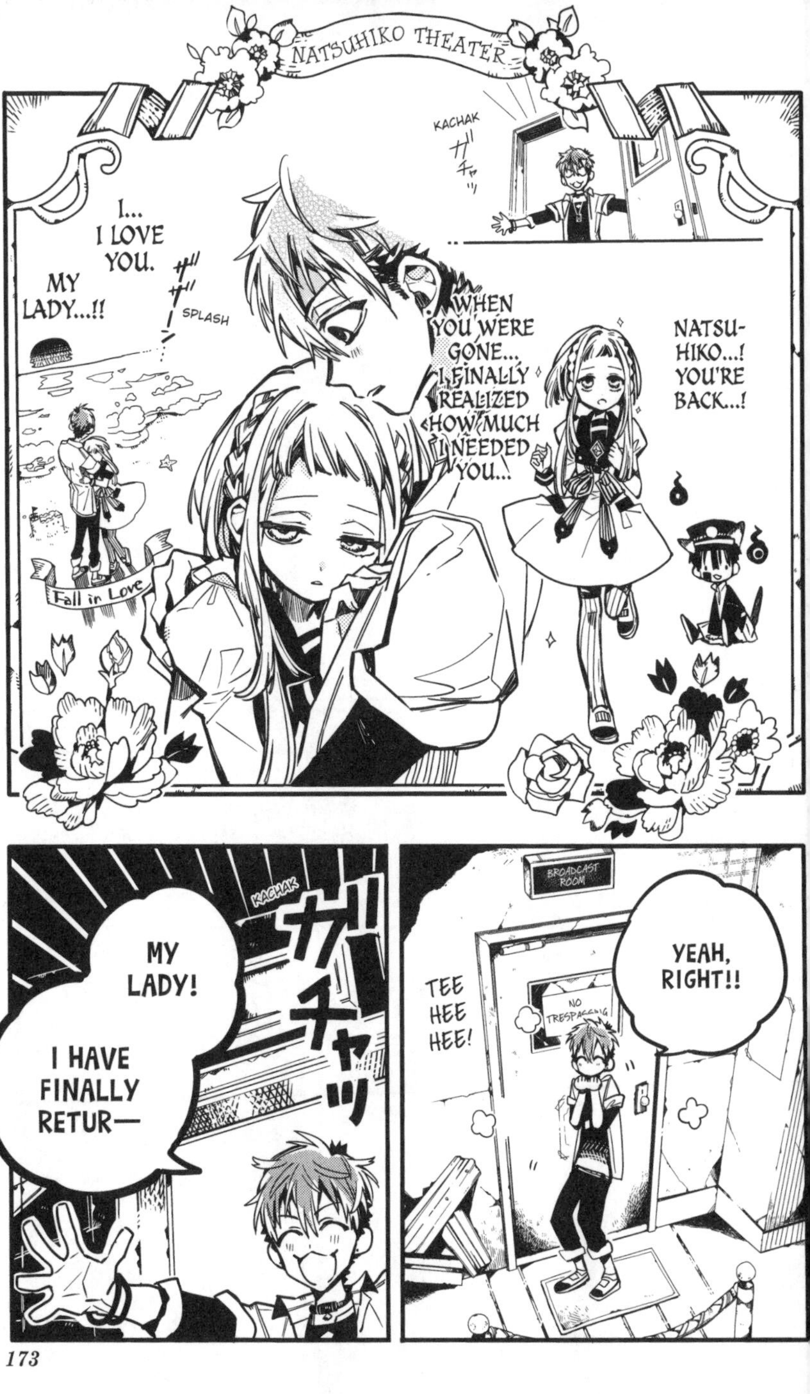
NATSUHIKO THEATER
KACHAK
ガチャッ
NATSUHIKO...! YOU'RE BACK...!
WHEN YOU WERE GONE... I FINALLY REALIZED HOW MUCH I NEEDED YOU...
I... I LOVE YOU.
MY LADY...!!
ザザー
SPLASH
Fall in Love
BROADCAST ROOM
YEAH, RIGHT!!
NO TRESPASSING
TEE HEE HEE!
KACHAK
ガチャッ
MY LADY!
I HAVE FINALLY RETUR—

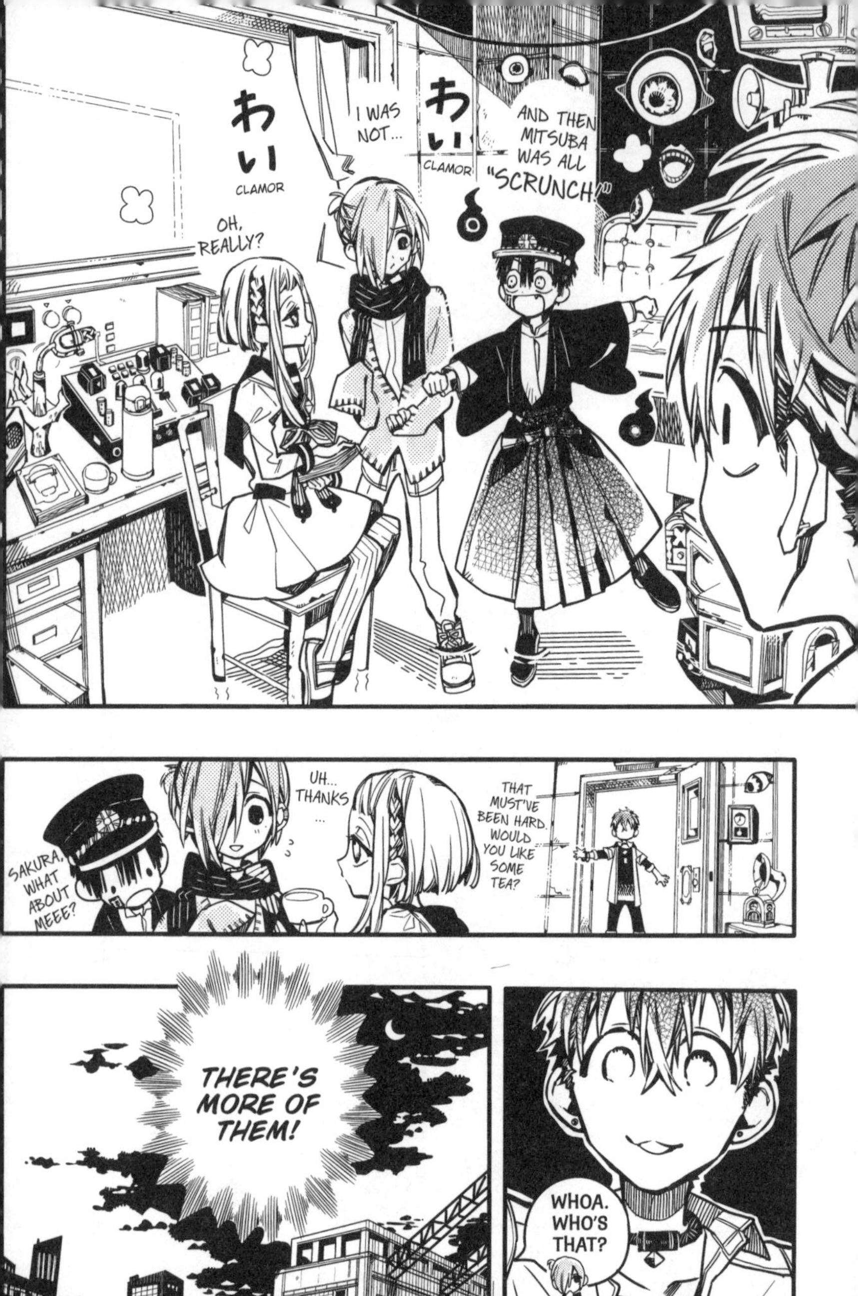
AND THEN MITSUBA WAS ALL "SCRUNCH!"
わい
CLAMOR
I WAS NOT...
わい
CLAMOR
OH, REALLY?
THAT MUST'VE BEEN HARD. WOULD YOU LIKE SOME TEA?
UH... THANKS
...
SAKURA, WHAT ABOUT MEEE?
WHOA. WHO'S THAT?
THERE'S MORE OF THEM!

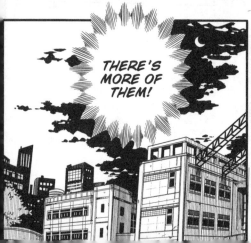

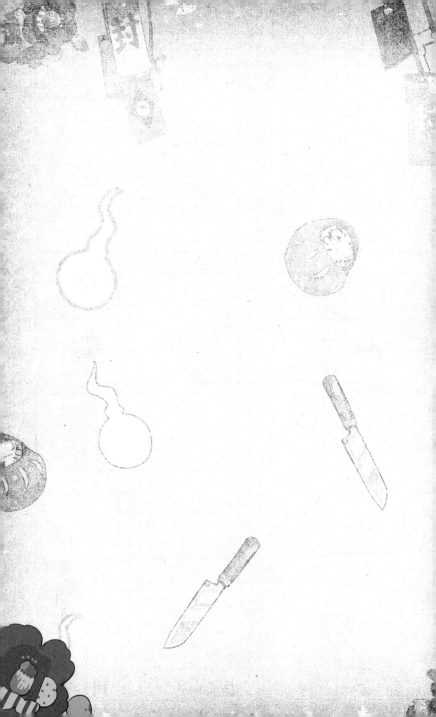

THE UGLY-RADISH INCIDENT — WITH KOU —

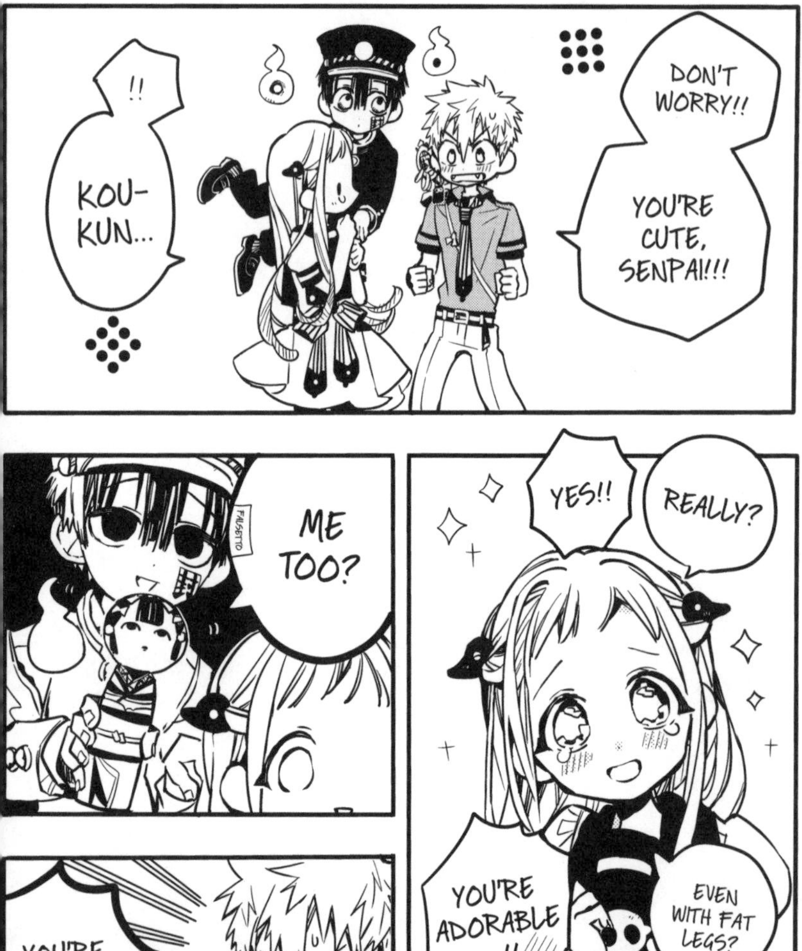
DON'T WORRY!!
YOU'RE CUTE, SENPAI!!!
!!
KOU-KUN...
REALLY?
YES!!
EVEN WITH FAT LEGS?
YOU'RE ADORABLE ...!!
FALSETTO
ME TOO?
YOU'RE SUPER-CUTE!!!!

REFLEX

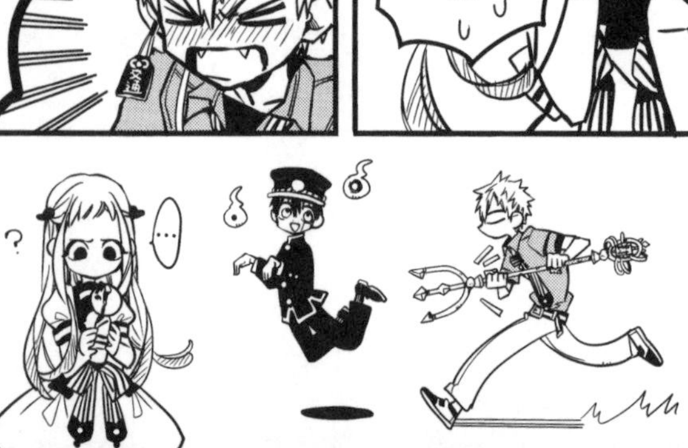
...
?

# TRANSLATION NOTES

**Common Honorifics**

**no honorific**: Indicates familiarity or closeness; if used without permission or reason, addressing someone in this manner would constitute an insult.

**-san**: The Japanese equivalent of Mr./Mrs./Miss. If a situation calls for politeness, this is the fail-safe honorific.

**-sama**: Conveys great respect; may also indicate that the social status of the speaker is lower than that of the addressee.

**-kun**: Used most often when referring to boys, this indicates affection or familiarity. Occasionally used by older men among their peers, but it may also be used by anyone referring to a person of lower standing.

**-chan**: An affectionate honorific indicating familiarity used mostly in reference to girls; also used in reference to cute persons or animals of either gender.

**-senpai**: A suffix used to address upperclassmen or more experienced coworkers.

**-sensei**: A respectful term for teachers, artists, or high-level professionals.

**Page 71**

*Echinococcus* is the genus name for a type of parasite commonly associated with foxes.

**Page 72**

*Kitsune* ("fox") *udon* is called this because the main topping for this dish of noodles is *aburaage*, deep-fried tofu. According to Japanese folklore, *aburaage* is a favorite food of foxes. It seems likely Hanako's recipe would replace the tofu with fox meat.

**Page 82**

*Neesan* is generally used to address young women whom the speaker thinks of as an older-sister type. As an ancient supernatural, however, Yako spells it with an outdated character that today is primarily associated with yakuza culture; Kou picks up on this with his response, "*ossu*" (translated as "Yo!"), a slangy greeting also often used by yakuza and other hoodlums. How Kou knew the way she "wrote" a word by hearing it is another question...

**Page 98**

Japanese superstition holds that sneezing is a good sign that, at that very moment, someone somewhere is gossiping about the sneezer.

# Toilet-bound Hanako-Kun 7

## AidaIro

Translation: Alethea Nibley and Athena Nibley
Lettering: Nicole Dochych

JIBAKU SHONEN HANAKO-KUN Volume 7 ©2017 AidaIro / SQUARE ENIX CO., LTD.
First published in Japan in 2017 by SQUARE ENIX CO., LTD. English translation rights arranged with SQUARE ENIX CO., LTD. and Yen Press, LLC through Tuttle-Mori Agency, Inc.

English translation © 2018 by SQUARE ENIX CO., LTD.

Yen Press
150 West 30th Street, 19th Floor
New York, NY 10001

Visit us at yenpress.com • facebook.com/yenpress • twitter.com/yenpress • yenpress.tumblr.com • instagram.com/yenpress

First Yen Press Print Edition: January 2021
Originally published as an ebook in August 2018 by Yen Press.

Yen Press is an imprint of Yen Press, LLC.
The Yen Press name and logo are trademarks of Yen Press, LLC.

The publisher is not responsible for websites (or their content) that are not owned by the publisher.

Library of Congress Control Number: 2019953610

ISBN: 978-1-9753-1139-1 (paperback)

10 9 8 7 6 5

LSC-C

Printed in the United States of America